Stylish Acclaim for
Leslie Caine's

DEATH BY INFERIOR DESIGN

"SPARKLES WITH CHARM, DESIGN LORE, AND A SLEUTH WITH A GREAT MANTRA. COZY FANS WILL EMBRACE THE DOMESTIC BLISS SERIES."
—Carolyn Hart, Edgar Award–winning author of *Letters from Home*

"Witty and smart, with HOME DECORATING TIPS TO DIE FOR!"
—Sarah Graves, bestselling author of the *Home Repair Is Homicide* series

"Leslie Caine deftly merges hate-fueled homicide with household hints in her 'how to/whodunit' mystery."
—Mary Daheim, nationally bestselling author of *The Alpine Pursuit*

"*Trading Spaces* meets *Murder, She Wrote!* TALK ABOUT EXTREME MAKEOVERS! Dueling designers Gilbert and Sullivan might want to kill each other, but no one expected anyone to try it. Who will hang the trendiest curtains? Who will choose the poshest paint? Who will come out alive? I'm not tellin'."
—Parnell Hall, author of *With This Puzzle, I Thee Kill*

a domestic
bliss mystery

DEATH BY
INFERIOR
DESIGN

Leslie Caine

A DELL BOOK

DEATH BY INFERIOR DESIGN
A Dell Book / November 2004

Published by
Bantam Dell
A Division of Random House, Inc.
New York, New York

ISBN 978-0-440-24175-1

Manufactured in the United States of America
Published simultaneously in Canada

OPM 10 9 8 7

For my fabulous agent, Nancy Yost,
to whom I along with every fictional character
I ever created give, in spirit, a resounding
and much-deserved standing ovation

acknowledgments

The author wishes to thank two immensely talented and generous designers who patiently answered hundreds of questions: Julie Thornton of Thornton Designs, Boulder, Colorado, and Emily Ferretti in Manhattan. Also thanks go to the Parsons School of Design and the Boulder Police Department. Thank you from the bottom of my heart to my wonderful, talented cowriter friends, especially Francine Mathews, Claudia Mills, Elizabeth Wrenn, Phyllis Perry, Christine Jorgensen, Lee Karr, and Kay Berstrom, whose encouragement and insightful comments were a beacon during my many months of writing and rewriting. I couldn't write anything at all without the support of my family, especially Mike, Carol, and Andrew. I'm enormously indebted to Kate Miciak, my wonderful and brilliant editor, and to all the terrific people at Bantam and, of course, to my aforementioned agent, Nancy Yost. There are dozens more people whose names aren't listed herein and deserve mention; please forgive me and know that your names and your many significant contributions are written in my heart.

DEATH BY INFERIOR DESIGN

chapter 1

Something was rotten in the state of Colorado, or more specifically, in this one Crestview neighborhood. Steve Sullivan's utility van, emblazoned "Sullivan Designs," was parked in my clients' driveway.

I pounded the steering wheel with the heel of my hand. "Not again! If he steals another client from me, I'm going to kill him!" I parked my silver van with the name of my business—Interiors by Gilbert—an inch behind Sullivan's bumper. "Gotcha!" Caught like a rat in a trap, Steve wouldn't be able to get out of the driveway without confronting me face-to-face.

I silently repeated my personal mantra: *confidence*

and optimism. My credentials were sterling—an MFA in design from Parsons, a four-year apprenticeship at the D&D Building in Manhattan, and two years of supporting myself through my own up-and-coming business.

The trouble was, Steve Sullivan had been running *his* home-design business in Crestview for three times as long as I had, and he had three times the number of referrals. Not to mention that the guy had a great eye and a sleek, contemporary style—and no sense of business ethics whatsoever. Not in a million years would *I* resort to stealing *his* clients.

But, again: *confidence and optimism.* I would ring that doorbell, march inside, and convince Carl Henderson that I, Erin Gilbert, was the best designer in town.

My biggest challenge was that Carl Henderson had hired me without ever looking at my plans for his bedroom and professed not to care. His exact wording had been, "What the hell difference does it make what a room you're sleeping in looks like? *All* rooms look alike once your eyes are closed." Redecorating the bedroom was a "surprise Christmas gift" for his wife, whom he'd sent to a spa for the weekend. The room had to be completed by eight p.m. tomorrow, when Debbie was due to return, and—Carl insisted—the transformation had to be made sans my fabulous team of home-improvement contractors.

I glanced at the upstairs window above the Hendersons' attached garage. The master bedroom that I'd *already been hired* to redecorate was located there, in the front of the house; the Hendersons had a splendid backdrop of the front range behind their home. This morning the sky was a cloudless sapphire blue. The distant peaks were snowcapped, though there wasn't a speck of snow in the city itself.

The glorious view of the Rocky Mountains was part of

the reason I had moved to Crestview two years ago to start my business. I'd also fallen in love with the variety of architecture and sizes of homes. Here I could spend the morning working on a mouthwatering century-old mansion on Maplewood Hill or an adorable eighty-year-old bungalow a few blocks north, and spend the afternoon in a brand-new spacious dwelling in the Cottonwood Creek neighborhood. Crestview was a designer's paradise!

I grabbed the sketches from my folder and strode up the brick walkway to the front porch. My bedroom design for the Hendersons would surpass whatever Sullivan had in mind. Sure, he was energetic, personable, charming—when he wasn't stealing clients or accusing me of naming my business with the sole intention of confusing his referrals. What was I supposed to do? Give up my last name of Gilbert just because there happened to already be a Sullivan Designs in town? In any case, I'd been pretty darned charming myself when working with Carl Henderson, even though my newest client had been surly in return. Carl was only redecorating "to get the missus off my back"—the kind of heartwarming sentimentality that brings a tear to any girl's eye. Carl did not *care* how good his bedroom design was.

So why was Steve Sullivan here?

During our initial meeting, the tall and angular Carl Henderson had insisted upon paying me a flat fee and stated that "Debbie wouldn't want a whole troop of strangers tromping through our bedroom." He vowed that he and a neighbor would be at my beck and call all weekend, and he'd even hired his stepson from his previous marriage, supposedly a professional carpenter, to make my custom-designed furniture on-site. Relatively on-site, that is. Carl had also said that "sawdust makes my wife's allergies flare up," so the workshop would actually be located across the street, at Randy Axelrod's house — the home of Carl's aforementioned helpful neighbor.

Even now, the name Randy Axelrod struck me as familiar in a worrisome way. In fact, the whole setup had given me a bad feeling that I knew better than to ignore. I'd wanted to postpone the project till after Christmas so that the customized furniture could be made in advance, but Carl had all but pounded on my desk in his refusal. "Debbie is already scheduled for her spa weekend. Taylor can handle whatever furniture you've got in mind." Taylor Duncan was his stepson, the carpenter. Then Carl had frowned and said, "I know this isn't how you're used to working. So I'll throw in another thousand bucks for being such a good sport."

The *ka-ching* of a cash register in my head drowned out my skepticism when Carl went on to say, "That'll make it more fair anyways, if you're getting paid the same —" He broke off and winced, and his cheeks hit a hue halfway between dusty rose and crimson. When I'd pressed him to continue, he'd babbled about my getting paid "the same as what I told Debbie the room would probably cost us eventually." Now, as I rang the doorbell and glanced back at Sullivan's shiny big van, that cute little cash register jingle in my mind was replaced with a shrill warning siren. What had I gotten myself into this time?

Many of the Hendersons' rooms were definitely in need of a face-lift, especially Debbie's home office. Just by looking at the woman's smiling likeness in the wedding photograph in their den, I'd gotten a sense that she was a nice, likable person, and I wanted to do an especially good job for her. The woman, however, was clearly not a neat freak. Carl could very well have decided to do a second room with a second designer in the same weekend while she was away. And, of all the designers in Crestview, he could have chosen my archrival.

A short, muscular man wearing jeans and a CU sweatshirt swept open the door. I smiled, wondering if this was Randy Axelrod, the helpful neighbor. The guy was certainly too old to be Carl's stepson; like Carl, he looked to be in his late forties. "Hi. My name is Erin Gilbert, and I'm here to—"

"Kevin McBride," he interrupted. Despite my casual, paint-splatter-ready attire, he gave me a slow grin and a visual once-over. His gaze lingered on my chest so long that I wanted to clobber him. "Carl didn't mention how attractive you were."

That sounded like a stale pickup line—perhaps a residue from the man's disco days—but I joked, "Didn't he? Darn! I was so certain that was on the things-to-do list I gave him."

Kevin chuckled and winked at me. "Come on in, Erin. Everyone's in the kitchen." He raked his fingers through his thick, graying hair as he said, "I'm afraid we've played a little trick on you. But I'll let Carl explain." Still eyeing me, he added, "Don't worry."

"Okay," I replied placidly, although in truth, nothing makes me worry quite as much as being told "Don't worry." I knew the Sullivan Designs van in the driveway meant trouble ahead.

Kevin McBride ushered me along a wear-marked path in the tan carpeting—past the living room and dining room and around the corner. Carl Henderson and Steve Sullivan were leaning against a kitchen counter, listening to a third man pontificate about who would "really kick butt" in the Super Bowl. The football expert had an enormous paunch, salt-and-pepper hair, and a white scrub-brush mustache.

I tucked a lock of my wavy auburn hair back into its ponytail. In spite of myself, my vision was drawn to Steve Sullivan, who—because life isn't so fair as to give human weasels beady black eyes and scrawny tails—was really *hot*. At roughly six feet, he was three or four inches taller than I and a couple of years older—thirty or so. He was wearing a black sweater—cashmere—and black jeans. He had gorgeous hazel eyes and light brown hair, slightly tousled in that arty, I'm-too-cool-to-comb-my-hair way that you just *know* takes twenty minutes in front of a mirror to arrange. His handsome face froze the moment he spotted me. Meanwhile, the large man beside him continued his football lecture and appeared to be in no hurry to acknowledge my presence.

"This is the other designer," Kevin McBride interrupted. "Have you two met?" He made a palm-out gesture to indicate Steve and me.

"Yes," Steve replied, not bothering to smile. "Our offices are both downtown. Hi, Gilbert."

I nodded. "Sullivan." No one else addressed me by my last name, but then, no one but Steve Sullivan had such a contentious relationship with me.

The overstuffed man gave me an appraising look while he smoothed his Fuller-brush mustache. "Aha. So we meet at last." He rocked on his heels. "Randy Axelrod. And, yes, I'm *the* Randy Axelrod. I live across the street."

Apparently his name should, indeed, have meant something to me, but it remained elusive—a mere pentimento of the memory banks. I decided to resist joking about being *the* only Erin Gilbert I knew personally and said simply, "Erin Gilbert. Hi."

Randy Axelrod made no move to shake hands. Instead, he stared into my eyes till I was finally compelled to look away. Kevin McBride was grinning while leering at my body as though he could see right through my black pullover and olive khakis. Although this was his house, Carl Henderson had the skulking, embarrassed demeanor of a man stuck holding his wife's purse in a lingerie department. What on earth was going on with these people?

Steve Sullivan held up his palms. "Before you jump to any conclusions, Gilbert, I'm not invading your turf. I've been hired to design the den for the McBrides, who live two houses down. Kevin left a note on his door telling me to come over here right away. So I'm here."

Carl piped up. "Kevin's wife has been nagging at him, too, about redecorating their house, so we got the idea of doing this as an early Christmas gift . . . sending the two gals off to this spa together and then surprising them. That way we both get this over with in one big crappy weekend."

"And who among us doesn't thoroughly enjoy the occasional big crappy weekend?" I couldn't resist teasing, but with a smile.

"The whole thing was my idea." Randy spoke in the same self-important tones he'd used to talk about football. "See, my wife is friends with their wives, and we three guys decided we might as well ship 'em out together. Then *my* wife and I were talking, and she's been after *me* to do something with the family room . . . always telling me to get my treadmill out of there and blah, blah, blah. I figured it'd be more interesting if we turned the whole weekend into a competition. So Carl and me decided to give you both the exact same amount of money to work with and hired the same carpenter, so everything will be fair and square." He chuckled. "Well, not square exactly. More like rectangular. Like your rooms." *The man was a real wit.*

"A competition?" I asked nonchalantly, keeping to

myself the plaintive shriek: *With Sullivan? Are you people insane?* This arrangement threatened to exceed even the powers of my confidence-and-optimism mantra.

Grinning, Randy crossed his thick arms and rested them on top of his stomach. Judging by his girth, his refrigerator door was getting a lot more action than his exercise equipment. "Yeah. I'm going to be your combination helper slash room-design judge. The winner gets hired to redo my family room . . . sometime next month, maybe. And I'll bring out one of the staff photographers and do a feature story on the winning design." He wiggled his eyebrows. "Maybe even a *cover* story."

I glanced at Steve's cocksure grin, and the sunlight finally burst through my mental shutters. Oh lord: Randy Axelrod was the editor in chief of *Denver Lifestyles*—a bimonthly interior design magazine.

Yikes! With no warning, my chic, romantic, decidedly feminine bedroom design had to compete against Steve Sullivan's den, with an influential male judge who kept his treadmill and blah blah blahs in the family room. A bedroom to a den is an apples-to-oranges comparison. Considering that this particular judge all but oozed testosterone, Sullivan's oranges would be hand-plucked, whereas my apples would be bruised and mottled from having fallen off the tree.

"Hope you're up for a friendly challenge, honey," Randy said to me with a wink.

I glanced at my handsome fellow designer, wondering if the man was capable of keeping "friendly" in the equation. Three months ago, while *filching the Coopers' job away from me*, he'd told Mrs. Cooper that he was mourning the loss of "his partner, Evan." Until then, I'd had the impression that the two men were strictly *business* partners, and furthermore I'd heard from more than one source that Evan was very much *alive* and had merely moved away. That conniving Sullivan had fed the Coopers a sob story to win them over and get the job. But that was all water under the bridge now. *Fetid* water, granted, but nevertheless located under the proverbial—albeit rickety—bridge.

Randy gave Sullivan's shoulder a playful jab, which the evil side of my nature hoped was painful. Randy should have planted his feet better. And swung at Sullivan's perfectly proportioned jaw. "Hey, Steve, Erin," Randy said. "You know what? With names like Gilbert and Sullivan, you two should form a team. I'm sure your styles would be in perfect *harmony.* So to speak." He laughed heartily.

"If we *did* become partners, it would have to be Sullivan and Gilbert," Steve said. "With a capital S and a lowercase G."

"Age before beauty, Sullivan," I fired back, and silently called him every four-letter word in the book; I could rename *his* business easily enough. He normally wasn't *this* hostile to me. The prize of a feature story was obviously bringing out the worst in him. Granted, I, too, would kill to get *Denver Lifestyles'* publicity for my business—but I would much rather kill with kindness. I gave him an angelic smile, secretly hoping that the incredible weight of his ego would cause his head to implode.

The doorbell rang. "Aha. That will be our carpenter, Taylor Duncan," Randy announced as he headed toward the door. "You two will share his services."

"Taylor's your stepson, right, Carl?" I asked, noting how polar-opposite he and Kevin McBride looked as they stood side by side. The short, solid Kevin was the shot glass to Carl's tall, thin champagne flute. "And he knows what he's doing? He's experienced enough to work on two different projects at once?"

"Absolutely. When it comes to carpentry, Taylor's a

real whiz kid." Behind Carl, however, Kevin McBride was shaking his head at me and giving a thumbs-down. "And just for the record, Kevin and I have a lot more riding on this competition than you and Steve here do."

Kevin nodded. "The loser has to watch the Super Bowl at home with Axelrod. The winner gets to watch the game live and in person—with a ticket to the big show itself."

Glowering at me through his wire-rimmed glasses, Carl spat out, "So you're not allowed to lose. Or else!"

"That goes double for you," Kevin told Sullivan.

A bear of a man—six foot five at least—lumbered into the room behind Randy. Taylor Duncan's head was shaved, and he wore work boots, overalls, and a spiked dog collar. His bare, corded arms were a mass of teal-blue tattoos, like a singularly ugly toile infused into his skin. "Hey, Carl. Kevin. Sorry I'm a bit late." He had received a split vote regarding his carpentry skills, but if this had been a lumberjack competition, Taylor would have been the man I wanted on my team.

"One more thing before we all get to work, folks," Randy announced. "Since I got a bad ticker"—he patted the left side of his chest as if to give us a visual—"I won't be able to do much in the way of heavy lifting. I'll keep an eye on the clock and keep things running smoothly at both houses. Come Sunday night, I'll be impartial, no matter what's gone on from now till then. I'll decide which of you two folks has produced the best interior design and which has the *inferior* design. My wife says she'll help out with the sewing and picking up after everybody. Understand?"

I *understood*, but I was boiling mad. This was one hell of a raw deal. No one would expect two football teams to play the Super Bowl with just five minutes' notice, yet these jerks had blindsided me into a direct competition with Sullivan. Would *Denver Lifestyles* have fun with the Gilbert-versus-Sullivan aspect and publicly reveal the *loser* of this competition? "I don't know how I feel about this," I began. "The thing is—"

"Let me show you something that might help persuade you." Steve snatched a notebook off the counter behind him and started to write furiously.

He ripped off the top sheet and thrust it at me. He'd written: *Hey, Gilbert! You earn $$$$ for 2 days' work! Even though you'll* lose!!

I crumpled the note into a tight ball while clenching my teeth. If a client hadn't been present, I'd have tossed the paper in his smug face. "You're on, Sullivan."

He gave me one of his cover-boy smiles and arched an eyebrow. "Bring it on, Gilbert."

Steve Sullivan and Kevin McBride left for Kevin's house; over his shoulder as he left the room, Taylor mumbled something about needing to get set up in Randy Axelrod's backyard. Seconds later, Sullivan was back, shouting through the front door, "Hey, Gilbert. Move your van. I've got to get mine out."

"Say please, Sullivan, and I'll oblige you," I shot back.

When he said nothing, my curiosity got the best of me. I stormed outside, weighing the notion of singing a line or two from a tune in *HMS Pinafore* just to bug him; the idea of polishing a door handle "so carefully" as to be made "the ruler of the Queen's navy" suddenly had a certain appeal. I found him standing by the garage. He was massaging his temples and had such a worried look that I almost asked if he was all right. He spotted me just then, cleared his throat and, turning on his heel and ignoring me, got into his van.

I backed up my van and parked in the space Sullivan had vacated while he drove a mere two doors down the street. Why hadn't he simply *walked* over here after finding the note on Kevin McBride's door? Could he have suspected something was up and been prepared to turn down the assignment and drive home? Had it just been his desire to defeat me in this wacko competition that made him stick with this job? If so, for a pair of interior designers, we were being disgustingly macho.

I decided to save myself a few steps later and bring some of my tools and paint supplies inside with me now. Opening the back doors to the van, I gasped when Randy Axelrod's voice unexpectedly boomed behind me, "Can I help you carry stuff in?"

"Didn't you just say you had a weak heart?"

"Sure, but I know when to take it easy. I'm not made of eggshells."

"You can carry the brushes, rollers, and pans."

"Will do."

I took my time stacking the supplies. I needed a moment to collect myself. "Aren't you worried about inspiring hard feelings between you and your neighbors by being a judge?" I asked Randy.

"Why would judging a couple rooms make anyone feel bad?"

"Someone might object to having their brand-new room deemed 'an inferior design,' as you called it."

"Ah, hell, that won't matter." He chuckled. "They already *do* hate me."

"Who? Kevin and Carl?"

"Yeah. And their wives, too."

I winced at the concept of that much discord so close to home, which should always be everyone's very *least* discordant place to be. As we headed up the walkway, I tried to send him the telepathic message: *Life's too short.*

"Don't look so concerned, honey," he said with a laugh. "It's not like I'm fond of them, either."

"Then why judge their rooms? And spend the weekend helping them remodel? Why subject yourselves to one another's company when it's not absolutely necessary?"

"Hey." He shrugged, opened the door, and held it for me with his foot. "Beats sittin' around the house, watching football." We stashed the supplies just inside the door. Randy tapped his chest. "Watching the Broncos lose is the worst thing I can do to my heart, if you ask me." He fidgeted with his mustache and surveyed our surroundings. "I never should've sold Carl this house in the first place."

"This used to be *your* house?"

"Up until five years ago. After my first heart attack, we decided to simplify—get a smaller place."

I looked across the street at the house, which appeared to be the smallest in the immediate neighborhood. Though this was December and not exactly the season in Colorado for lush yards and bountiful gardens, it was clear at a glance that someone was taking immaculate care of the grounds. Gigantic plastic candy canes had been placed to either side of the base of the driveway. An old-fashioned wood sled adorned with a lovely evergreen wreath and bright red bow leaned against the gray house—a simple but immensely elegant decoration. The sight made me yearn for a white Christmas. "That's your house over there?"

He snorted. "Home sweet home."

"Nice."

"On the outside." He gestured for me to follow him outdoors. "Come and meet the missus. I told her I'd let her know when we're starting work. She seems to think she can help, but the woman's all thumbs. Taylor had better not let her near his power tools, or she'll likely cut one of those thumbs of hers clean *off*." He chuckled at his gruesome imagery.

Curious to see the house that, if I won this inane competition, I could soon be redecorating—and keenly aware that our excursion would allow me to suck up to the judge a little—I replied, "Sure. Thanks," and headed across the street with Randy.

He let me inside his home, allowing the storm door to bang shut behind us. I took in my surroundings without making it obvious that I was doing so. As a designer, I'm voraciously curious about people's homes, but I've found that if I make it even the slightest bit evident that I'm checking out a room, the homeowners become nervous. This small living room could be made cozy, but at the moment, it was far too cluttered. The walls were a cavelike gunmetal gray and sported small pictures with a hodgepodge selection of frames. The fabric patterns were all over the map, with no consistent color palette. These were common problems that were easy to rectify, and it struck me as odd that this man edited an interior-design magazine.

"Randy? Is that you?" a woman's voice called.

"Last time I checked."

"I caught Taylor Duncan poking around in our refrigerator a couple of minutes ago! You need to go out back and—" A trim, fifty-something woman in a Waverly floral print cotton dress rounded the corner. Spotting me, she froze and stared slack-jawed at me.

Assuming she was simply caught off guard at suddenly finding herself face-to-face with an unexpected guest, I smiled and said, "Your husband suggested I come over and meet you. I'm Erin Gilbert. I'm going to be redecorating the Hendersons' bedroom."

"Pleased to meet you, Erin," she said, and stepped forward to shake my hand. She let her grip linger an instant longer than necessary, studying my features all the while. "My name's Myra. Myra Axelrod."

"Have we met before? If so, I'm sorry, but I—"

"No, no. You just remind me of somebody. My, uh, sister. When she was your age. I—"

"Erin's got to get cracking," Randy told his wife before she could say more.

"I'm all set, too," Myra said, grabbing a tan cardigan from the arm of the sofa. Her piercing gray eyes stayed on my face. "I'll come with you, Erin, and be your personal assistant for the weekend."

Before I could respond, Randy decreed, "No way, Myra. We need to start at the McBrides' house."

"But I—"

"No, Myra." He shook his head.

They held each other's gaze. Or rather, they held each other's glare. All things considered, I decided, this was my worst-ever send-off for a new job. "It was nice meeting you, Myra, but I *do* need to get cracking. . . ." My voice faded as I pondered the expression. When it comes to interior design, cracking is rarely a good thing.

"We'll catch up to you later, Erin," Myra replied with a warm smile.

The moment the door shut behind me, I could hear the bass and contralto rumblings of their argument. From my vantage point across the street, I got a good look at the McBrides' house and could see that it was half again as large as the Hendersons' place. Subtle clues in the roofline—now adorned with icicle-light strings—and weathering of the cedar shingles indicated that the McBrides, or maybe the house's previous owners, had made two significant additions to the original structure. Odd that homeowners who could afford to put that kind of money into their property would hire a designer for a surprise one-weekend makeover. Then again, *everything* in this neighborhood felt slightly odd.

Making a mental note to never again let mercenary

concerns override my instincts, I returned to the Hendersons' bedroom. Taylor was there, helping Carl clear out the room. I stole a moment to scan the bedroom, both as it existed and as I envisioned it, which was an ability that I considered one of my most precious gifts. My spirits soared at the notion of how, in just one weekend, I'd be able to take this space from blah to wow.

Carl had told me that his wife was a voracious reader, and there were books stacked like the Leaning Tower of Pisa along the wall beside her side of the bed. I planned to convert the small closet by the entrance into a floor-to-ceiling bookcase that would be hidden behind the closet door. Despite the richness that neatly arranged books bring to any room, "neatly arranged" was the operative phrase, which obviously wasn't Debbie's strong point.

The Hendersons already owned an exquisite eight-drawer alder chest with a lightly distressed stained exterior. That one piece was worth several thousand dollars—roughly ten times the value of all their other furniture in the room combined. When I was done, Debbie Henderson would have a fabulous custom-designed alder bed with maple accents in a light finish that complemented the showpiece chest. Curtains would hang between the bedposts and hide the new headboard's shelves so that she could keep them in whatever state she wished and not spoil the visuals of the room.

As for color schemes, the walls were now bone white. When my work was complete, they would be faux-finished with a gold base and a burgundy top coat, which would create a warm, romantic hue reminiscent of a Tuscan sunset. Floor-length honey-gold raw silk draperies would really pop against the wall's dark color. Crown molding, which echoed the lines of the chest, would enhance the height of the room.

Now that my cruddy send-off was behind me, I suddenly relished the chance to sink my teeth into this job. And if I got to force Sullivan to eat some humble pie in the process, all the better.

The three of us had soon moved the furniture into the guest room, and while the two men carried out armloads of paperbacks, I removed the corner bead from the aspen paneling on the accent wall. The sensation of ripping out boards has always greatly appealed to me. For one thing, it marks the no-turning-back-now portion of the journey, just like breaking a bottle of champagne on a ship's bow. For another thing, the nails as they're wrenched free make a really cool noise.

This paneling, which the Hendersons faced from their bed, was on a short wall that they had to round in order to reach their dressing area and bathroom. The floor plan necessitated that the large chest remain against this south wall, but placing wood furniture against a wood wall in nearly identical tones is a mistake. My remedy was yummy wallpaper with an elegant pattern that had a light burgundy—claret—background and champagne gold as the accent color.

I began my demolition on one side of wall, Carl and Taylor on the other. They were making short work of the task and had about half of the boards removed when Taylor asked, "Hey, Carl? Mind if I keep these boards and use 'em in my trailer? I'll burn the cracked ones in the fireplace 'n' install one of those kinds of decorating thingamajigs where the paneling comes halfway up the wall."

"Wainscoting," I couldn't help but interject, alarmed that a supposed first-rate carpenter wouldn't immediately know that term.

"You may as well, Taylor," Carl answered. "Might

make Debbie feel better to know someone was getting some use out of it. This paneling was her favorite thing in the room."

"Wait a minute, Carl!" I cried. "Why didn't you tell me that when I was asking you what your wife might want?"

He shrugged. "You're the designer. I didn't want to cramp your style. 'Specially not when there's a Super Bowl ticket riding on it."

"But this is your and your wife's room! I'd have been happy to forgo the wallpaper and work the paneling into my design." Horrified, I looked at the pile of thin tongue-and-groove boards we'd made. Most were cracked and dented. "Now it's too late. . . ."

"Then there's no sense sweating about it now, Gilbert," Taylor said with a sneer.

I glared at him and almost sniped, *Thanks for the advice, Einstein*, but for once kept my mouth shut, realizing it wasn't in my best interest to antagonize my time-share carpenter. "Please call me Erin, not Gilbert."

I went back to ripping out boards with a vengeance. One short board suddenly fell off the wall before I'd even touched it.

"Uh-oh," I said. "This had better not be a dry-rot problem." I knelt to take a close look.

"What's that?" Taylor asked, leaning down to look over my shoulder.

"Looks like a secret compartment," Carl replied.

"Weird," Taylor muttered.

I reached inside the small cubbyhole, which looked as though someone had punched through the drywall and then chipped at its edges. The opening was roughly eighteen inches above the floor and was large enough for me to reach my arm through past the elbow and touch the floorboards. The first thing my fingertips brushed against felt like a delicate chain, and I managed to pinch it between my fingers and lift it out. It was a necklace—a lovely onyx cameo on an old-fashioned chain of gold links. The intricate carving of a woman's face in profile against a pink coral background was stunning. With the delicacy of Belgian lace, the gold setting framed the petite carving beautifully. This cameo appeared to be a family heirloom, as opposed to a priceless possession. Why would someone hide such a beautiful personal item inside a wall?

"Is this Debbie's?" I asked Carl.

He shook his head, but his cheeks had gone crimson and his jaw looked tight enough to crack his teeth. I reached inside again and pulled out a sheaf of folded papers. They were tied with a red satin ribbon. Love letters, no doubt. I set the stack on the floor near my feet and reached one more time into the cubbyhole to determine if there was anything else behind the drywall, but the letters and necklace were everything.

" 'My dearest,' " Taylor read, crouching down by the pile of letters, " 'You were constantly on my mind today—' "

"Stop!" I cried. "You have no right to read those letters, Taylor! They belong to somebody else."

He ignored me but did at least read silently. After he flipped over the first page, he said, "It's boring anyway. Signed, 'Love always,' and the letter *M*."

"I don't know any *M* people," Carl muttered.

"Unless it's really *H* for Henderson." Taylor's voice was mocking.

Carl grabbed the letters from Taylor's hands. "That's an *M*. And even if it *is* an *H*, it's not *my* love note. I'd remember if I'd been stashing love notes inside my bedroom wall, for God's sake!" The muscles in his jaw were working.

He paged through the letters, and this time I couldn't object—they'd been found in his house, after all—though I grew increasingly uneasy. If they were Debbie's, I found myself hoping Carl wasn't the violently jealous type.

"The paper looks really old," Carl remarked. His features and voice revealed some relief. "I'll bet Randy or Myra put them here. Hey! *M* for Myra!"

But wouldn't Myra have remembered this stash in the years since they'd last lived here? Discussing the Hendersons' design project, if nothing else, surely would have sparked a memory. How hard could it have been to sneak upstairs and remove the contents before I arrived? "I have to plaster up that hole and have it dry in time to hang the wallpaper," I said, thinking out loud.

Taylor went back to work tearing down paneling while Carl carried the letters and the pendant to some other room. I idly turned over the board that had been covering the hole to see if the back half of the groove had been filed away.

In a rectangular, carved-out indentation that would have lined up with the cubbyhole was tucked a small photograph of a smiling toddler with red hair. She stood next to a blue-and-green checkered umbrella stand. I stifled a gasp.

I glanced up at Taylor. He was paying me no mind, absorbed in his work. I peeled the picture loose and pocketed it. My pulse was racing so fast that I felt faint.

I'd seen an enlarged image of that photograph sitting on my mother's piano every day for sixteen years of my life. The baby in the photograph was me.

chapter 2

I felt as though I'd been sucker-punched. I continued to rip out the paneling, grateful that this activity allowed me not only to stare at a wall, but to treat that wall with no small degree of violence.

What was my baby picture doing here? And how the heck had someone gotten hold of it? My adoptive mother was dead; my adoptive father had moved to California more than a decade ago. Only my birth parents could have had copies of that photograph.

Memories of my mother's death two years earlier made my eyes sting with tears. My chest ached, as it had throughout those two months of hospice care when my mother lay dying, the worst time of my life. My hopes and prayers had focused on the desperate, futile longing that I could somehow give my breath to my mother—could prevent her congenitally diseased lungs from filling with fluid—taking her from this world and from me when she was just forty-six years old.

To make the end more comfortable and less impersonal, I'd brought her home, only to discover that the apartment she and I once shared and loved swiftly mutated into a mini-hospital, rife with the odors of disease and despair, pungent antiseptic, and medicine. My mother had been my first and ongoing client long before I'd enrolled at Parsons, and yet every design decision I'd made suddenly mocked me—every speck of color and vitality in our home made her look all the more ashen and frail and her hospital bed more stark. Even fresh flowers became merely funereal; light seemed a taunting exposure, so we spent those somber weeks with curtains closed, shrouded in heavy shadows.

One evening after the meal that she couldn't force herself to eat, she reached for me. "You have to promise me one thing, Erin." Her voice was a halting, barely audible rasp, which tore at my heart.

"Of course, Mom. Anything."

"You have to promise me you won't *ever* look for your birth parents, under *any* circumstances. Do you understand?"

I didn't, not for a moment, but I replied without hesitation. "We agreed to that years ago, Mom." Her hand had become frighteningly cold in mine.

"I know. But you must promise not to change your mind once I'm gone."

"I promise, Mom. But why is it so important to you?"

She returned the oxygen mask to her face for one more shallow breath, then, closing her lovely blue eyes—the only feature of my mother that still resembled the woman who'd always been my one true parent—whispered, "I can't explain, Erin. I've got to rest now."

Although she'd languished for another nine days, it seemed to me that she'd poured what little strength and resources she had into asking me for that final promise. Afterward, she said less and less, until she fell silent for good.

Now I resented the hell out of whoever had forced me to relive this heartbreak. Jeannie Gilbert—my mother—had been a vibrant, optimistic person in life, and that was the part of her I wanted to keep in my heart and in my memory. I could almost hear her spouting one of her cheerful aphorisms: "There's a reason God gave us eyes in front of our head and not in the back, Erin, so that we can *always* look ahead."

Maintaining an eyes-forward approach had been a second promise of mine to her. It was one that, although unspoken, I also fully intended to keep.

I wrenched my thoughts away from the past as I pried the last piece of aspen off the wall. Taylor announced that he happened to have some scrap pieces of Sheetrock in his truck, and I always carried mud and tape in my van for just such an emergency. Soon we had squared off the hidden hole and patched it.

After an inordinately long absence for someone ostensibly putting away a few items, Carl returned to the room. He'd had enough time to read every word in those letters a dozen times. Suspicious that, despite his innocent act, he could have been the one to set this trap for me, I assigned him the miserable and messy job of sanding off the wall texture in preparation for the wallpaper. Even if it turned out that his wife was cheating on him and he'd had nothing to do with my photograph being inside his wall, he'd been a grump to work with; he deserved a nice coating of grit and white dust, I decided with petty satisfaction.

I turned to Taylor. "Are you ready to get started on the new furniture and built-ins?"

"I'll get to 'em eventually."

" 'Eventually' has rather tight limitations when the homeowner is supposed to return to a finished room in thirty-three hours. Even though the bedposts and legs have already been lathed, the headboard has a slanted backrest and an attached bookcase that'll take a chunk of time to build. Let me show you my drawings."

He made a derisive noise. "So you're in this big hurry, but suddenly you want me to look at your artwork?"

"I'm talking about my *sketches* of the pieces I need you to *build* for me!" I took a calming breath and made a quick note to myself to adopt a new mantra for the weekend: *be nice to the carpenter.*

I showed him my neat and precise diagrams, which he creased and stuffed in his pocket. He ignored me completely when I asked if he needed help unloading the boards from my van. Instead he called past my shoulder, "Hey, Carl! I'll give you a hand with sanding that drywall."

Pointing out to Taylor that he was our *carpenter* and had yet to do any actual *carpentry* would not help matters. The upstairs guest room was now crammed wall to wall with furniture, so I went downstairs in search of a temporary sewing room. I needed to assemble the drapes, skirts, pillows, and duvet.

Once alone, my thoughts returned unbidden to the photograph. What kind of person would hide a baby picture under a piece of paneling for the grown child to discover? Was the whole thing a cruel joke? Or was someone trying to draw me into some weird psychological game?

In any case, I vowed, would *not* renege on my promise to my mother.

Furnishings and wall treatments absorb the auras of their inhabitants as surely as heavy kitchen curtains soak up cooking smells. The less-than-ideal ambience of the Hendersons' home now struck me. This place all but screamed of marital friction, of two people existing more apart than together within the same quarters. Although Christmas was right around the corner, there wasn't a speck of holiday decoration. There were no conversation nooks, no groupings of chairs in this house. The wear marks and cushion indentations on the left side of the sofa indicated that Carl was a television junkie—and that the Hendersons didn't rotate their cushions with enough frequency. The cheery yellow and robin's-egg blue chintz love seat in the sunroom was obviously where Debbie came to relax and dream; the brass floor lamp was adjusted to aim its light over one armrest, and a fluffy periwinkle-and-gray crocheted afghan had been draped over the sofa back. Their bedroom makeover might prove to be taking place in the nick of time, and I vowed that I would focus all my thoughts and energy toward the job at hand.

I decided to put my sewing machine on the oak dining room table at the base of the stairs. There I could avoid most of the airborne plaster particles but still have convenient access to the front door for hauling supplies, and I could also race up the stairs whenever necessary. I wanted to begin with the draperies, knowing the new ones would be a massive improvement.

Debbie Henderson—or perhaps one of the Axelrods, if the window treatments had come with the place—had made the common mistake of neglecting to pay attention to the curtain rods themselves. Floral fabric had been hung on metal hoops from a two-inch-diameter chocolate-brown rod, which sported oversized plastic finials on either end that resembled horizontal pagodas. That curtain rod had the same effect as a long, black heel mark in the center of an otherwise stunning travertine tile floor.

After a few minutes, while I was immersed in pinning and cutting, I overheard Carl say, "Hey, Taylor, I've been thinking. You know anything about that hiding spot?"

I instantly pricked up my ears.

"Course not. Why would I?"

Carl replied, "It just doesn't seem like something Myra or Debbie would do . . . build a secret compartment in a wall. Randy either, for that matter."

"You think *I'd* put love notes and some chick's necklace in your wall?"

There was a pause. I didn't move a muscle for fear that I'd miss their words. I *hate* to snoop on my clients, but my personal investment in their not-so-private conversation had been purchased in full by the photograph of me now tucked in the back pocket of my khakis.

"I was thinking you might've been hiding something of a completely different nature. Back when you were housesitting while Debbie 'n' I went to Europe last summer."

A *different nature?*

"I was staying in the *guest* room, not your room."

"That's beside the point. You were alone in my house for over a month."

"Get real, Carl. I told you, I got set up! By that big, fat sack of shit *you* seem to be too scared of to—"

"Watch it, Taylor!"

After another pause, Taylor told Carl, "Mom believes me. Why don't you?"

"Because I can see you more clearly. *She's* your mother. She lets you get away with murder."

"You saw for yourself! All that was in there were those

stupid letters and some dumb necklace. It's not like Gilbert found my bong or anything. *That* sucker's still missing."

"Oh, for Christ's sake, Taylor! You promised your mother you were off the drugs!"

"I am! I was just kidding! Jeez, it's like nobody can take a joke anymore!"

"Not about you and drugs, no, we can't. Not just three months after you got out of jail."

I clicked my tongue. So Taylor had a problem with drugs—or he had once had a problem. That was all well and good, but couldn't they get back to discussing the hidden compartment? I wasn't eavesdropping to give my ears a workout; I wanted to learn the who and why behind *my* baby picture having been stored in the wall of people I barely knew!

"Tell me the truth, Taylor. It doesn't matter now, either way. Did you put that hole in my wall?"

"Thank you," I whispered, craning my neck toward the stairwell.

The doorbell rang, and I jumped in my seat and pricked my finger with a pin. The conversation upstairs became unintelligible murmurings. The doorbell rang again. Carl called down, "Erin? Can you get that?"

I called back, "Sure thing," then stuck my bleeding finger in my mouth. This was what I got for eavesdropping. Later, I would just come right out and ask Carl if he'd figured out who put the hole in the wall. Not that he'd tell me the truth. Or that, without revealing my own vulnerability, I'd be able to offer a reasonable explanation for why it mattered so much to me who owned the love letters I'd discovered there. *Oh, well, you see, Mr. Henderson, I'm simply dying to know whether or not your wife is cheating on you, and your voices just weren't projecting over the doorbell. Speak up, man!*

Kevin McBride was at the door. He gave me his usual lascivious once-over as I invited him inside. With his eyes riveted to my breasts, he said, "Sullivan asked me to come over here and fetch Taylor. As a matter of fact, he insisted that I tell you to—quote, unquote—'quit hogging the carpenter.' We've got an entertainment center for him to build."

Typical of Sullivan, to try to sabotage my progress by grabbing Taylor. "How do you like Steve's room design so far?"

"It's great. Though I gotta admit, all I really care about is the new, top-of-the-line Barcalounger."

"Steve Sullivan is putting a *Barcalounger* into your den?" I all but shrieked. Sullivan's designs were usually so sleek and clean-lined—something of an Americanized Asian style. It was not like him to choose a chair with that much bulk and curvature. "Was that at your request?"

"You bet. And it's going to be fantastic! Leather, built-in footrest, and storage places under the armrests for a couple of beers and the remote control. Steve says it'll be delivered tomorrow. I can't wait." Grinning, Kevin added in a conspiratorial voice, "Sorry to tell you this, sweetie pie, but Steve described the chair to Randy, and it's all over for you. The guy's ten shades of *green*. Randy practically started drooling on the spot!"

"Maybe his weak heart was acting up," I snapped. Damn it! If I was going to lose this competition to Steve Sullivan, it had better not be on the basis of one testosterone-soaked recliner! "Those chairs are really expensive. I'm surprised he had enough money in the budget for materials for an entertainment center."

Still grinning, Kevin said, "I know. But he said somebody owed him a favor and sold it to him at cost. He said it was a real *steal*."

I ground my teeth. It's a truism in this business that a

designer is only as good as his or her sources. Trust Sullivan to suck up to exactly the right one.

"Just wait till I rub this in Carl's face!"

"Congratulations, Kevin. I'm sure your wife will love her new chair."

"My *wife?*" The compact, muscular man froze on the staircase and pivoted to face me. "But it's *my* chair! It's . . . leather. You know. *Leather.* Cattle hide." He made a motion as though he were cracking an imaginary whip. "Manly stuff. Cowboys and Indians, and all that. Besides, Jill doesn't even *like* beer."

"But the room design is your Christmas present to Jill, isn't it?"

"Not the Barcalounger, though. I mean, she couldn't possibly . . ." His face had paled visibly. "Cripes! You're right. If I claim the major new item in the room, Jill's going to have a hissy fit." He raked his fingers through his hair. "I should've asked Sullivan if he got us any other new seats for Jill."

"Even if he didn't, you can always ask Steve to change his design, you know. Maybe he could provide matching recliners for you and your wife. After all, maybe his friend at the Barcalounger store owed him *two* favors." I fought back a grin at the idea of Sullivan being forced to integrate not one but two Barcaloungers into his design.

Looking a little panic-stricken, Kevin stomped upstairs to find Taylor.

Okay, that hadn't been very nice of me, and I especially had to assign myself negative brownie points for chuckling the moment Kevin had left the room. Having the homeowner get cold feet about a plan in progress is one of a designer's toughest challenges.

Upstairs, Kevin grumbled, "Taylor, Steve needs you to put in equal time here. He's got some stupid entertainment center and a . . . coffee table, or something. He's waiting for us at Axelrod's."

"Yeah, all right. See you later, Carl."

"Jeez," Kevin muttered at me as he slunk down the stairs, Taylor lumbering ahead of him. "I can't believe you ripped out the paneling I put up."

"*You* installed the paneling?" I asked.

"Yeah. Myra asked me to, a few years back. The Axelrods used to own this place. Randy never got around to putting the stuff up himself. But Debbie loved that paneling, big time. She even had me come over and spruce up the finish on the wood just a few months ago."

My heart sank. A half-dozen people had apparently had access to the paneled wall. With that lack of privacy, the letters and necklace might as well have been stuck to the refrigerator door. I said to Kevin, "Since you and Taylor are heading across the street anyway, would you two mind unloading the lumber in the back of my van?" Earlier I hadn't gotten anywhere with this request to Taylor, but a brief stint as my pack mule was the very least Kevin owed me for leering at me so rudely.

He said, "We'd be happy to."

"Thanks. Please be especially careful with the bed-posts." The tiger-maple legs and headboard posts had been the one item I'd managed to have premade, despite the busy time of year, and I was protective of them and proud of my design. I tossed Kevin my keys.

Taylor had been waiting at the front door listening to our exchange. Now he asked Kevin, "So I'm s'posed to build an entertainment center? What, like, a shelf unit for the stereo and TV?"

"No, Taylor," Kevin grumbled as Taylor opened the door. "We want you to build us an entertainment center, as in a series of trapezes and a water slide. My wife, Jill, happens to be a chimpanzee." He rolled his eyes at me as he shut the door behind them.

An hour later, Carl had finished sanding the wall, and we primed it with an acrylic wallpaper primer. Carl wasn't a naturally chatty person, and I eventually gave up on trying to draw him into conversation, most of which had been geared to my private agenda about determining who was responsible for the hidden photograph. The only salient points that I managed to glean were that it had been Randy Axelrod who'd insisted upon hiring me to work on this house, and that Randy and Myra had always lived alone.

Randy, it seems, had told Carl that he was familiar with my work by virtue of his having inside information as the editor of a design magazine. As much as my ego begged me to accept that explanation, the photograph burning a hole in my pocket suggested that he'd used his editing job as a convenient ruse. My hunch was that Randy Axelrod had arranged this whole contest as a means to get me to discover my own photograph, which he'd planted there himself. But why? Could he have fathered me? If so, why be so devious? And why had he been conspicuously absent all morning? If this had been a trap, wouldn't he want to be present to see if I'd take the bait?

While Carl applied the matte base coat for the faux finish, I returned to my sewing. An hour later, I decided to dash across the street and make sure that Sullivan wasn't going to keep Taylor so busy on *his* carpentry projects that the latter neglected *mine* completely.

The temperature had warmed to the mid-forties, and the sky above the white-capped mountains was a glorious azure. Even without the Rockies' majestic backdrop, I'd have moved here for the pleasure of being able to live beneath such a divine shade of blue, I decided as I crossed over to Randy Axelrod's backyard.

Taylor was hunkered over his saw, a cigarette hanging from his lips. Pacing nearby, Steve Sullivan seemed to be trying to stay upwind of the smoke. The boards I'd purchased were stacked by the Axelrods' back door, and on top of the stack were my keys, which I pocketed.

Steve's brow furrowed the moment he spotted me, and he stormed toward me. "Nice work, Gilbert."

"On what? My bed design?"

"On making my client nervous about the Barcalounger. I'll be sure to return the favor, first chance I get."

"You can try. It won't do you any good, though. Carl Henderson couldn't care less how his bedroom turns out."

Sullivan snorted. "So I guess you win this round. But let me warn you: you *don't* want to play hardball with me."

"Oh? And why is that? Because *you* have no professional ethics whatsoever, and I do?"

"Hey, I have—" He stopped his protest and shut his mouth, his eyes blazing. Then he said grimly, "The Cooper job had extenuating circumstances, Gilbert. If it makes you feel any better, though, I'm sorry."

I hid my surprise at his having not only admitted to the transgression of having stolen the Cooper account from me, but apologizing for doing so. "What 'extenuating circumstances' are you referring to?"

He shot a glance at Taylor, bent over his noisy saw. "Now's not a good time to go into that." He crossed his arms and glared at me.

His haughty behavior couldn't spook me. "Fine, but

you owe me a full explanation if you expect me to accept your apology."

He merely arched an arrogant eyebrow. Taylor shut off his saw, so we both turned our attention to him. "I was wondering how my projects are coming," I said to the carpenter, ignoring the fact that I could see for myself that all my materials were a few steps away, and untouched.

Taylor swiped his big palm across his shaved pate. "Haven't started 'em."

"Can you give me a time frame? If you can just cut the pieces for the bed and the TV stand, I could have Carl stain them tonight, so they'd be dry by tomorrow. And I'd love to have the closet shelves today, so we can paint them."

Taylor took a long drag on his cigarette, leaned toward me, sneared, and blew the smoke directly in my face. Grinning as if daring me to object, he replied, "No sweat, Gilbert."

"Good," Sullivan immediately interjected, to my surprise. "Because if you can't handle the work, Taylor, I'll have one of my people replace you even before you can get your tools reloaded in your pickup."

"I can handle the job just fine, dude." Taylor shot a visual dart in my direction and crushed his cigarette under the heel of his boot. "You'll have your closet shelves in an hour, Gilbert, soon as I finish with Steve's project."

"Thank you," I replied in Taylor's general direction, but I kept my eyes on Steve Sullivan. His bland expression didn't change. I turned and headed back across the street. Sullivan had just bailed me out of a jam. If he hadn't been there, I very well might have made the same threat to Taylor, but my threat to replace him would have been a bluff. Sullivan, however, had the connections to back up his assertions. Why was he being so nice? He was probably trying to lull me into a false sense of security.

Carl was in the living room, rummaging through my fabric pieces. With his tall, thin, and stooped frame, he resembled a curved-over contemporary floor lamp. One that never lit up, that is. "Painting's done," he muttered glumly.

"That's just the first coat. We'll put the burgundy coat on for the faux finish later this afternoon. The frottage technique is a two-person job, with one person rolling on the paint and the second person placing the plastic on top of it. It's a subtractive procedure that . . ." Speaking of glazing, his eyes had started to glaze over. "The point is, I'm hoping that by then, Randy or Myra will come over to give us a hand. I need to hang the wallpaper at some point. In the meantime, I could use some help with the sewing. Especially with the pillows. It's really a simple job, and I can show you how."

Carl grimaced, then grabbed his keys. "I don't sew," he declared. "I'll go get us some reinforcements."

"You have more people who can help us out?" I asked.

"No, I meant I'll go get us some lunch. What would you like? A burger?" Before I could reply, he continued. "You're probably more the salad type. How 'bout I get us something from the noodles-to-go place?"

"That sounds great. Thanks, Carl."

The garage door rumbled open and then closed behind his car. It was the first time I'd been left alone in the house, and after a couple of minutes, I decided to take a break. I'd inspect Carl's painting and the patch job we'd done on the hole.

Upstairs, I knelt, closed my eyes, and ran my palm over the smooth surface of the repaired wall. To my delight, only the coolness of the still-damp plaster gave me any indication of where Taylor had taped over the new seams. This surface would make a perfect blank canvas beneath the sublime wallpaper that I was so eager to hang. I opened my eyes and admired Carl's paint job. The gold walls were already catching a lovely slant of light through the windows. This new bedroom was going to be the absolute ultimate Christmas gift, wrapped in luxurious, warm red-and-gold walls.

The garage door opened again. Carl must have forgotten something: his wallet, perhaps. I grinned and waited for him to enter the house, planning to call down to him that he'd done an excellent job on both the sanding and the painting.

"Oh, my God!" a woman shrieked. "We've caught them in the act!"

I scrambled to my feet and raced out of the bedroom, making it to the landing of the stairs. Below me, I instantly recognized Debbie Henderson—an attractive, round-faced woman with strawberry-blond hair—from the wedding picture, although her delightful smile was now absent. Next to her stood a rail-thin bleached blonde. She wore a stunning heather pin-striped suit that was obviously an Armani. She had to be Jill McBride, Kevin's wife.

"It's okay," I said, trying to mollify them. "I'm supposed to be here, Mrs. Henderson. I'm a . . . guest of your husband's."

Debbie cried, "I knew it! Didn't I tell you, Jill? We caught them in the act! She was coming out of the *bedroom*."

"Your husband was paying me to . . ." Come to think of it that didn't sound good. "Mr. Henderson hired me to—"

"We know full well that you're a designer," Jill McBride cut in firmly. The woman reeked of old money in her upper-crust Bostonian accent and her every movement. "Don't deny it."

"I wasn't going to." How could I? My only other option would have been to claim I was a hooker. One who'd brought a sewing machine and fabric to her trick's house.

Debbie grumbled, "I suppose Carl thought I'd enjoy being surprised. As opposed to having some input in what my own bedroom looks like . . ."

"I've got to get home," Jill said. Her face was ashen. She gave Debbie's arm a squeeze and drew a shaky breath. "If Carl's having your bedroom redone, Kevin's probably destroying my den as we speak. Honestly! He knows I handpick people to do that sort of thing for me!"

Despite the gravity of the situation, I couldn't help but smile at the notion of Jill's handpicking people to destroy her rooms.

"Go. Hurry." Debbie gestured Jill toward the door. Peevishly, she brushed past me and marched up the stairs.

"I assure you, Mrs. Henderson, I've been trying to take your personal taste into consideration as I—"

"Oh. My. *God!*"

I raced after her into the room. Although the other walls were already much improved—at once livelier and truly elegant in their new golden hue—my client's wife was gaping in horror at the blotchy accent wall.

Debbie Henderson snatched up my crowbar and whirled to face me. "Whatever possessed you to tear out my paneling? What kind of an idiot designer *are* you?"

chapter 3

The aspen paneling was really nice," I said to Debbie, hoping that "really nice" was apt flattery for something that she'd loved and that I'd just hacked to bitty bits during her brief absence from home. "You and I share an appreciation for unpainted, quality wood. Unfortunately, your husband didn't mention that the paneling was your favorite part of the room until it was too late. The good news is I'm installing magnificent wallpaper that's an absolute work of art and is going to look positively sublime. . . ."

But Debbie was still too agitated to hear me. She was now examining Taylor's and my patch in the wall as if she were assessing the aftermath of some terrible accident.

At least she'd dropped my crowbar to do so, and I toyed with the idea of nudging it farther away from her with my foot. "Why is *this* here?" she asked me in accusatory tones.

"It's a repair job from the hole in the Sheetrock that we discovered when we removed the panels."

"Why would there have been a hole in the wall? And why wouldn't my husband or I have known about it if our walls were crumbling all around us?"

"The hole was put there deliberately. Somebody had apparently been hiding several letters and a necklace in it."

"Letters?"

"Love letters."

Her angry expression instantly changed to a startled one, and then she looked worried. "That's very strange, to say the least. If there were letters here, they must have been put there long before Carl and I got married and bought the place." She paused. "Did my husband happen to see them?" she asked, too casually.

"Yes, he was with me at the time. He put them away in another room."

"In the guest room?"

"I don't know."

She sighed, then muttered under her breath, "I should have seen this coming."

Below us, I could hear a man's heavy footfalls, and Carl's voice soon called up the stairs, "Erin? You didn't happen to see my wife, did you? I could have sworn she and Jill took *Debbie's* car to the spa, but—"

With her hands fisted, Debbie marched out of the room.

"Debbie!" he cried.

"Carl."

I rushed into the hallway behind Debbie. Carl was holding two containers from Noodles and Company and staring up at his wife. His facial expression reminded me of the way my cat, Hildi, had looked up at me when a former neighbor carried her home by the scruff of the neck after Hildi had snuck through a window and attacked his canary cage.

"What are you doing back so early?" Carl asked his wife.

"Jill and I got to talking during the drive about some of the peculiar things you and Kevin have been saying lately. We put everything together and realized what you were up to. Then we decided we'd never be able to really relax at the spa anyway, so we turned around and came home."

He glanced at the food containers in either hand, then at the front door. I'm pretty sure he was considering dropping the lunches and bolting. Instead he sighed, pointed at me with his chin, and told his wife, "This was supposed to be a Christmas gift. Merry Christmas."

"You let her tear down my paneling!" Debbie stomped her foot. "What *were* you thinking?"

Carl hung his head. "I didn't realize why no one else touching the paneling was so important to you, or—"

"What do you mean, *why* it's so important? Because I just happen to like the look of natural wood, that's why. I didn't know any more than *you* did about the cubbyhole in there till just now, when . . . when your designer told me."

"Erin Gilbert," I supplied, realizing that I'd neglected to introduce myself. "Mrs. Henderson, let me just show you the wallpaper and my design for your room, okay?"

"It looks great to me," Carl interjected with a careless shrug.

"You don't know an ottoman from an armoire," she scoffed. "You'd be just as happy if our furniture were made out of cinder blocks and particleboard."

"Hey! I've gone along with every one of your decisions without complaint. I've never objected to a single stick of furniture you brought into the house. And I agreed to toss nearly every piece of furnishing *I* owned before we moved in here."

She flung up her hands. "Because *all* of it was constructed from particleboard and cinder blocks!"

"And I'm *agreeing* with you!"

She rolled her eyes, then sighed and stared at her shoes. After an uncomfortably long pause, she met my eyes. "Hi, Erin." She held out her hand. "I'm Debbie Henderson. Welcome to our home." Her smile was sincere.

We belatedly shook hands and exchanged pleasantries. "I'm sure you can't tell this from looking around the place," Debbie told me, "but I have a true *passion* for interior design."

"Sure I can. For one thing, I'm completely smitten with your eight-drawer chest. Not everyone would recognize such high-quality craftsmanship."

"Thank you. That was one of the items I purchased specifically for this house, five years ago. I love it. That's why I put it at the foot of the bed, where it's the first thing I see when I wake up every morning."

Hmm. That chest needed to be moved to one side to improve the overall balance and flow of the room. It would still be the first thing she saw upon waking, though . . . if she didn't mind tilting her head a little. For the foot of the bed, I'd selected a stunning, gilt-framed oil painting of a narrow cobblestone road in a quaint French village, the terra-cotta housefronts all brimming with colorful flower boxes. I could always return the painting, though, if she preferred having the chest there. I donned my warmest smile. "Let me show you my plans, Debbie."

I soon found Debbie Henderson to be every bit as engaging as I'd assumed her to be from the sparkling blue eyes and warm smile in her wedding picture, as well as from the exquisite taste she'd shown in purchasing that eight-drawer chest. We decided to go over my plans for the room at the kitchen table while Carl and I ate our lunches. Debbie liked every single one of my ideas and selections, and actually squealed with excitement when I showed her the new antiqued bronze curtain rods with their ivy leaf finials that echoed the curved lines in the wallpaper pattern. Carl, meanwhile, when pressed by his wife, would give my drawings an occasional nod. They say in the design business that all rooms need "peaks and valleys," and although Carl was physically built like a peak—or at least like a hat tree—moodwise he provided whatever room he inhabited with a perpetual valley.

Halfway through lunch, Taylor wordlessly stepped inside the front door and dumped the new shelves in a heap, so I showed Debbie how well they worked in her bedroom closet. She was effusive with her praise and hugged me. Having clients appreciate my ideas for sprucing up their living spaces is one of my favorite things about this job. Having to listen to the occasional bickering between spouses is one of my least favorite aspects, but what job is perfect?

After lunch, we discussed the tasks that still remained to be done, and the Hendersons volunteered to apply the final coat—the burgundy—for the faux finish. Carl wanted to be in charge of applying the paint, so I showed Debbie how to smooth three-foot squares of plastic onto the wet paint, then peel the plastic away, which gives the walls a wonderful marbleized appearance. The two of them were working with confidence and good rhythm. I cautioned them to stick to the same task throughout; switching the painter and the person handling the plastic leads to noticeable differences in the finished appearance. Then I went downstairs to sew the drapes.

I had purchased premade sheers, but even so, the raw silk drapes would, if left unlined, fade dreadfully in direct sunlight. Carl had told me that Debbie was a light sleeper, so I was using a high-density blackout lining. The panels would use butterfly pleats, and with the sheen of the fabulous fabric, the new curtains would glow like liquid gold against the walls.

The doorbell rang. It was Myra and Randy Axelrod, who announced that they were "here to lend a hand."

"Great," I replied with sincere relief as I ushered them inside. Randy was such a large man that I had to flatten myself against the wall to allow him to squeeze past me. "I'll gladly take all four helping hands."

"I've really only got the one free hand at the moment." Randy raised the half-full Budweiser bottle he was carrying. He laughed at his lame joke, then headed upstairs to check the progress of the room.

Although I offered to show Myra the room, she declined. "No, no. That's quite all right. I can see it tomorrow, when you're a little farther along." She was searching my face again with the intensity of an antiques expert studying a potential purchase for signs of fraud. Her avid curiosity about my appearance sent a shiver through me; could *she* be my mother? Facially, we looked nothing alike. We were both thin, however, and were roughly the same height. Myra had gray eyes, unlike my dark brown ones, but her graying shoulder-length hair held the same hints of auburn hues you could see in mine.

Before we'd had the chance to exchange more than a

couple of mundane comments, Randy tromped back downstairs and announced, "Making good progress up there. You'd be even farther along, except we spent so much time today at the McBrides'. They're applying Venetian plaster," he continued. "It's a lot of work."

"What color?"

"A darkish, lightish green."

I nodded. If he was so unable to describe a medium shade of green, the man surely didn't write his own articles in *Denver Lifestyles*. Venetian plaster is not available in myriad hues. Sullivan was probably applying Behr's Fox Glen, which, unfortunately for me, I'd yet to see come out poorly: the deep, rich hue could magically enhance a room with cooling and refreshing powers reminiscent of a desert oasis. I was sorely tempted to create friction between client and designer by suggesting to Kevin McBride that what would *really* tie Sullivan's room design together would be a Salvador Dali–like melting-clock mural on his ceiling. . . .

Randy was eyeing the dining room table. "Nice cloth."

"Thanks." The fabric he was referring to happened to be a luxurious maroon-and-bronze patterned chenille, as soft as butterfly wings, which complemented the wall treatments magnificently. The thick fabric could encase the down comforter that the Hendersons already owned or serve alone as a bedspread during summer months. With maroon-and-gold cording on the four throw pillows—two bronze-colored velvet and two made from the duvet fabric—I was confident that my clients and I would love the finished results. Well, *Debbie* and I would love it. Mr. Death Valley would no doubt point out to me again that once his eyes were closed, the room was pretty much a solid *black*.

"This cloth goes great with the curtains," Randy muttered, examining my nearly completed drapery panels. He'd used the word *cloth* twice now, when everyone in the industry referred to it as fabric. Was this man really editing a design magazine? "I like what I'm seeing in both rooms. You gals are neck and neck at this point."

"Which gals are you referring to?"

"Gilbert and"—he made a downward flick of his wrist and added in a lisp—"*Sullivan*, of course, sweetcakes." He chuckled.

"I have to tell you that I find gay jokes extremely offensive, Mr. Axelrod," I said without stopping to think. I was shocked at myself for letting that slip out. Sullivan was surely the last person I needed—or wanted—to defend.

"Do you? And what if I *have* to tell *you* that you might have just cost yourself the contest?"

"Randy!" Myra cried.

He chuckled and gave my arm a painful squeeze. "Just kidding. I already told you I was going to be strictly impartial, didn't I?" He shifted his focus to his wife. "Myra?" He snapped his fingers and pointed at the sewing machine. "You're up, girl."

I felt like grabbing the man by the collar and giving him a piece of my mind for treating his wife like a golden retriever, but Myra merely plopped down in the chair by the machine and asked cheerfully, "What am I sewing here, Erin?"

"You really don't have—"

"Myra likes sewing. Says it relaxes her."

"That's true. I make most of my own dresses."

"I'm impressed," I said honestly, while making a quick assessment of the situation. My interests were best served by keeping my nose to the grindstone. That meant not wasting my time trying to enlighten an oaf like Randy Axelrod. And not allowing someone with unauthorized access to my personal history to yank me around like some mad puppeteer. That's certainly what my mother would have advised. Ignoring Randy, I showed Myra the measurements for the new duvet.

With a sly grin Randy asked, "So tell me, Erin. Have you and your bro been working well together?"

"My 'bro'?" I repeated, bewildered.

"Yeah, you know . . . Taylor Duncan."

"That's just a figure of speech, Erin," Myra explained. She glared at her husband with laser eyes. "Randy uses it all the time. Don't you, dear?"

"All the time." He stared so intently at me that I got the impression it was a test of wills, so I just stared right back. I tend to like most people, and especially most people who share my passion in interior design. Randy Axelrod, editor of *Denver Lifestyles* or no, was an exception. "I see you ripped out the paneling. Did that go okay for you?"

He couldn't have missed seeing the repair job during his tour of the room minutes earlier. That was even *assuming* he hadn't already heard about the hole from Taylor or Kevin, let alone if he hadn't put the hole there himself. Nevertheless, I replied breezily, "Just fine, thanks. No problems."

Though I lacked a shred of hard evidence, or even soft evidence, I was now absolutely certain that Randy was the one who'd hidden my picture on the back of the aspen board with the intention of my discovering it.

"Glad to hear it." He swiped some dots of perspiration off his brow. I realized suddenly that his face looked a little pallid. "Where's the wood you pulled off the walls?" he asked me.

"Taylor stashed it in the back of his pickup, I believe. Why?"

"I'm gonna see if any of the boards are salvageable.

They're mine, after all. I was the one who picked 'em out and paid for 'em."

"They came with the house," Myra scolded over the whir and rhythmic chugging of the sewing machine. Her pressure on the pedal was steady and in perfect synchronization with her hands as she confidently fed the burnished material through the machine. It was obvious that this woman was better at sewing than I am—and I'm no slouch. "The wood from the paneling belongs to the Hendersons, and you know it, Randy. Same with their old curtains, so don't get any ideas there, either."

He snorted but made no reply. I decided that Myra had no idea about the booby-trapped paneling, whereas Randy wanted to find the one rigged board and ensure that the photograph had indeed been removed.

He took another swig of beer, then grimaced and glanced at the bottle. "This stuff tastes a little funny. Must've been a bad batch. I should take the whole six-pack back to the store and complain." Again, he swiped at his damp forehead. "The alcohol's making me dizzy."

Without looking up from her work, Myra suggested, "You've been looking a bit tired all afternoon. Why don't you go back home and rest?"

"Yeah, I think I'll do that. See you gals later."

The faux finish came out beautifully, much to Debbie's and my delight. Carl's response was, "Nice. Hell of a lot of extra work just to get a batch of *streaks*, though. Used to be a job like this would lead to the painter getting fired."

Debbie patted him on the back and said, "Ah, yes, Carl, that's got to make Erin feel just terrific. You're quite the charmer, all right."

Letting them bicker quietly, I found myself surreptitiously studying the room with an eye for ways that I could warm up and romanticize the space even further. Candles. Lavender incense. A mixed tape of Vivaldi and Marvin Gaye, maybe? When I was done, this room would be a snug refuge for Debbie Henderson, a room in which she could read, sleep, or just daydream.

To my utter lack of surprise, minutes later Carl declined to volunteer when I said that I could use some help hanging the wallpaper. He grumbled that he needed a break and was going to watch some TV in the basement. By then, Myra had finished sewing the duvet and pillows and called it a day, with my blessings. She'd done a wonderful job. She'd lined the vibrant fabric with thin sheets of cotton batting, which keeps pillows from getting lumpy, and attached the cording to the edges, up to the openings. All that remained of the sewing chores was stuffing the pillows and then hand-stitching their openings in the seams. The plump pillows and duvet would be truly sumptuous.

Wallpapering is a task that's particularly conducive to conversation. A teacher of mine at Parsons once mentioned that he'd known of many couples who blamed their divorces on wallpapering stints, so perhaps those conversations aren't always *pleasant*, but Debbie merely asked me to tell her about the headboard, which seemed innocuous enough.

Their headboard would be the room's unifying piece. Last week I'd found them a night table so exquisite that the instant my gaze lit upon it, I realized that if I were to drop dead that very minute, that night table was the item I would want to take with me so I could wrap my body around it for all eternity. Clients get a little freaked out when I describe their furnishings in those terms, so I merely explained to Debbie that their to-die-for transitional contemporary night table was crafted of tiger maple, whereas their very traditional showpiece chest was alder. Therefore, their new bed would be magnificently crafted from alder, but with warm, golden-hued tiger-maple accents. Or at least it was magnificently crafted in my *mind's* eye. If Taylor managed to wreck that hand-selected lumber with its sumptuous pattern, Carl—by God—was going to have to fork over the bucks for my own craftsmen to redo the piece from scratch. "We're going for the same distressed finish on the headboard that's on your chest of drawers," I told Debbie.

"Distressed finish, hey? That's appropriate. I'm pretty distressed myself these days."

"I guess the holidays have a way of doing that to people." That was as noncommittal a response as I could think of at the moment. Perhaps I should have heeded my teacher's warnings and insisted on doing this job alone. But then I hadn't realized that decorating the Hendersons' bedroom was going to be an emotional minefield. Debbie tucked her red hair behind her ear and muttered, "Why should the holidays be any different than any other time with Carl?"

"You're having problems, I take it." I wasn't a good enough actress to feign surprise, but I didn't have to fake my concern.

"It's not easy playing second fiddle in your marriage. Especially when there aren't even any children involved."

I made a sympathetic noise. If she wanted me to understand what she was talking about, I knew she would elaborate.

"I guess he deserves some credit for finally agreeing that it was time to do something with our bedroom. And for hiring you," Debbie added generously.

Reaching for my somewhat dicey arbitration skills, I said, "You and Randy did an absolutely fantastic job on the paint. It looks fabulous."

"It sure does. And I already love the wallpaper. I'm so glad now that you stuck to your guns and put that up, in spite of whatever trauma it caused me earlier."

I said nothing. I would much rather have kept the paneling and never discovered that damned picture.

That brought a question to mind. If Randy Axelrod had deliberately hidden my picture there for me to find, how could he have known that I would be the one to remove the paneling? Had I been too hasty to conclude that he was the culprit? Then again, he could have gotten me to find that picture either way; he could have easily claimed to notice that there was a loose board and feigned discovering it himself in my presence.

Aiming at safer conversational grounds, I said, "I hope Taylor is making progress on your furniture."

"That sounds a bit like wishful thinking, unfortunately."

"Do you know your husband's stepson well?"

"Too well." Debbie rolled her eyes. "Carl told me while we were painting that Taylor was the one who built that hiding spot behind the wall. He used it as a drug stash when he was house-sitting for us during a long vacation we took in Europe." She sighed.

A new theory occurred to me, and my heart started hammering. Randy had referred to Taylor as my "bro." Could I be Taylor's older sister? Could Taylor have known that fact somehow and put my photograph where, for some unfathomable reason, he'd intended for me to find it? "So were the necklace and letters his as well?" I asked casually.

Debbie pursed her lips, then shook her head. "I doubt Taylor would have the energy or motivation to read a whole letter, let alone write one."

She avoided my eyes. She knew more than she wanted to tell me.

Was Mom watching over me right now? If so, she was probably screaming at me to hold my tongue, but I *had* to know more. "Taylor is Carl's ex-wife's son, right?"

"Emily's son. Yes. Emily and Carl were married for twelve years, and Carl treats that boy like his own son. Sometimes I think that Emily . . ." She sighed again. "Let's just say that Emily and I don't get along all that well." She added in a slightly choked voice, "Not that it's surprising, since we're both in love with the same man."

Now I understood her earlier remark about playing second fiddle. It wasn't the first time I'd glimpsed the vicious battles that could rage between a man's first and second wives. "I'm sorry, Debbie," I said. "That must make it awfully hard on you, if she still hasn't let go of him."

She gave me a peculiar expression but merely replied, "The way Emily spoils Taylor, it's lucky she only had the one son."

Was there an emphasis on the word *son*? This was maddening: someone in this house's intimate circle of visitors or owners knew more about my family tree than I did. I didn't know Debbie well enough to confide in her, plus she clearly had troubles of her own. "Emily only had the one child?"

"Yes. And Taylor's real father cut himself out of the picture right after he was born. From what I understand, they married young, split up . . . and then *he* split the scene."

"I see." If that was accurate, Taylor and I were probably not full siblings. I gritted my teeth. I was ignoring my final promise to my mother again by trying to guess my birth parents' identity.

The doorbell rang, then the door opened, and a moment later, a voice called, "Don't worry. It's just me."

"Come on up, Jill," Debbie answered.

She swept into the room and greeted us both warmly. To my eye, Jill McBride was a refutation of the old saw that you can't be too rich or too thin. Her face *was* very pretty, though, despite her apparent anorexia. She did a slow three-sixty, her eyes wide in delight. "These walls! The finish, the wallpaper! This bedroom is absolutely to die for! Are you putting up crown molding?" She touched my shoulder.

I couldn't suppress a proud smile. "To match the trim of Debbie's chest of drawers."

Jill looked at Debbie. "The Guy Chaddock chest that I gave you last year?"

Blushing and averting her gaze, Debbie mumbled, "Mm-hmm." I was stunned. For no apparent reason, Debbie had lied to me. She'd told me she'd bought that chest herself when she and Carl had first gotten married.

Jill clutched her hands over her heart. "Divine. Simply divine," she gushed.

"And you should see the fabric," Debbie said, mimicking Jill's behavior by also touching my shoulder, although my feelings of camaraderie with Debbie were now greatly diminished.

"Oh, I *did*," she replied. "I peeked at it on my way up the stairs. It's absolutely *yummy*. Take a look at my eyes, ladies. I kid you not. They are positively green with envy."

"Speaking of green, how's your new room coming?" I asked.

"Quite nicely, thank you. Though to be honest, it's much more in Kevin's taste than in mine."

Debbie clicked her tongue. "Carl doesn't seem to have *any* opinion whatsoever when it comes to our house."

"I know. You're so lucky." Jill lowered her voice and asked, "Is Carl here?"

"He's glued to the TV set downstairs."

"Good thing." She took another step toward Debbie, then added, sotto voce: "Hate to tell you this, but *she* was here again." Jill kept an eye on the stairs, as if fearful someone would come pounding up them any second.

"Emily?" Debbie asked with alarm.

Jill frowned. Then she nodded. "An hour ago. I spotted Emily across the street, talking to Taylor."

Debbie grimaced. Looking at me, she explained, "Carl's ex-wife is, as usual, trying to find an excuse to see Carl. Emily manages to come over whenever I'm not around. That's the other reason Jill and I decided not to go to the spa today." To Jill, she muttered, "Naturally, with me gone, she *would* use the excuse of her son's being here all weekend to see Carl."

"Well, rest assured, her plans didn't work out this time. Carl's been here with you, and *I* drummed up an excuse to pull Taylor away from her. I made it clear we were all far too busy to chat. For once, she took the hint and left."

"Bless you!" Debbie said, giving her a little one-armed hug.

"Oh, don't mention it, darling. You've done the same sort of thing with you-know-who on my behalf. Countless times."

"I don't know how you put up with it. Or why."

Jill arched a nicely shaped eyebrow. "Well. Kevin has his other qualities. And we have a comfortable relationship." She turned to me and chuckled. "My, but we're giving you quite the unsolicited earful, aren't we, Erin?"

"That's quite all right. I'm just minding my own business."

"Good for you, dear. Perhaps I'd better warn you,

though, that you're going to have to lean hard on your carpenter if you actually expect that boy to do anything resembling *work*. Steve Sullivan's all but keeping Taylor in his back pocket. If you don't do the same, he'll do as little as possible on our room, but nothing whatsoever on yours."

"That was nice of you to warn us," Debbie said with a laugh. "Considering the circumstances, I mean."

"You mean, considering the contest the men have going?" Jill flicked her wrist. "That's their silly little diversion, not ours. There's really no deadline now that we've already forced them to unveil their little surprise."

"Except that my schedule for Monday is pretty full," I interjected. I was keenly aware that, for the sake of my sanity, I needed to finish this bizarre job as quickly as possible. "And I'm sure that Steve has other jobs scheduled for Monday as well."

Jill made an exaggerated "oops" face, then joked, "In that case, never mind. Rest assured that Taylor's a regular whirling dervish and is painstakingly dividing his time right down the middle."

"I guess I'd better go speak to him as soon as I'm finished."

"Too late," Jill replied with a hint of malice. "I saw him drive away as I headed up the driveway just now."

Frustrated and finding my confidence-and-optimism mantra increasingly ineffective, I decided to call it a day myself. I thanked Debbie and Carl for all their hard work and headed straight for the Axelrods' backyard in the hope that Taylor might be there, even though his truck was gone. My lumber was still untouched, neatly stacked by the back door.

Cursing under my breath, I returned to my van for

some plastic sheeting. In the event of an unpredicted storm, there was a small roof that would offer the stack some protection, but I couldn't risk water damage to the unfinished wood.

The back doors to my van were unlocked. "Jeez, Taylor! Thanks a lot!" I grumbled as I reached inside and grabbed a roll of plastic.

I heard an engine idle as a vehicle came to a stop behind me. Whirling around—this job had made me ridiculously jumpy—I saw Sullivan roll down the window in his van. "Hey, Gilbert. How about letting me sabotage our contest and get you drunk tonight?"

The invitation was totally out of character. Where was the arrogant Sullivan I'd come to know and loathe? I walked up to his van, mulling my response. There was nothing I would like more than to compare notes on our clients. But for all I knew, Steve Sullivan could have known both the McBrides and the Axelrods long before he accepted this job. Maybe, in fact, he'd been in on the whole thing from the beginning. If he was unscrupulous enough to swipe a client, he might have been willing to help rig a high-stakes contest. "Tempting as that sounds, I'd better say no," I told him coolly.

"Suit yourself, Gilbert," he said with a grin, "but don't go saying I never asked you."

He started to roll up his window, and that's when the panicked, chest-constricting feeling hit me again with the blunt force of a tidal wave. In its aftermath, every iota of my confidence and optimism instantly deserted me. "Steve?"

"Yeah?"

What was I thinking? I'd just called him "Steve," as I would if we were *friends*, not ruthless competitors. I couldn't reveal myself to him like this. To mention the photograph meant letting him see through my veneer.

Steve Sullivan didn't need to know that I was adopted. That my father had deserted my mother and me when I was twelve. That my mother's death was as painful to me as though it had happened only yesterday. That despite all of my mother's best efforts, a part of me would always ache to know why my birth parents had given me away at eighteen months, as though they'd discovered some irreparable flaw in me that made me permanently unworthy of their love.

I forced a smile and met his hazel eyes. "Oh, nothing. Have a nice night, Sullivan."

"You too, Gilbert."

I watched him drive away.

chapter 4

> "Just before you wrap your gifts, spritz
> the inner side of the paper with
> cologne. This will give your loved ones
> a delightful sensuous bonus as they
> open their presents."
>
> —*Audrey Munroe*

DOMESTIC BLISS

Garages and driveways are a rarity in the historic district of Maplewood Hill, but I never complained. Having to park on the street and negotiate the slate walkway always allowed me to fully appreciate the rich grandeur of the late-nineteenth-century house in which I rented a room. My short stroll was especially wonderful now that the grand, stately homes and their tall, majestic spruce trees sparkled with Christmas lights. More than any other season, Christmas was a time of hope and love, when we could loosen the reins on our hearts. I paused on the walkway, took a deep breath of the sweet, crisp air, and looked down the street. Despite the intense challenges this day had brought me, I couldn't help but smile. The view was glorious. In my mind's eye, I enhanced the beauty even further: the asphalt was buried in a blanket of glistening snow. Tree branches and roofs were frosted with white powder.

Still smiling, I entered Audrey's house through the arched oak door. The magnificent foyer, which I'd decorated myself, was so beautiful that I loved to linger here. Tonight, however, the French doors to the parlor had been left wide open and, at the sight before me, I gasped aloud.

Audrey Munroe, my petite, sixty-something-year-old landlady, was kneeling on the richly grained antique-pine floor. She'd shoved the furnishings aside, rolled up the exquisite oriental navy-and-claret rug, and laid down a sheet of thick plastic in its place. In some sort of twisted art project gone mad, she was taking a box cutter to the sublime custom wallpaper that I'd custom-ordered for her dining room.

Horrified, I crossed the room toward Audrey. My sleek black cat, Hildi, had been sitting beside her but, accurately assessing my mood, promptly pranced out of the room.

Audrey glanced up at me, then did a double take. "Don't worry, dear. I've decided not to hang this wallpaper after all, so I'm putting it to good use elsewhere. Much as I love it, I've decided instead to go with wall treatments based on renewable resources . . . sea grass on three walls and cork on the fourth. We're doing a Dom-Bliss segment on sustainable resources in January."

Dom-Bliss was Audrey's nickname for the local television show that she hosted: *Domestic Bliss with Audrey Munroe.* Audrey was the first to admit that her morning show was "your basic Martha Stewart knockoff."

I struggled to find my voice. "Audrey. I ordered twelve double rolls for you. We had the manufacturer alter some of the colors in their pattern to match your window treatments. That paper cost an ungodly amount of money. We won't be able to return any of it. I explained all of that to you. Remember?"

"Of course I do, dear, and I wouldn't dream for one minute of cheating those lovely people who make such delicious designs. I had no choice but to use their paper as gift wrap. Tomorrow's show is called 'Wrapping Paper Alternatives.' I find store-bought wrapping paper to be so . . . *unimaginative,* don't you?" She studied my still-horrified expression, then returned to her wanton slicing. "Two of my wrapping paper alternatives are wallpaper and fabric remnants. So I checked the contents of my storage room, and alas, I'd cleared out all of my scraps."

"But why didn't you ask *me* for some? I have enough wallpaper scraps to cover every carton and box in Crestview. I would have been more than happy to give you all the wallpaper you possibly could have wanted."

"Oh, well." She brushed back the bangs of her ash-blond highlighted hair. "I enjoy spending my money on fabulous wallpaper, regardless of how it eventually gets used."

I sank into the closest chair, a Martha Washington

upholstered in lustrous leather. "Buy all the wallpaper you like, Audrey; that's terrific. But please don't hack it to bits like this. Chopping up untouched Scalamandré wallpaper for Christmas wrapping in my presence is like . . . like lopping a calf's head off in front of a Hindu."

"My goodness." She reached over and patted my knee. "I had no idea you'd get so upset. Do you feel as strongly about that shiny metallic paper you ordered for the accent wall?" she asked innocently.

Through gritted teeth, I asked, "The hand-hammered copper paper from Farrow and Ball? The paper that we put the rush order on . . . which had to filter all the way to their craftsmen in China? Do you mean *that* shiny metallic paper?"

"Well, I can tell by that unpleasant shrillness in your voice that the answer's going to be yes, so you may want to avert your eyes whenever you go past the Christmas tree in the den."

"Oh, dear lord," I murmured. I gripped the sturdy mahogany arms of my chair and watched as Audrey marked the dimensions of a shirt box on the back side of the amazing work of art that she was blithely mutilating. "Not to criticize, Audrey, but that wallpaper is too stiff to fold easily. Not to mention that the cost of the wrapping paper is going to exceed the cost of the gift inside it. You'd be better off wrapping the present in an Hermès scarf."

She sat up and gave me a big grin. "As they say, 'Great minds think alike.' That is precisely one of my alternatives! A gift within a gift, if you will." She rose—barefoot beneath her elegant black-and-gold kaftan—and did some sort of plié to stretch her muscles. Many years ago, Audrey Munroe had been a dancer with the New York City Ballet. Nowadays, the woman metaphorically brought her own stage with her wherever she went. Audrey had an innate gracefulness and flamboyance that I greatly admired, although she conquered every room she entered so thoroughly that, even inside this cavernous room with its twelve-foot ceilings and just the two of us present, it sometimes felt crowded. "Let me show you the results, sweetie."

She headed toward the kitchen, and I trailed after her, detecting a faint scent of onion, as well as pine, in the warm air. Unlike me, Audrey loves to cook extravagant meals. Her kitchen, like her foyer, is absolutely stunning. The design and contents of all the other rooms in the house, including, sadly, my sitting-room-cum-bedroom, were subject to her whimsical changes of mind and spur-of-the-moment purchases. Not to mention her tendency to treat the materials that I'd purchased for her home at her behest as though they were dime-store ingredients for one big sloppy science project.

I asked, "The Sunday comics are going to be another alternative wrapping paper, I presume?"

"Exactly. After I cover them in clear cellophane. And, of course, I'll be doing a segment on using vegetables to turn that plain, *boring* tissue paper that clothing stores use as box liners into beautiful handmade wrapping paper, and—"

"Vegetables?"

"Yes. After they've been carved into ink stamps." She started to hand me a potato that had been sliced in half, the white surface cut into the silhouetted shape of a teddy bear, which I recognized as having originated from one of her cookie cutters. Then she hesitated. "You're not . . . unnaturally *connected* to potatoes, are you, dear?"

"No, Audrey, I have no ethical problems with cutting up vegetables. Making ink stamps out of raw potatoes is a terrific idea. I used to do that myself as a kid."

"I'm doing some abstract designs with celery stalks too. I was already in the kitchen to collect the potatoes, and I thought, why not use vegetables as paint-brushes?" She gestured at the stove, where some half-full pots were burbling. "So then I decided to make some natural paints—red from sugar beets, amber from onion skins, and green from spinach."

"Nice." On her Caledonia granite countertop, she had spread out fragrant boughs of cedar and fir trees, along with pinecones dusted with glitter. These items were obviously intended as decorations to augment the gift boxes. She had also preserved some oak and maple leaves, which she would probably spray-paint gold; the telltale paint can was nearby.

"I've cut some photographs out of old magazines and calendars to do decoupages in interesting de-signs," Audrey informed me as she refreshed her water glass. "And lastly, I'll show my audience how to make those dear little fabric gift bags. So *charming,* don't you think?"

Knowing what was coming, I gripped the cold, smooth edge of the beautiful granite countertop as she retrieved several squares of fabric from another room. All had been cut from the elegant toile drapery fabric that we'd special-ordered from Christopher Norman. Her eyes sparkled. "Oh, and Erin? Just wait till you see how pretty the fabric for the sheers is now that I spray-painted it! I've turned those sheers into the *loveliest* ribbons imaginable!"

chapter 5

The next morning, I awoke in a foul mood. By accepting Carl Henderson's job, I'd given up one of my precious, leisurely Sunday mornings spent wrapped in my feather-soft angora afghan with Hildi curled in my lap as we perused the home and garden section of the newspaper and furniture-ad fliers.

My night had been dreadful, my inadequate sleep interrupted with unpleasant dreams. To make matters worse, I'd been awakened at dawn by what sounded like a town hall meeting in the den, only to stagger into the blinding lights of what proved to be a film shoot for Audrey's show. Although her fictitious living room in the Denver television studio had a marvelous, lavishly decorated blue spruce (I should know; she'd had me select the tree and decorate it myself on-site just three days earlier), Audrey had decided she preferred the backdrop of our *actual* Christmas tree and den for her alternative-wrapping-paper show. She apologized for forgetting to warn me about the crack-of-dawn photo shoot and soothed, "You'll have the whole house to yourself for the rest of the day, dear. After this, we're filming a segment in Vail, where there's actually some snow. I'll be lucky to get home before midnight."

While grumbling to myself such nasty remarks as "Domestic bliss my ass," I smeared on makeup to hide the dark circles under my eyes and compensate for my plain lavender turtleneck and blue jeans, stashed my baby picture in my back pocket, in case the opportunity arose to confront anyone about it, and left for work.

To my surprise, Taylor's pickup truck was already in the Axelrods' driveway when I arrived. The sharp growl of a table saw buzzed away behind the house. I crossed the street and rounded the house, greedily inhaling the intoxicating scent of freshly cut lumber.

Taylor had his back to me as I approached, but my initial pleasure at finding him at work on the oak television stand faded when I saw where he was making his cuts. "Taylor, stop!" I shouted over the noisy saw. "Stop!"

He shut it off and said, "Yo."

"These lengths don't look right to me."

"They're what you told me," he said with a shrug.

I ran my tape measure along the length of the board. "This is four inches too short!"

"Hey! You told me you wanted 'em thirty-six inches! That's what I cut 'em at."

I checked my sketch, which I found on a folding table he was using as a flat surface, a claw hammer serving as a paperweight. Sure enough, my measurements had been correct for the two-shelf stand. "I told you forty inches, just the way it's written here on my drawing."

"That's *not* what you *said*."

"It is too!"

"Is not!"

Be nice to the carpenter, Erin. I sucked in a deep breath of chilly air, but the aroma of newly sawn lumber had lost its magic. We certainly *sounded* like siblings, if nothing else.

"Anyways," Tyler said, "you were coming out short one board if I'd made this four inches higher. So *you* head back to the lumberyard, or *I* make your table thirty-six inches high 'stead of forty inches."

"There's no way I'm short a board."

"Search the yard if you don't believe me. Frisk me if you want, Gilbert, but I promise you, you ain't finding no missing board. Face it. You underordered your materials. Tough luck."

I was too sleep-deprived to be nice, and I was itching to strangle the guy, even if he *was* eight inches taller than I and outweighed me by some one hundred pounds of solid muscle. "I bought five of these boards, Taylor, and all five were here last night when I covered them with plastic. How many boards did you start with this morning?"

"I dunno, Gilbert. Nobody told me I was supposed to count boards. I'm a carpenter, not a mathematician."

And counting to five is hardly calculus! I closed my eyes and let out a quick growl to vent before replying.

This stand for Carl's thirteen-inch TV had been the only aspect of my design that Carl had commented on when he'd nixed my armoire design—tiger maple to match the night table with knobs that were identical to the alder chest's. With it, the entire room would have created a fabulous, unified feast for the eyes. Carl, however, had objected. "My TV can't be closed in, or I'll lose emergency access to the rabbit ears when the cable's out!" He wanted me to simply stack their two oak reproduction icebox nightstands and set the TV on top of them. This forty-inch-tall oak stand was my compromise between perfection and an eyesore.

Slightly calmer, I decided to reason with my carpenter. "Okay, Taylor. Explain something to me. If you didn't add up the total length of the boards you had available, how did you *know* you were going to come up short?"

"That was just experience talking, plus a bit of luck." Pride lurked in his voice. "I remembered you told me yesterday to make 'em thirty-six inches high."

Breathe, Erin, I reminded myself. *Take nice deep calming breaths.* Then *grab a two-by-four and smack the guy upside the head.*

I looked at the lumber he was using. There did indeed appear to be only four boards. It was extremely unlikely that some random thief had stolen a single board. Randy or Myra could have taken a board into their house, but *why?* Then again, I seemed to have been asking myself that question nonstop ever since Carl Henderson first walked into my downtown office last month.

Taylor tapped his wrist, indicating an imaginary watch. "Time's wasting. What's it gonna be? Do I fall behind schedule and start over once the lumberyard's open—in, like, three hours—or do I make this hunk of junk thirty-six inches high?"

I decided to let the "hunk of junk" remark slide, largely because, in my exhaustion, my wittiest comeback would have been—*Oh, yeah? If that's a hunk of junk, you're a hunk of punk*—and I had too much pride. That darn board had to be someplace. Maybe Taylor had simply misplaced it. More likely, Steve Sullivan or Kevin

McBride was trying to get a leg up on the Super Bowl bet by messing with his competitor's plans.

"Well?" Taylor prompted.

"You can wait the two minutes it'll take me to try to locate the missing board, then I'll let you know."

"Suit yourself, Gilbert, but it's too late now. I already cut up two of those boards."

Nothing under the table. No boards wedged alongside the concrete pad by the back door. This backyard was roughly half an acre, but there was no place for an eight-foot board to get misplaced. "At this point, I just have to know what happened to the thing, even if it's too late to get what I want."

The only reasonable possibilities were that (a) I was losing my mind; (b) Taylor had recognized his mistake earlier and had chopped one board into shims and tossed them to avoid having to admit to his error; or (c) someone had maliciously removed one board from my stack of supplies to mess with my design and my head. The first option was probably something of a given, but I'd never let a mild case of insanity stop me before. Options b and c were in a dead heat.

"Gives me a chance to take my cigarette break anyway," Taylor mumbled. He then plunked himself down on the tarp that covered a stack of lumber tidily marked "Sullivan."

"Could you sit someplace else, please? I need to go through that stack to look for my missing one-by-six."

"This is Sullivan's stuff." He kept his perch and lit his cigarette.

"And what's the obvious place to hide a board? With other boards. Give me a hand."

We started restacking Sullivan's materials from top to bottom so that I could handle each piece of wood and ensure that there didn't appear to be one odd man out that resembled my wandering board. A third of the way through a half dozen Italian black walnut boards we found a lone one-by-six of oak. Eureka! Kevin or Sullivan *had* tried to throw me off by hiding one of my boards! How low could you get? "This is it."

"How do you know, Gilbert? Did you mark each one with your lipstick?"

"No," I shot back, the tone of my voice more than implying the word *jerk-face*, "but when you're at a lumberyard, you load the boards as you select them from the racks. You wouldn't suddenly stick one board into the middle of a group of . . ." A brown bottle on the ground, partially hidden by the tarp, suddenly caught my eye — especially the skull and crossbones prominently displayed on its label. My pulse quickened. "Oh, my God," I said. The bottle looked exactly like a container I'd stowed in my van a couple of months ago, just before moving in with Audrey. My ex-boyfriend had bought the cyanide for a metal-plating project that we never actually got around to starting before he became my ex. I hadn't known where to dispose of the stuff, hadn't wanted to bring a bottle of poison into Audrey's home and risk Hildi's getting into it, and the bottle was so safely packaged and nicely tucked away in my spacious van that I hadn't given the matter a moment's thought in weeks.

"What's wrong *now*?"

"What's this doing out here?" I demanded, showing him the bottle.

"That?" he asked as if seeing it for the first time.

"Yes, that! It's cyanide! Do you know if this is my cyanide?"

He shrugged. "Guess it must be. It was in your van."

"What were you doing with it?"

He puffed on his cigarette before replying, staring impassively at the little bottle of poison I clutched in my hand. "I didn't want the glass to break when I was unloading wood."

"I had it carefully packed inside a heavy-duty plastic bag, inside a sealed metal container filled with kitty litter in case of spillage! And I put the *can* inside a box packed with foam. Just to make sure that it *couldn't* break open!"

He took another drag on his cigarette, squinted at the smoke. "So I guess I got curious."

"Jeez! This was an unopened bottle! Someone's broken the seal!"

"Like I said, I got curious. I've never seen real cyanide before. I wanted to know what it looked like."

"You had no right to go through the stuff in my van like that!"

"You told me to unload your materials."

"I told you and Kevin to unload the *wood*. What kind of nutcase would have put *wood* inside a cardboard box inside a can that was filled to the brim with kitty litter?"

"Beats me. Maybe the same kinda nutcase who carries around bottles of poison."

"Someone *gave* it to me when we . . ." I gave up. I didn't need to explain myself to the likes of Taylor; after all, he was the one who'd swiped the bottle out of my van. "I don't like anyone to touch it, for obvious reasons. That's why I keep it locked away, inside my van." Which, come to think of it, Taylor had left unlocked all of yesterday afternoon.

"And yet you go tossing your key to Kevin," he retorted. "After you'd talked to the guy for all of ten minutes."

"Where do you get off, criticizing me for—" I stopped. This situation was getting out of control. I was all but hopping up and down in my anger. "If anything should happen to anyone in this entire *city* that's linked to cyanide poisoning, I'm going to tell the police about this."

His face remained inscrutable. He took one last pull on his cigarette, then dropped it and crushed it under his heel. "So what's the final word on the length? Do I start over again this afternoon or use what I've got now?"

Through gritted teeth, I retorted, "Neither one. We're going with plan B." I flipped my paper over and quickly sketched out what I wanted, very carefully explaining each aspect to him. This was an idea that I'd almost opted for in the first place—to have a twenty-inch shelf unit sit on top of one of the reproduction iceboxes that the Hendersons already owned. That ought to make Carl happy. Part of the design had, after all, been his idea.

Taylor flipped on the motor of his saw and fitted his safety goggles back in place. "I like that idea better anyways. See? I knew I was cutting these boards right."

"I'm locking the cyanide in my van," I shouted over the ruckus. "And we'll keep my board right where it is now, in Sullivan's stack."

"Knock yourself out," Taylor said, and resumed cutting, sawdust scent wafting in the sweet morning air. "Just be sure 'n' keep the stuff available. The way this weekend's going, I might just want to mix myself a Mazel Tov cocktail and put myself out of my misery."

"Molotov cocktail," I muttered to myself, certain that was what he meant, although that particular "cocktail" was a type of bomb and not a poison. At this point, he was welcome to either one!

I ducked into my van and carefully opened the bottle. My heart sank. Had there really been this little of the white powder in the container? The contents should have been a full inch higher.

I'd skimmed the literature sent with the bottle when I

first received it. An inch was probably enough poison to kill a grown man. I packed the bottle away again. The name of the chemical company on the outside of the box must have piqued Taylor's interest; he'd probably hoped it contained recreational drugs. If only I'd done an inventory before heading home last night . . . or, better yet, researched how to safely dispose of the stuff right away instead of leaving it in my van for months. Maybe I should join Taylor in a Mazel Tov cocktail.

My head was pounding. My van had been unlocked all Saturday afternoon. Yesterday that cyanide bottle could have been in someone else's possession for half of the day. Who would want it? And why?

"Erin?"

I jerked upright and twisted toward the voice. Steve Sullivan was watching me through the van's open double doors. He had what I could only describe as a smug smile on his face. "Is everything all right?" he asked.

How did he manage to appear whenever I was off balance? "Just fine, thanks. I'm taking a quick breather."

He raised an eyebrow and studied me as I scooted past him to jump from the van. "Guess the pressure's off now that the jig is up, hey?" His hair was in its usual annoyingly sexy-looking faux disarray. Today he wore a tan V-neck sweater and blue jeans.

"I suppose so. I'm still going to try to finish the job by this evening, though." I glanced at the Axelrods' house. Maybe it wasn't Sullivan or Kevin who'd moved my board to my competitor's pile, but rather Randy, who really seemed to relish messing with people's heads. On the remote chance that the lone oak board really did belong to Sullivan, I asked, "You didn't happen to bring a one-by-six eight-foot length of oak with you for this job, did you?"

"No. Why? Do you need one?"

"Not anymore," I said.

"Uh-oh. Has Taylor been playing fast and loose with your work orders?"

"Something like that."

"Quite the carpenter we've got here." He waggled his thumb over his shoulder. "If we just needed him to tear down walls for us, we'd be all set."

"Is that a reference to my fiasco yesterday with removing the paneling?" I snarled.

"I admit I heard about that from Kevin, but I simply meant that the guy's built like a bulldozer," Sullivan said placidly. "Don't be so defensive."

"Sorry. The undercurrents in this neighborhood must be getting to me."

"You mean the simmering Hatfields-and-McCoys aspect?"

"Exactly." So he'd noticed it, too.

He nodded. "I've never seen people who so obviously rub one another the wrong way choose to spend so much time together." He paused. "Kind of like you and me."

That we rubbed each other the wrong way was an understatement, but hearing him say that aloud made me unexpectedly sad. He pivoted and headed toward the McBrides' house before I could get a read on his expression.

"Good luck, Sullivan."

I'd meant good luck with Taylor's not botching his jobs, but he must have taken my remark to mean more, because he gave me a mock salute over his shoulder as he continued to walk away. "Yeah, you too. May the best designer win."

"I'm just hoping for a tie," I blurted before I could stop myself.

I was already framing a rebuttal to his anticipated joust, but he made no reply.

Taylor and Carl carried the cut-to-size boards for the bed to the Hendersons' garage at a few minutes after ten. Carl excused himself to install the shelves in the closet while I measured the headboard pieces to make sure that they, too, weren't four inches too short—at which point Taylor would no doubt try to convince me that the room would look nicer with a double bed instead of the existing queen. To my relief, this time everything was sized perfectly.

"It looks great, Taylor," I told him, bubbling with enthusiasm. "Any idea of when you can start putting the headboard together for me?"

"Monday or Tuesday. I'll let you know by the end of the day."

"It's got to be finished tonight. That's written into my signed contract with Carl."

"No way. I'm not knocking myself out for my stepfather. I can come back later and finish it up."

"No, actually, I have to have the room done by eight p.m. I thought you knew that."

"Yeah, originally, sure. Hate to tell ya this, Gilbert, but I have a feeling the surprise Christmas gift was spoiled the moment Debbie got back and saw it. Get real."

I grabbed fistfuls of my hair to stave off an impulse to grab his thick neck. "Never mind. I'll finish the wood and assemble it myself."

"Whatever," he called over his shoulder as he headed back toward the Axelrods' property. "Course, the TV stand is gonna be a while. The glue's gotta dry."

While Carl installed the closet shelves, Debbie and I turned the garage into a workshop. She worked on staining the crown molding, while I completed the headboard, deciding that I could just as easily stain and poly the wood *after* the bed was fully assembled—and this way, I comforted myself, I'd at least have the illusion of having made more progress.

When I paused from tapping the boards for the bookcase into their notches, Debbie said, "I really love everything about your design. I'm sorry I was so panic-stricken when I came home yesterday. I wish I hadn't yelled at you like that."

"That's all perfectly understandable."

She frowned. "Well . . . but my fib about where I'd gotten the alder chest was inexcusable. I was just so embarrassed . . . coming home and finding a professional designer in my dreadful, messy house. I just couldn't stand to give Jill all the credit for the one thing in my home that you were actually impressed by."

"Believe me, Debbie, *my* house is messy more often than not, and your alder chest is hardly your most impressive possession. Your entire sunroom is marvelous— the white antique wicker rocking chair, the breakfast nook, the brass lamp. . . . It's all I can do to walk past the doorway and not drop whatever I'm doing, curl up on that cushy yellow-and-blue loveseat of yours, and just stare out the picture window and dream the day away."

She put her hand over her heart. "Really? That's my favorite room in the house, too! Or, rather, it used to be. I already like the bedroom a hundred times better. And I hope you win the contest."

"I do, too, of course, but I have a feeling Steve Sullivan's a lock. He's really very good"—*damn him*—"and Randy seems to be all agog over the recliner that Sullivan picked out."

"It *would* be just like Randy to base his decision on a new chair." Her voice was sour, and she'd narrowed her eyes. She forced a smile. "He's not so bad, actually. And Myra's got a really good heart. I don't think anyone could blame her for being so . . . eccentric, considering the life she's had."

"Oh? What kind of life has she had?"

She considered her answer. "Let's just say . . . lonely, and sad."

Carl rejoined us before I could ask Debbie any more questions. He announced that the closet shelves were installed, then looked at me working on the headboard, and said, "Why are you doing that yourself?"

"Taylor said he was behind schedule with Sullivan's coffee table, so he needed to—"

"Bull. I'm getting Taylor over here if I have to drag him by the ear."

Minutes later, Carl returned with Taylor and Myra in tow. Beaming, Myra said, "Good morning, Erin." She added, "And Debbie. Beautiful day, isn't it?"

"Isn't it?" Debbie replied.

Myra gave me a searching look. "I'm not much with power tools, but I can do the last of the hand stitching on the pillows."

"Thanks. That would be a big help."

Taylor crossed his arms on his chest. "Like I already said to you guys, I've got stuff to do for Sullivan. He's waiting for me at the McBrides' right now. In two or three hours, I'll get—"

There was a thud directly over our heads. It sounded disturbingly like someone taking a header in the master bedroom.

For a moment, nobody spoke, and I realized we were all taking a mental survey of anyone who could possibly be inside the Hendersons' house. "Wait. Where's Randy?" Myra sounded alarmed. "He said he was coming over here ten minutes ago."

"Oh, my God. . . ," Debbie murmured. "His *heart!*"

We raced into the house. Taylor took the lead, taking the steps two at a time. I darted into the bedroom just behind him. A couple of steps into the room, Taylor stopped so abruptly, I bumped into him. He stared down at Randy Axelrod's sprawled body.

Randy's face was ice blue. Scattered on the floor around him were the love letters and the cameo pendant.

chapter 6

andy!" Myra cried. "Oh, my God! Randy!" She stood frozen in shock, the Hendersons flanking her.

Wordlessly, Taylor rolled Randy over onto his back. I knelt and felt his neck for a pulse, but my hands were shaking so badly, I couldn't trust my judgment. Other than my nursing stint at my mother's bedside, I knew nothing about medical care or first aid.

"He's not breathing," I told Taylor. "Do you know CPR?"

He said, "Yeah," and tilted Randy's head into position.

"I'll call nine-one-one," I said, rising and dodging past

Debbie, Carl, and Myra, who merely gaped mutely at Randy with ashen faces.

I sprinted downstairs, grabbed the phone in the kitchen, and dialed. I told the dispatcher what had happened and gave her the Hendersons' address. She told me to stay on the line till the paramedics arrived, but I insisted that I needed to tend to Randy myself, which felt true in spirit; I couldn't stand being downstairs on the phone while a man was clinging to his life just a short distance away. I hung up and rushed back upstairs.

Taylor was bent over Randy, still trying to resuscitate him. If his efforts were having any effect at all, I couldn't tell; Randy looked lifeless. Myra was clutching her husband's hand and crying—a low, keening moan that sounded almost inhuman. Debbie was at her side, patting her back, reassuring her again and again that everything would be fine. Carl still lurked by the doorway, looking both flushed and flustered.

"The ambulance is on the way," I told Myra, kneeling beside her.

She murmured, "I *knew* he shouldn't be here, climbing up and down those stairs all the time. His heart wasn't strong enough."

I felt helpless. Was this my fault for not confronting Randy and instantly refusing to continue work the moment I found that picture of me? Had I done so, he probably wouldn't have kept coming here, climbing up and down the stairs. I glanced over at the letters and necklace, still scattered on the tan carpeting. The only thing missing from the secret stash was my photograph, which I'd confiscated.

Randy still wasn't breathing on his own, even though Taylor appeared to be doing an excellent job at CPR. "Taylor, do you need a break? Should I try to take over for you?"

He gave me the finger and kept ministering to Randy. "I'll take that as a no," I muttered.

Myra stared at the items on the floor next to her husband, only just now noticing them. She reached across her husband and grabbed one of the letters and the necklace. "What's this?" she asked.

"I found those inside the wall when I removed the paneling," I explained, surprised that she hadn't heard about the discovery from one of her neighbors, if not from Randy himself. She dropped the letter and cameo onto the floor again, disinterested.

Carl said, "I stashed that stuff in a dresser drawer yesterday in the guest room for safekeeping. I don't know why Randy was going through our things."

"That's the least of everyone's worries right now," Debbie said rigidly, watching Taylor's attempts to resuscitate Randy. "When he recovers, we'll ask him."

Myra pursed her lips and said nothing. Despite Taylor's efforts, Randy didn't seem to be breathing. I felt sick.

Outside, sirens wailed. "Thank God! I'm going to go down and let them in," I said, seizing the opportunity to leave this appallingly silent room.

My thoughts whirled. Randy, as I'd already suspected, had to have been the one to stash everything in the wall, after Taylor had built the hole in the first place. Otherwise, how could Randy have known to search through the Hendersons' drawers?

The ambulance tore into the driveway. Two paramedics emerged and rapidly unloaded equipment. "Hurry," I told them. "He's not breathing."

Carl had apparently followed me downstairs and was now sitting on the single step that made the living room sunken and delineated it from the dining room. He said nothing as I ushered the two men upstairs, and after a moment's hesitation, Debbie told Myra that she thought it would be best to keep out of the way. Leaving Myra with the paramedics, Debbie and I went downstairs to join Carl. The three of us waited in anxious silence in the living room, listening as the paramedics questioned Myra about her husband's medical history.

After a minute or two, Taylor thumped down the stairs. There were beads of perspiration on his shaved head. I rose and said to him, "Thank you for your efforts up there. You might have made all the difference."

He wiped his brow and grumbled, "Whatever. I'm going home. Don't nag me about your damned headboard, and tell Steve to lay off, too, or I'll tell you both where you can stick your furniture."

Brusque as he was, he'd earned the right to vent, and I merely replied, "No problem."

"We're not going back to work today, Taylor." Debbie's voice and expression conveyed a sense of bone weariness. "I wouldn't dream of asking anyone to soldier through. Not after what's happened . . ."

Taylor ignored her. "Carl, I'll check in with you in the morning," he muttered. The door closed behind him.

The room fell silent once again. Moments later, the doorbell chimed. Almost simultaneously, Jill and Kevin McBride burst inside. "We heard the ambulance," Jill cried. "What's going on? What's happening?"

"Randy collapsed," Debbie answered. "The paramedics are upstairs with him and Myra now."

"Must be his heart. Is he still alive?" Kevin asked Carl.

"I don't know. We were all in the garage when we heard him collapse. Taylor tried his best to revive him, but . . ." Carl's voice faded.

Kevin patted Carl on the back, then sank down in a chair at the dining room table.

Jill called up the stairs, "Myra? Is Randy doing any better?"

Grim-faced, Myra came down the stairs. "I'm going to the hospital with them." She didn't, I noticed, answer Jill's question about Randy's condition.

"He'll do great, Myra," Kevin said, rising. "Randy's strong as an ox. Remember how he insisted on driving himself to the hospital during his first heart attack? He'll do great."

Myra, face pale and eyes blank with shock, simply nodded.

The paramedics were carrying Randy out on a stretcher, awkwardly navigating the stairs. At the sight, Myra's composure shattered. She began to sob. Turning to us, she wailed, "Quit being such hypocrites! I know you've always hated him! Well, he's still my husband, and he's all I've got in this world! You miserable people should have thought of that before you treated him the way you have!"

Chagrined, confused by her violent outburst, and not knowing what else to do, I held the door for the paramedics and mutely watched as Myra stabbed a finger at Carl and Kevin. "You don't think we both knew about your cruel side bet? Of seeing who was going to have to be *stuck* with his company during the Super Bowl? Well, it seems neither of you turds will have to worry about *that* now."

Kevin moved toward her as if to embrace her but froze when she shrank back from him. Gently, he said, "Myra, we're sorry. If there's anything we can do . . ."

Myra took a halting breath and scanned our faces; the McBrides and the Hendersons were staring at her with jaws agape and color rising in their cheeks. "You people put him in this condition in the first place! I'd say you've done plenty. Wouldn't you?"

She stormed out the door. Through the glass, we watched the ambulance tear away, siren slicing through the Sunday morning quiet.

Silence reverberated accusingly in her wake. Debbie sank her head into her hands and murmured, "I don't think I've ever felt this bad about myself before." Her voice was choked with tears. "What have we done?"

"None of this was your fault," Carl said, but he made no move to go to her side. "That Super Bowl bet was *my* idea."

"That's not true, Carl. It was mine," Kevin said firmly. "I was the one who got just the one ticket on eBay and decided to throw it into the kitty. *I'm* the one who should feel bad."

"Let's go home," Jill said quietly to her husband, who nodded. They brushed past me and out the door.

I had no idea what to do now. How to react after having someone collapse in the very room that you were in the process of redecorating was not a topic that had been covered in any of my design classes at Parsons.

Fueled by the disharmony in this neighborhood, a horrible thought now wormed its way into my brain. *Was* this really a heart attack? Could Randy have been poisoned?

I felt sick with fear that the paramedics and everyone else's assumptions could be wrong—that Randy hadn't fallen ill due to cardiac arrest but rather because of cyanide poisoning. But that was absurd, I told myself, and surely just the insane by-product of my sleep-deprived brain. Even so, a man's life was at stake, and I couldn't let my knowledge that there had been a container of potassium cyanide on Randy's property go unreported.

No way would I risk possibly fueling a killer's fire by talking about poison in front of the McBrides and the

Hendersons. "I have to use your bathroom," I muttered. I turned the corner and entered the family room. Giving a quick glance over my shoulder to ensure that my actions weren't observed, I grabbed the cordless phone and Crestview directory from the open shelf by the fireplace and brought them into the bathroom with me, closing and locking the door behind me. I looked up the number for Crestview Community Hospital and dialed, turning on the fan to drown out my words. Thankfully, the phone was answered by an actual person and not an automatic system. In a half whisper, I said to the woman, "My name is Erin Gilbert. I called nine-one-one a few minutes ago for Randy Axelrod, who appears to have had a heart attack. The ambulance is on its way to the hospital now. I just want to let the emergency room staff know that there was an open bottle of cyanide on his premises earlier this morning."

After a brief pause, the woman said, "Let me transfer you to the police, ma'am."

"No!" I cried in a harsh whisper. There was no way I could pull off a prolonged phone conversation. "I'll contact the police myself. I just wanted the emergency room personnel to know that it's possible Mr. Axelrod was poisoned."

"What was your name again?"

"Erin Gilbert," I replied, and hung up.

I splashed water on my face; my hands were trembling. I opened the door and peered out. The family room was empty. I tiptoed inside and returned the phone book and phone. If it was poison, Taylor was surely innocent. He wouldn't have worked so hard to resuscitate Randy if he'd poisoned him himself. Or would he? Had that merely been a show? Had his CPR techniques been *intentionally* ineffective?

Debbie and Carl hadn't changed positions in the

living room when I returned. "I'm sorry," I told them, "but I'm going to go home now, too."

"Of course you should, dear," Debbie said with so much kindness that tears filled my eyes. "You can't possibly think about decorating at a time like this, and neither can we. Carl and I will make do with our bedroom as is for as long as you need."

"As long as it's ready by bedtime tomorrow," Carl amended. "Sleeping on the guest bed is killing my back."

"Oh, honestly, Carl!"

"We'll compare everyone's schedules tomorrow and try our best to make that happen," I intervened, before another marital spat could explode.

"Good," he replied bluntly. "I'll take the day off and give you a hand. I'll call my boss at the agency first thing in the morning and let him know I won't be in."

"You work at an agency?" I asked in surprise. Somehow the image of the staid, uncongenial Carl Henderson as a real estate agent was utterly incongruous.

"Insurance agency. I'm an actuary."

The thought popped into my head: Carl might know about Randy's life insurance beneficiaries. I pushed it away; this was, after all, probably natural causes, a heart attack. I said my goodbyes and left.

To my surprise, Steve Sullivan was pacing on the sidewalk just beyond sight from the Hendersons' living room window. The collar of his pea coat was pulled up. The wind had tousled his hair even further and brought color to his cheeks. His body English indicated he'd been waiting for me.

"You heard about Randy, I take it," I said to him.

He gave a slight nod. "From the McBrides, when they returned home. Are you all right?"

"Not really." I glanced up at the window of the master bedroom and spotted Carl watching us. He must have raced upstairs the moment I'd left. He instantly stepped back out of view, as though I'd caught him with his hand in the cookie jar.

That was the final straw. If I didn't tell someone soon what was happening to me, I would go crazy.

I searched Sullivan's eyes, hoping to discover some kindness there. "Can we please bury the hatchet... preferably not in anyone's back?"

"Of course. You look like you need to talk. Can I take you out for lunch?"

I was stunned: Sullivan seemed to have read my mind. "Okay. Thanks," I said lamely.

"My pleasure. McDonald's or Burger King?"

"Can't respond to jokes right now. Sorry."

In a somber voice, he replied, "There's a decent Mexican restaurant just a mile or two from here. Let's take my van. We'll come back for yours afterward."

I moved my van out of the driveway, checked that the damned cyanide was still in the back, then locked the doors. We drove to the restaurant in silence. At eleven thirty on a Sunday, we had the place almost to ourselves. Cumin and chili spiced the warm air inside, which, despite the morning's trauma, I couldn't help noting was decorated in a predictable southwestern style—maroon, tan, and forest-green upholstery over lodgepole pine.

The waitress came over with a basket of chips, salsa, and two ice waters in red plastic glasses. I declined a menu and told Sullivan, "I'm not really hungry. I think I need to break my usual rules and have a liquid lunch."

"Sounds good to me."

I ordered a margarita, and Sullivan ordered a Michelob. To his credit, Steve didn't rush me. Imbibing some alcohol seemed to take the edge off my shattered nerves.

I watched him take a sip of his beer and teased, "Figures you'd get a macho drink."

He gave me a small smile. "Beer? Macho?"

"Sure. According to the TV ads, all you guys have to do is get a bottle of suds, and gorgeous women throw themselves at you. Presumably to get at the beer."

"Is that right?" He peered at his bottle. "Huh." He gave me a slow, sexy grin, and to my astonishment, I felt myself blush. "Are you trying to hint at something? Making a personal suggestion?"

"Not at all. Just idle conversation." Although, I admit it, I *was* idly curious about his sexual orientation. Sullivan had told the Coopers he was gay, yet in a crowded bar six months ago, I'd spotted him with a leggy brunette draped over him like a chintz slipcover. Either way, I needed to find myself intrigued by my soulless archrival like I needed to go color-blind. I licked a small clump of salt off the rim of my drink, took a sip, and added, "You're not my type."

Maintaining eye contact, he leaned across the table. "So, what exactly *is* your type, Gilbert?"

"Men who don't say that the name of my business should have my last name spelled with a lowercase *g*," I snapped, without thinking.

He lost his smile and straightened up again. "So much for our truce."

"Sorry. It was unfair of me to bring that up right after I'd asked you to bury the hatchet. It's just that this has been one of the worst days of my life. And I've had some real doozies."

"Seems to me you need to talk, right? So go ahead and vent."

I took a healthy sip of my drink, then set the glass down. "I'll just start at the beginning. I was adopted, and I don't know anything about my birth parents."

"Wow. That *is* the beginning. This could take a while. Are you sure I shouldn't order us some lunch?"

Despite myself, I chuckled. "Skipping forward twenty-plus years, yesterday I found my own baby picture carefully framed inside a slat of the tongue-and-groove paneling in the Hendersons' master bedroom. It was directly over a hole that someone had carved out from the drywall."

His brow furrowed. "Could you have been mistaken? It's probably not PC to say this, but *all* babies look alike, especially in those hospital photos."

My age at the time of my adoption was my Achilles' heel, and it was excruciating to have to reveal that weakness to him—a professional rival who resented my having set up shop in his town. "It wasn't a birth photo. The picture was from when I was eighteen months old. Shortly before I was adopted. My mother . . . my adoptive mother, I mean . . . took the photograph herself." I reached into my back pocket. "Here. I'll show you."

Sullivan smiled as he took the picture from me and studied it. "Cute. But what's that blue-and-green checkered thing in the background? A flowerpot? A wastebasket?"

"I think it's an umbrella stand. It's quite a monstrosity, whatever it is."

"Maybe you were predestined to become a designer . . . to protect future clients from such eyesores."

"Maybe so." In a way, that was the nicest thing Sullivan had ever said to me. He must really have been taking pity on me. He handed the picture back, and I tucked it into my pocket and forced myself to continue. "My adoptive mother died two years ago. In our last conversation, she made me promise never to look for my birth parents, no matter what happened."

"Did she say why?"

I shook my head and slowly swirled the contents of my glass to keep my hands occupied. "It doesn't really matter why, or if she even *had* a reason. In any case, it was my mother's dying wish. I can't go back on my promise."

"How about your adoptive father? Were you able to discuss this with him?"

"My parents got divorced some fifteen years ago, and my father remarried and moved away. I was always a lot closer to my mother anyway. He did come back for her funeral, though. And I see him once a year or so."

"Did you ever tell him what your mother said about not looking for your birth parents?"

"No. Frankly, the whole issue just . . . didn't seem that important. Till now." I rolled my eyes, thinking that just two days ago I never could have guessed how important my ignorance regarding my birth parents was destined to become. "I guess I always figured that my mother knew some reason for me to feel bad about my gene pool . . . so I was in no hurry to discover whatever that was." I frowned. "*Now,* of course, I feel as though I've been forcibly dunked into the whole putrid mess. There isn't a single person we've come into contact with this entire weekend who anyone would especially *want* to be related to."

Sullivan snorted. "Yeah, I'm with you there. Debbie seems pretty nice, though. Jill and Kevin have nothing but good things to say about her."

"Debbie *is* nice, but she and I don't have a single physical trait in common." That wasn't entirely true; although my auburn hair was much darker than hers, we both had red hues. "Anyway, there's more." I sighed. "I have a poison bottle in my van, and this—"

"Come again?"

"I happen to have a container of potassium cyanide. It was unopened." I added under my breath, "Or at least it was, until today."

"Why would you be driving around with a bottle of poison? Is it rat poison or something? Working some seedy jobs lately?"

That stung. We both knew Sullivan got the better clientele. "No, my ex-boyfriend gave it to me, actually."

He regarded me solemnly over the edge of his glass. "Your ex-boyfriend gave you poison. Well. I can see why he's your ex. Was this a you-broke-up-with-me-so-now-I-want-you-dead-you-bitch present?"

I fought back a smile. "Not exactly, though I hear Hallmark is starting a line of greeting cards for just that occasion. He's a chemistry student at CU, and he was always searching for various get-rich schemes. We'd been out looking at antiques, and—"

"If this guy's an undergrad at CU, I suppose I would qualify as an antique myself."

"He's a Ph.D. candidate. Anyway, we saw this cast-iron bear-claw bathtub with chipped paint, and he asked me how much it would cost to restore it." I took another sip of my margarita, and my sip became a couple of gulps. I was going into way more detail than necessary and, if I gave myself permission, would prefer describing that antique-hunting trip to Lyons to this talk of poison and shattered loves. "The long and short of it is, he thought we might be able to invent some sort of metal plating, using cyanide as a hardening agent, and go into business together. So he got me the cyanide as a birthday present . . . this symbolic gesture of our venturing off together in pursuit of the lucrative and fascinating world of bathtub repair, or something. Shortly afterward, we wound up getting into a fight and breaking up."

He mulled my explanation over and tried to hide his smile, which I appreciated, even if his effort was largely unsuccessful. "Pity you let *that* one get away, Gilbert. It's not every guy who'd give his girlfriend a bottle of poison for her birthday." He clicked his tongue. "And they say romance is dead."

"The point is, this morning I discovered my bottle had been taken out of its packaging and had migrated into Taylor's work area. Taylor claims he grabbed the poison when he unloaded my materials yesterday afternoon, and that he opened the bottle because he was curious."

"A man's in the hospital. He may be dying. And you're worried that someone could have siphoned off your arsenic."

"Cyanide, actually."

"Whatever. And this could all be connected to your baby picture being hidden inside a wall."

"Nice summation, Sullivan. What's your point?"

"You have to go to the police."

"I know. I called the hospital and reported the cyanide before I left the Hendersons'. I told the receptionist that I'd tell the police, and I will, eventually. But Randy seems to have had a heart attack. With any luck, he'll be treated and released, and finally learn to lose those extra pounds and take better care of himself."

Steve was staring at me, unsmiling. "At the very least, you should call your father and tell him about this . . . see if he can shed some light on anything."

"I suppose. My thoughts are so jumbled right now, I'll have to go home and look up his number in my address book. I only keep business numbers on my Palm Pilot."

"I have one of those, too. Aren't they great? They're expensive, breakable, and less convenient than a spiral notebook."

Again, I battled back my smile; Steve Sullivan was unknowingly tugging at my weakness for men who could make me laugh. "Yes, but they smack of success . . . of

our ability to throw money away on electronic gadgets."
I drained my drink.

Steve polished off his beer, too, then asked, "Should I
get us another round?"

"No, thanks. I got so little sleep last night that two
drinks would flatten me. Thanks for listening. I'd better
get home and get this phone call to my father over with."

"Want company?"

I raised my eyebrows in surprise.

He lifted his palms. "You said you wanted to bury the
hatchet, and you've had more than your fair share of
trauma the last couple days. It seems to me some company might help. We can go pick up your van, and I'll
follow you to your place."

If this had been anyone else, I'd have leapt at the offer. Audrey would be in Vail, so only Hildi would be
there to greet me, and Myra's sorrowful wails were still
echoing in my brain, taunting me that my birth father
might at this very moment be at death's door. But Steve
Sullivan was the man who'd called me three or four
times my first year in Crestview and harassed me about
how he was losing clients who'd gotten "Gilbert" confused with "Sullivan." The man who'd ridiculed me in a
drunken tirade at a social function last fall. Who'd lied to
the Coopers to steal their business out from under me.

"Thanks, but I'm fine."

He nodded. He looked expectantly at me after he'd set
some money on the table to cover our drinks, probably
waiting for me to either rise or say that I'd decided to order something else after all. I felt paralyzed. I neither
wanted to stay or to leave, but Sullivan was right about
one thing: I was definitely not ready to be alone.
Babbling, I said, "I live in an amazing house. It belongs
to Audrey Munroe."

"Of *Domestic Bliss with Audrey Munroe?*" Steve's eyes widened.

"The one and only. Audrey lets me have a room, and in exchange, she uses me for design consultations and services on her mansion. Which is great, because she changes her mind so frequently on what she wants done that it's a never-ending job. One day she'll be decorating the parlor to resemble a drawing room from the Château de Versailles, and the next day she'll be doing it up like the jungle room from Graceland."

He grinned. "Sounds fun."

"It is. Except I never know what furniture I'll have in my home one day to the next. She's always buying things or giving them away on whims. Two weeks ago, I walked into the den, and the camelback sofa was gone. As it turns out, a friend of hers had visited that morning and praised it to the sky, and *poof.* Audrey got someone with a pickup to haul the thing to the friend's house."

"Wow. I've got to make nice with this woman. I could use some free furniture."

I had to resist a sneer. Sullivan *would* want to take advantage of Audrey's generosity. "I'm sure you already have lots of exquisite furniture."

"To tell you the truth, Gilbert, I'm into minimalism these days. I lost a lot of my stuff." He clenched his jaw and his fists and said with unmasked bitterness, "Thanks to Evan."

He'd said his former partner's name with pain rife in his voice. Clearly I'd misinterpreted his role regarding that woman I'd seen clinging to him in the bar. So his ex-partner had taken most of the furniture when he'd moved out. "Evan Cambridge?"

Steve nodded. "He cleaned out our accounts and ripped off some of our clients, big time. I had to max out all my credit cards and go way into debt to cover for him.

It was either that or lose the business entirely, and I just . . ." His voice had been rising, and now he stopped himself and regained control. "Anyway. That's your 'full explanation' regarding the Cooper account. I'd bid on the Cooper job already, before they called you to get a second designer's input. Then Mrs. Cooper called me, after she'd agreed to hire you, to say that she'd loved both of our designs but had gone with yours because yours was slightly less expensive. I had to have the money, so I pleaded with them to give me the work at the same price that they'd agreed to pay you. I learned my lesson from that experience. I felt so crappy about the whole thing that it just wasn't worth it."

"Jeez, Sullivan. If you'd just called me and explained your predicament, I would—"

He held up his hand. "There are things I know I should have done differently. I was pretty crazed at the time."

"I'd have been crazed, too. Who wouldn't be? Did you report this to the police and to the BBB?"

"Yeah. Evan appears to have fled the country. Let's just say that the odds of my finding him and getting my money back aren't great."

"But what about your insurance? Surely your errors-and-omissions policy would cover at least . . ."

He was shaking his head. "Guess who was in charge of supposedly paying the insurance company?" He blew out a puff of air. "I was head over heels at the time, and I trusted Evan implicitly. Meanwhile, he emptied all my accounts and ran everything I'd worked my whole life for into the ground."

The poor guy! Come to think of it, I *had* heard some murmurings of Sullivan's having some trouble, but that was right after his drunken vitriol toward me at the party and immediately followed by his stealing the Cooper account, and I hadn't wanted to listen to a sob story on his behalf, which would have spoiled my perfectly justified indignation. I stared at him, stunned. "I don't even know what to say."

"Nobody ever does. I've been a real joy to have around at parties and social gatherings, let me tell you."

"Well, maybe you're not exactly Santa Claus or one of his merry elves, but—"

He snorted and grumbled, "I'm not even one of his reindeer."

"But on the other hand, you probably make everyone else feel better about their own lives in comparison. I know *I* feel better."

"Good." He grinned, rose from the table, and gave me a slight bow. "Then my work here is done, milady."

To my near mortification, I actually blushed and giggled like a schoolgirl as I got to my feet, too. Well, then, as my mom would say, live and learn. That's what came of my imbibing alcohol in the aftermath of someone collapsing in a client's home.

Maybe Steve Sullivan wasn't quite as bad a skunk as I'd come to believe. Then again, everyone who'd ever met the man, myself included, knew how charming Sullivan could be whenever he wanted to be. And a skunk's fur is beautiful. So what?

chapter 7

Audrey's parlor remained in the same state as it had been in last night, the contents shoved with abject indifference against the walls. In times of stress, I'm drawn to certain pieces of furniture — regardless of their setting — the way some people are drawn to certain types of food. The parlor's sage sofa — its plush velvet impossibly soft to the touch — was a haven for me. I curled up against its arm, the cordless phone in my hand, and gathered my courage.

Just as I felt resolved and ready to act, Hildi sprang onto the far end of the sofa and began to navigate a nonchalant course over the plush cushions toward me. Too nervous about my impending phone conversation to have my cat on my lap, I rose. Hildi promptly hopped back onto the antique-pine floor. Her indignation at having been treated so ignobly was evident in her every movement. She flicked the white tip of her tail at me as she strode past me toward the kitchen, in a feline gesture that I chose not to interpret at the moment.

I dialed my father's number, half hoping there would be no answer. I waited through the first three rings, my stomach in an unpleasant flutter. My father picked up. At least it wasn't Angie, his wife, or their twelve-year-old daugher, Jessie. Forcing a measure of gaiety into my voice, I said, "Hi. It's Erin."

"Well, hi there. I was just thinking of you."

The greeting would have been flattering, except that was what he always said, and yet he contacted me so seldom that it was impossible for me to believe.

"The strangest thing happened yesterday, and I need your input. I was removing the paneling from a wall in a house in north Crestview and discovered a hiding spot in the wall. A copy of that baby picture of me that Mom kept on the piano was inside."

There was a long pause. "Did you ask the owners about it?" His voice was utterly unemotional.

"No. Mom made me promise never to look for my birth parents. But do *you* know who they are? If so, you don't have to tell me their names, but . . ." I faltered. Staring unseeingly at the floor, I asked, "Do you have any idea why my *not* finding them was so important to her?"

"Erin, as you know, when I met your mother, she'd already adopted you."

I chewed on my lower lip. He could sometimes take a hundred words to give a simple yes or no.

"I didn't even know for the longest time that you weren't really hers—that she hadn't given birth to you herself. All I ever knew about the circumstances was that she adopted you from a friend when she was living in Colorado. It was a sore subject with her, and I chose to never upset her by prying into it."

I frowned, frustrated. That she'd adopted me from a friend and that, even though I'd been eighteen months old at the time of my adoption, she'd known and loved me from when I was just six weeks old was all she would ever tell me as well. She never explained why six weeks or why this friend had given me up, aside from the gentle, pat answer: "She knew I would take better care of you than she could."

"You never asked? Was the adoption even legal?"

"I'm sure it was all legal and aboveboard."

I completed a full circle of the parlor. Even while this phone conversation was so critical as to make me hang on my father's every word, I still managed to silently admire the painstaking stitch-work that was evident on the back of Audrey's rolled-up hand-knotted oriental rug. "But . . . how *could* it have been? She was just twenty-one and single. I was already eighteen months old. That's not your standard, legal adoption. Is it?"

No reply.

"There's something you're not telling me."

"I've always told you the truth, Erin."

"You say that, Dad, yet it's so hard to believe that, once you found out I wasn't her biological child, you simply let the subject drop. Who would *do* that? How could you be so complacent about your own family?"

"You know what they say about curiosity and cats."

Though impatience and anger had already crept into my father's voice, I had to ask the question that had haunted me for the last two decades—ever since my mother first admitted I was adopted. I'd dragged that much out of her when she'd been unable to produce any pictures of me as a newborn, which my second-grade teacher wanted for a which-child-is-which-baby guessing game. From that day on, her meager answers had only brought me more questions and doubts. None of the circumstances surrounding my adoption had been typical. Neither of my parents was ever willing to explain them fully. My mother's dying wish had been for me never to look into my past.

"Erin? Are you still there?"

I slid a wing chair toward me to reach over its back and reposition Audrey's divine coral harlequin table lamp so that its ivory shade was no longer being crushed. I took a deep breath. "Dad, is it possible . . . that I was an abduction?"

"Absolutely not," he fired back, suddenly furious. "How could you even think such a thing of your mother? Or do you mean that you think *I've* been lying all these years, and that I snatched you from your real parents?"

My emotions fluctuated between rage and despair. The retort that I couldn't bring myself to say aloud blasted through my brain—*Do you honestly think I'm trying to hurt you, Dad? Can't you see this from my side for once—what it's been like for me? Not to know such basic truths as who I am and where I came from? To always have my most soul-baring and painful questions met with an angry barrage?*

I leaned against the entrance to the kitchen, the only spot on the wall that wasn't blocked by Audrey's repositioned furniture. Over the lump in my throat, I persisted. "Look at this from my perspective, Dad. Certain things about my adoption never made a whole lot of sense to me, but that didn't ever really matter till now. I had a good, happy childhood." More or less.

"Yes, you did. You did indeed. And you went to the

school that you wanted, and you got the career that you wanted."

I clenched my teeth. He'd neglected to mention that my going to the school that I wanted had come to me thanks to a generous scholarship and my part-time job, so neither he nor my mother had been forced to pay for my education.

He went on in a simmering tone. "And yet, even so, out of all the places to live in the entire country, you chose to move to Crestview, where your mother went to college. Why? Did you secretly want to find your biological parents, despite your mother's explicit request?"

"No!" This was so unfair of him. He was playing what I'd just now told him against my wounded emotions at the loss of my mother. Or was I in the wrong here? This was why I hated talking to my father about anything of a serious nature; I instantly felt trapped into being the same heartbroken twelve-year-old that I'd been when he'd moved out. It was impossible to see the forest for the trees when the branches kept jabbing me in the eye. I heard myself yammer, "Mom always talked about how pretty Crestview was. After she died, I just . . . wanted to see the place, and I wound up staying and starting up my business here. That's all."

He sighed heavily in my ear. "Erin, if you're asking my opinion, just do what your mother asked. *Stay away* from these people! Perhaps your mother had more than her fair share of secrets, but everything she did was in your best interest. Always."

"That's the one thing I'm sure of," I replied, feeling a little better from the reminder of that one cornerstone from my past.

"Erin, I . . . This isn't a good time for me to talk." That was a frequent response from my father. I doubted that we'd had a single phone call in which he hadn't uttered it at least once, including those rare occasions in which he had been the one to place the call. In a bad case of overkill, this time he added, "You caught me on my way out the door. I've got to go. Just . . . let someone else finish this . . . this room you're working on, and stay away from those people."

"I can't quit work three-quarters of the way through a project."

"Erin," he said firmly, "the one and *only* thing I know about your birth parents is that one time your mother told me that they were dangerous."

"But you said she got me from a friend. How could she consider a *friend* of hers to be dangerous?"

"I don't know. I've got to go. Just . . . be careful. And good talking to you, Erin. Thanks for calling."

He hung up before I could reply. Good talking to me? That was what he says about a conversation like *that? Hey, Erin. Your mysterious birth parent might want to hurt you. And it sure is shitty of you to worry that you may have been kidnapped at eighteen months. But it was good talking to you. I've got to get back to my real daughter now.*

I slammed the handset into its cradle on the mahogany console, currently wedged behind the chesterfield sofa. My cheeks felt red-hot. It was immeasurably painful not to believe my own father. His studious avoidance of this subject matter was, I was certain, the mortar of the brick wall he'd built between us. If only there were some other relatives—aunts or uncles—I could tap for information . . . But my mother had been an only child, and her parents passed away about twenty years ago.

My father hadn't asked for the name of the homeowners for my design project. Surely that meant he didn't know my biological parents' last name. That was an infinitely kinder possibility than its alternative—that he knew the name and just didn't care.

If only I could remake my own personal interiors as easily as I could a dwelling space, could keep only the useful or the lovely or the fondly sentimental. That simply wasn't possible. *Yes, Mom, we do indeed need to look forward and not behind us. But how can we understand where we are without ever understanding where we've been?* I'd never thought to ask her that question when she was alive.

With no one answering the phone at either the Axelrods' or the Hendersons' houses, around six o'clock that evening, I drove to the hospital. A sense of foreboding overwhelmed any cheer that I might normally have gleaned from the decorative lighting on the houses and trees I passed. I was now certain that Randy Axelrod was my biological father.

Having run the phone conversation with my father through my head so many times that my brain was getting wear marks, one possibility could tie everything together: Randy was something of a bully. My biological mother and my adoptive mother had been friends, perhaps at CU. According to my father, I had been given away to protect me from a dangerous parent. Perhaps Randy had been abusive, and Myra and my mother had conspired to get me halfway across the country to keep me safe. Maybe my mother's last wish was *also* geared toward keeping me safe. Perhaps she simply never wanted me to find out that my father was a despicable human being.

If the Axelrods *did* turn out to be my biological parents, at least Myra seemed to be a nice enough woman. She had to be scared out of her wits right now. A quick visit to let her know someone was thinking about her and her ailing husband was just the natural, human thing to do.

I walked through the main doors and did my best to stifle the torrent of memories that the antiseptic-laced air brought me. A shiny blue garland rimmed the receptionist's desk. Below the garland, a slightly faded cardboard Santa had been captured in a permanent "Ho, Ho, Ho." On the credenza, a two-foot-high artificial tree was laden with red, blue, silver, and gold balls on its forest-green scouring-brush branches. I asked the receptionist for Randy Axelrod's room number.

She glanced at her computer screen and asked, "Are you a family member?"

I hesitated, thinking that the truthful answer—I don't know—would not go over well. "No. If that's a problem, is there any way I could get a message to—"

Just then I caught sight of Myra. Her chin was held high as she entered the lobby, and her lips were so tightly pursed that they were white. She did a double take and then came over. "Erin, hello. It's so good of you to come. You must have heard the news."

Confused, I studied her face. She had a drugged-out glaze to her gray eyes that might have been shock. "I . . . was there when your husband collapsed."

She shook her head. "Randy passed away. Two hours ago. Heart attack." Her voice was emotionless.

Frustrated, I balled my fists. With him had died my only chance to get to know the man who might be my biological father. What little I did know of Randy Axelrod, I hadn't liked, and now that was all that would remain of him in my memory banks. My own concerns and emotions were meaningless, however, when face-to-face with his new widow. "I'm so sorry," I told her, staring into her eyes and hoping that she could sense my sincerity within such a well-worn response.

"Thank you."

We stood there in the hospital lobby in silence. Myra wrapped her tan cardigan tight around her shoulders, clutching the garment with both hands as if it were a security blanket.

"Can I . . . give you a lift home?" I asked.

"That would be lovely. Thank you. I was just about to call for a cab."

"Come on. My van's in the parking lot." She gave me a small smile of gratitude as I touched her shoulder. We walked side by side toward my car in silence. Was this woman my mother? Was my having been kept in the dark all these years now robbing us both of the chance to comfort my own biological mother upon the death of my father? The agonizing questions made me so tense, it was hard to breathe.

"The cold air feels nice," she murmured. "Refreshing."

I opened the door on the passenger side without comment. What could I say?

Myra sat in silence as we pulled out of the lot. Then, as if reading my mind, she said, "I should be more upset than this, I know, but I've had a long time to prepare myself. This was Randy's third heart attack. We both knew it was coming eventually, and that it would probably be his last."

"I guess it's good, then, that you've had time to adjust."

She sighed. "Truth be told, Erin, I tried to leave Randy half a dozen times, but he'd always track me down . . . promise me that he'd changed, plead with me to stay. The first two times I left him, I found jobs teaching high school chemistry." She added by way of explanation, "I was a professor at CU when I met him, but he made me give that up. He was insanely jealous of all the men I would come into contact with at the university. By the third time I'd left him, my past record with the school district was suspect—those abrupt midsemester departures. After a while, I guess I lost the desire to even bother to leave him. Sooner or later, I'd give up and return to Randy . . . he'd come find me."

My stomach was churning. Her story was confusing; I'd seen no evidence of Randy being jealous.

She gave a mirthless chuckle. "I'd have been better off if we'd never met in the first place. At least I outlived him. Despite . . . everything."

What could I say? *Congratulations on the achievement of outlasting your miserable marriage?* If this was the worldview my biological parents had to offer, it was no wonder Mom had made me promise not to find them. Then again, I didn't even look like Myra or Randy. I was probably leaping to wild, baseless conclusions.

There was a slight noise as I turned the corner into Myra's neighborhood. Something in my tool box was rattling around. With a pang, I remembered that the container of cyanide was still back there.

A wave of guilt all but paralyzed me then, and I drove the rest of the way to Myra's home in bewilderment, thoughts roiling. The numerous houses decorated for the holidays now not only seemed cheerless to me, but mocking. Myra had said it was a heart attack, and maybe so. But what if my message had never been delivered to the emergency room by the hospital receptionist? What if the doctors' efforts to revive Randy had been impeded by cyanide in his system? Could my failure to report the cyanide to the police have cost the man his life?

Taylor's explanation had made no sense. Some of the poison had been removed. Besides, if he'd been curious about what cyanide looked like, why not just leave it in my van and sneak a quick peek there? Why bring it to his work area and drop it on the ground? The bottle was sure to be discovered whenever Steve removed the tarp from his materials. It seemed to have been staged—the cyanide put there deliberately for someone to find it there.

Could Taylor have been lying to protect someone else?

Maybe cyanide poisoning could push someone with a weak heart into cardiac arrest. All that Bill, my chemist ex-boyfriend, had taught me about poison was that it worked by shutting off oxygen to the body—or rather by interfering with the way oxygen is processed. He'd explained something about the cyanide itself taking the place of some other substance and thereby blocking the step that traps the energy gleaned from the oxygen. *See, Bill?* I told him in silence, *I was listening.* He had been the one who'd had no interest in *my* job. As if a glorious French bergère chair in chocolate Italian-leather could possibly be boring in comparison to the chemical-bonding process of phosphates!

We pulled into her driveway. Myra turned toward me. In a matter-of-fact voice, she said, "Now that he's gone, I'd like to hire you to decorate my entire house, instead of just the one room. Would you accept that kind of challenge, Erin?"

Surprised and caught off guard, I answered, "I'm not sure." My father had warned me just a few hours ago to stay away—that my birth parents were dangerous. Even setting my own issues aside, there was that old cliché about grief talking. Myra surely hadn't given herself enough time to weigh the consequences of a complete interior transformation in the home she'd shared with a spouse who'd died just hours ago. But she was waiting for me to go on. "I'm very flattered. But I'd really have to think about that, Myra."

She frowned. "Is there a problem?"

"My schedule is hectic for quite a while, and I doubt I'll be able to take on more jobs just now."

"Well." She rotated in her seat to face front. "There's no great rush. I could have you get going on this as soon as tomorrow or as late as six months from now. I'll let you think about it for as long as you need."

"All right. I'll do that. Thanks."

She reached for the door handle.

"Are you . . . going to be okay alone tonight, Myra? Is there anybody I should call? A relative, or somebody?"

"No, I wouldn't know who to begin to suggest, even if I did feel as though I needed some company. But don't worry, my dear, I'll be just fine."

"If you're sure . . . Take care. And good night."

"You, too. Goodbye." Her voice remained impassive. I've had clients take the news that a sofa delivery was going to be delayed with far more emotion.

I almost asked again if she couldn't at least ask Debbie Henderson or Jill McBride to come over for a while. But I held my tongue and watched as Myra opened her front door and slipped inside the darkened interior.

Although I kept an eye on the place in my rearview mirror, Myra still hadn't turned on any lights by the time my van rounded the corner and left the neighborhood.

I had every intention of heading straight home but couldn't sway whichever portion of my brain was steering. I turned and headed south on 30th Street toward the police station, the very last place on the planet I actually wanted to go. Nevertheless, I had told the receptionist at the hospital that I would talk to the police about the cyanide because, like it or not, that's what needed to be done. With just a modicum of luck, all my fears about Randy being poisoned would prove unfounded.

The police were using the same bargain-basement style of Christmas decorations that the hospital had. The metallic-paper garlands here were silver, and they'd hung silver and white paper snowflakes from the ceiling. I stammered my story to the receptionist and then to a bald, uniformed officer, who let me get as far as the word "cyanide" before he held up a hand and said, "Lemme have you talk to the detective on duty, miss."

While he ushered me into the official areas of the police station, my path happened to cross with an attractive, young female officer who looked familiar. Our eyes met. She smiled at me and said, "It's the stemware lady."

I realized then who she was, though she looked quite different now, wearing a police uniform. Last week she'd attended a presentation on selecting glassware that a local store had hired me to give. "Linda, right?" I remembered her because she'd shown genuine interest in my talk. Plus, there had only been five glassware shoppers in attendance; the rest of my audience had come disguised as empty chairs.

"Right." Linda glanced at the bald officer at my side, then back at me. "Trouble?"

"Someone . . . collapsed in the house I was redecorating. Probably a heart attack, but . . ."

"I'm going to have Detective O'Reilly speak to her," the male officer beside me explained.

She nodded and touched my arm. "My last name's Delgardio, Erin, if you need anything." She continued on her way but added over her shoulder, "The guys here all call me Del."

It was nice to discover that I had an acquaintance in the police department.

The other officer ushered me to a small room and told me to wait there a few minutes until Detective O'Reilly finished making a call. There was nothing in the room to occupy myself with. A rectangular table topped with dark brown linoleum had cheap aluminum legs that matched the black plastic-and-metal chairs. A large mirror on one wall that was bound to be one-way glass. The smoke-gray, industrial-grade carpet was a short-fibered polyester that, installed, retailed for $11.99 a yard.

To amuse myself, I mentally redecorated the space. By the time a tall, thirtyish, mustached man wearing a cheap, gray flannel suit entered, he was crossing a lovely Berber carpeting toward me. I was seated in the conversation nook—gently framed to either side by ficus trees—comprised of two comfy contemporary club chairs upholstered in a geometric art deco pattern and an elegant, oversized leather ottoman that doubled as a cocktail table.

The image was shattered as he slapped his notepad on the table and said, "I'm Detective O'Reilly. And you are . . . ?"

Suddenly scared half to death, I mentally replied, but said, "Erin Gilbert."

I told my story of the past weekend. It was slow-going; he stopped me every other sentence and made me repeat myself. Afterward, the detective seemed to be more interested in attempting to stare me down than in uncovering any further information about Randy's death. There was something about being watched this way that made me unbelievably nervous. I half felt like confessing—to anything at all—just to get his pale eyes off me and end this conversation.

Detective O'Reilly sighed. "That's it? Nothing to add?"

"That's all I can think of."

He leaned back in his chair, regarded me for a moment, then rose and said, "Sit tight for a moment. I'll be back in a minute."

Once again, he was gone for so long that I had time to mentally refurbish the room twice, and was in the process of redesigning it into a romper room for cats, complete with climbing structures and cubbyholes and a multitude of dangling cat toys, when he finally returned. He kept smoothing his mustache as he studied a piece of paper in his hand. He reclaimed his seat, then put the paper facedown on the scarred table. "Well, Miss Gilbert. I just got some interesting news."

I waited, with increasing anxiety, but he didn't continue. Finally, I felt compelled to say, "Oh?"

He gave me a solemn nod. "Because of your call to the hospital this morning, the lab ran some preliminary tests . . . blood workups and so forth."

The mention of blood work made me sit up. I so hadn't wanted to hear that there was any possibility of the cyanide in my vehicle having had anything whatsoever to do with Randy's death. "Mr. Axelrod *was* poisoned?"

" 'Fraid so."

"Oh, God. Someone actually did pilfer the cyanide from my bottle. I never expected anything like this to happen, *ever*, or believe me, I'd have called someone . . . found some safe way to dispose of the poison."

O'Reilly shook his head. "It wasn't cyanide that they found in his system." He was staring into my eyes again. "Miss Gilbert, what reason would you have had to be carrying around arsenic?"

"*Arsenic?*" I repeated in confusion. "No, no—it was cyanide."

He said nothing.

My heart was racing. "I think arsenic can also be used

as a hardening agent for metal plating, but I've never used either cyanide or arsenic. And I'm sure it was cyanide in my bottle—in *the* bottle," I added firmly.

"So you don't use arsenic in your line of work? Just cyanide?"

"No." Had that been some sort of trick question along the lines of *When did you stop beating your wife?* If so, I'd just flunked. My mouth felt dry, and it was an effort to swallow.

He said nothing.

"It's not as if I do metal plating, along with designing interiors," I heard myself yammering. "Like I explained before, the cyanide was a . . . gift from my ex-boyfriend."

He nodded, removed his notepad from his jacket pocket, and jotted down something.

Great. If I were in his shoes, listening to me babble, I would arrest myself right on the spot.

While he wrote, he muttered, "That's what the victim died from. Arsenic poisoning."

"Arsenic?" I echoed. "Not cyanide?" My mind flashed back to my conversation with Steve Sullivan. Hadn't he mentioned my container of arsenic when he'd meant to say cyanide? Surely that had just been a meaningless slip of the tongue.

Detective O'Reilly flipped his notepad shut, then leaned forward in his seat. "That would be a real clever ploy, to suggest someone died of one type of poisoning when all the while another type of poison was the killer. Might be a nice way to frame someone else and make *yourself* look innocent."

chapter **8**

> "When opened, draperies are picture frames, meant to enrich and enhance the view by providing a touch of texture and a splash of color. When closed, draperies are the artwork itself."
>
> —*Audrey Munroe*

"Whew!" Audrey wheezed, dropping into the seat beside me as she waltzed into the living room, her complexion ruddy from the cold night air. "I am *positively* exhausted. I'm like that little skunk from the Bugs Bunny cartoon show. As the French would say if they were Americans, 'I am Pepe Le Pooped.' "

The remark was so silly, it made me laugh in spite of my troubles. Despite her words, Audrey appeared to have more energy than I did—and it was easy to picture her thirty years younger, having just now danced off the Broadway stage to thunderous applause.

In sharp contrast, too keyed up to sleep upon returning home from the police station, I'd taken it on myself to unroll her rug and rearrange her parlor. I'd then done my best to relax by cuddling into my favorite corner of my favorite sofa and reading a novel, but I'd merely held the book open and stared at the page, unable to command my eyes to read the words or my brain to comprehend them.

"I'm glad you're still up, Erin. I wanted to enlist you to do a guest spot on my Friday show."

My pulse quickened with the beginnings of stage fright at the mere suggestion of appearing on television. "No, uh-uh, Audrey. Can't do. I've got far too much on my plate these days."

"If you don't do it, dear, I'm going to have five minutes of dead air." In the *Here, kitty, kitty . . .* tones that I used to call Hildi when it was time to take her to the vet, Audrey added, "The topic is one of your pet subjects—curtain rods."

"Thanks, but no thanks, Audrey."

Her jaw dropped. "Who else am I going to get to talk about curtain rods at length?" she demanded theatrically.

"Is that a pun . . . talk 'at *length*' about curtain rods?"

"No, and don't try to discourage me from choosing you by making lame remarks. You have *got* to get over your shyness in front of the camera, Erin. I'll be with you, and you can pretend we're having a regular conversation, just the two of us."

Though I'd never told her in so many words about my stage fright, she'd seen through me. I could speak in front of groups of people without fear, but to do so on TV was another matter entirely. I replied, "A sizable portion of our 'conversation' will need to be spent looking out at the *camera* instead of at each other."

"What's hard about that? Pretend the camera's the third person in our conversation. With a bad case of laryngitis. And one big eye in the middle of his or her forehead." She patted my knee. "My show would be marvelous publicity for you."

True, but irrelevant; I morphed into a blathering idiot in front of a camera. "You know who would be terrific for the job? Steve Sullivan. He's a fellow designer I've been working with this past weekend."

Talking about Sullivan brought the day's horrific events to mind. *I should tell Audrey the whole story tonight: she might never forgive me if she heard it secondhand, and it was bound to make the headlines in tomorrow's newspaper.*

She asked, "Would *he* be willing to talk for five minutes about curtain rods?"

"Probably not, now that you mention it. But he could talk about coffee tables instead. His designs are—"

"It *has* to be curtain rods, Erin, not coffee tables. And I need *you*."

I shuddered at the notion of myself on a TV screen. "There's bound to be someone at a window treatment store who'd be dying to do something like this."

She rolled her eyes. "Fine, fine. Just help me prepare for the interview. Tell me what I'll need to ask my curtain rod representative."

I rubbed my forehead. "Do you really want to do this now? Can't it wait until tomorrow?"

That was a stupid question for Audrey. For someone who changed her mind every two seconds regarding her room designs, she was adamant about her show's topics and never one to procrastinate.

Indeed, she shook her head as she fished her Tiffany notepad and Mont Blanc pen out of the pocket of her scarlet jacket. "Didn't you once sell curtain rods to the trade in New York?"

"Briefly. Among other things."

She donned her reading glasses. "Just give me the basics so that I can be an informed interviewer."

I sighed, loathing the very idea of talking about this now. I hatched a plan to make my every statement as dry and clinical as humanly possible and bore the woman to tears. I'd already been manipulated by Detective O'Reilly tonight. By gosh, if *I* wasn't able to enjoy this conversation, *she* wasn't either. "Okay. Let's see. You'll want to ask about materials."

She nodded and peered over her reading glasses at me. "By 'materials,' you mean the fabric for the curtains?"

"No, as in wood versus metal rods. Wood is traditional, metal more contemporary. But be sure whoever you interview talks about other factors that go into the decision—the overall balance of the room design, etcetera. You'll want to ask about how to select the size, as well. Standard curtain rods are one-and-three-eighths or two-inches in diameter. The size of the window determines the size of the rod. Everyone knows a large window needs a large rod and a small window requires a small rod, but the length of the curtain needs to be considered, too. A wide but short window with curtains that extend only to the sill or apron can seem out of balance with a thick rod, and—"

"Good lord!" Audrey cried. "You're putting me to sleep here!"

I pretended to be offended by her statement and clicked my tongue. "It's nearly midnight! Doesn't sleep strike you as *appropriate*?"

She rolled her eyes a second time and continued scribbling notes. Then she looked up at me and inquired, "What about those doodads at the ends of the rods?"

"They're called finials. Finials are especially important. They can augment a window treatment and enhance the overall design of a room."

While writing, she muttered, "Maybe it's just as well that you aren't going to do the interview. You're sounding like advertising copy now."

"Thanks so much, Audrey."

She gave me a regal smile. "Which is not to say that I don't truly appreciate your help, dear." She sighed. "Only that this segment is never going to win me an Emmy."

"That *is* a bit beyond the scope of even the finest-quality curtain rod."

She gestured at me with her pen. "Go on, Erin. Fill me in on finials."

Deliberately sounding as close to a computerized voice as I could reasonably hope to get away with, I rattled off: "Finials are often sold separately from the rod. They're made out of glass, wood, or metal, and there's a wide range of prices. Low-end finials are made out of plastic, but you should tell your viewers to avoid them unless they intend to paint them. That's a great way to save some money. A crappy-looking rod can be painted a color that looks wonderful with the curtain fabrics, or the finial can be covered in fabric."

She grinned. "At last. Some information that's actually going to be helpful." She looked up from her notepad. "Anything else?"

The perfect opportunity to change subjects and tell her about the traumatic events of my day. Realizing I wasn't up to the task at this hour, I replied, "That's it. Just that decorators need to consider not only the pattern, if there is one, in the curtain fabric, but the patterns and lines of all the upholstery and accessories, and especially the wallpaper and molding."

Audrey nodded, and as she scribbled, she said, "Right. All lines. Especially wallpaper and molding." She gave me a beatific smile that I instantly knew was a payback for my affectations while answering her questions. "Thank you, Erin." She returned her beautiful notepad and pen to her pocket.

Feeling a little guilty, I said eagerly, "Hey, Audrey? I do

have *one* fun suggestion for the show. You might want to close the segment by saying something along the lines of: 'Spare the rod, spoil the drapes.' "

She gave me a look that clearly said, *You poor dear,* patted my knee, rose, and swept from the room.

chapter 9

Long after Audrey had retired, I remained awake—my second night in a row unable to sleep. Detective O'Reilly might have lied about Randy Axelrod's cause of death to see if I would confess or point the finger at some murderous co-conspirator. After the detective had all but accused me to my face of poisoning Randy, I'd insisted on giving O'Reilly the container of cyanide. He could consider it evidence or not, but I wanted it out of my possession.

What festered in me throughout the night, however, was the suspicion that someone had murdered my biological father all but in front of my eyes. Even if I was destined to never know my paternal roots for certain, I did know that Randy Axelrod deserved justice, and I wasn't going to sleep well until his killer was behind bars. I waited until eight a.m., then, determined to do whatever I could to help solve his murder, I called Debbie Henderson and arranged to arrive an hour later, vowing to myself to keep my eyes and ears open for clues.

At nine o'clock on the nose, I rang the Hendersons' doorbell. Carl answered. He was wearing a suit and tie. So much for his promise yesterday that he would take the day off to help me. Before I could even say hello, he said, "Taylor got your headboard out of the garage. He needs to know what you need done to it."

My instructions were clearly spelled out in the drawing, and I couldn't begin to understand why Taylor would choose to haul it across the street again, but I bit back an irritated response and merely replied, "Okay."

"I've got some eggs cooking on the stove. Excuse me." Carl closed the door in my face.

Advising myself not to read anything into his brusque manner, I tightened the belt of my black leather jacket and went across the street in search of Taylor. The air was sweet and crisp. I glanced over my shoulder; a bank of clouds had cloaked the mountains and much of the sky in gray.

Myra emerged from her front door as I walked up the driveway. Had she been watching me through the window? She wore a pretty cotton skirt and a periwinkle shell underneath her tan cardigan. For the first time since I'd met her, she had on makeup, and her gray hair was neatly fastened into a French twist. All told, I thought, she looked as far from a recent, grieving widow as one could get.

"Good morning," she said. "How are you doing, Erin?"

"That's just what I was about to ask you."

"I'm fine." She smiled at me. "Absolutely wonderful, in fact."

Wonderful? Just half a day after her husband died? I battled through a mental flashback of Randy complaining about the taste of his Budweiser and forced myself to return her smile. "That's good to hear. I noticed Taylor's truck is parked in your driveway. Is he going to keep his workshop over here, do you know?"

She nodded. "We discussed moving it to the Hendersons' or the McBrides', but that seemed like such a waste of time."

Taylor specialized in wasting time. He'd carried a heavy headboard out of its owner's garage and clear across the street.

Myra continued. "He should be out back. Can I make you a cup of coffee?"

"Thank you, but no, I'm fine." No way was I accepting food or beverages from anyone in this neighborhood. "I'll just see how Taylor's doing and then I'll get back to work at the Hendersons'."

I let myself through the gate of the split-rail cedar fence. Taylor was not in sight, but the odor of cigarette smoke was so strong that I couldn't have missed him by much. He'd probably gone into Myra's house to use the bathroom.

I passed the workshop area to examine the headboard, which was atop a plastic sheet on the lawn. It was fully assembled, and Carl and Debbie must have completed the staining and sealing work yesterday. Even in this incongruous setting, the headboard was beautiful—and looked as though it must weigh a hundred pounds. Now, thanks to Taylor, I would need to get him and another strong individual to carry it back over to the Hendersons'. Could he be stalling? Deliberately keeping me here on the job until he could slip something into my water glass? Good heavens, I was getting paranoid!

I surveyed Taylor's workspace. The vise grips of a Black & Decker Workmate held an Italian black walnut coffee table, the pieces clamped in place while the glue dried. The table was very handsome—simple and stunningly elegant—with tapered legs and a small shelf below the tabletop for magazines. The piece was characteristic of a Sullivan design, relying on the sublime wood grain for its distinctiveness.

There were still some materials under Steve's tarp. Curious, I peeked under the tarp and noted that all of the boards had been cut and their rough edges sanded smooth. These had to be the makings for the entertainment center that Kevin had fetched Taylor to begin on Saturday afternoon. In contrast, my own stack of wood was gone, yet there was no sign of the oak television stand. Maybe that was now in the Hendersons' garage, but if so, I had no idea how Taylor had assembled it so early in the morning. Maybe he'd come back last night and worked after all.

Taylor slid open the back door and stepped out. He spat on the ground. "Checking up on me again, Gilbert?"

Carl had been the one to tell me to come over here and give Taylor the instructions he needed. My paranoia was raging, and I felt a prickle of fear as the muscular young man approached. Today he wore his spiked dog collar again, along with the same overalls and work boots he'd had on all weekend. His scalp, however, was sporting a five-o'clock shadow, as was his chin. "The headboard looks great," I praised. "Now all we have to do is assemble the rest of the frame, *after* it's in the bedroom. I'm sure you've already noticed that the stairway is too narrow to angle this through otherwise."

"Yeah. No shit." The false bravado in his voice combined with the suddenly super-innocent facial expression made me very glad that I'd mentioned it.

"Is the TV stand assembled?"

"Yeah. But it still has to be stained and sealed. I brought that over to Carl's garage for you this morning, when I was picking up the bed."

"Thanks." I couldn't help but glance at the much heavier headboard as I said, "So . . . this is ready to go *back* across the street now and up to the bedroom, I take it?"

"Yeah, I just brought it over here 'cuz I thought the boards were too long by an inch or so and needed to be cut again. Didn't want you flipping out again like you did with that TV stand. But, turns out, everything's gonna fit fine."

"That's why I keep a tape measure with me." I showed it to him. "They're so portable." *Especially when compared to a massive headboard with an attached bookcase. Not to silently beat a dead horse.* "Are you going to be able to help me install the bed and the crown molding this morning?"

"Nah. Still got a shitload of work to do for Sullivan. But I already cut the molding, and it's all in Carl's garage, so you can go ahead and get that up yourself. So long as you can handle a nail gun."

"I can manage."

"I got Carl one for Christmas last year. I'm pretty sure he's never used it, though."

As Taylor brushed past me, another disturbing memory returned to me. The first time we met, Myra had said that she'd caught Taylor poking around in her refrigerator. Maybe he'd been doctoring Randy's beer. I resisted the temptation to babble to Taylor that I was an excellent shot with a nail gun to give him the impression that I knew how to defend myself.

He turned on his saw and started to cut a chunk off what looked like a piece of scrap board to me, so I was quite certain that this was his gentle way of bringing our little chat to a close. While mulling Taylor's backward approach to carpentry—for simplicity's sake, molding is generally cut to size as it's being installed—I headed through the side yard. The odds that he'd sawed all of my precut crown molding pieces correctly were comparable to my happening across a winning ticket for the Colorado state lottery.

Debbie was standing on the bottom step of Myra's porch, looking up at Myra. I was about to greet them, but hesitated when I glimpsed their expressions. Both women were obviously very upset with one another. I took a step back, so they couldn't see me.

"Myra, please. I'm asking you to forgive and forget," Debbie pleaded.

Her voice redolent with hostility, Myra replied, "I forgive you, Debbie. After all, it's not like I loved the son of a bitch. But asking me to *forget* is a different matter entirely."

They fell silent. Deliberately making a noisy approach, I came toward them. Debbie gave me a quick glance, then looked up at her neighbor and said, "Again, Myra, if there's anything at all Carl and I can do . . ."

"You'll be the first to know." In much lighter tones, Myra said, "Erin, don't hesitate to ask for help with finishing up the room, either. These days, I would just as soon stay busy, rather than allow my thoughts to wander."

I thanked her, and she said goodbye and went back inside her house. Meanwhile, Debbie Henderson combed her fingers through her red hair and said, "It's so good of you to come again so soon. We were all so shaken yesterday. . . ."

"It was upsetting, all right, but much worse for you, I'm sure. You knew Randy so much better than I did."

She pursed her lips as if biting back a reply. "I'm afraid Carl left for work already, so I hope you aren't counting on his help." Crestfallen, she added, "He suddenly changed his mind about taking the day off."

To offer some cheer, I said, "I should be able to complete your bedroom today or tomorrow. My calendar's fairly open. All I've got scheduled this week are quick jobs—decorating homes for holiday parties or assisting with furniture shopping for Christmas presents."

"Myra was under the impression that you were really swamped."

This is why I hate telling white lies—they darken of their own accord, like unstained cherry cabinetry. "Myra has a major job in mind that would take me well past New Year's to complete."

We headed up her driveway. Debbie said, "Myra told me about your hospital visit yesterday. Jill and I went there ourselves, but Myra said Randy wasn't in any state to see us. She told us to leave."

"I must have happened to come along at exactly the right time, then."

"Apparently so." Her face was inscrutable, but I detected a hint of bitterness in her voice.

"I hope it doesn't seem as though I'm getting in the way of established friendships here," I said, feeling sorry for her.

"Not at all. Heavens!" She hesitated as we stepped through the front door. "I can't begin to imagine how this must all seem to you—a perfect stranger—walking into all this . . . bickering among friends. Not to mention having someone collapse in the room you were working so hard on." She glanced upstairs, then added, "I know this is selfish of me, but . . . thank God he died at the hospital and not in my bedroom. I don't know what I'd do. The room is so beautiful now, but I know all I'd be seeing when I closed my eyes would be Randy's corpse."

I hadn't stopped to consider the nightmarish images that she'd been left with in the wake of finding Randy sprawled on the floor of her room. If Debbie now had indelible negative emotional connotations, my design wasn't going to be successful, no matter how good it might be otherwise. "Are you going to be okay with your new room if we stick with the original design? Or would you feel more comfortable if we started over fresh and tried to get rid of any mental associations?"

"No, absolutely not! I love what you've done with the room. It was a horrible coincidence that . . . his heart gave out in my house, not in his own. But I don't feel as though the room is cursed. And it's so lovely!"

"Good." Over the years, something unexpected had happened in nearly every room I'd ever worked on; it was just part of the process. However, truth be told, if ever a project of mine was cursed, this was the one. Among the potential disasters decorators envision, *death* is not high on the list.

I wished I felt comfortable enough with Debbie to ask her for her theories on what had happened. Why had Randy been carrying the letters and necklace? He had to have been in severe pain from the effects of the arsenic. Had collecting those items been so urgent as to be his final action? And what had happened to the letters and necklace afterward? Had Carl collected them and hidden them for safekeeping?

"After the crown molding is up, I'll need to hang the window treatments and move the furniture in. Normally I have furniture movers do that for me. That headboard is going to be really heavy, and the bed frame needs to be assembled, which requires two or three people. I'm going to have to find someone other than just Taylor to help me."

"I'll bet the three of us could manage, don't you think?"

"Yes, but I just can't ask you to do that. It seems so . . . unprofessional. This is the one stage where the homeowner shouldn't lift a finger, let alone a two-ton headboard. It's unfortunate that Taylor moved it back over there while it was still in pieces, but he thought he might have to make some alterations." A plausible—if inadequate—explanation for his actions suddenly occurred. "Oh. I'd forgotten about your allergy to sawdust when we were working in your garage yesterday. I hope you—"

"Pardon?"

"Aren't you allergic to sawdust? That's what Carl told me."

She shook her head, her features hardening. "That's *Emily.* His first wife. Any kind of dust or fine particles makes her sneeze. Supposedly. She's quite the princess."

Debbie had such rancor in her voice that it felt as though I'd just let a cat out of the bag, and I automatically did my best to stuff kitty back into place. "I'm sure Carl simply made up the story about your having allergies to explain to me why the workshop was being set up at a neutral site. The men didn't want Steve and me to know until after we arrived that we were in a competition. Kevin probably gave the same excuse to Steve Sullivan about Jill."

The sparkle returned to her blue eyes and she chuckled a little. "In *Jill's* case it would have been accurate. She's allergic to dirt and messiness. I love her like a sister, but how that woman ever got through the child-rearing years, let alone childbirth, is beyond me."

"She and Kevin have children?"

"Twins. They're both college freshmen. They'll be coming home for winter break soon."

I smiled and nodded, but shrank a little inside. The nagging questions about my lineage had returned. I tried to stave them off by saying cheerfully, "Let's take a look at the stand that Taylor built. He said he put it in your garage."

While we headed toward the garage, she said, "We won't have any trouble getting another person to set up the room with you. Myra sincerely wants to help. And there's . . ." She paused, and her eyes lit up. "You know what would be great fun? If I go help Steve Sullivan complete Jill's room, and she helps you with mine."

"I'm game. We can see if that works for them." I flipped on the light and was impressed to see that Taylor—or perhaps Carl—had brought down one of the iceboxes that would form the bottom half of the TV stand. The unfinished piece had been put into place on top. The curved lines of the top ledges matched perfectly, and after the shelf unit was stained to match the icebox, the two pieces would look as though they had always been one complete stand. Remarkable. Once again, despite Taylor's apparent thickheadedness, his craftsmanship had been superb. The man seemed to be something of a carpentry idiot savant.

Something in the corner of my eye caught my attention, and I took a couple of steps closer to investigate. A paintbrush was sticking out of the open can of polyurethane. Next to that container, the can of stain had also been left open. I grabbed the brush handle, and the can of polyurethane came with it, having hardened around the gray foam brush. My second, smaller brush, intended for touchup work, was ruined, too. "Someone must have forgotten to put this away last night."

Debbie clicked her tongue. "That was Carl. I reminded him, just before I went to bed." She stomped her foot. "What the hell is wrong with that man? He's been in a fog ever since I got back from the spa!"

"I'm in no position to complain. I know better than anyone to put away my supplies, and yet I took off yesterday without giving the work in progress in your garage a second thought."

"Yes, but Carl and Taylor have been in the garage off and on since dawn today. They *had* to have noticed this, yet nobody said a word to me. *I* haven't been out here myself today until just now."

"I'm afraid this does change my schedule somewhat. I'll have to run to the store and replace the supplies, then the oak needs to be stained, dry for at least four hours, then sealed."

"I'll have Carl run out and get the supplies during his lunch hour, to make up for his ignoring the matter last night. We can always stain the wood then, and seal it this afternoon."

Debbie and I installed the crown molding and remade the two pieces that Taylor had cut at a reverse angle. The job took all morning, but I had to admit, doing so much of the work myself as opposed to having it done by allied professionals added an extra element of pride to this project. However, it was wreaking havoc on my schedule. I was beginning to suspect that it would be tomorrow, after all, before the job was complete.

Carl came home for lunch while Debbie and I were stitching shut the openings in the pillow seams. He had brought the new can of wood stain with him, but had forgotten the polyurethane. He and Debbie squabbled about whether she'd told him to clean everything up or had told him that *she* would take care of it. I decided to take this opportunity to go see how Sullivan felt about trading homeowners for the finishing touches.

Sullivan's van was now parked in the McBrides' driveway. Yesterday he'd bought me a drink and listened to my problems. Today I was worried sick that the police considered me a murder suspect. I so dearly wished that I could trust at least one person. The truth of the matter, though, was that I was in this alone and could trust no one.

A gong resounded when I pressed the McBrides' doorbell. Moments later, the door was opened by Jill, dressed in black wool slacks and a gray cashmere sweater, a string of pearls gleaming lustrous against the ensemble. Suddenly the khakis and black V-neck sweater under my leather jacket seemed especially shabby.

She ushered me inside with a gracious smile. As I stepped onto her stunning travertine tile, I took in the understated elegance of her foyer—its succulent, honey-hued walls, how the circular mahogany table captured the high sheen of the staircase banister ahead, and that the crystal bowl on the table seemed to lovingly echo the curves of the pendant ceiling fixture.

Jill touched my arm. "You look so tired, Erin. You poor dear. You, too, must have been too rattled by yesterday's events to sleep last night."

Normally, being told that I looked tired made me bristle. But this time it was so true that I appreciated the note of sympathy. "It must have been much worse for you and your husband."

"Yes, it was terrible. Just as we were starting to come to grips with everything, the police came by to interview us. At ten o'clock last night."

Ten o'clock was a couple of hours after I had gone to the station house—when O'Reilly had implied that I was his prime suspect. A chill ran down my spine. "They did?"

She nodded. "There were 'suspicious circumstances,' according to one officer, but that's all he would tell us. They spoke to all three households—us, Myra, Debbie, and Carl. . . . Didn't anyone mention any of this to you?"

"No." My pulse and my thoughts, once again, were racing. I'd only exchanged a few words with Myra and Carl this morning, but I'd worked side by side with Debbie Henderson for a good three hours. Why hadn't she said a word about the police coming to her house just last night, questioning her and her husband about a death that we'd both, essentially, witnessed?

Was she embarrassed? Afraid? Or guilty?

chapter 10

J ill smiled, touched my arm a second time, and said, "I was just about to fix myself some lunch. Would you care to join me?"

"No, but thank you for offering." Now that there had been a poisoning in the neighborhood, it seemed as though everyone was trying to get me to eat or drink something. "Do you think I could interrupt Steve Sullivan's work for just a minute?"

"He's not here, I'm afraid. Heaven help him, but he said he had to *discuss* something with Taylor. They must both be over at Myra's house."

"Oh, okay. I just wanted to run a suggestion that Debbie made earlier past you and Steve."

"I'm intrigued." She beamed at me. "By all means, run this suggestion past me first. And, while you're doing so, I'll give you a peek at the room in progress. You're undoubtedly curious to see the design of one of your colleagues."

"I am, actually."

"Maybe by the time we're done with your dime tour, Steve will be back," she added. "You can leave your shoes right by the door there with the others." She pointed at her own feet, clad in Italian leather pumps. "These are my house shoes, with which I *never* step outside."

I obediently left my shoes on the edge of the tile and stepped onto the white wool plush carpet, enjoying its cushy softness, and she led the way deeper into her home. Those were real holly boughs at the base of each rail in the banister, I realized; although the carol made decking "the halls with boughs of holly" sound joyful, those nasty, barbed leaves could stab straight through thick gardening gloves.

In the living room, which was graced with a striking cathedral ceiling, I greedily drank in the pine aroma from a ten-foot-high, lavishly decorated tree. Here the carpet had given way to the ochre tones of a maple floor, and the honey-hued walls looked buttery in the light that streamed through the windows. A grand piano stood in regal splendor at the opposite side of the room. I sang my praises, telling Jill in all honesty that this room should be featured in *Architectural Digest*.

After she'd thanked me and we'd moved on, I returned to our previous conversation. "Debbie suggested that we switch helpers for the final room installation . . . you would help me, while Debbie helps Steve set up your den."

"How marvelous!" Jill exclaimed. "When will your room be ready?"

We passed a set of closed French doors that afforded me just a glimpse of the McBrides' khaki-colored parlor, where I was delighted to see that their built-ins were full of the kind of knickknacks that I love and Sullivan detests. "Anytime, I suppose, although the TV stand won't have had time to dry properly until tomorrow."

"That would be perfect. Steve has to practically *sit* on Taylor Duncan to get any work out of him, so Steve doesn't think our room will be completed until tomorrow either."

I was briefly distracted at the sight of a stunning formal dining room on the opposite side of the hall, but we'd reached the den. Kevin's prized new Barcalounger and a Chesterfield sofa in matching bomber-jacket-brown leather were back-to-back in the center of the room, carefully tucked under protective plastic. I could tell at a glance that the room was going to be on a par with the other gorgeous rooms within this glorious home. My eyes were every bit as green with envy as the walls were with Venetian plaster. On the opposite wall, there was a fabulous fireplace made of salvaged redbrick that Sullivan was helping to accentuate with a new hearth and mantelpiece.

"As you can see," Jill said in museum-curator tones, "the walls and ceiling are finished. However, the custom furniture that Taylor is building hasn't been completed yet."

"Everything looks wonderful so far. Do you happen to have a copy of his finished plans?"

"Oh, heavens, yes. That was the first thing I insisted upon seeing once Debbie and I arrived home on Saturday." She fluffed up her blond hair. "I was looking at them again just a moment ago. I'll be right back."

I mentally drew some furniture plans in her absence, knowing that, if this were my project, I would want to soften the somewhat butch colors and lines of the leather sofa and Barcalounger by draping a lilac cashmere throw on the Chesterfield and setting at least one large, dramatic floral arrangement with pinks and purples on a side table. There was zero chance that my vision for accessorizing would match Sullivan's, but I would be willing to wager my entire salary that he was going to add a spectacular area rug, centered by the fireplace on the west wall, to draw the eye away from the recliner and Chesterfield.

"Frankly, the design is a bit masculine for my taste, but I'm adjusting," Jill said as she returned and handed me the watercolor renditions of the finished area.

I had to resist the urge to cry "Aha!" The drawings supported my expectations exactly: there was indeed going to be an oriental rug centered lengthwise along the west wall. He'd used a classy, asymmetrical furniture placement. It was the entertainment center for the north wall that he'd sketched out that was truly exceptional, though. The tapered lines were simply exquisite—a gentle flair accentuated the open spaces of the piece, imbuing the work with a grace and lightness. In lesser hands, this would have been a typical shelf unit—box-like and bulky.

"This one room has become Kevin's den of late," Jill explained, "and the more that I think about it, the more that I like the idea of its staying that way. Now, he can have his room, and I can have the thirteen others."

"It's beautiful," I murmured and, alas, meant it, although I'd noticed one puzzling item in Sullivan's plan. "Is that a mounted fish that Steve's drawn above the mantel?"

She grimaced. "It's a blue marlin Kevin managed to hook on some male-bonding fishing expedition he went on years ago. I've been hiding it in the attic, with the ex-

cuse that I was saving it for the vacation home we've yet
to purchase."

I couldn't help but smile; having to incorporate a
mounted fish in his design must have irked Sullivan to
no end. He must have selected the nicest area rug imaginable to distract focus from *that* item.

"The coffee table and entertainment center Steve has
designed are too bland for my tastes," Jill announced. I
disagreed but said nothing. "But otherwise, I agree that
the room is handsome, if not exactly 'beautiful.' Steve
Sullivan has a fine sense of style, even if he doesn't quite
have that Manhattan panache that I so adore. Excuse me
a moment." She swept out of the room and promptly returned, a Palm Pilot in hand. "Let's say eleven thirty tomorrow morning then, shall we, for our joint venture in
room design?"

"I think I can arrange to be here then."

"Great. I'll check with Debbie and Steve, so just be
sure to touch base with me today, before you leave, to
make certain we're all on the same page."

"That sounds . . . very efficient."

She laughed and brushed her pearl necklace with a
manicured fingertip. "Kevin's always telling me that I
missed my calling . . . that I enjoy organizing everyone so
much, I should have been secretary of state."

She ushered me to the door. "I'm sure Debbie will be
free—her work schedule is always flexible, since she's
self-employed. As long as Steve doesn't have a conflict,
we'll be all set for tomorrow at eleven thirty."

I thanked Jill and left, ruminating about Sullivan's design as I headed toward the Hendersons' house. With the
exception of the blue marlin, that room had been very
nearly perfect; I could quibble with Sullivan's Spartan
accessorizing, but I would like to believe that I'd have
made many of the same choices in all other design

aspects. The realization, though, that I wouldn't have been capable of visualizing those furniture designs—the coffee table and entertainment center—nagged at me.

Manhattan was where I had trained, which Jill had probably gleaned from chatting with Debbie, and so Jill had made her remark about the city's stylishness to flatter me. In all honesty, I couldn't really claim to be more stylish than Sullivan. When it came to the "wow" factor—the reaction of entering a room that took one's breath away—Sullivan had me beat, although I was making strides. But I did a better job at getting into my customers' heads to understand their likes and dislikes. A Sullivan room could impress a guest, but a Gilbert room made the guest say to the host, "This room is so *you*." Or at least, that's what I'd been told more than once. I treasured the compliment, for it was really important to me that my finished rooms reflect the people who dwell in them.

Across the street, Myra had been standing in front of her glass door and promptly opened it as I neared. "Erin?" she called. "Have you got a few minutes to talk?"

"I suppose so. Sure." Truth be told, Myra was the last person I felt like sitting down and chatting with at the moment. My vivid imagination was running a bit amok, making me ask myself: if Myra had sent me away as a baby to protect me from Randy's abuse, could she have resorted to murder to protect me a second time, all these years later? Then again, *I* seemed to be Detective O'Reilly's prime suspect. Could the police have specifically told Debbie and Carl not to speak to me? Was that why Carl had all but slammed the door in my face this morning?

Myra led me to her living room, telling me to have a seat. I sat down on the floral brocade sofa, and she eyed me as she perched on the overstuffed chair across from me. "Are you all right, Erin? You look so worried."

I was *now*. These dark gray walls in such a small space truly were oppressive. "I just . . . learned from Jill that the police were here last night, asking about your husband's death."

"They're just being thorough."

Her dismissal only raised my warning flags further; the police were "being thorough" because her husband had been poisoned and therefore most likely murdered. Was Myra really unaware of that fact? Last night at the hospital she'd been the one to tell me that he'd died of a heart attack. Had she been misled, or was she trying to mislead *me*?

She leaned toward me, elbows on her knees, and held my gaze. "Erin, tell me something. I've given this a great deal of thought, and I've decided I do indeed want to re-decorate my home as soon as possible, from top to bottom. Not to be heartless, but I want this place to finally be able to reflect *my* tastes. And, despite your reluctance, I think you'd be the perfect designer to help me figure out what my tastes are, after thirty years of a stifling marriage."

Instantly, I was torn. Under vastly different circumstances, hers was precisely the type of challenge I most relished, plus it would be an excellent opportunity to observe the people in Randy's life and, perhaps, uncover the motive for his murder. On the other hand, I had my father urging me to stay away, I'd sworn to my mother that I wouldn't try to find my birth parents yet could well be sitting across from my biological mother at this very moment, and the police considered me a murder suspect and would no doubt find me all the more suspicious if I accepted a job redesigning the victim's house.

That was three reasons for declining and two for accepting. I felt like tearing out my hair in frustration, but answered reluctantly, "I'm going to have to pass. It's . . . such a big job, and things start getting really hectic for me in January." That last was something of a fib, but it seemed much kinder than the truth.

Myra pursed her lips and said nothing. If I *was* her daughter, as she'd hinted, my refusing her offer like this was a slap in the face when she most needed support. It felt horrible to hurt her . . . and to know that I was simultaneously turning my back on a terrific career opportunity.

I glanced around at the cluttered room. An ugly black ashtray when neither of the Axelrods were smokers. Ostrich feathers in a copper urn. A table lamp with seashells glued to its base. A faded watercolor of a mallard in flight and an oil painting of a rain-slick street. Did these items have special meaning? Had they been accumulated during vacations? Garage-sale visits? The objects that we choose to keep—to surround ourselves with—reveal our souls. The fibers that formed the tapestry of my biological parents' lives could very well be right here before my uncomprehending eyes.

I swallowed hard and met Myra's gray eyes, trying to remember now if Randy's had been dark brown, like my own. "I'd really love to do your house, Myra, if only I could. There's nothing I love more than doing a whole house at once, starting over fresh, but . . . the timing's all wrong. I'm terribly sorry."

"What if you were to just do half of the rooms? Maybe just the rooms on the main floor? Would you have time to tackle that?"

It felt to me as though I had equally compelling reasons to accept or decline this job. Half the house was a reasonable compromise. I glanced heavenward and asked silently, *Right, Mom?*

No answer in my mother's voice, but no lightning bolts zapping me, either.

To Myra, I replied, "I'll think about it carefully. And, no matter what I ultimately decide, thank you very much for considering me for this job."

She grinned. "That's what I was hoping you'd say! That's why I took the liberty of inviting Steve Sullivan over here. To discuss sharing the duties."

"Sharing?" I all but shrieked. There was no way sharing could work. Steve Sullivan would be a distraction; we'd bicker over design decisions when I could be uncovering clues. "I assumed you meant you would just . . . do half the house now and the rest later. It's very, very difficult for two designers who've never worked together before to blend their tastes and also listen to what the homeowner—"

The doorbell rang. "Ah. That will be Steve now." Myra hopped to her feet. "You two could be 'Gilbert and Sullivan' after all."

"Sullivan and Gilbert," I muttered to myself as Myra went to the door.

"Hi, Myra. Taylor seems to have things under control now, so I have . . ." Sullivan's voice faded. "Gilbert. I didn't know you were here."

His obvious disappointment at seeing me made me suspect that he felt our relationship was back to square one. Maybe that was true; my recent epiphany that I couldn't trust him was wise. I fired back, "Now you do."

"Erin and I were cooking up a plan just now," Myra told him as she reclaimed her seat. "We were thinking that you two could pool your considerable talents and work together on remodeling my whole house."

He kept his expression inscrutable but gave me a quick glance. I shook my head at him to indicate that Myra's wording was a far cry from how I would have described matters. At least I hoped he could gather that from a mere head shake; it didn't seem prudent to make circular gestures against my temple in attempt to signal that Myra was a bit off her rocker.

He gave her a warm smile, back to being the charming Sullivan clients gushed about, and sat down stiffly in the icky orange plaid–upholstered chair. "It's really not a good idea to have two designers on the same project, Myra. You know what they say about too many cooks spoiling the broth."

"You two wouldn't be working on the same broth, exactly. I was thinking separate rooms, or floors, even. Erin could do the main floor, and you could do the upstairs, for instance."

"But, you'd surely want Erin to do the bedrooms. That's her specialty."

"Not necessarily," I interjected. His haughtiness in banishing me to the nonpublic rooms was making me sizzle. "I wouldn't say that I specialize in bedrooms. If I *had* to pick a specialty, it would be accessorizing."

He grimaced. "Ah, yes. Accessories. Also known as dust catchers. Pillows and throws and bric-a-brac . . . full walls boasting nothing but family photographs . . . big floral arrangements."

"I happen to believe that rooms are more comfortable and appealing when they are designed to be *lived in*, as opposed to having a sterile, museum-like quality."

Sullivan turned toward Myra and gestured at me with an upraised palm. "There you have it. Erin and I cannot work together. I admire Erin's work, and I think she's perfect for you, even if she's far too froufrou for my tastes.

Neither of us have any intention of being half of Sullivan and Gilbert Designs."

Froufrou? Me? I hated to be described as anything that rhymed with doo-doo and snarled, "You can say *that* again." *And it's Gilbert and Sullivan, darn it!*

He raised an eyebrow and studied me, as though sincerely perplexed that I'd taken offense. "Gilbert, all I'm saying is that I'm into more masculine a design than Myra would like."

"The best solution, then," I said to Myra, ignoring Sullivan, "would be for you to find a third designer. There are scores of them in Crestview."

Sullivan's jaw dropped a little. "Wait. You're . . . not interested in accepting the assignment yourself?"

I said nothing and merely met his gaze.

He rose and gave Myra a sheepish smile. "Erin and I need to discuss this for a minute, Myra. Could the two of us step outside and rejoin you in a minute or two?"

"Certainly," Myra said.

With our borderline boorish behavior, we would be lucky she didn't lock the door behind us and refuse to let us back inside.

The moment we were out of earshot, he snapped, "You're *also* turning the job down? Why?"

"Last night on the phone my father said that my biological parents were dangerous and warned me to stay away. Now someone's dead. All I have are a batch of unanswered questions about my birth parents and why someone set me up to find my picture." I hesitated, but while staring into those gorgeous hazel eyes of his, I decided I might as well be up front with him. "I went to the police station last night. According to the detective who's handling the investigation, Randy Axelrod didn't die of a heart attack after all."

Sullivan raised his brow. "So was he poisoned?"

"Apparently. But by arsenic, not cyanide . . . unless the detective was just yanking my chain to see if I'd blurt out that it was definitely cyanide. He seems convinced I'm guilty. In any case, I've been on the fence between taking Myra's job and seeing if I can dig up some answers myself in the process, or bugging out of here entirely, like any sensible person would. But there's no way I can do my best work while constantly looking over my shoulder. So I'll bow out and let you accept Myra's job."

Sullivan was shaking his head slowly, looking thoughtful. "Here's what we do, Gilbert. We *both* accept the job. It'll take us until after the holidays to get full swing into the assignment. By then, the police should have discovered whoever killed Randy. If not, and things start to get too hot to handle, we'll back out . . . say that we can't take on the project after all."

"By 'too hot to handle,' you mean, for example, that our client has been arrested for murder?"

He straightened his shoulders and studied my face, his own expression instantly growing somber. He said in a half whisper, "You think Myra killed him?"

"Maybe. She had the best motive . . . the most to gain. All I know is, I was enjoying life a lot more before I showed up to work here on Saturday morning."

He raised an eyebrow and said under his breath, "Can't say the same's true for me." He gestured at Myra's door. "If we take this job, we might be able to salvage a feature story from the new editor at *Denver Lifestyles*." He gave an apologetic shrug. "I know that's callous of me, but it sure beats losing my business."

Our gazes locked. It would be so nice to know that I wasn't in this alone, after all. But *Steve Sullivan*, of all people? My temporary *partner*?

"Besides," he continued, "the bottom line is, I'll never

feel right about the Cooper account if I were to pull *this* whole job out from under you as well. We both know Myra asked *you* first. What do you say?"

I averted my gaze, which fell on the sled adorned with the evergreen wreath. "I don't know, Sullivan. It feels as though I'm dragging you into my troubles this way."

"It's a job, like any other job. Aside from Axelrod's poisoning . . . and your finding your baby picture inside a wall . . . this is as run-of-the-mill as an assignment can get." He winked at me. "Seriously, what's the worst that can happen?"

"One or both of us will stumble onto something incriminating, and we'll wind up getting murdered, too."

He winced. "Ouch, that's bad. But . . . I'll be here to watch your back and make sure nothing like that occurs. And hey," he joshed, "what's the *second*-worst thing that could happen?"

"I could discover that my birth father was abusive to me and to his wife, and that my birth mother is a murderer."

"My God, Gilbert. For someone who designs such warm, soul-cheering rooms, you've got a hell of a lot of gloom hidden inside you."

"You think my rooms are warm and soul-cheering?" I exclaimed. "What happened to being too froufrou?"

"You caught me." He spread his arms. "Yes, that was a compliment. Which I don't give very often. Now you expect me to *repeat* it?"

"I've always really admired your designs, too. They're—"

The door creaked open and Myra called, "Aren't you two starting to freeze out here by now?"

"We're almost through discussing our options," I replied promptly.

Sullivan said, "Tell you what, Myra. Let us work up

some initial thoughts on what we'd like to do, and we'll see how it goes. If you've decided to go in a different direction by then, that will be perfectly understandable, and there'll be no hard feelings."

"Which will be something of a change in pace for you two, apparently," she replied, studying us. "It sounds to me as though you two have had bad blood between you for quite some time."

Sullivan and I exchanged guilty glances. It was distressing to think that I'd made it so obvious that I had some problems with a fellow designer.

"Gilbert and I share a healthy competitive spirit that will actually work out in your favor, Myra. We'll give collaborating on your home our best effort."

They were both looking at me, awaiting my reply. "Absolutely." I could only wish that I felt the enthusiasm that I'd put into my voice, but my intuition was screaming at me to walk away from this assignment. If I'd listened the last time my instincts had advised me to decline a job, I never would have been in this neighborhood in the first place. And Randy Axelrod might still be alive.

"Wonderful," Myra said, smiling. "Where do we begin?" She held the door for us, and we went back inside. Now that we'd come in from the crisp air, the musty odor of the house hit me. If nothing else, we needed to replace this worn, blah-brown wall-to-wall carpeting.

Sullivan replied, "We'll compare schedules and make an appointment with you so that we can take some photographs and measure the rooms."

"Wonderful," she said again. "If you've got a few minutes right now, I can take you both on a quick tour. That way, you can get a running start later."

Again, he and I exchanged glances. He said, "Fine," and I nodded.

"How about if we begin with the upstairs bedrooms?" I suggested in as happy tones as I could muster. "I'd like to get an idea of what *Steve* has in mind."

There was a hitch in his step. "We'll work out all the details of who's doing what as we get a little further along . . . before we develop a working plan."

Myra ignored my suggestion to begin upstairs, and we instead started in the family room, where Randy's dusty exercise equipment still held court. A five-foot-high Christmas tree, decorated with popcorn strings and numerous tiny teddy bears, had been placed on the treadmill. Almost none of the furniture was salvageable, except the wing chair, which had good bones.

Myra led us to a second room and opened the door. "This was Randy's office," she said.

If you needed one word to describe Randy Axelrod's office, that word would definitely be *hideous*. The furniture looked to be discards from a scratch-and-dent sale. No attempt whatsoever had been made to balance or harmonize the area; it looked more like a room-sized storage bin than a place to work in, surrounded by lovely and meaningful possessions that give the soul sustenance.

"Terrific natural lighting in here," I said, looking at the bay windows. It's always best to voice the positives. Keep the negatives private until they can be framed in terms of how the new design will eliminate them.

"Was this office your husband's exclusively?" Sullivan asked. "Do you want to keep the computer and shelves and use it as your own office?"

"Or we could convert it to any type of room you'd want," I said. Myra had a strange, tense expression on her face when I turned to face her, but I continued. "A library or sitting room, or if you have any collectibles you'd—"

"Actually, the more I think about it, the more I'm thinking that maybe this is the one room I don't want anyone to touch."

"Fine," Sullivan said easily, not at all thrown by her sudden change of mind. "And I'm assuming you aren't thinking of doing anything with the basement, either, right?"

"Right. We'll leave that unfinished."

"Do you have a ballpark budget in mind?" he asked, stepping aside so that Myra could lead the way.

I was burning with curiosity to know why Myra had such a bewildering change of heart regarding this room. She'd made no secret of the fact that she was eager to expunge her recently deceased husband's things from her home. There wasn't one item in here that was worth holding on to for anything other than sentimental reasons. And sentimental reasons were precisely what this woman seemed to lack. . . .

Just as I turned to close the door behind us, I saw the ugly blue-and-green checkered umbrella stand in the corner.

chapter 11

You look like you've seen a ghost," Sullivan said to me as we left Myra's house.

"No, I'm just . . . distracted, I guess." Although my past *was* haunting me. Myra had whisked us out of that office to prevent my spotting that umbrella stand. She must have forgotten its significance until she saw me standing near it—that it was in my mother's earliest photograph of me, and so I was likely to recognize it.

He peered at my face, then grabbed my elbow and ushered me across the street and out of sight of the Hendersons' and Axelrods' front windows. I was too surprised to object. "Out with it, Gilbert. What did you see in Randy's office? Another baby picture?"

"Why do you ask?" I snarled.

"Because I don't want to see you get . . . Because I'm nosy."

I clicked my tongue. "You were about to say that you didn't want to see me get hurt. Which would have been nice for me to hear. You know, Sullivan, just because you got screwed by a con man doesn't mean you can't be nice to anyone ever again. It's not like *everyone* is looking to rip you off. You don't have to go around being the big bad wolf."

He laughed. "If I'm the big bad wolf, does that make you one of the three little pigs?"

"Nice avoidance tactic," I snapped.

He pointed at me with his chin. "Back at you. So what exactly did you see in Myra's house?"

I frowned and held my tongue, but Sullivan's probing eyes were relentless. "There was a checkered umbrella stand behind the door of Randy's office. It's the same one that was in the photograph, I'm sure of it."

"Jeez. No wonder she acted so weird all of a sudden. Do you think *she* might be your mother?"

"Maybe. I wish I didn't have to think about it. Everything was just fine by me with never knowing who my birth parents were."

He combed his fingers through his light brown hair. "What the hell's going on? Taylor Duncan's had a big chip on his shoulder toward you from the get-go. I get the feeling he knows something and is just playing dumb."

"Yeah? Well, *I'm* pretty sure that's not an act."

He chuckled. "Maybe you're right, on second thought. But, you know, once he gets going on some carpentry project, he's not half bad."

"I've noticed that, too."

We shared an awkward silence. Sullivan said, "There's

not much more I can do here till Taylor finishes a project or two. I'm calling it a day. How 'bout you?"

"I have about two thousand feet of garland to hang this afternoon for a Christmas bash in Foothills Park."

"Decking the halls, hey?"

"Something like that. Which reminds me, Jill and Debbie agreed to act as our assistants when we install our rooms. Debbie's going to work with you, and Jill with me. Tomorrow morning at eleven thirty."

"Eleven thirty, hey? The time of day is already scheduled for me?"

I'd forgotten to get his approval for our plan, which was rude of me, and he would probably chew me out now. I shrugged. "Jill's rather . . . efficient."

"So I've noticed. Okay, then. I'll fit my schedule around it." He took a couple of steps in the direction of the McBrides' house. "I'll see you tomorrow. Maybe we can get together for dinner afterward."

"Are you asking me out?"

"Not dinner like on a date. I'm not your type, remember? I just meant we could eat while we discuss Myra's home."

"Oh. Sure. That'd probably be okay." To my surprise and annoyance, I wasn't nearly as repulsed by the notion of dating Sullivan as I knew I should be. The guy was probably not even interested in women, for crying out loud! And, even though he was now being nice and Evan's betrayal made Sullivan's recent bad behavior understandable, that didn't explain his initial shabby treatment of me. This was the man who'd stormed into my office three months after I'd set up shop and snarled, "Let me give you some advice, Miss Gilbert. You want to succeed, you'd better learn to do so on your own merit, not by tricking Sullivan Designs' clients into hiring you!" The memory still rankled.

We headed to our respective clients' homes to let them know we were leaving. Debbie came to the door, carrying a stack of paperbacks balanced in a shoe box. "Come on in, Erin. Carl told me to tell you that the TV stand is stained, and he said he'd apply the polyurethane when he gets home at five. I'm just putting these away upstairs in my closet."

I faked a stern expression. "You know, Debbie, you're breaching my policy of never allowing my customers to move things themselves back into the remodeled room."

She chuckled. "I couldn't wait. Besides, these books weren't in the bedroom before. They were in my office. So technically, I'm not moving anything *back* into the room."

"Ah. Well, that eases my conscience a little." I glanced at my watch. I had fifteen minutes to spare before I had to leave for another client's home in Foothills Park. "I'll give you a hand."

"Thanks. I've got two more loads after this one. I can't believe how much extra storage space for books that closet gives me!"

I followed her upstairs and glanced around at my nearly completed design. The ambience of a calm, cozy oasis that I'd hoped to achieve was starting to come together. It was frustrating to have to wait clear until midday tomorrow to see this room in its final state.

Debbie had triple-stacked books on the deep shelves and had me help her stash them without rhyme or reason. This hidden shelving was infinitely better than having knee-high stacks along the walls, but she would have a devil of a time finding a particular title this way. If only my room design hadn't initially been a surprise, we could have discussed other options, such as a floor-to-ceiling book carousel in the closet. As we descended the stairs again, I had to adopt yet another temporary mantra—*Let it go, Erin . . . let it go.*

There were only another twenty or so books remaining in her office. While helping her to box them, my vision fell upon a small stack of papers next to the printer. The printout was titled "Window Treatments—A Whole New World."

"Oh, hey," I said with a big smile. "When Carl told me you were a technical writer, I assumed that meant computers and high-tech equipment."

She stuffed a tress of her red hair behind her ear. With her back to the computer, she replied, "That *is* what I write."

"But you sometimes do freelance work on home design articles?"

Her eyes flew wide. She whirled around to look at the printout. "Oh, uh, no, I don't. I didn't write that article myself, I just printed it off the Net weeks ago. For use when planning my own bedroom."

How odd. If she'd printed the article off the Net, it should have contained Internet print headings. I read the existing headers. "Oh, that's one of Randy Axelrod's pieces for *Denver Lifestyles*." He must have sent Debbie one of his yet-to-be-published articles.

She followed my gaze. "Oh, yes, indeedy. That's Randy's article, isn't it? I'd forgotten." Avoiding my eyes, she scooped up the box of books. "I'll carry these. Can you turn out the lights?"

"Sure."

She had borne that same expression and demeanor when she'd been caught in the lie about how she came to possess her chest of drawers. She was lying about something again. I scanned the first paragraph of the article. It was the typical voice that Randy had used in his magazine editorials.

I followed Debbie up the stairs, wondering. Could she have ghostwritten those articles? That would certainly explain the disparity between Randy's written and speaking voices. Not to mention his complete lack of interest in design.

As we were putting away the last of Debbie's books, she said, "Seeing Randy's article just now got me to thinking . . . I wonder if I should go ahead and talk to someone at the magazine about that story Randy promised to do on you and Steve Sullivan."

"Or on the contest winner, rather."

"Well, yes, but now we can rethink Randy's decision. In fact, I could have our subscribers vote on which room they liked the best. That way you'd *both* get plenty of positive publicity."

Our subscribers?

Her expression changed to alarm as, obviously, her own words registered. "I . . . used to do a lot of freelance work for *Denver Lifestyles.*"

"I see." There was obviously more to this than she wanted to divulge, but I decided to let the matter drop. "Jill told me she was interviewed by the police last night."

She nodded. "They spoke to Carl and me, too. They're suspicious about the circumstances of Randy's death, but I can't imagine why. I mean, yes, the man had enemies. Randy enjoyed rubbing people the wrong way. But his heart condition was a ticking time bomb, and he stubbornly refused to adjust his lifestyle. There's no way he would have lived all that much longer, regardless."

Maybe the killer had an even-louder ticking time bomb to deal with, I thought.

Just before noon the next day, I was sitting alone on the floor beside the glossy new night table in the Hendersons' master bedroom. Jill had excused herself to make an important phone call a minute earlier. The bed had been assembled and the chest of drawers moved into place, but it was the night table that currently held my attention.

I indulged myself and ran my palms over the top. It had a heavenly smoothness to the surface. I took a deep breath as I opened its breakfront and slipped some books inside. There was nothing quite like the scent of new fine wood case goods. This had been a pricey purchase but worth every penny—a limited-edition artisan-style breakfront in rich tiger maple. It was absolutely exquisite, with a sleek, gentle flair in its legs and sexy lines. I lovingly closed the breakfront doors. From the doorway behind me, Jill chuckled.

"Caught in the act," I murmured, and scrambled to my feet.

"That's quite all right. I don't blame you in the least. That nightstand is divine. Believe me, Erin, if I'd have seen how beautifully that table went with my old dresser, I never would have let Debbie have my dresser in the first place."

"I've always had a weakness for nice furniture," I confessed. "My high school friends were drooling over pop magazines that showed Brad Pitt naked from the waist up, while I was poring over the legs in *Architectural Digest,* and *House and Garden.* 'Oh, sure,' I would tell them, 'the man has gorgeous blue eyes, but try holding up a Murano indigo glass bottle next to his cheek sometime and see which color is more spectacular.' Pop stars come and go. But a solid cherry cabinet with dovetail joinery? Now *that* will outlive us all."

She continued to smile at me, her blue eyes merry. "And were your friends impressed with that argument?"

"Not really."

She laughed. "I wouldn't think so."

"It probably goes without saying that I wasn't voted Most Popular in high school."

She smiled a little and turned away. "Let's get your window treatment up now, shall we?"

"Oops. Did I hit a nerve just now, Jill? Were *you* voted Most Popular?"

She laughed again, clearly delighted that I'd picked up on her body English. "What can I say? High school was a good time for me." She said wistfully, "My family lived in a mansion in Massachusetts. That's where I grew up . . . in Lexington. Our home was filled with the antiques—Hepplewhites, Sheratons . . . I'm sure you'd have appreciated its interior. I should show you photos sometime."

"You really should. What was the house design? Colonial? Federal?"

"Federal. Every room had these marvelous high ceilings and fireplaces. The estate had such a grand presence that it positively reeked of elegance and grace. It's hard sometimes to adjust to the more contemporary style of homes we have out here in Colorado."

"Do you get to go back and visit, at least?"

She frowned and shook her head. "We wound up selling the place when my parents passed away."

"I'm sorry."

"Me, too. About that whole situation. Losing my parents and their estate. But Randy needed the money."

"*Randy?*"

"Kevin." She giggled unconvincingly. "I meant my husband, of course. Slip of the tongue. Randy's death's so heavy on my mind, I guess." She made a fluttering motion with her fingertips, as if to flick away any discomfiture at her flub. "*Kevin* needed the money—venture capital funding—for his latest get-rich-quick scheme."

"I had a boyfriend who was always trying to discover

some quick way to make his fortune. And I'm sure one of these days he'll manage."

She put her hand on my shoulder. "Was he an electrical engineer, like my Kevin?"

"No, a chemist."

She nodded thoughtfully. "That's probably just as bad . . . their noses always in these ridiculous books with mathematical equations." She rolled her eyes and released a heavy sigh. "Do yourself a favor, Erin. Marry a man with the same interests as you. You'll keep each other's hearts much longer that way."

So the McBrides' marriage was in trouble, too, just like the Hendersons' was. These couples didn't need designers so much as marriage counselors!

Jill proved to be a less-than-ideal helper. She was clearly more used to giving instructions than to receiving them. We managed, however, to hang the sheers and the drapery panels on both windows and across the bedposts. The bronze curtain rods with their carved ivy leaf finials were every bit as big of an improvement as I'd expected them to be. The draperies were now a tapestry to delight the eye.

While I hung the oil painting, Jill put together the second nightstand on the far side of the bed—Carl's side. To save money, I had gone with a flea-market purchase of a simple table with an open shelf. This is a nice trick of the trade—let one nightstand or corner table be merely functional by virtue of lovely, sin-concealing fabric. A large number of books could be hidden underneath the raw silk skirt I'd chosen.

We put the television set into place. I couldn't hide all three jacks—the cable, phone, and electric outlets—behind this one small oak unit, so I'd created wallpaper covers for the outlet plates. The large oil painting worked so well in this room and drew the eye so nicely that I almost didn't mind having the little black TV set with its dreadful aesthetics exposed to one side of the painting's ornately gilded frame.

Next came the accessories, which for me was tantamount to conducting the orchestra in the final performance or adding the final tantalizing ingredient to a heavenly recipe. At this stage, I always have everyone leave the immediate area, because I can't tolerate the slightest interruption, so I ushered Jill firmly from the room.

For a needed touch of femininity, I placed a delicate pattern of Belgian lace on the tiger-maple nightstand. I'd noticed a lovely pitcher that wasn't being suitably shown off in the kitchen; this I would use for fresh flowers. The flowers were tulips—magenta with delicate white edging to each petal—and looked spectacular against the burgundy-and-gold glazed wall. I placed them on the nightstand on Debbie's side, using a coaster I'd cut with pinking shears from an old plastic placemat.

I "borrowed" a bentwood chair from the sunroom that was suitably aged but had great bones and would look terrific under the window, as well as being a comfortable place to sit and read or just daydream. I set a reasonable and appealing number of books on the headboard shelves and parted the silk panels so that the folds curved deliciously. I arranged the fluffy pillows and draped a cream-colored cashmere throw so that its tassels dangled invitingly over the edge of the tiger maple footboard.

To provide an extra splash of color, I nestled a small pillow of aubergine velvet among the chenille ones we'd made. To highlight and echo that color burst, I placed an aubergine hand-blown art glass piece on the round table on Carl's bedside. The slant of early afternoon sunlight that now graced the room was lovely and serene, and the lighting would be even nicer in the morning. Then the art glass would catch the sunlight with an intensity and warm glow reminiscent of a glass of fine claret at a mid-summer day's picnic.

Speaking of wine, I arranged a bottle of Merlot and two crystal glasses, along with a corkscrew, on the round table next to the art glass. In a subliminal message that I was certain Debbie would pick up on, I retrieved a hardcover copy of *Far From the Madding Crowd* from her closet and centered it on the shelf. Lastly, for an extra touch of romance, I placed and lit three sandalwood-scented candles.

I called Jill back inside, and although she said nothing at first, the look of unabashed envy on her face was heartwarming. After she turned a full three-sixty, she looked at me and said quietly, "Regrettably, Kevin made me promise I won't redo rooms until a full year has passed, which isn't the case with our master bedroom. Expect a call in *four* months." She sighed, then turned on a heel. "I'm going to go see the final results of my den and send Debbie over."

"I hope she likes it."

"She'll love everything. Trust me. It's *Carl* who's impossible to please," she called over her shoulder as she descended the stairs.

Alone again, I checked the room from all common angles, except while sitting on their bed; once a bed was fully made and pillows in place I had a superstition about that, and the last thing the Hendersons needed was bad luck. I positioned the arms of the brass sconces partway out and hid the remote control along the very back edge of books on the bottom shelf of the bed. Jill's reaction had made my heart sing, and I had to admit that this was the nicest bedroom I'd ever been in—warm, elegant and yet cozy and inviting, and extraordinarily romantic with its rich, deep Mediterranean hues.

To my surprise, I heard a male voice along with Debbie's as the front door opened below. Debbie called, "Erin? Carl came home for lunch. Are you ready for the great unveiling?"

I came down to the landing and said, "Go on up. I'll be there in just a moment." I always prefer to give homeowners a minute to absorb how different their interiors have become before expecting them to give me their response to them.

Debbie was hugging Carl when I stepped back into the room. Hearing my footsteps, she immediately pulled away and said, "Erin, you're a genius! I never imagined this room could be so *stunning*."

"Do you like it, Carl?" I asked, inwardly bracing myself.

He fidgeted with his glasses. "This is . . . really something. Dang! I didn't want to hire you. As far as I could tell, the room was just fine before, but jeez . . . I don't even know what to say. I mean, this is so . . . neat." He stared at the television set on its stand. "Look at that, Debbie! We can look straight at the TV now, without craning our necks!"

"Hurray," she said in a deadpan voice.

"It was just an observation," he muttered. "I'm not saying . . ." He scanned the room in an obvious attempt to find something else to comment on. He fixed his vision on the round table in the corner. "Oh, hey. You gave us some wine. Great!"

"I'm delighted you like the room."

"We love it," Debbie assured me. "I don't know how to thank you enough."

"You just did. Enjoy. I'm going to go home now, but

I'll call on you tomorrow to make sure you're completely satisfied."

I went downstairs. As I collected my purse and grabbed my keys, I heard Carl say, "I think I'll take the afternoon off. Would you like some wine, my dear?"

"I'd love some," I heard her reply.

I pumped a fist and breathed a triumphant "Yes!" as I let myself out the door.

And yet I hesitated when I got behind the steering wheel of my van. I was sky-high now and dying to see Steve's completed design. I decided to just brazenly go over there and ask Jill to show it to me. I made the short drive to the McBrides' and parked behind Sullivan's van.

Kevin McBride answered the bell and immediately said, "Erin! Come in and see my room."

He put his arm around my shoulders as, after kicking off my shoes, I headed inside. "Steve Sullivan might not be as easy on the eyes as you are, but he did one heck of a job for us."

"I'm sure he did. He's very talented." Even barefoot and with Kevin in his indoor shoes, I was an inch or so taller than he. I jerked my shoulder just enough to signal him that I didn't appreciate having his hand there, and he wisely let go of me as we rounded the corner into the den.

Well, rats. This interior was drop-dead wonderful, and I had to catch my breath as I took in my surroundings. It was a Sullivan room, and he was a master of clean lines and understated yet dramatic visuals; what had I expected?

Jill and Sullivan appeared to be in consultation about the entertainment center along the north wall. She was working the hardware, which allowed the pocket doors that hid the television set to slide out of sight to either side of the TV, but was saying to Sullivan, "I just don't know." She saw me in the doorway, stepped back to give me a view of the piece, and said, "Erin, what do you think? It's just so . . . plain."

The shelving echoed the clean lines of the coffee table, and I knew at a glance that all that the piece needed to meet with Jill's approval was an eye-catching and expensive-looking vase or sculpture. "I love it! The top shelf is at just the right height to showcase beautifully your favorite figurine or sculpture."

"That's exactly correct," Jill exclaimed. "Kevin, let's go get the Ming vase from the study."

The moment we were alone together I expected Sullivan to bite my head off for stepping on his toes, but he whispered instead, "Come downstairs with me for a moment."

"Why? What's going on?"

"You'll see." I followed him to the study, where, under Jill's watchful eye, Kevin was lifting the blue-and-white vase as though it contained nitroglycerin. If that was a *real* Ming and Kevin were to drop and shatter it, Jill would no doubt strike him dead where he stood. Sullivan told them, "I want Erin to look at something for me. Would you mind terribly if I showed her your basement?"

Jill flashed a panicked look in her husband's direction, then returned her gaze to Sullivan. "Is there something wrong that you're not eager to share with us? A crack in our foundation?"

"No, it's nothing important. Really. Your foundation is rock solid. I just noticed an unusual wire connection when I was down there earlier today and couldn't get the phone jack to work. Erin knows way more about wiring than I do."

"Go right ahead, then."

We went downstairs, and he shut the basement door softly behind us. I muttered, "I don't know diddly-squat about wiring."

"That was all I could come up with off the top of my head. If they ask, the problem's caused by a carpenter's staple through the phone wire. That's actually the truth." He led me through an unfinished room into an enormous partially finished workshop. Wall-length shelving was filled with gadgets and jars of various sizes and contents. "I was down here an hour ago, and it's like a miniature science lab. I decided to check the labels on all these bottles, just in case. I found one that'll interest you."

We were obviously looking for a container of arsenic, but just as I'd started to read the labels, I heard someone enter the room behind us. Kevin had somehow managed to follow us down the stairs, unheard.

"Hey, Steve," Kevin McBride asked. "What's this about some sort of trouble with our wiring?"

"It's nothing major." Sullivan replied, "The phone jack in the den doesn't work. I wanted to trace it down . . . see if I could fix it." Man, he was a smooth liar!

"I'm more than capable of doing that by myself."

Kevin was glaring at us, and I was absolutely certain he'd caught us scanning his shelves and not the wiring along the floor joists above our heads. "This is quite a workshop you've got here, Kevin," I said, surveying the area and trying to send icy thoughts to my cheeks, which were nevertheless growing warm. "Your wife said you're an electrical engineer, right?"

He drummed his fingers on his crossed arms and replied sourly, "That's right."

I headed across the room to feign interest in a

schematic that was spread across the top of a large oak table. "Wow. This is impressive. You even design your own circuit boards?"

"Yeah. I'm trying to start up my own company." His roving eyes focused on my breasts again. Considering that we'd been caught snooping, for once I appreciated his ogling me as a much-needed distraction to him. "It's been a lifelong dream of mine. I think I've hit upon a new invention that could sell like hotcakes. Once I get some more financial backers to help with the production, that is."

While scanning the wiring along the ceiling, Sullivan asked, "What is it? Your invention, I mean."

Kevin gave him a jab in the shoulder. "Can't tell you that, man. Loose lips sink ships and all of that."

"Hey, I understand." Sullivan held up his palms. "Not that you have to worry about me, in any case. All I know is fabrics and color palettes. Wouldn't know how to wire up a circuit if my life depended on it. That's why I had to trust Gilbert here when I wanted to know if it was okay to drive a big staple right through a phone wire like that." He pointed at something above his head, hopefully the carpenter's staple.

"Which I told him it isn't," I replied firmly.

"I see." Kevin looked at me, then at Sullivan, and rocked on his heels. "So why were you looking at my bottles?"

"I'm a collector of rare old bottles," I lied instantly. "There are a couple of bottles on your shelf that happened to catch my eye."

None of those bottles appeared, at a glance, to be more than ten years old. Still scrutinizing the ceiling, Sullivan hastily interjected, "Someone must have been a bit careless with the staple gun."

Kevin followed his gaze and replied, "Taylor, I guess."

He looked at me with a raised eyebrow and, for some reason, winked. "Jill hired him do some odd jobs around the house last week. I didn't connect Taylor's recent handiwork with the fact that the phone in the den hasn't been working."

"I'll take care of it," Sullivan promised.

"That's okay. Really. I'll fix it myself later. As you can surmise, we hardly ever use the phone in that room anyway. My wife prefers the cordless from the kitchen."

"Even so. I'll get some phone cord and redo this for you," Sullivan said. "I like to make sure my rooms are perfect."

"That's really not necessary." Kevin paused, rocked on his heels again, and regarded us coolly. "So. How long are you two going to keep this up?"

"Keep *what* up?" Sullivan asked, innocence personified.

"This crap about both of you coming down here to look at the one staple in the cord. Do you really think you're fooling me?"

"Pardon?" I asked, affecting the same look of innocent ignorance that Sullivan had donned.

Kevin ignored me. He said to Sullivan, "Jill assumes you're gay, but I've seen the way you look at Erin when her back is turned. You two have a thing going, don't you?"

"He caught us, Erin," Sullivan said.

He strode over to me and rested his arm around my shoulders, and I played along and flung my arm around his waist. He was every bit as well toned as he appeared to be.

My cheeks were growing ever warmer, and I babbled to Kevin, "It helps Steve's business sometimes when his female customers think that he's gay. They're more willing to listen to his ideas about fabrics and colors."

"Hence the ruse," Sullivan added.

Kevin gave me another of his patented lascivious grins, still undressing me with his eyes. "Can't say as I blame you one bit, dude."

"What did you think?" Sullivan asked as we left the McBrides' home several minutes later. An icy breeze greeted us the moment that we stepped away from the ell of their house.

"You did a terrific job. I liked everything about your room." I couldn't help but tease him: "Especially the mounted fish. That was a really nice touch."

"I *meant* about the arsenic in the basement, and don't push my buttons, Gilbert. There was nothing I could do about the stupid fish and you know it."

We stopped by the door of Sullivan's van, parked next to mine in front of the McBrides' garage. "I never actually saw that arsenic bottle."

"It was on the second shelf," Sullivan replied, "half-hidden behind other bottles. No way is their having arsenic a coincidence. Kevin or Jill must have killed Randy. I should go to the police, don't you think?"

"You might only succeed in turning yourself into their new chief suspect. Which is about all *I* accomplished by going to them about the cyanide."

"Yeah, but . . . it's so suspicious, that bottle of poison in Kevin's workshop."

"Which is why it's so weird that Kevin or Jill would have simply left it out in the open, if they knew about its being there. Someone else could have sneaked into the McBrides' house at some point and stashed the bottle there to frame them."

He shook his head. "I don't think anyone framed them. I think that's why Kevin was so anxious not to leave us alone in his workshop. He had no way to know anyone would be looking around there before he had the chance to get rid of the bottle. The guy's a lech, and I wouldn't trust him as far as you could throw him."

My attention wandered to a blue sedan on the street that had slowed as it drew closer to the house. It seemed to me that the neighborhood was overdue for another police visit, and I wouldn't have been at all surprised if this turned out to be an unmarked police vehicle. The driver backed up and parked on the street, then a stocky man with a dark complexion climbed out of his vehicle and headed toward us. My heart sank. A police officer. He was in a suit and tie, but the casual attire of Crestview made this almost as obvious a police uniform as the standard blues.

He glanced at the "Interiors by Gilbert" on the side of my van and then at the "Sullivan Designs" on Steve's as he stopped in front of us. "You Erin Gilbert?" he asked me, a hint of a smile on his face.

"Yes, I am." My stomach was instantly in knots.

"And are you Steve Sullivan?"

"Yeah. Can I help you with something?"

"Maybe. I'm Detective Martinez." He fished out a pair of business cards from his pocket and handed one to each of us. The half smile remained. "I'm investigating a possible homicide in this neighborhood."

"Yeah, we know about that . . . Randy Axelrod," Sullivan said. "Erin spoke with the police already. A detective told her Randy died from arsenic poisoning."

Martinez's expression didn't change. "Come down to the police station this afternoon. We'd like to ask you both some questions."

"Together?" Sullivan asked.

"Or separately. Whatever works best for you."

Never would work best for me, but I wisely kept the

thought to myself. The concept of the police possibly considering me a suspect in a murder terrified me into silence.

Detective Martinez turned to walk away. Sullivan looked at me with raised eyebrows, as if to ask if he should mention the arsenic. When I shrugged in reply, he said, "Officer? You might want to get a look in the McBrides' basement workshop. I was down there earlier and spotted a bottle of arsenic on the second shelf of their bookcase."

The detective eyed Sullivan for a long moment. "Be sure to come to the station house. *Soon.*" He stabbed at the McBrides' doorbell.

Sullivan made a poor show of unlocking his van in super-slow motion while we watched to see what would happen next. Jill answered; she and Martinez spoke quietly, then she and I locked gazes for an instant before she ushered him inside. The fierceness in her expression chilled me to the bone.

Sullivan and I stood there in silence for a moment or two after the front door had been shut. Sullivan chose to ignore our brief exchange with the detective entirely and said, "We're still on with Myra at five tonight, right?"

"Right." That was when we had scheduled our initial visit with Myra to take "before" pictures, measure the rooms, and get a feel for what she was looking for in her redecorated household. Sullivan hadn't repeated yesterday's suggestion of dinner, but if he remained mum on the subject by the time we left Myra's tonight, I vowed to myself that I would take the initiative. He was being a true gentleman now, and it was high time for me to forgive his boorish behavior last year and make nice.

I drove home, my mind in a whirl. I wasn't going to go back to the police station of my own volition. Detective Martinez hadn't set an exact time or stated that my visit was mandatory. No way was I willing to sit in that sterile environment and be stared at like bacteria under a microscope. The police could come to me if they wanted more information, and anyway, there was nothing more for me to tell them, was there?

chapter 12

> In the blink of an eye, our babies become adults, and minor keepsakes from their childhoods become our greatest treasures.
>
> —*Audrey Munroe*

"Splendid," Audrey cried as she rushed into the foyer before I could even close the front door. "You're home precisely when I need a practice audience."

She waited impatiently as I removed my coat and stored that and my purse in the closet. I rarely had the chance to watch Audrey's show and enjoyed my occasional gig as guinea pig for her five-minute show segments. This, however, was a rare break for me in the middle of an intense day, and I weighed the notion of telling her that I had too much on my mind. Realistically, though, all I felt up to doing for the next five minutes or so was sitting and staring at a wall, so I might as well stare at Audrey.

I followed her into the kitchen, and we took our standard positions—Audrey behind the island and me seated in the breakfast nook. Today her sewing machine was out, so obviously this segment had something to do with fabric.

With no how-are-you-doing-today preamble, she flashed me her TV smile and launched into her show persona. "If you're like most parents of young children, you dearly enjoy recording your little ones' heights. You can buy premade plastic charts for upward of twenty dollars, or you can make and personalize one for the cost of a couple of yards of fabric, a measuring tape, and a few odds and ends such as rub-on letters that you probably already have in your junk drawer."

Who has rub-on letters in their junk drawer? I wondered, but knew better than to interrupt. Audrey would tolerate criticisms *after* her demo, but not during.

"And for us aunts, uncles, and farther-up-the-growth-chart parents, personalized height charts make a wonderful baby shower or Christmas gift." She reached below my line of sight and lifted up some off-white fabric. "My first tip is to be sure that you make separate growth charts for each child. We parents well know that the last thing children need is one more source of comparison and competition. Besides, the chart that you make will be a lovely, wonderful keepsake you'll always treasure . . . with pictures of your child and his or her name on top. One chart for two or more children simply *won't* do."

I couldn't help but smile and nod.

"You'll want to buy thick, heavy fabric with a coarse weave, such as this stiff interfacing or this canvas." She showed me the fabrics as she spoke. "Purchase two linear yards of fabric. With the standard thirty-six-inch widths, you can cut the fabric in half lengthwise for two eighteen-inch-wide charts—the perfect dimensions." She unfolded the canvas to reveal that it was actually two pieces. "We'll attach a measuring tape to each chart. Plan on mounting your finished chart on the wall so that the bottom of the tape is precisely twelve inches above the floor. Unless you're measuring the height of Fido, Fluffy, or your ficus, those bottom inches are wasted space. And if your child is well over six feet tall, chances are that he or she is too busy playing basketball to be measured anyway."

I chuckled, but then my mind started to wander as Audrey demonstrated how to hem the fabric and put eyelets in the top corners. Audrey was the only person I knew who actually preferred to sew standing up like this; she'd once explained to me that it felt better on her back, though Audrey had so much excess energy, she probably simply couldn't stand to sit down long enough to sew.

Talking loudly over the whir of her machine, she showed how to attach the measuring tape along the right edge of the fabric. She'd first lopped off the bottom foot of the tape, altered the numbers one through twelve on that piece to read sixty-one through seventy-two inches, then fastened it to the top of the tape.

Audrey continued. "If you need to pinch pennies,

rather than purchasing tape measures from your local fabric store, you can print a free measuring tape from Web sites such as LLBean.com. Just be sure to use high-quality cloth paper, or to laminate your everyday paper when you print out your measuring tape." She held up a second chart that she'd already started using this method, which she completed by gluing the last segment of tape into place on the interfacing.

She gave me, as the virtual camera, a beatific smile. "Let me show you the wonderful keepsake I made from my son's growth chart." Again she reached down, retrieving a beautiful cedar container, roughly the size of a shirt box. "As you'll be able to tell from his six-one height, Michael inherited my first husband's genes." She removed a folded cloth from the container. "By the way, I'm expecting him to be available quite soon. He lives near Washington, D.C. He married this shrew of a woman two years ago, and naturally the marriage is falling apart. I tried to warn him that he should never choose a woman whose main hobby was—"

"You're going to talk about your son's marriage on TV?" I yelped.

"Of course not, dear. That was an aside to *you*."

As she spread out the wall hanging, I was so impressed that I rose involuntarily and stepped forward for a closer look. "Audrey! That's absolutely adorable!" She'd sprayed a clear polyurethane over the surface of the cloth to keep the dates and marks preserved and had lovingly cut out pictures of her son at two- to three-year stages. She'd embroidered his name at the top and done a lovely cross-stitch pattern along the entire edge of the piece. She'd also used fabric paint to augment some of the blank spaces with delicate designs. From bottom to top, the photographs began with her newborn son at the hospital and ended with him looking very, very handsome in his cap and gown.

"Thank you, Erin. That's truly sweet of you to say. But you know, my real audience isn't allowed to leap up and rush the stage for a closer look." She glanced at her watch. "Oh, shoot! You've thrown off my timing."

"Surely that was already thrown off when you started trying to fix me up with your son. Michael's still a married man, you know. Even if he gets divorced tomorrow, he'll need to decide on his own when and if he's ready to start looking again. He's a grown man of—"

"You make a good point, Erin," Audrey interrupted. "No need to keep *jabbing* me with it."

"Sorry. Please continue." I meekly reclaimed my seat while Audrey cleared the counter of everything except the sewing machine.

A dazzling smile was instantly back on her face, and I recognized it as her we've-just-returned-from-commercials expression. With the identical intonations that she'd used before, she began, "If you're like most parents . . ."

chapter 13

Three hours later, I arrived at Myra's house a minute or two early and rang the doorbell. Though there still wasn't any snowfall despite this being mid-December—Christmas was just a week away—there was a decided chill in the air, and I didn't feel like waiting for Sullivan to arrive and having to idle my motor to keep the heater going. Now that I was no longer required to move or stain furniture or paint walls, I had dressed up in autumnal colors—an A-line wool skirt suit, silk blouse, and silk scarf.

Myra, her complexion ruddier than usual, threw the door open and said, "Oh, look, everybody! It's Erin." Her words were slurred. "Come on in."

I entered, hung my red blazer on the coat tree, and saw that "everybody" consisted of Debbie and Jill, seated on Myra's faded floral sofa. "Ladies' tea party," Debbie explained, " 'cept with strawberry daiquiris instead of tea. Want to join us?"

"No, thanks. I'm afraid I don't drink very much alcohol."

"Oh, well, alcohol is nothing to be afraid of, my young friend," Jill said. "Especially not at a time like this."

"Sit. Sit," Myra demanded of me. Her gestures at the turquoise overstuffed chair were considerably broadened by her alcoholic buzz. I noted that Myra had been serving the drinks in brandy snifters, which were nice and large but not exactly ideal for daiquiris. One quick glance at Jill and Debbie assured me that they were already a few sips past caring about their glassware, however.

As I dropped into the well-worn chair, Myra explained, "We're having a send-off party for me."

"Oh, Myra," Debbie chastised, "we are *not!*" She clicked her tongue and then explained to me, "This afternoon, a police detective managed to give Myra the impression that she's going to be thrown into jail at any moment. But they don't have enough evidence to do anything of the sort."

"Of *course* they don't," Myra said sternly as she knelt down on the rug and picked up her glass from the clunky coffee table, "because I am *innocent.*" She looked at me. "The coroner says Randy was poisoned. They cleared out my refrigerator to take everything to the lab for testing. Everything they took will have my fingerprints on it, since *I'm* always the one who puts the groceries away. Randy can never be bothered to—"

She broke off abruptly, set down her glass and gripped

the edge of the table as if for ballast, then hung her head and started to weep. In a small voice through her tears, she moaned, "Oh, God. Listen to me, still carping about him. I keep expecting him to walk through that door any minute now and tell me this was all just a big mistake. You know?"

"It's going to be fine, Myra," Jill said, placing her hand atop Myra's on the coffee table.

Debbie, too, leaned closer to poor Myra. "Of course it will. Jill's right. We won't let the police do anything bad to you." She grabbed Myra's glass and refilled it from the half-full blender on the coffee table. "Let's all drink to your eventual vindication."

I had to admit that if I were hosting a party prior to my imminent arrest for murder, I, too, could well be serving straight from the bottle, let alone a blender. And my guests would be lucky to get glasses, as opposed to straws for a vat's worth of mimosa.

Myra blew out a puff of air and wiped her cheeks, though the tears kept falling. "I couldn't believe the police the first time they spoke to me. I was so sure it was his heart. He was not a perfect man—not even close—but he didn't deserve to be murdered. Who could have done such a horrible thing?"

I glanced longingly at the door. It wasn't that I was uncaring and couldn't relate to her pain—quite the opposite. It was just that this scene was not what I had prepared myself for. I'd brought my portfolio, camera, notebook, and tape measure and was deep inside my designer mind-set. This felt like arriving at a party in black tie, only to discover that the event was a Halloween party.

I brushed my hair back from my forehead to sneak a surreptitious glance at my watch. Five o'clock. Steve Sullivan should be arriving anytime now.

Waiting until Myra regained her composure, I asked

gently, "Myra? Have I gotten my times wrong? Weren't we supposed to meet Steve here? I was under the impression that we were going to share some of our thoughts about your interiors."

"You're quite correct, as always, my dear," she replied, clearing her throat. "But after my talk with the detective, I called you both and asked if we could reschedule."

"I'm sorry. I checked my voice mail just prior to driving here, but I never got the message."

She touched her forehead with trembling fingers, and her eyes widened. "Oh, dear. That's right." She took a couple of gulps of her drink. "After I got off the phone with Steve, I'd told myself that *he* was going to call and tell you I'd canceled, like he offered. But I was in such a tizzy, I forgot that I'd told him *I* would be the one to call you." She set her drink down but misjudged the distance a little, causing some spillage. She dried the last of her tears. After a moment, she managed a smile and said to me, "That young man is *so* cute. Is he gay?"

"I'm not sure. We don't know each other very well."

Debbie let out a bark of laughter. "I *know* he isn't gay. Haven't you seen the way he looks at Erin when he thinks no one's watching? He obviously has a *huge* crush on her."

Though this was the second time I'd heard that Sullivan ogled me surreptitiously, I hadn't believed it either time. Even so, Kevin had probably told Jill about catching Sullivan and me together in the basement. I had to hold my tongue.

"Let's take a quick vote, shall we?" Jill asked. "Who agrees that Steve finds Erin wildly attractive?"

All three women promptly raised their hands.

"There you have it, Erin." While speaking, Jill rotated in her seat and knelt on her cushion to reach the bottom shelf of a sofa table directly behind her. She emerged with an empty brandy snifter and said, "You'll drink to that, too, Erin. These daiquiris are wonderful, and you can always pretend it's a Shirley Timple." Her eyes flew open wide. She swatted Debbie, who was pouring me the pink liquid and nearly spilled it, and laughed. "Did you hear that? Shirley *Timple*." Jill took custody of the half-full glass from Debbie and thrust it at me. "Shirley *Temple*, I meant to say."

My thoughts lingered on what they'd said about Sullivan, but I couldn't take the matter seriously. The source was three women who were three sheets to the wind. I took a sip of my drink and couldn't help but cough. This had to be the stiffest drink I'd ever had. I'd assumed that its watery viscosity was due to melted ice, but this concoction was basically white rum with an innuendo of strawberry.

Jill laughed merrily for no apparent reason. "Myra, if you break out the coffee for us later, let's just be sure that it isn't almond-flavored, all right?"

For a moment, nobody spoke or moved. Debbie's face paled. Myra set her glass down and glared at Jill. "What's *that* supposed to mean?"

"I was just kidding. . . . Isn't arsenic supposed to taste a bit like almonds?" Jill asked Debbie.

Debbie set her glass down. Evenly, she said, "Jill, you've had too much to drink."

"No, I haven't had nearly enough." Jill laughed again, hysteria edging her voice. "I can still see and think straight. *That* will never do." She drained her glass. "You have nothing to worry about, Myra. *I'm* the one who's got cause for ulcers."

Not knowing what else to say, I said to Debbie, "I take it the police were here this afternoon."

Jill replied on Debbie's behalf, "They were taking things as evidence. Someone planted an arsenic bottle in Kevin's workshop."

"He had arsenic?" I asked, feigning surprise.

"It wasn't Kevin's," Jill said rashly. "Someone planted it there."

"How do you know that someone planted it?" Debbie asked.

"Kevin told me."

"That must make it true, then," Myra grumbled. "Anyway, Erin, point is, my schedule got all thrown out of whack, along with my day, when the police suddenly appeared."

Jill reached over and patted Myra's hand. "Don't worry. You're among friends here. We all know what Randy did to you."

Myra wobbled to her feet. "Randy didn't do anything to me. I don't know what you're talking about."

Jill froze. Debbie's cheeks had grown red and she was staring at her shoes. Jill said, "I think that we should . . ." Her voice faded. "Maybe I *have* had too much to drink. I've forgotten my entire train of thought." She forced a laugh. "Dear me."

Debbie stood up and said to Jill, "Time to go, don't you think?"

"Are you going to be all right alone, Myra?" I asked, also rising, only too happy to desert this entire scene and my too-stiff drink.

"Of course I will. Thanks for coming, and I apologize for forgetting to call you."

The three of us grabbed our coats and departed together. "She probably just wanted to see you again," Jill said to me the moment the door was shut behind us. "I think you remind her of—"

Grabbing Jill's elbow, Debbie interrupted. "Let's both go over to my place, shall we?"

"Myra told me I reminded her of her sister," I said, testing their reactions.

"Did she?" Debbie's smile seemed forced. "That's nice."

"I didn't know Myra had a sister," Jill muttered.

"We're all full of surprises tonight then, aren't we?" Debbie said. "Good night, Erin. Nice to see you again."

I wanted to blurt out that I knew full well that I "reminded" Myra of the daughter she'd given up for adoption, but instead I said only, "Yes, you too. Good night."

The next morning, I worked on two small assignments—one quick floor plan for a referral who simply wanted advice on furniture placement in the family room of her new house, and some guest room accessorizing in preparation for a nervous new wife's first extended visit from her exacting mother-in-law. At lunchtime, I returned a call to one of my oldest clients in town and reached her husband, who was so like Carl Henderson in terms of his lack of interest in his room design that we'd only met once before, despite this being the fourth time that his wife, Susan, had hired me. He offered to take a message. "Please just tell her that Erin called about your guest room makeover, and I'll call again later."

"Oh, right. Erin Sullivan. How are you?"

Sullivan? "My last name is Gilbert, actually, but I'm great. How are you Mr. Jameson?"

"Got it wrong again." He chuckled. "I can't remember that for the life of me. Susan must have told you that whole story, right?"

"*What* story?"

"How we'd already signed on with this designer named Sullivan and given him a deposit, but my company's finances took a turn for the worst, and he was nice enough to let us put a hold on everything for a few months. Only it turned out to be a full year till we got back in the black . . . and then Susan and I got Gilbert confused with Sullivan."

Alarmed, I sprang to my feet and began to pace.

He went on. "We assumed you were his assistant and that we'd forfeited our deposit after all that time. Took Susan a full month to realize our mistake, and by then, she figured it'd just be easiest to explain the mess to Sullivan."

"Oh, my God! Nobody ever told me!"

"Ah, like they say, all's well that ends well. Susan said Sullivan was nice as could be about it and said you were both terrific designers. Anyway, I'll tell Susan you called."

I muttered, "Thanks," and hung up, sick to my stomach. *I* was the bad guy? I *was* the bad guy!

Two years ago, I'd done something I truly believed I would never do; I'd stolen Sullivan's client! Not *knowingly*, certainly, but I *had* ignored the inexplicable change in tenor from Sullivan's initial friendly joshing over the Gilbert-Sullivan thing to his nasty rancor a couple of months later, when he'd yelled that I needed to rely on my own merits. I'd written him off as an asshole, demanded that he leave my office that instant, and had never stopped to ponder that some misunderstanding had, *of course*, occurred.

How the hell had I been so stupid? Which was not to say that Sullivan had been the innocent party throughout and hadn't foolishly rushed to his own snap judgments, but bottom line: *I* had cast the first stone, not the other way around.

The sound of imaginary glass walls breaking echoed in my brain.

That afternoon I drove to the Hendersons' for the twenty-four-hour follow-up visit that I always make to ensure that my customers are thoroughly pleased. I spotted Carl's hunched-over figure across the street. Myra appeared to be setting up a substantial garage sale, which was odd timing. Could she perhaps be deliberately getting rid of evidence? Surely the police would object to her selling off Randy's personal effects during an ongoing investigation. Maybe it was time for me to give Officer Del—Linda Delgardio—a quick call.

I parked on the street and promptly went over to make sure that she wasn't selling any quality furniture that I might want to encourage her to keep. I glanced around quickly for the umbrella stand, but it was nowhere in sight.

Myra looked up and smiled as I approached. "Erin, you're just in time. Do you ever collect people's old furniture and recycle it?"

"Sometimes."

"I put some of Randy's things for giveaway in the garage. Carl's going through everything. I'm afraid he was here first, so he gets first dibs."

Carl seemed intent on ignoring me, which was a bit strange, considering he knew we had an appointment scheduled to begin right now. "Morning, Carl," I called.

"Erin," he replied with a nod. "Debbie sent me over. She wants to put a second desk or a crudoza in her basement office."

" 'Crudoza'?" I repeated. "Do you mean a credenza?"

"Whatever. Got to figure out how to get it across the street by myself, since she ran out of printer toner and had to rush out. Just expects me to hoist the thing on my back and mule-train it home somehow. I don't suppose you've got a dolly, have you, Myra?"

"The two of us can carry it," I interposed. "I don't mind."

Carl glanced at Myra, then gave me a long look. "The cops were just here again. They were asking questions about you. The officers seemed to think we were lying about there not having been a prior connection between you and Debbie and me."

"Really?" I replied, feigning disinterest although a chill ran through me. I opened a drawer in the credenza as a distraction, surprised to see that it wasn't empty.

"What were the police talking about?" Carl pressed.

Myra was staring at us with rapt attention. I replied to Carl, "I found an old photograph of me in your house. It had been taped to the back of the paneling that hid the cubbyhole."

"What?" His eyes widened. "How is that possible? And why would anyone do such a thing?" He sounded sincerely puzzled.

"I don't know." I turned my attention to Myra, who was clearly struggling to regain her composure. "Shouldn't we at least empty out the drawers before taking the desk?"

Carl removed a stationery box from the open drawer. "Hey, what's this?" he asked, giving the box a shake.

"Oh, that's just some old stationery," Myra replied. "It's Randy's. If you want anything in the desk, just take it. I'm keeping the computer, but as far as I'm concerned, everything else can go in the trash."

"This looks strangely familiar," Carl grumbled under his breath as he examined the stationery. I peered at it and noted that the paper had the same thin, faded lines as did the letters we'd found in Carl's wall. He pitched the box into the trash can. Then, without so much as a cursory inspection, he removed and dumped the contents of each desk drawer. All the while, however, the muscles in his jaw were working furiously.

We carried the desk across the street, and Myra excused herself to go back inside her home. I kept brooding about how she had nearly fainted at the news that I'd found my own picture in the Hendersons' paneling.

As we made our way down his driveway, Carl glanced over his shoulder at the Axelrods' house, then asked, "You're a designer. You probably know about aging techniques that make things look older than they really are, right?"

"I know some antiquing techniques, yes."

"You can age paper, right?"

"Yes."

"How?"

"The classic method is to soak the paper in lemon juice and then let it dry in the sun, or sometimes directly on a heater, which can cause the lemon juice to turn slightly brown. Or to use weak tea water."

"That's what I thought."

His voice was so sad that I suspected he had come to believe the secreted letters were his wife's, written by Randy, despite their having been signed *M*, as in Myra. *M* could have been the initial of Debbie's pet name for Randy, however. "That stationery isn't all that unique, Carl. Any number of paper companies produce it. There have to be thousands upon thousands of similar-looking boxes of stationery sold here in Colorado alone."

"Yeah. Sure." He paused, and we set down the desk on the front porch to rest. His shoulders were once again badly stooped over, and he fidgeted with his glasses as he searched my eyes. "Has Debbie said anything to you about . . . me? Our marriage?"

"Not really. I barely know your wife. And what I do know of her, I like."

"We've only been married for five years." He rubbed his forehead. "My ex-wife cheated on me. When she started, Emily showed some of the same behavior that Debbie is suddenly exhibiting now."

"I don't know how to respond to that, Carl. I've never been married myself . . ." I floundered.

"If you're smart, you'll keep it that way."

"You don't honestly believe that your wife and Randy were having an affair, do you? Debbie's made it clear to me that she didn't like him."

He gave me a look revealing that his answer to my question was yes. "Myra and Debbie got into a spat just a month or so ago. Debbie admitted to me it was because Myra had walked in on her and Randy in a . . . lip-lock. She swore to me that it was just the one time, but . . ."

That indiscretion must have driven Debbie's apology to Myra that I'd overheard the other day. "Carl, it's a tough row to hoe, not trusting your spouse. And Randy's dead, so I don't see how productive this can possibly be for you."

He sighed and fumbled again at his glasses. "True. True. I just wonder about this whole mess. Why my wife would suddenly want to keep some office furniture of *his*."

"I'm sure it's more the need for surface space than anything else."

"Yeah, you're right." He made a derisive noise as he stared at the credenza. "I guess not too many people would get attached to this hunk of junk as a memento of a former lover." He sighed again. "Anyways, I really appreciate the great job you did with my room. I'm sorry it didn't land you the feature story you deserved."

"Thanks. Actually, although the whole thing pales in

comparison to Randy's death, Debbie did mention that since she freelances at *Denver Lifestyles*, she might be able to get an article about your bedroom published after all."

Carl set the clasp on the pneumatic door closer to keep the storm door propped open. "Debbie's a lot more than a freelancer. Hell, she practically . . ." He let his voice fade and he grabbed his end of the desk, so I followed suit. "Getting the feature published would be a snap for her to arrange. Now that that windbag Axelrod is out of the picture."

I tried to let the insult to the man who was probably my biological father slide off me; after all, Carl suspected the man had been having an affair with his wife. "He did strike me as somewhat arrogant," I murmured when we set the desk down in the foyer so that Carl could shut the door behind us.

"Thought he was God's gift to magazine writing. But the guy couldn't spell *cat* if you spotted him the *c* and the *a*."

"Really?"

"Yeah. He claimed it was his spell-checker that let him be lazy."

That did seem strange. It was also strange that his home had so few books, and that he'd been rather inarticulate for a writer and editor. Not to mention the lack of any interest in interior design, all of which led me to further suspect that Debbie had been ghostwriting for him. "Had he always been an editor? For as long as you knew him, I mean?"

"Nah. He was out of work when we bought the place from him . . . something like five years back. I think he used to be a gym teacher." He snorted. "I guess they call themselves *fitness instructors* now." He shook his head and muttered, "Must've had one hell of a good insurance package. Otherwise, Myra couldn't have hired you."

I helped Carl carry the desk into Debbie's basement office, and by then it was starting to feel very heavy indeed. Nevertheless, with Carl's help, we got the credenza nicely situated behind her existing desk.

"Do you mind if I take one more look at the bedroom?" I asked. "I'd like to take some photographs for my portfolio, too, if that's okay."

"I suppose that'd be all right. Did you ask Debbie if it was all right with her?"

"If what's all right with me?" Debbie asked, coming down the stairs to join us.

I repeated my request to take photographs.

"Heavens. Of course it's fine with me. I'm flattered. In fact, please give my name to as many people as you'd like, anytime you need a reference."

She led me upstairs and into the room, leaving Carl to catch his breath on the sofa. "I've got to tell you honestly, Erin," Debbie said. "At first I was so nervous about this! It was just such a shock to see that Carl had done something like this . . . hired a decorator without my knowledge or checking any references."

"I'm sure he checked my credentials—"

"Oh, probably so. I just meant that it all seemed to be done in great haste. Not at all the way I like to do things. It's just—"

The doorbell rang.

Debbie hollered, "Carl? Are you getting that?"

She continued to rave about the wallpaper. I heard the low rumbles of male voices downstairs, but ignored them to take my shots and get a 360-degree view of the room. Just two frames into the task, however, heavy footsteps came tromping up the stairs. Carl entered, followed by two uniformed officers.

Debbie cried, "Carl? What's going on? What are the police doing here?"

"That's my wife, officer." He looked at Debbie and explained, "They have a search warrant."

"A *search warrant!* For what? What do you want to search my house for?" she demanded of both officers.

"We need to look inside the north wall, ma'am," the officer closest to us said. "You'll be reimbursed for any repairs."

"Repairs?" she shrieked, and we both stared at the sledgehammer that the second officer was carrying. "Oh, my God! My beautiful bedroom! You're going to tear it up?"

"We have to search the hiding space for evidence that might help us to identify your neighbor's killer," the officer explained, nearing the wall with his sledgehammer. "Sorry, ma'am."

"There's no *evidence* in my walls!" Debbie cried.

"Your husband found some items that could be linked to our investigation."

"Carl?" she screeched.

"I already burned the letters." He shrugged. "And they picked up the garbage this morning, so the necklace is gone, too."

Debbie grabbed her head. "But why—"

"We have to check inside the wall, ma'am," the officer with the sledgehammer interrupted, his eyes gleaming at the sight of my beautiful work.

In what I'll confess will not go down in history as one of my more dignified moments, I did a spread-eagle against the wall and blocked his path. "Wait! You can get to that space from the other side. By knocking a hole through the back wall of the closet!"

"She's right!" Debbie cried. "Please, please do it that way!" She looked pleadingly at Carl, who stood motionless by the entrance, as if none of this affected him directly.

The two officers exchanged glances, then peered around the corner into the dressing area. "Looks like they're right, Tony," one policeman said to his partner. "So, why do you suppose someone put the opening in the *middle* of the bedroom wall instead of in the *back* of a closet wall?"

"Maybe he didn't want to get all the clothes in the closet dirty," I suggested, even though I knew at once that the real reason was that it was easy to hide a hole behind paneling, but not in an unadorned closet wall. "The plaster dust from the drywall is a total bear to get out of clothing."

"You live here too, miss?" the not-Tony, non-sledge-hammer-wielding officer asked me.

"No, I'm the interior designer. I plastered up the hole and hung the wallpaper."

"Nice," the officer said with a nod as he studied the wallpapered surface.

"Yes, it is," I said desperately, "so please be sure not to swing—"

Debbie gasped, and we both jumped back a little as the sledgehammer suddenly slammed through the wall from the other side.

chapter 14

Oops," the officer with the sledgehammer muttered, just as I continued sadly, ". . . too hard."

"No-o-o-!" Debbie screeched. "My wall, my beautiful wall! The paper is *ruined*!"

"Sorry, ma'am, but—"

She balled her fists and raged: "Do you people have any idea how long I fought to get this project done? *Five* years! Ever since the day we bought this place, I've been telling my husband that I wanted it fixed up. I didn't even want to move *in* until the walls were painted something other than . . . than primer white, but no!" She pointed at her husband, still standing in the doorway.

"Carl insisted that it'd just take a couple of hours to re-paint it, and there was no sense holding up the closing date just for that. He promised he would paint it himself, the very next weekend. It has taken me *five* years of *pleading* and *cajoling* to get a bedroom that I love, and I only had the chance to sleep in it *once*! Just *once*! You *idiots* just put a sledgehammer right through my *dreams*!"

Carl, his face reddening, reseated his glasses, but maintained his stubborn post by the door. "Debbie, calm down. It's—"

"Shut up, Carl! Do you know how infuriating it is to be told to calm down? As if I hadn't realized all on my own that I was upset! As if that would make me go"—she smacked her own forehead—" 'Oh, *that's* what I need! I need to *calm down*! Thank heavens my husband was here to tell me that, or I might have *raised my voice!*' "

"It's really okay, Debbie," I interjected desperately. "I have an extra roll of this paper with the same dye lot in my van. I always overorder by at least two lengths, in case of disaster—"

"Oh, thank God," Debbie exclaimed, pulling me into a hug. "I love you. I will adopt you right now on the spot."

The words were unnerving. I said as evenly as I could, "We'll just plaster over the hole again, let it dry overnight, then I'll pull down the one sheet and put up another—"

Another blow reverberated, promptly ending our hug. Debbie shrieked again. A second hole appeared in the wall. This time, a second panel of wallpaper was ruined.

"Jeez, Tony!" his fellow officer complained. "What did you go and hit it that hard for?"

"What are you doing?" I hollered at the sledgehammering officer. "That's a good two feet over from where the cubbyhole was located!"

"Figured we're going to have to check the whole inside of the wall. That means we're going to have to bust through all the sections between the studs."

"I'm going to be sick," Debbie wailed. "I can't watch this."

"Neither can I," I agreed, but watching the wall destruction was something like spotting the aftermath of an accident at the side of the road: my eyes seemed to be glued to the scene of their own volition.

I glanced at Carl to see if he was going to go comfort his wife, but he'd averted his gaze and pretended to be transfixed by a magazine that had been lying open on her side of the bed. Debbie shuffled down the stairs alone. I waited through one more blow from the closet wall and gasped as the hammer merely dented the wallpaper this time and just missed banging into the back corner of the chest.

"Watch it!" I shouted through the wall at Officer Tony. "This chest is worth thousands of dollars! I can repair the freaking wall, but not the furniture!"

"Sorry, miss," he called back, unrepentant. "It won't happen again."

I studied the dent in the paper. That section of Sheetrock would also have to be repaired. The wallpaper would need to be removed, the Sheetrock patched or perhaps replaced, and the wallpaper rehung. If the store happened to be out of this dye lot, I'd have to exchange my emergency roll and start over again, replacing the paper for the entire wall.

I went downstairs to console Debbie. She was the picture of a woman in a deep state of shock. She was seated at the table in the kitchen, staring straight ahead with unfocused eyes. She didn't even blink when I came into the room and pulled up a chair across from her.

"I'll get another double roll of wallpaper, and we'll

send the bill to the police. If I have to, I could do a patch
behind the chest that—"

"No. There's no point. I should have known better. It
wasn't meant to be. There's no way to build the bedroom
of your dreams when you're sharing the bed with a man
who doesn't love you. He can't even keep me straight
from Emily. I'm in a sham of a marriage that was over before it even started!"

"Oh, Debbie. I'm sure you don't really mean that!"

"I do." She gave a sardonic laugh. "Ironic choice of
wording." She sighed. "It was the *first* time I said 'I do'
that was wrong."

We said nothing for a full minute or two. "What are
you going to do now?" I asked at last.

"Move out, I suppose. Maybe I'll ask Myra if I can stay
in her guest room for the time being."

Her statement shocked me. Carl strongly suspected
that Randy and Debbie had been lovers. If that were
true, she surely wouldn't want to move in now with his
widow. Unlike me, however, Carl had actually read the
love letters; he was in a far better position than I to know
who the author and the recipient were. "Those love letters . . . were they yours?" I asked Debbie gently.

"No." She brushed her red hair away from her face
brusquely and clenched her jaw. "I'm sure they were
Emily's. Carl probably couldn't bear to part with them,
so he brought them with him to our new home and hid
them. And then he forgot about them."

Hadn't the hiding spot been built just a few months
ago? By Taylor? Trying to weigh Debbie's mood against
the possibility that she was lying to me, I asked, "You
didn't read them yourself?"

"Carl wouldn't let me. But I glanced at them when
Taylor was trying to revive Randy, and it looked like
Emily's handwriting."

"But . . . just today, Carl gave me the distinct impression that he thought they were yours . . . written *to* you. He found some stationery in Randy's desk that he thought was the same paper."

She shook her head. "In a weak moment, after a fight with Carl, I wound up in Randy's arms—for all of two seconds. Literally. Ever since then . . ." She shuddered. "Anyway. Emily's handwriting and mine are very similar. I wouldn't be half surprised if Carl's gotten us confused in his head once again. In any case, *Randy* didn't write them. As if that man would ever write a love letter!"

I tried to make sense out of her explanation. If Emily had written the letters to Carl, he would be intimately familiar with their contents. He couldn't possibly think that his *current* wife had written them. "Could they have been from Emily to some other man? To Kevin, perhaps?"

"Then what would they have been doing inside *our* wall? Emily and Carl were, of course, already divorced when Carl and I got married and bought this place."

I frowned. This wasn't any of my business. Even so, the letters seemed to be a major factor behind the terrible troubles in the Hendersons' marriage, and the two of them could erroneously be pointing fingers at their spouse. "Maybe Kevin wrote them and put them there to get Carl's goat for some reason."

Debbie shook her head again. "Kevin is an incorrigible flirt, but he would never do anything so foolish as to write love letters to another woman. If one of those letters were to find its way to Jill—aka Miss Moneybags where Kevin's concerned—he would lose his precious funding for his vast plans."

She released a heavy sigh and dabbed at a tear. "It's not as though I could blame him, really. Dreams are important. You lose them, and what's left? You find yourself in your fifties with no goals, no plans, no children or grandkids to dote on. You just . . . do what I did, eventually. Marry some man you think you love and hope he'll fill in what's missing. When that's impossible. What you're missing is your own soul, and nobody else can find something like that for another person."

I felt horrible for this woman. I watched helplessly as she struggled to regain her composure. "Are things really that bad for you, Debbie?"

She nodded, blinking back tears. In a halting voice, she said, "I shouldn't talk about this to you; we barely know each other."

"Maybe that's why you *can* talk to me about it."

There was a considerable racket around the corner as the three men came down the stairs and Carl ushered the officers out the door. I wanted to give them a few seconds to get in their patrol cars, then I intended to beat a hasty retreat myself. The Hendersons needed some privacy.

Carl lumbered into the kitchen and began to pace in front of us. "Well, crap," he said before I could excuse myself from the house. "Looks like Taylor's in big trouble now. They did some sort of test where chemicals they put on the inside of the wall changed color if there were drugs—even the smallest of traces—and it turned, all right. Taylor had been stashing drugs in our wall, just like he said he was."

I was confused: Taylor had already served time for the drug possession. Right now, however, I was more concerned with getting out of here. I pushed my chair back from the table. Debbie looked up at him, a blank expression on her face, and said, "I want a divorce."

As if Debbie had never spoken, Carl continued. "They didn't find anything other than the drug traces. But they only came clear through the wall the two times . . . when you were there, too, and saw it. Erin, you've got enough on that extra roll to replace two pieces, don't you?" His face was slowly growing flushed as he spoke. I wanted desperately to get out of here. Unfortunately, Carl was standing directly in front of the doorway, blocking my exit.

"Carl, I want a divorce," Debbie repeated firmly.

He pushed his glasses against his nose and looked at her. "Stop saying that, Debbie! If you'd wanted a divorce, why would you have sent me across the street to get you some free furniture?"

"Do you think I'd stay married to you just because you got me a *free* desk?"

He spread his arms. "Why would you ask me to re-model the bedroom one day and then leave me the next? I didn't care what the damned room looked like in the first place!"

I got up from the table and muttered, "I'll let myself out."

"I'm coming, too," Debbie replied, rising.

Carl snorted. "No, you're not. You can't just say, 'Carl, I want a divorce,' and then leave with the interior de-signer. You don't even know each other from a hole in the wall. That doesn't make any sense!"

She swept up her purse from the kitchen counter. "I'm going to ask Myra to let me stay with her for a cou-ple of days."

"But I built you your damned bedroom! Why would you want to leave me *now*? I thought you'd finally be happy!"

"Carl, we're a terrible match. You don't care about anything. I care about too many things at once. It's bet-ter this way."

A marriage was breaking apart in front of me, and there was nothing I could do to reverse the tide. Yet another situation that had never been covered in my education at Parsons. "Sorry to run out on you like this, but I'll call about the . . . wallpaper." I strode out the door as quickly as social decorum allowed—just short of an all-out sprint.

Reading the *Crestview Sentinel* had kept me informed of the key details regarding Randy's funeral. Though I'd been so exhausted that I had finally slept solidly, my nerves were shot throughout the morning service. There was a twitching muscle beneath my left eye that was driving me nuts, and I kept rubbing at it, to no avail. At least that gave me the appearance of having to dry my eyes, unlike anyone else in attendance. My raw feelings were probably due to my deep suspicion that we were laying my biological father to rest.

A total of twenty people had come, including myself and Sullivan, Debbie and Carl Henderson—sitting at opposite corners of the room—and Jill and Kevin McBride, along with Detectives O'Reilly and Martinez. I much would have preferred my one threadlike connection to the Crestview police—my fellow glassware aficionado—Officer Linda Delgardio. *She*, at least, was a warm, easy person to talk to.

I still hadn't spoken to Sullivan about the Jamesons—our former mutual clients—even though my recent insight into Sullivan's and my past history had changed the tint of my recollections the way that a sunbeam changes the color of wall paint. I'd merely told him in passing that we needed to talk later, left the service, and headed to my tiny—but very nicely decorated, if I do say so myself—downtown office.

My office was a one-room, loftlike space; the flight of stairs leads directly into my room, and I'd just begun my bookkeeping when I heard someone coming up the stairs. It was Steve Sullivan, who muttered, "Thought I might be able to catch you here."

Knowing how much he deserved my apology, my nerves were instantly on edge. "Yeah. Hi. I'm just getting caught up with my paperwork."

"You took off kind of fast from the service." He sat down in the beautiful Sheraton armchair in front of me. My mother and I had refinished that chair ten years ago; she'd done the floral cross-stitching on the cushion and padded seatback, a wonderful Victorian design. "I would have sat next to you, but when I saw how few people were there, I thought it'd look better attended if we spread out a bit."

I nodded. "It was a sad situation."

"Pathetic, even."

"His wife must have been his entire family."

"Yeah. And *she* was almost cheerful. Not a wet eye in the place, in any case."

Everyone had at least worn dark clothing. Steve was dressed in a black turtleneck, black jacket, and black jeans. I was wearing a black cable sweater and my brown suede skirt and leather boots. "At least the Hendersons and McBrides came." Albeit the Hendersons had arrived separately and stayed that way throughout the service.

"Along with a dozen people from his magazine. I did a bit of networking." He pulled a half-dozen business cards out of the breast pocket of his black jacket and sorted through them in silence. Watching him, I reminded myself that he wasn't all *that* much less at fault over our misunderstanding than I was. Here he'd been trolling for work at a man's funeral service.

"And two detectives," I grumbled. "I recognized them, sitting in the back."

"Yeah. I talked to them yesterday." He glanced again

at the business cards in his hand, frowned, shook his head, and tossed them into my trash can. Then he made a derisive noise and grumbled, "Time to get a grip on myself, once and for all. This was what I've lowered myself to . . . looking for work at a man's funeral like some kind of ambulance chaser. Not to mention revealing to the Coopers that Evan had left me high and dry in order to gain their sympathies. And—"

"Wait. Didn't you tell the Coopers that Evan had *died* and you were left . . . bereft?"

His eyes widened. "Come again?"

"Mrs. Cooper told me that you were grieving over Evan's death, so she just couldn't bear to hire me instead of you."

"God, no! I told her the truth . . . that he'd given me the shaft and left town. She must have misunderstood. Or was so embarrassed about changing her mind that she overstated my situation to you. I'm not *that* desperate for work."

A perfect segue. "Speaking of misunderstandings, Sullivan, I owe you an apology . . . long overdue, as it turns out. I didn't know until yesterday, when I happened to talk to Susan Jameson's husband, that they were already under contract with you when I accepted my first job with them. Almost two years ago."

Obviously perplexed, Steve furrowed his brow and held my gaze. "Yeah, you did, Gilbert. Come on. I told you that myself, when I . . . kind of barged into your office that one time."

Kind of? I shook my head. "Actually, I never picked up on what you were talking about. I thought you were just griping at me in general terms. About locating Interiors by Gilbert two blocks away from Sullivan Designs."

"But I'd have to be some sort of raving lunatic to . . ." He paused. As if thinking aloud, he said, "That was just the second time you and I had met. I was sure you knew about the Jamesons' mix-up, but figured you'd just look the other way. I mean, you were being so self-righteous and everything when—"

"*I* was being self-righteous? Excuse me?" Livid, I gripped the edge of my desk. "*You* were the one who came storming into my office like, as you said yourself, a raving lunatic, accusing me—"

"Hey!" He shot to his feet and stabbed his finger at me. "*I* wasn't the one who had clients already under contract with another designer sign a new contract and give a new deposit! I mean, how could the Jamesons *possibly* not have known you were separate from Sullivan Designs?"

Unwilling to yield the power position, I stood up, too. "They *didn't* know, though. They thought the whole agreement with you was null and void because they'd reneged a year earlier!"

Sullivan whacked his chest with his palm. "How would I have known that?"

"I can't hardly answer for you at this point, now *can* I? All I know is, yesterday Jameson said that Susan *told* you that at the time!"

He threw up his hands in disgust. "Jeez, Gilbert! In other words, you assumed I just flew off the handle and made baseless accusations. Just like you think I would sink so low as to outright *lie* to the Coopers about someone's *death* just so that—"

He broke off as someone banged open the door and noisily tromped up the stairs. Taylor Duncan entered. He hadn't come to the funeral and was wearing a bright red T-shirt that sported a cartoon mouse holding its middle finger aloft, a tattered and faded plaid shirt as a jacket, and grungy-looking jeans. At least the cooler weather had inspired him to wear a shirt. There was a slight hitch in his step when he spotted Steve. "Oh, hey. You're both here. Cool."

Considering that Sullivan and I had been on the verge of throttling each other, Taylor's words struck me as so ironic that I had to smile. I reclaimed my seat, and Sullivan followed suit. "What can I do for you, Taylor?"

"Came to ask for some work, actually. I was hoping one or both of you could use a carpenter or woodworker for some contract jobs, maybe."

Surprised, I replied, "I don't think I have anything for you right at the moment, but if you leave your card . . ."

He snorted. "Yeah, like I have business cards." He folded his impressive—although tattooed beneath the flannel—arms and looked at Steve. "What about you, dude? I'm a little short for Christmas. I'd take just about anything at this point."

"Let me make some phone calls, then get back with me tomorrow and we'll see."

To my surprise, Taylor let out a puff of indignation. "Aw, come on, man! At least be honest about it! You have no intention of helping me out . . . neither of you does." He dragged his palm across his again clean-shaven scalp. "I can't even get shit jobs now that I've got this damn police record hanging over my head."

Why, I wondered, was he suddenly so talkative about his arrest record? Could he be intoxicated at two thirty in the afternoon?

He dropped into the Windsor chair next to Steve. "This is all that asshole's fault!" Taylor growled. "None of this would have happened in the first place if he'd have just minded his own damn business!"

"What are you—"

"Axelrod set me up!" he interrupted. "Oh, sure, I was dealing a few drugs. So what's the big freakin' deal? I wasn't hurting anyone. And it's not as if I had customers follow me into the neighborhood and traipse across his lawn."

"But *you* were the one who was breaking the law, Taylor, not Randy," Sullivan interjected.

"Maybe so, but, like, he was the one who did all that breaking and entering." He paused. "Okay . . . so maybe he didn't *break* anything, but he sure as hell *entered*."

I remained perplexed as to why Taylor would march into my office asking for work, only to volunteer all this adverse information about himself. But I was also dying to hear anything he was willing to reveal about Randy Axelrod. "Didn't Randy have a key to the Hendersons' house?" I asked him.

"Sure, but nobody *gave* it to him. Randy just kept hold of it without telling Carl he still had it from when the place was his."

"Taylor, I—"

He cut Sullivan off and snarled, "That son of a bitch turned me in for no reason! Kept bargin' into the house, checking out what I was doing whenever I wasn't there."

He stood up, his eyes widening. "Hey, don't, like, get me wrong. I didn't kill him. But no way are the police ever going to believe that. Not after all the bad blood between me 'n' Axelrod."

Sullivan said, "I didn't even realize you two had any problems. I mean, you decided to set up shop in the man's backyard."

"No shit! Randy practically begged me to set everything up in his backyard, to forget about our 'past differences.' Easy for him to say. *He* wasn't the one who spent three months in jail," Taylor scoffed. "He said it wasn't personal, that he was just trying to keep the neighborhood free from *potheads* like me. It was just the one time. I got a little high and forgot to replace the board that covered the opening in the wall. Next thing I know,

I'm selling a couple of grams to a narc, and they arrest me."

Sullivan leaned back in his seat and laced his fingers behind his neck. "If you're considering this a job interview, Taylor, I've got to tell you that you might want to reconsider your presentation skills."

I fought back a smile. "If I have a need for your services, I'll get your number from Carl," I told him.

Taylor said, "Yeah, yeah. I won't hold my breath. But . . . can I tell my parole officer and social worker that you both gave me job interviews?"

That explained his bizarre behavior: he needed to prove he was looking for work, but he'd sabotaged his "interview" to prevent his having to start work.

"Sure," we answered simultaneously.

He nodded his thanks and thumped down the stairs. After a moment, I said to Sullivan, "Well. He was just so charming and personable that it *killed* me to have to break his heart and give him the brush-off like that."

"I know," he replied with a dramatic sigh. "A designer's lot is not a happy one."

I grinned at him. "A modified lyric from Gilbert and Sullivan."

He shrugged. "I was the set designer for *"Pirates of Penzance"* back in high school." He pulled out a notebook from his jacket pocket. "So, Gilbert. Let's try to let bygones be bygones and bounce around some ideas for Myra Axelrod's house."

Later that day, I arrived at the Hendersons' home, having changed into jeans and armed myself with a steamer and scraper, along with the necessary Sheetrock-repair accoutrements. Despite Debbie's admonishes last night not to bother, I couldn't knowingly leave a design of mine in that state of disrepair. After a long wait for the doorbell to be answered, Carl pulled the door open by twelve inches or so and stuck out his head.

In an attempt to ignore his odd behavior, I gave him my nicest smile. "Good evening, Carl."

Although we'd made this appointment by phone just an hour ago, he stared at me with blank eyes and made no move to let me inside. He was panting a little, and his forehead sported beads of perspiration.

"I'm here to patch the holes in the drywall," I reminded him.

He reseated his wire-frame glasses on his nose. "Right. You called about that."

Worry niggled at me. "And you said that this would be a good time, but if—"

"Right. Right. Come on in." He stepped back, and I caught sight of his right arm for the first time: it was in a cast from his fingertips to his elbow.

"Oh, dear. What happened?"

He said nothing and trudged up the stairs. I followed, noting the half-tucked-in, half-out state of his dress shirt and that he was in his stocking feet; we stepped around both of his black wing tips en route. My nervousness grew, and I sighed with relief when I entered the bedroom and saw that his bed was neatly made and empty; I'd started to suspect that I had interrupted a rendezvous with his ex-wife, Emily.

"Here it is," Carl mumbled. He flicked on the light, and I gaped at the condition of the accent wall. Instead of two holes, there were now four—the two I'd seen, plus a large fist-high hole in the wall and a second smaller one. "The cops, uh, put in a couple more holes after you left."

"Huh," I muttered noncommittally. Carl himself had said that the hammer only went clear through the wall twice. Besides, this time the impact had obviously come from the front and not the back of the wall.

He watched as I filled my steamer and plugged it in. "Truth is, Erin, I kind of lost my composure and put my fist through the wall. Well, technically, I only went clear through the wall once. The *second* time I hit the stud."

"That's how you broke your hand?"

" 'Fraid so."

"I can fix it. The wall, that is, not the hand. No problem."

His expression swiftly changed to one of unmasked fury. "Well, it sure as hell was a problem for *me*!"

Shocked, I took a step back. "Pardon?"

"You're a terrible designer! You destroyed my life!"

If nothing else, your accusations are something of a non sequitur. I said gently, "I'm sorry you've run into some bad times. It really wasn't my bedroom design that was at fault, though."

"Oh, no? I've got no wife and a broken hand. None of this would have happened if you hadn't come onto the scene and torn down the wood paneling!"

Okay. Maybe this wasn't the best time for me to be stripping the man's wallpaper. Afraid to turn my back on him even for an instant, I yanked on the cord to unplug my steamer, hoping it would make a good defensive weapon if Carl was to try to grab me. He was so enraged I really did fear he would attack me. "For what it's worth, I dearly wish I'd left the paneling in place. This hasn't been a vacation for me, either."

"You don't seem to have lost *your* spouse or broken *your* hand. And you made money on the deal. *I* had to pay big bucks for the privilege of getting my life trashed!"

"I'm sorry about the way things turned out for you, Mr. Henderson."

"Are you? Is that supposed to make me feel better? My

wife's called a lawyer, and they want *me* to move out so *she* can have the house. Want to guess why?" He took a step toward me.

I shrank back, bracing myself a little to clock him with the wallpaper steamer when he took a swing at me. Quietly, I guessed, "She likes the new bedroom?"

"Bingo!" He snorted. "You got it right on the first try. She *likes* the new bedroom. Which you designed. So I'm supposed to move out of my own home. My wife has an affair with my neighbor *again*, and I am supposed to give her *our* house because she loves the damn bedroom you made for her. Where's the justice in that?"

Again? Debbie been extremely convincing when she'd claimed to me that the letters weren't hers. Carl might have been allowing his ragged emotions to make his decisions for him. "It's a difficult situation, all right," I agreed tersely.

"You know what? She wants the bedroom, let's let her have it." As I watched in horror, he smashed his elbow into the wall. Another hole appeared in the beautiful wallpaper I'd chosen with such care.

"Carl, this isn't going to—"

Carl growled, "By the time I'm through with it, she'll—" He kicked the wall with his stocking foot and yowled, "Ow! Oh, crap! I hit the damned stud again!" Then he crumpled onto the floor, holding his injured foot aloft.

Not knowing what to do, I watched him writhe in agony for a moment, then asked, "Do you need a ride to the hospital?"

"No! Not from you! You're my bad-luck charm. I'd have to sit in the death seat, and you'd probably *crash* the car!" He grimaced with pain.

I started making my way to the door. "Carl, this is obviously not a good time for me to be trying to repair the wall. Let's just go with the flow for a little while here and see where we wind up. Okay?"

He was yipping and rocking himself as I hurried down the stairs and out the door.

Early the next morning, I was climbing Myra's porch steps for our rescheduled appointment just as Sullivan drove up. I waited for him, noting that he was looking especially handsome in his perfectly fitted black suit jacket over a gray mock turtleneck and black slacks. I, too, was dressed to the nines in a cream-colored Armani skirt suit. Being well-dressed was such a solid job requirement that I felt our high-end wardrobe should be tax-deductible. Decorating clients are buying an upgrade in their home's appearance and deserve the whole package—a designer who knows and cares enough about appearances to dress the part.

"Ready, Gilbert?" he said without greeting me.

"Sure, Sullivan."

His hand smacked into mine as we simultaneously reached for the doorbell. He gave me a lopsided grin. "Sorry. Go ahead."

"No. By all means, you take the honor."

He hesitated, but pushed the button. Some partnership. We couldn't even agree on who would ring a doorbell.

Myra was bubbling with enthusiasm as she let us inside. Sullivan and I managed to settle into her living room without stepping on each other's toes, and the three of us began our discussions. We weren't—unfortunately—redesigning the kitchen or bathrooms, and we all agreed that Myra's walnut-colored rosewood dining room set was lovely, so aside from the living room, we needed only to discuss her requirements and vision for the family room, the office, and the two upstairs bed-rooms. Steve and I immediately agreed that we'd like to remove the existing wall between the living and dining rooms and replace it with a half wall.

Myra rose and walked over to that wall. "I guess that makes sense. We can put a shelf on the half wall."

"That would look great," I said. "It will open the area up, but the half wall will still give the rooms definition."

Steve tapped on the wall, judging where the studs were located. "We'll need to put a support post here . . . right where the wall ends. We'll have to contract that work out," he told Myra. "We shouldn't have any prob-lem finding someone to do this after the holidays."

"That reminds me. The floor is making an unusual squeak right here," Myra said. She stood in the center of the room and shifted her weight from foot to foot, which did cause an unduly loud squeak as the plywood subflooring creaked beneath her. "Do you hear that? It doesn't sound like a piece of loose plywood to me, somehow."

"It doesn't to me, either," I agreed. "Steve, I'm going to head downstairs and check the structure. There should be a beam going across the ceiling in the base-ment right about where you're standing. We need to make sure the support beam is in good shape before we start any major renovations."

Myra escorted me to the basement door. I asked, "It's unfinished, isn't it? Your basement?"

"Yes."

She flipped on the light, and I went down into the musty-smelling basement. Myra came down partway with me but waited on the stairs.

"Can you tell where I'm standing?" Sullivan called down to me.

"Yes."

"The noise in the floorboards does sound a bit odd," he said in a half shout. "It's probably my imagination, but there seems to be too much give."

There was a loud cracking sound just over my head, as though he were turning the floor above into a trampoline.

"Erin, don't you think—" Myra started to say.

I couldn't hear her above the noise. Just as I stepped toward her, the massive support beam almost directly above my head gave way.

chapter 15

I dived onto the concrete floor. The impact jarred through my body as my jaw smacked shut and pain seared through my rib cage and abdomen. The wind was knocked out of me, and I struggled against intense pain to catch my breath.

I managed to prop myself up on my elbows and look back. Miraculously, nothing heavy had fallen on top of me, just splinters and rubble. I'd been very lucky, and I stared at the devastation around me in disbelief.

The entire support beam that ran straight across the ceiling had collapsed.

Myra was screaming. She'd turned away, but remained on the basement stairs, her arms covering her face.

"I'm okay," I called, as much to reassure myself as Myra.

As I stumbled to my feet, Steve raced down the steps past Myra. "Erin! Are you all right?" he asked as he rushed to me. His face was white.

It hurt to talk, but I answered, "Fine. Just bruised." My cream-colored Armani was now dirt-colored. My panty-hose were a complete casualty. Coughing, I tried to wave away the considerable cloud of dust that the falling beam had kicked up.

"Erin! Thank God you're all right!" Myra cried. "For a moment there, I was so afraid you'd been killed."

I examined the fallen support beam. The wood was a perfect, sawed-off rectangle; the timber was an engineered, glue-laminated piece. Only the top inch of the end was jagged where the beam's weight combined with the pressure of traffic above forced it to give way. Steve's stomping on it from above had apparently done the trick.

"The beam's been cut," Steve said as Myra cautiously made her way over to us.

I ran my hand along the slight arc-shaped marks left by the circular saw. "And there's some flaking here along the bottom edge. Someone sawed through the beam on both ends and then caulked it so no one would notice. The house was booby-trapped."

"That's . . . that's impossible! Who would do such a terrible thing?" Myra asked. Her eyes were wide with fright.

She'd recently learned that her husband had been murdered. Why would she think it was impossible for someone to have sabotaged her house?

Steve said, "Just on the off chance that the rest of the house is about to collapse on top of us, I suggest we all get out of here." He grabbed our arms to hasten us along. "Thank God the subflooring held," he told me as we climbed up the basement stairs, "or I'd have landed right on top of you."

"Yeah. That was lucky for both of us."

The nearest exit was through the garage, and Myra opened the door for us. The skies had clouded over, and the temperature had plummeted. Myra was shivering, and I dully realized that I was, too, despite my now-filthy suit jacket.

"You need a coat," I told her. I glanced at the front door and bit back a curse. My leather satchel was inside her living room, along with my portfolio, my digital camera with its hundreds of stored photographs, and my notebook. Without those items, I was essentially without the database that I'd been developing for years.

"Steve, I have to go back inside. I left my satchel with my portfolio—"

"Get it later. It's not like you don't have any backups in case . . ." His voice faded as he studied my features. "No backup? Jeez, Gilbert!"

Being chastised by Sullivan was the last thing I needed, and I grumbled, "I'll be right back."

He grabbed my arm as I tried to walk away. "No. I'll go."

"You weigh more than I do. You're likelier to crash through the floor."

"It's my house," Myra said. "I should be the one to go in."

"No! I'm going! You two are getting on my nerves. I will walk softly, get my satchel, and be right back."

"Stick to the outer walls."

"I'm not a spider!"

"I meant, don't go near the center of the house."

"I know, Sullivan! I'm not stupid . . . just overly optimistic"—a personality trait that my experiences in this particular Crestview neighborhood were stripping from every fiber of my being.

Despite the scene in the basement, nothing seemed amiss when I gently stepped through the door. There was no noticeable sagging of the floor, nor were there any toppled furnishings. My satchel and all its precious contents remained exactly where I'd left them—on the floor next to the worn-out turquoise velour overstuffed chair. Gingerly, I crossed the room and snatched up the handle, then started to collect Sullivan's things from the coffee table, only to hear him bellow through the glass outer door, "Hey, Gilbert! Leave it! *I* have backups!"

"Too late, Boy Scout," I snapped, and swept his portfolio and notebooks into my arms. Just to spite him, I took yet another step deeper into the house to retrieve his briefcase.

Under his watchful—if angry—gaze, I returned to the doorway and grabbed a coat of Myra's from the Victorian coat tree. Sullivan held the door for me. "Real smart, Gilbert. Remind me never to get caught in a fire with you. I'm sure you'd insist on going through the flames to rescue your shampoo."

"Probably so. I buy high-end, salon-quality products, and they're pricey." I thrust his things into his arms, all but hurling them at him. "Here. And you're welcome."

Myra was standing at the very edge of her property. It wasn't as if the place were going to implode and suck us into the rubble, I thought ungenerously. I gave her the coat.

Myra asked, "Can you and Steve fix this?"

"No. But we can hire someone who can."

"We've got a major construction problem ahead of us now," Sullivan interjected, striding toward us. As if we needed *him* to lend an authoritative voice to our discussion. "We'll have to keep everyone out of the house, first off, and get a crane and winch to replace that beam before there's any further damage. I can call some trust-worthy contractors and get you a name."

"Maybe you'll be able to find someone willing to check out the premises today and see if they can put up a couple of temporary posts," I suggested. I glared at Sullivan, silently daring him to disagree. Whether or not he deserved my wrath, I'd nearly had a house collapse on top of me. I'd paid my dues for the day.

He made no comment.

I asked Myra, "Was anybody operating power tools downstairs recently?"

She shook her head. "I don't think so. I don't know for sure, because we went to Aspen during Thanksgiving week. Last year I gave both the McBrides and the Hendersons keys to our front door, in case of an emergency. With Randy's heart condition, that seemed prudent. And anyway, Randy was always building things and sawing down there." She paused. "Come to think of it, I don't know why he made Taylor set up a workshop outside, when Randy had a perfectly good workshop already in place in our basement."

"Maybe he just didn't want to allow Taylor access to his private tools," Steve replied.

Myra pushed a stray tress of gray hair back from her forehead. Her face was still very pale. "True, but now that I think about it, Randy hadn't been going into the basement as often as he used to. . . ."

"You think your husband might have sabotaged his own home?" I asked. "Why would he do something like that? He'd be putting *himself* in danger."

"But maybe he didn't care about that, since he knew he didn't have long to live anyway," Myra said. Under her breath she added, with a touch of venom, "And it wouldn't be the first time he's tried to kill me."

There was an awkward pause, and Steve and I exchanged anxious glances. Conflicting theories occurred to me at once—an explanation for Jill's drunken remark about knowing "what he'd done" to her—that Randy had tried to frame Myra for his murder with the sawed-off beam and then ingested the arsenic intentionally, or that Myra had staged everything and wanted to kill me.

"The police need to know about this right away," Steve said, reaching for his cell phone.

"That's okay," Myra replied. "I'll use Jill's phone. And I'll have to let Debbie know that she can't stay in my guest room after all."

She turned and started to walk toward the McBrides' house, then stopped and faced me. "Erin, I am so, so sorry about what just happened. I feel so responsible. I don't know how I'd have been able to carry on if that beam had killed you."

"Better than *I* could have, I'm sure," I retorted, in what was nothing more than a nonsensical babble. It seemed to suffice. Myra gave me a kind smile and turned back toward Jill's house.

Once she was out of earshot, Steve asked me, "Do you think she'll actually call the police? Should I call them, too, just in case?"

"I don't know. Right now, the only thing that I'm certain of is that I'm taking the rest of the day off. And I'm not taking another minute of my precious life for granted."

"Should we bag this job right now?"

"Pardon?"

"It's your call, Gilbert. We can tell Myra we've reconsidered, and thanks but no thanks. We agreed we'd turn the job down if it looked like things were getting out of control. You just nearly got killed. If that's not out of control, I don't know what is."

I sighed and looked up into his grim face. There was no way I could walk away from all of this now. I had to know who killed Randy and who'd inadvertently come so close to killing me. "Maybe so, but I just can't believe I was the intended target. The only person who could have pulled that off would have been Myra, and that means she had to have been walking around in her house aware that the floor could collapse at any moment. Let's see what happens over the next few days while Myra's getting her house repaired. Maybe the police will have arrested Randy's killer by then."

Steve frowned. "Maybe." He was obviously unconvinced.

My weekend was blissfully uneventful—thanks in no small part to the Dom-Bliss goddess herself. Audrey'd decided to enjoy a brief vacation in Aspen and left me alone in her soul-restoring house. My time was spent in glorious fashion. Saturday morning, I fixed up the den and, despite my time constraints and nonexistent budget, put the whole room more on a par with its stunning Christmas tree. By swapping some furnishings among the living room, parlor, and den, I was able to harmonize the den and improve the balance of all three rooms. On Audrey's regal marble fireplace, where we'd hung our stockings, I decorated the mantel with some of her excess homemade gift-wrap materials.

When I plugged in the tree lights that evening, I felt a surge of joy. All those shiny, nicely textured gifts that Audrey had overdressed in custom wallpaper and fabric did indeed look fit for a king. Four of the presents were, however, for me, making me suspect that she'd violated our agreed-upon spending limit. My money for *her* gift had gone to fourteen-karat gold earrings, which I knew would be sheer perfection when worn with her favorite caftan. To my consternation, Sullivan's voice whispered in my head: *What is it with you, Gilbert? Why are you always accessorizing?* I told him off, however, and he kept his mouth shut from then on.

With the setting arranged to my satisfaction, I could finally enjoy watching television in this room. A bowl of popcorn beside me and Hildi on my lap, I channel surfed and watched some design shows, which are my own personal version of a spectator sport—I talk back to the TV the way men do during football games. On Sunday morning, I drank cocoa and pored over the furniture ads and home-store fliers. Later, I was thrilled when a pair of friends back in New York called, and we yakked for nearly two hours.

Rejuvenated, my work on Monday morning was a breeze. Although my work was mostly of the basic-business-operation—and unpaid—variety, I so loved it that I was the proverbial kid in a candy shop. A sales rep came to my office to show me his company's new lines for spring. I researched the three *f*'s—fabrics, finishings, and furniture—for my source library of catalogues, pictures, and materials. The day's schedule also gave me a chance to have my by-appointment-only office open to walk-ins. Not that I got many walk-ins anyway, tucked away as I was on the second floor between two clothing stores. Unless you knew to look for it, only the sharpest eye could spot my door with "Interiors by Gilbert" painted in white on the glass door.

The phone warbled, and it was Myra.

"Good news," she declared. "The house is structurally sound again."

"*Already?*" I asked.

"Already," she repeated, her voice bubbling with cheer.

"I paid extra for an emergency construction job. The contractor Steve recommended to install the temporary posts was able to build a permanent fix. Since the beam was cut so close to the basement walls, they were able to install new posts and anchor them to the walls. Everything's good as new, so we're ready and waiting for you and Steve to start work again."

"Who is 'we'?"

"Debbie Henderson. She could be renting my guest room for quite a while. We were both hoping that you would be able to duplicate your design at her house for her room in my house."

My heart sank at the mere suggestion; the one thing I never liked to do during the course of my work was repeat myself. "The two rooms have completely different floor plans and natural lighting. I might be able to repeat certain design elements, though."

"Whatever you choose to do will be wonderful, I'm sure. We'll let Steve handle the living room, and you and I can delve right into the guest room."

She paused, but I said nothing, not yet able to phrase my reaction in a positive way. My shouting *Trade a living room in the front of the main floor for a tiny guest room upstairs? Over Sullivan's dead body!* would not be the best way to go.

"Steve's going to be calling you later this morning to discuss this with you himself, but can you make it over here at one o'clock this afternoon?"

My entire afternoon was free, although I'd planned on doing some Christmas shopping. "I suppose so."

"Wonderful. I'll see you then, Erin."

She hung up before I could reply, and I went back to work, but in somewhat of a dour mood. I tried to restore my spirits. No matter who would be lead designer on which room, there was no harm in my doing a little planning on the guest room; Sullivan and I could hammer out which of us actually did what later.

Several minutes later, Taylor lumbered up the stairs. He was wearing a white T-shirt underneath his overalls, but no jacket, although the temperature hovered in the thirties. He asked, "Is Sullivan here?"

"No. He might be in his own office."

"He isn't. That's where I came from, just now." Taylor met my eyes. "I kind of . . . wanted to let you both know that I'm serious about needing some work. Something important has come up, and I really do need some dough. My mom could use my support."

He did seem to be completely sincere this time and, despite my better judgment, I felt a pang of sympathy for him. "Okay, Taylor. I'll think about it. I doubt I'll have much work right away. . . ." I let my voice fade, remembering that we *were* going to need a carpenter to remove that wall and install the new half wall at Myra's. I would need to think long and hard to decide if I trusted Taylor well enough to forgo my usual contractors in favor of him. "But if anything comes along, I'll let you know."

He held my gaze for a long moment, frowned, and muttered, "I only did what I had to do, Gilbert. A guy's got to stand up for himself. You know?"

"Taylor, I have no idea what you're talking about."

He scowled. "Just watch out. You think you're, like, protected somehow. But you're not. You're getting taken for a ride like you wouldn't even believe."

With that, he pivoted and slammed down the stairs.

"Wait! What are you saying?"

He kept going.

I raced to the staircase. He was already pushing out the door. "Wait!" I cried.

He didn't. I ran after him and spotted him turning down the red-brick walkway of the Spruce Street Mall. "Taylor, stop. What are you talking about?" I called after him.

Finally he stopped, and I trotted up to him. Taylor could flatten me with one punch. There was some old saw about discretion being the better part of valor, but Mom had never stocked that particular piece of advice in her arsenal. I asked him point-blank, "Did you put that photograph in the paneling?"

He snorted. "No way."

"You're the one who built that hiding spot in the wall, though. No one else even knew it was there."

"Randy knew. Like I told you the other day, he was spying on me and turned me into the police. I was keeping drugs stashed in it. I sure as hell didn't put someone's baby picture in it, though."

"Then *Randy* put the picture there?"

"Who knows? Randy's dead. But I'd bet my last dollar it was intended for someone else to see."

"How did you know about it if you weren't the one who put it there in the first place?"

Taylor stared at me as though I were an idiot and retorted, "You just told me!"

"All I said was that it was a photograph. I didn't say anything about a *baby* picture."

He clenched his jaw and glared at me for several seconds, but then said, "I saw you take it out and put it into your pocket."

"So, what did you mean by 'it was intended for someone else'?"

Fury suddenly marred his naturally fierce features. He stabbed a finger in my face. "You think you're so much smarter than me, bitch, *you* figure it out."

Once again, not the best possible exit line for a job interview, I thought sourly as I returned to my office, mind
racing.

I arrived fifteen minutes early for our scheduled fact-
gathering appointment at Myra's and decided to stay in
the car and review my notes and sketches. Debbie
Henderson pulled up and parked next to my van in the
driveway. I gave her a smile as she emerged from her car.
Opening my door, I explained, "I'm early and thought
I'd go over some things."

"Come on inside with me. You'll be more comfortable there, and Myra won't mind in the least."

"Thanks. That would be great."

"I'm so glad to hear you're going to do Myra's guest
room," she said.

"I actually *haven't* agreed to that yet. Steve's coming
over, too, and eventually we'll discuss who's doing what."
I studied her, noted the weary sadness to her features as
she unlocked the door, and found myself wondering how
wise it was for her to move in across the street from her
newly estranged husband. I wondered, too, what had become of the argument I'd overheard between her and
Myra the morning after Randy had died. How had they
put aside their differences so quickly?

"Can I get you some coffee or anything?"

"A glass of water would be great." As long as I watched
her pour it from the tap, water would be safe to accept.

The living room was identical to how I'd last seen it—
no collapsed floor and no pizzazz. Debbie led me past
the living room, and I stepped gingerly around the one
wall to the dining room, just above the newly repaired
support beam. Debbie suddenly froze, and I almost

bumped into her. An instant later I saw what had stopped her in her tracks.

With Myra at his side, Kevin McBride had obviously been trying to slide the back door open quietly, intent on making a hasty exit. His neck was smudged with lipstick.

He gave us a sheepish smile. "Oh, hi, Erin. Debbie. I was just checking the runners on the screen door for Myra." He made a show of sliding the screen back and forth. "You just need a couple drops of oil in the wheels, Myra. That's all. I'll bring some over next time I think of it."

"Thank you, Kevin." Myra was, avoiding everyone's gaze. "That's extremely considerate of you."

"Don't mention it."

"I'll be right with you, Erin," Myra said, clearly flustered. "I just need to duck into the bathroom for a moment. . . ."

Red-faced, Kevin turned to Debbie and me. "The, uh, carpenters did a great job on the beam," he told us. "It's good as new now."

Debbie crossed her arms and muttered, "It's nice to see that you're worrying about a squeaking screen door, Kevin. That's downright neighborly of you." Her face was frozen with malice.

"Yes. Well. I was just making a handyman's visit, wanting to make sure everything's safe and sound. The house has sure made me nervous, after Erin, here, was nearly conked on the head by that huge beam."

"Yes, Kevin," Debbie agreed scathingly. "You're nothing if not helpful to Myra."

"I'd better get home, then. Excuse me, ladies."

"You might want to button up your shirt collar before you see Jill," Debbie said, rubbing her own neck where Myra's lipstick had marked Kevin's. He took the hint: he was scrubbing away the plum stains with a tissue from his pocket as he left.

Debbie had apparently forgotten about my glass of water and started to brew some coffee. I asked if it would be all right if I headed upstairs to take a quick look at the guest room. "Go ahead," she said. "First door on the left."

I leapt at any chance to see a soon-to-be-redone room by myself and without distraction. This is a phase of my job that I love—when a room feels like a blank canvas that needs a burst of color here or splash of fabric there to be completely transformed.

At a glance, there was no way I was going to do the guest room in a burgundy faux finish. This room faced the mountains, and I just knew the view cried out for buttery yellow walls.

The furniture was in a sorry state of repair. A book was propping up the nightstand; one of its three-inch-tall back legs was missing entirely. I glanced at the word *Chemistry* in the book's title and instantly thought about Randy's poisoning. I extracted the book and let the top of the table gently lean against the wall. It was some old chemistry textbook, the cover now badly dented from years of service as a table leg. Myra had said she'd taught chemistry at CU and in high school.

Out of idle curiosity, I opened the book to see if the pages, too, were dented. They weren't, and as I started to set the book aside, something fell out of it.

I knelt and stared, my heart racing. This couldn't be happening again, surely. Another trap, another photograph for me to happen to stumble across. And yet, this time my happening to pick up and almost drop that one book was too unlikely for this to have been staged; no one could have known that I would find this picture.

Incredulous, I picked up the photograph that had fluttered to the floor and slowly got to my feet, staring aghast at the three people seated on a sofa in the celluloid image. I recognized my mother. Seated on the other side of the sofa from my mother was a young Myra Axelrod, who must have been just about the same age I was now. Between them sat a bright-eyed, smiling baby, maybe a year old. Although I'd never seen photographs of myself at that age, I knew at once that the baby was me.

"Erin!" Myra cried.

Startled, I gasped, and she stormed through the doorway toward me. "You're poking around in my personal possessions!"

"This photograph just fell from a book."

Crimson splotches stained her cheeks as she snatched the photograph from my hand. "Huh. Must have been some friend of mine and her daughter. From when Randy and I were first married." She let out a little laugh. "I can't even remember her name."

She handed me back the picture and whirled on her heel to abruptly leave the room.

"*I* do," I called after her. "She's my mother."

Myra stood frozen in place, her back toward me. When she finally turned and looked at me, her expression was one of tremendous pain.

Only one conclusion could be drawn: Myra was my birth mother. An all-but-forgotten childhood fantasy flitted past my mind's eye—my beautiful, gracious birth mother would pull up to the schoolyard in her limousine, and my classmates would watch slack-jawed in envy as she whisked me and my ecstatic parents off to live with her in her palace.

In this face-slap reality, I'd outgrown the need for happily-ever-after fairy tales, but to my shame and surprise, the need to hear that I hadn't been fundamentally unlovable at eighteen months of age nagged at me even all these years later.

I swallowed the lump in my throat and said, "My mother made me promise that I would never try to find my birth parents. Apparently *you* found *me*, however."

Tears ran down Myra's cheeks. "It's too late now," she said softly. "It's been too late for the last twenty years. Jeannie let me know that in no uncertain terms."

I was unable to keep the bitterness out my voice as I asked quietly, "So you remember her name, after all."

She nodded. "Of course I do. Jeannie was our live-in nanny for more than a year." She swiped at her cheek with the back of her hand and took a ragged breath. "It's not easy to forget someone who takes your only child away from you to raise as her own."

chapter 16

It felt as though all the air had been sucked out of my lungs. Myra's words terrified me. Had my beloved mother kidnapped me after all? If so, I didn't want to know that. Not now. Not ever.

My legs felt wobbly. I knelt and turned my face away from Myra as I put the photograph back into the book and slipped the book back under the base of the night-stand.

"I'd thought that was the perfect hiding place for that picture," Myra said wistfully.

"Why did you have to hide it?"

She didn't answer, but rather, gave me a sad smile.

"Your mother was a very decent and kindhearted woman, Erin," she said.

I closed my eyes for a moment and sighed with relief.

"I heard that she died recently."

"She did." I rose. "It was two years ago, but sometimes it feels like it was just yesterday."

"I'm sorry."

"So was I." I finally managed to meet her gaze. She was searching my face with a pitiful longing in her expression. I'd seen that look on more than one mother's face as they'd showed me the former bedrooms of their now grown children.

"And . . . your father?" she asked gently. "I never met him. I don't even know his name."

"He lives in California. He remarried. The divorce was several years ago."

So. Myra Axelrod was indeed my biological mother. She had a flatter, broader profile than mine; perhaps she had some Native American genes. Maybe I'd inherited my thin frame from Myra and some yet unrecognized facial characteristics from Randy. He might not even have been the father, though. *My* father, I reminded myself.

"If there was any way I could have kept you, Erin, I would have. But Randy said . . ." She paused and swiped the tears off her cheeks. "You have to understand. I did the only thing I could do. There was no way I could protect you from that monster. I had no choice." She struggled to keep her voice steady.

"What monster? Do you mean Randy?"

She closed her eyes and said nothing.

My God, this was weird—speaking to my biological mother, the woman who'd given birth to me. "Myra, I don't understand—"

"All these years, I tried to find you. But I never could." She gritted her teeth and snarled, "It *would* have to have been *Randy* who managed the feat. It's almost funny, under the circumstances."

"What circumstances?"

Again, her gray eyes took on that wistful longing as she met my gaze. "Randy knew he didn't have much longer to live. He'd told his doctors that he'd decided to forgo the bypass surgery that they all insisted he needed. He told me he wanted his last weeks and months in this world to be on his own terms. And, I guess, that included finally getting to know his daughter."

But now he was dead. Murdered. This was all to much to handle. Simultaneously I longed to learn the answers to questions that had gone unanswered for most of my life and to leave this house and strike everything about the Axelrods from my memory banks.

"I . . . just can't do this now, Myra. I'm sorry. I have to go . . . be alone for a while."

She nodded, her arms folded tight against her chest. "Of course. When Steve arrives, I'll tell him that we need to reschedule. But can you come back, Erin? At four this afternoon? Please?"

I wasn't at all sure that I wanted to reenter this house. Ever. "I don't know. . . ."

"It would mean a lot to me if we could just . . . move forward with everything, go on with our lives. I don't want to feel like now you can't even bear to treat me like a client."

I hesitated. Her request was phrased precisely as my real mother—the woman who'd mothered and loved me for more than a quarter of a century—might have expressed it. That connection tugged at me. Yet I'd just found out that Myra had given birth to me. How the hell was I supposed to treat her like any other client? "I don't know how I feel yet," I told her honestly, and saw her flinch. "I'll wait for Steve outside, and we'll decide about rescheduling later." Without waiting for her reply, I brushed past her.

This had been as far removed from my childhood-fantasy reunion as possible. I felt all turned inside out. I wandered down the sidewalk awhile, then slumped down on the curb shivering, trying to get my heart out of my throat.

Steve Sullivan drove up just then and parked. He slowly made his way down the sidewalk toward me.

"Gilbert? You okay?"

Not looking up, I murmured, "Oh, absolutely. Confident and optimistic. Just like always."

He crouched to lower himself to my eye level. His pea coat was unbuttoned. He looked dashing and handsome. Must be nice to just arrive at work without having your heart ripped out and handed to you. "What's wrong?" he asked gently.

"Myra's just confessed that she's my birth mother. So. It seems that my biological mother is a bit of a loon, and my father was an abusive bully with a bad heart—both literally and figuratively—who was murdered almost in front of me, and I suspect by my mother's hand. That's setting aside the fact that a booby-trapped beam fell in their house and narrowly missed killing me." I gritted my teeth, determined to shrug off this gloom. If there was one thing my mother had taught me over the years, it was that self-pity does much more harm than good. "But then, I guess everyone's family is a bit dysfunctional, right?" I got to my feet and brushed myself off, and Steve rose as well. "On the bright side, at least if I ever decide to host a family reunion, my guest list will be really, really short."

"I . . . wish I knew what to say. I'm sorry."

"There's no need to say anything. But I do need a couple of hours to sort this through. Myra suggested we return at four this afternoon. Can you make it back here then?"

"*I* can, but what about you? Are you really sure you want to go ahead with this job?"

"I'm not sure about a single thing right now. Except that I need to be alone for a while. Unless I call and cancel, let's just meet here at four."

"Erin," he said softly, and touched my shoulder.

I shrank away, not looking at him, and headed for my van, saying over my shoulder, "Thanks, Sullivan. I'll see you at four, then." No way was I going to let myself break down in front of him; if I decided later that I needed company, this was strictly girlfriend-commiseration territory, after all.

I drove to Audrey's house, parked, and sat in the van, lost in thought. Given any choice, I never would have looked for Myra and Randy, but *they'd* found *me*. Had I unconsciously hoped for some sort of reunion? Otherwise, as my father had said to me over the phone, I wouldn't have chosen to move to Crestview, Colorado, in the first place.

Now I had to face up to the simple fact that I was inexorably *myself*—that I wanted and needed to know the answers even to painful, soul-baring questions and to make peace with whatever happened next. I had to know who had murdered my birth father, or at least the man who'd apparently taken me into his home and served as my father for the first eighteen months of my life. I had to know, too, why the Axelrods had allowed their young, unmarried live-in nanny to adopt me.

Furthermore, I had to prove to my birth mother—the woman who had hired me—that I was one hell of a designer. I was going to squeeze every iota of experience and creativity out of myself and Steve and give Myra Axelrod's house a stunningly brilliant design.

A little less than three hours later, just as I'd pulled into Myra's driveway, my cell phone rang. I answered, and Steve said, "Hey, Gilbert. It's Sullivan. I'm almost at Myra's. It's not too late to cancel the job at Myra's, you know. Are we in or out?"

"In. So let's be brilliant."

He chuckled and said, "If you insist. And I'm right behind you." I glanced in the rearview mirror: he was. We hung up.

I took a deep breath and imagined myself dispelling all the bad thoughts from my body as I exhaled—a self-help technique I'd picked up someplace. I had to admit, to myself at least, that on this particular job, I was glad to have a partner.

Despite some obvious awkwardness between Myra and me, the first half hour of our information-gathering meeting went very well. Debbie, Myra, Steve, and I checked out the repaired beam, and the carpenters had done a good job. Although retracing my steps put me on edge—I refused to stand underneath the beam—the experience was somewhat cathartic. Debbie then excused herself to do some writing on her notebook computer in her bedroom.

Myra told us what her budget for redoing the entire house was, and it was a workable figure—enough that we would be able to make significant improvements, but not so much that we would be tempted to gut the place and rebuild from scratch. We signed the contracts and received our retainer, and listened to Myra's requirements and preferences for her new design. The three of us then attempted to get some ideas flowing in earnest.

There are trade-offs in all interior design decisions; otherwise, there wouldn't be a need for more than one designer in the entire world, who could answer everyone's questions from an 800 number. Question: what's the best floor plan for a thousand-square-foot main floor that includes a kitchen, living room, family room, and dining area? Answer: a great room with a kitchen island, Berber carpeting in the combination living/family room, hardwood floors in the dining room and kitchen. One large great room can prevent multiple, claustrophobic rooms and utilize space efficiently.

But what if the clients object to being able to see the dirty dishes on the kitchen counter when they're relaxing or entertaining in their living room? Also, kitchen islands can cut into floor space that might otherwise provide for a table large enough to seat eight diners in elegance and comfort. Hardwood floors are durable but have poor acoustic qualities. And they're grueling on the legs when, for example, a gourmet cook spends long stretches at the stove. Rugs wear out faster and are harder to maintain than other floor coverings but are much more comfortable on the feet and to sit on, as I'd seen for myself that Myra liked to do.

The key to doing my job well was being able to get inside the client's head—to learn what she most valued, what activities made her the happiest. By asking Myra about her daily routine and listening as she described how she loved to sit every morning with her coffee and pore over the *Crestview Sentinel* for up to two hours, it was obvious that she needed a large sitting area at the kitchen counter. The space needed to be opened up somewhat; hence the proposed half wall that had led to Steve's nearly crashing through the floor on top of me.

Steve and I determined that the new wall would be three feet high and feature an oak shelf and an elegant, simple oak post for structural support. This compromise between a full wall and no wall would give Myra's public areas definition, yet a more open feel than its current design.

After grinning at each other about how smoothly our programming phase was going, Steve then said, "Now let's talk about the front room—Randy's office. There I'd like to consider removing the wall entirely and incorporating the space into the family room. You'd be able to make good use of the bay window in the former office, maybe build a window seat and turn it into your own private nook."

Much as I personally agreed with Steve's proposal, Myra's face was not lighting up at the idea. In fact, her upper lip was curling the way Hildi's did just before she coughed up a hairball. My hunch was that Myra wanted to transform her overbearing late husband's room into *her* space. "Or," I interposed, "you could get some of that same spaciousness and openness with French doors. You'd be able to turn that room into a sewing room and close it off from the public spaces of the house whenever you wished, yet still be able to look through the doorway from nearly every spot in the living room and see that terrific bay window."

"Oh, I love that, Erin!" Myra cried. "That would just be *wonderful* for that room. Thank you so much for suggesting it."

"You're welcome."

Steve's features had tightened almost imperceptibly, and he said, "Or we could convert your guest room upstairs into a sewing room. Then you'd have enough floor space in your living room for a grand piano, even."

"I don't play the piano, Mr. Sullivan, and my guest room is currently occupied." Decisively, she pointed at the closed door to the office. "French doors. Sewing room."

He flashed an unwavering smile at her. "That will

look fantastic." The smile turned to a glare the moment she looked away and his eyes shifted to mine. Drat! I'd flubbed an obvious rule of working in tandem—never show up your partner. I should have said that Steve and I would gladly entertain other ideas from her if she wanted to keep that room intact, and then steered the conversation so that the sewing-room idea seemed to be *her* suggestion. "Should we talk about the upstairs bedrooms now, or—"

Myra shook her head. "Why don't you two just surprise me with what you work up on your own? After all, Erin, you know how much I'd like to see something similar to what you did for Debbie and Carl."

"Yes, and thank you. But we're not going to repeat it exactly. For one thing, the floor plans are very different. Did you like the bed best, or the faux finish . . . the fabrics . . . ?"

"It would be impossible to choose, so you decide for me. I trust your taste and judgment implicitly." She rose and turned her attention to Steve. "And you're very good, too. Thank you both so much for coming."

As Steve and I gathered our belongings to leave, the tension between us was palpable.

"How soon until we can get started?" Myra asked, looking directly at me.

Steve replied, "We'll need a few days to develop our presentation plans for the rooms. We'll have a better idea of the overall time frame by then, after we talk to the contractors that we hire."

She furrowed her brow. "You mean you won't be doing the work yourselves, like you did for the McBrides and the Hendersons?"

"No, that was an exception, for both of us," I said.

"And you aren't willing to make an exception in my case?" Myra asked, staring directly into my eyes.

I was caught off guard, but Steve said with a gracious smile, "We can discuss that later on in the week as well."

We thanked her and left. On our way to our vans, I stammered, "I'm not used to working with a partner. That was really bogus of me to just blurt out the idea about—"

"Forget about it, Gilbert," he said icily. "We were gathering information about Myra's likes and dislikes, and you just got the jump on me. Good for you."

He opened the door of his van with more gusto than was required. I hesitated, mulling over whether I should apologize again and offer to buy him a beer, or leave him alone to fume for a while. Before I could decide, I was distracted by something in the Hendersons' driveway. "Huh. There's a car in Carl's driveway that I haven't seen before," I told Steve. "Maybe I should go over there right now to repair his wall. If he's got company, he'll be on his best behavior."

"What do you mean? What's the matter with the wall? And when *wasn't* he on good behavior?"

"Didn't I tell you about that?" I asked, then realized that, obviously, I hadn't. The thought of Carl Henderson smashing holes in the walls of a room that had come out so superbly still rankled. "On Thursday, after Randy's funeral service, I went over to repair damage the police caused while searching for evidence. But Carl had been drinking and punched more holes in the wall, and he accused me of ruining his life. I'm sure he's calmed down by now, though, and I need to see if he wants me to arrange to have the drywall replaced." Over my shoulder, I said to Steve, "I'll talk to you later," and crossed the street.

Sullivan slammed his van door shut. "Gilbert! Wait up a second. It'd be a good idea if I came with you."

"Why? He's not going to go berserk and kill me on his front porch, for God's sake."

"Probably not, but if he was punching holes in a wall, it's possible that he might greet you with a right cross."

"Nah. There's no chance of that. He's got a cast on his right hand, so it'd have to be a left cross."

"That cements it. I'm coming with you."

"How very gallant of you, Sullivan. Just don't get any ideas about keeping this up for long. I'm an only child. I need my space."

He bowed slightly. "Lead on, O independent one."

I rolled my eyes but allowed him to accompany me to Carl's house. "Don't you think this will look weird to Carl? Your shadowing me, I mean?"

"Not at all. I'll explain that I didn't get the chance to see the completed room, albeit with a few holes in the wall, and that I'd like to see it now. Which happens to be true, by the way."

"Are you just curious? Or are you checking out your competition?"

"Both, I guess," he replied with a shrug.

I rang the doorbell. The door was swept open by a woman I'd never met. My jaw dropped slightly as our eyes met. She was in her forties and was my exact height and coloring. We had the same long neck, even.

I fought to collect myself. This was merely a product of stress, playing weird psychological games with me. Myra had just now told me that I was her daughter. I'd dragged the information out of her, after happening across a well-hidden photograph. She would have had no reason to lie.

"Hello. My name is Erin Gilbert, and I—"

"Your name is Erin?" The woman's face paled. She stared at me.

"Erin Gilbert, yes, and I—"

She relaxed and interjected, "Oh! you're the interior designer Carl hired."

"That's right. And this is Steve Sullivan, a colleague. Is Carl here?"

"Who is it?" Carl called. He came limping up on crutches, his foot in what looked like a removable cast. He frowned as he spotted me. "*You* again? Haven't you taken your pound of flesh already? You cost me an arm and a leg! Literally!"

"Carl," the woman chastised, "stop it! It's hardly her fault that you're such a hot-tempered ignoramus that you've broken some bones by pounding on a wall!"

"It may or may not be her fault, but I sure as hell am not letting her back inside my house. I might break my *neck* next time!"

"Come in," the woman told us, swinging the door wider.

"Hey! This is *my* house, not yours!"

"Point taken." She rolled her eyes. "I'll come outside, then." She stepped onto the porch beside us. With a jerk of her head, she indicated Carl and explained, "I'm playing temporary nursemaid and was about to leave. He has a hard time driving his car in that cast."

"Which doesn't give you the right to invite people off the street into my house!" he called indignantly through the glass door.

She again rolled her dark brown eyes. "I'm Carl's first wife. Emily Blaire."

"Nice to meet you. This is a fellow designer, Steve Sullivan," I said, introducing him, I belatedly realized, for the second time.

They shook hands, Steve turning on the charm as they exchanged pleasantries. I returned my attention to Carl, leaning on his crutches as he glared at us through the glass. "I just wanted to see if you wanted me to hire someone for you to repair the drywall," I called to him.

"No! I'm paying Taylor to do it tomorrow. Emily! You coming in or going home?"

"Going home," she growled as she trotted down the steps. She got into her car and started the engine.

Jaw agape, Carl watched her leave as if unable to believe she wasn't going to change her mind and come back inside. As she drove away, he yelled, "Fine! Goodbye!" Carl attempted to slam the door by whacking it with one crutch, but lost his balance. He toppled to the floor.

Steve and I rushed into the house to help him up. His glasses had gone flying, and while insisting that he didn't need any help, he lost his balance a second time and mangled the frames. Carl, in turn, accused me of having "blinded" him. I apologized, and after a minute or two of cajoling and being assured that he was fine by himself, Steve and I left.

Partway down the walkway, I hesitated and snapped my fingers. "Oh, darn! I forgot to ask him if he'd mind writing me a letter of recommendation. Think I should go back and ask?"

Steve laughed heartily. Then he accepted my offer to buy him a drink, seeing as he'd paid the last time.

We decided to have dinner, along with our drinks, at a downtown restaurant. After the plates had been cleared and we were partway into our second round, I said, "I think I know why my mother felt it was so important for me not to look for my birth parents."

"Because she knew that they and their neighbors were raving lunatics?" Steve asked.

"Exactly."

Steve fidgeted with his napkin. Then he finally met my eyes and said, "Emily Blaire sure acted strange. She nearly passed out when she first saw you."

"Yeah, but that's the same reaction I got when Myra saw me for the first time. Myra claims I'm *her* biological daughter and that my mother was her nanny, which makes sense. Mom always said she knew me from the time I was six weeks old. My hunch is she got to know Myra when she took a class from her at CU." I took another sip of my beer.

Steve said nothing; his eyes stayed on my face.

"*What?*" I asked, annoyed.

"Erin, do I really need to point out to you that you and Emily Blaire look a lot alike? And when I say 'a lot,' I mean a *whole* lot."

I squirmed a little in my seat. So he, too, had detected physical similarities. I scraped at the label on my beer bottle with my thumbnail. "Not so much that Carl Henderson ever noticed. If it was anything other than a coincidence that she and I happen to look a little similar, you'd think her ex-husband would have noticed at some point."

"He's not exactly Mr. Perceptive. He seems to have tunnel vision about everything."

"But Debbie didn't notice, either. Nor did Jill or Kevin. And they all know Emily. Plus, why would Myra lie about something like being my biological mother?"

"Maybe because she's nuts or has some evil plan. Maybe she fed her husband a whopping dose of poison and lies about *everything*."

While sipping my Michelob, I mulled over Steve's words, unable to dismiss the possibility that he was correct. "If Emily Blaire was my birth mother, that makes me Taylor's sister. Or half sister, at any rate. Yet he and I look nothing alike."

Steve leaned back and squinted at me. "Hmm. Maybe if you grew a foot, shaved your head, took some anabolic steroids, and went into bodybuilding . . ."

I grinned. "Now, *there's* a coincidence. Your suggestions for self-improvement happen to be precisely what's already on my Day-Timer as personal resolutions for New Year's."

He laughed.

I widened my eyes and feigned offense. "I'm serious. It's going to be a whole new me come January. I'll be six-eight, bald, built like a Mack truck, and competing for the title of World's Strongest Woman."

"Far be it from me to object." His hazel eyes sparkled. "By all means, go for it. My prospective customers won't have such a hard time remembering if it was Sullivan Designs or Interiors by Gilbert that they want. As of next month, I'll be able to explain that I, *Sullivan*, am the male, eminently qualified, and highly sought-after designer. Whereas *Gilbert* is the two-hundred-pound, bald, Amazon woman designer who works down the street from me." He laughed. "Come to think of it, I think I'll start doing that right away, regardless."

"Very funny."

A moment later, though, the humor left me as Steve's words about Emily Blaire sank in. *Could* Myra have been lying to me after all? Was Emily my actual mother? The sudden awareness of birth parents in my life was all so foreign to me.

"Anyway, the thing is, Steve, when you come right down to it, this is all just genetics. The people I consider my parents are the ones who raised me. They're the ones who influenced me, shaped me into who I am. I mean, what difference does it make who my biological parents are?"

"Nature versus nurture," he replied thoughtfully.

"They've done studies on that, you know, with identical twins separated at birth. A lot of personality traits are actually inherited."

"Yeah, yeah. And that's what allows people to feel sorry for themselves . . . to say, 'This is the way I am, and I can't change.' My mom, my *real* mom, that is, was this terrific person. She had a degenerative lung disease, and giving birth would have exacerbated the illness. As it was, she died when she was forty-six. But she taught me that what matters is now—the present. She knew from her twenties on that her life expectancy wasn't the best, so she made the most out of every day she had. When her marriage fell apart, she was sad, but she picked up the pieces and she moved on. None of us has any guarantees in this world."

"So your philosophy is to live for the moment? To do whatever feels good now?"

I gave a little shrug, worried that the natural follow-on to that do-whatever-feels-good philosophy might lead me to make some really stupid choices. "It's that the present is whatever I make it be . . . lemonade out of life's lemons, and all of that."

Steve nodded and lifted his glass. "I'll drink to that."

I regarded him for a moment, thinking about his own situation. "It's probably a lot harder for you to move forward than it is for me. After all, I'm not the one whose partner took him for all he was worth."

He frowned and muttered, "You don't know the half of it." He forced a smile. "But one of these days, I might catch up to Evan and get him to give me my money back. If not, I'll rebuild the biz one more time from the ground up. That's what I had to do the first time, before he and I hooked up. It's easier now that I've got an established reputation."

I winked at him. "Especially now that Gilbert of

Interiors by Gilbert is going to turn into this bald Amazon who'll scare the bejeezus out of anyone who wants to hire her."

"Right," he agreed with a chuckle.

I had to admit to myself that the more I got to know Steve Sullivan, the more I was tempted to like him. "How did you get interested in interior design?"

Instantly he got a wistful, faraway gaze in his eyes. "I was originally going to be an artist—the next Picasso. And I still paint—that's my big hobby. I love working with oils, mostly. But maybe it was growing up in such a noisy household that did me in . . . so there's your nurture factor for you. My artistic bent wasn't inherited, I can tell you that much. Anyway, being the middle kid of five—two brothers, two sisters—and living in a three-bedroom house, I was always fighting for my own private space. I had to share a room with my younger brothers, so when I was in high school, I built a partition."

"And it turned out well?"

"Yeah, it really did. It wound up being really cool . . . a makeshift wall, even, with an accordion door. My sisters asked me to do the same thing in their room, and next thing I knew, I was helping them redecorate their entire room with their pooled babysitting earnings. My first semester at Colorado Art Institute, I took a design class just as something of a lark, and by the end of the class, I was hooked." He shrugged and grinned. "How 'bout you? How'd you get into the field?"

"It's always been my passion. My mom was a big influence. When my dad moved out, we had to go to a smaller place, a two-bedroom apartment in Albany, New York, and Mom said we were going to make it gorgeous on the inside, since the outside was a lost cause. That became our big mother-daughter activity—for years, actually—looking at textiles and paints, envisioning how this would look with that. There was never a question what I'd study after high school."

Smiling, he searched my eyes, then averted his and drained his beer. Weird. If I hadn't known better, I'd think he was battling an attraction to me.

The waitress came to our table to ask if we needed anything else. Steve looked at me, and I shook my head. "It's time to call it a night, don't you think? I might be getting a little tipsy," I said as I threw down a twenty and a ten to pay for the drinks and my dinner.

Steve gallantly offered to pick up the entire tab but finally relented. "Are you okay to drive?" he asked as we got to our feet.

"Oh, absolutely."

"I'm going to follow you home, just to be sure."

"There's no need to—"

"Hey, it's more or less on the way to my place, anyway."

"So are *you* okay to drive? I hope you don't think I'll be lenient if you wind up rear-ending my van just 'cuz I was the one who bought your beers."

Steve smirked at me. "I'll be extra careful, Gilbert," he promised.

We left the restaurant. The evening air was chilly. I pulled my wool coat closer, but I felt a glow that I knew wasn't entirely a matter of the two beers I'd consumed. We walked so close together that our coat sleeves occasionally brushed. We discussed the logistics of his following my van, and parted to go to our separate vehicles. I'd managed to find a space on Eleventh Street, and Steve had parked in the outside lot for the restaurant.

As I slid behind the wheel and started the engine, I scolded myself aloud. "Get ahold of yourself, Gilbert. No way are you *ever* going to fall for Steve Sullivan! It would never work out." I glanced into the rearview mirror and said, "Are you listening to yourself?"

Just then the headlights of an approaching car flashed in my mirror—a couple of points of light appearing on the wall of my van. Thinking my eyes had deceived me, I turned and looked back as a second car headed north on Eleventh. Something was wrong with the side of my vehicle. There seemed to be two holes in the metal.

I got out to look at the holes from the outside, still not quite believing my eyes.

One hole had pierced the letter G in *Gilbert*, and the second was dead center in the letter *b*. And I knew without question that they were bullet holes.

chapter 17

Just then Steve's van was turning the corner of the parking lot, which looped past my car toward the exit gate. I waved frantically with both arms, and he braked and opened his window. "Someone shot at my van!" I called.

He hesitated, said, "Be right there," and backed up to reclaim his parking space. Jogging over to me, he asked, "Did I hear you right just now? Were you saying that . . . ?"

His voice faded. Then he ran his fingertips over the damaged metal. "This might just be a random prank . . . some teenager, showing off his shooting prowess to his buddies, maybe."

"No way. Why hit two letters in my last name, and no place else?" My voice sounded odd in my ears. I had to struggle to catch my breath. "I think it's a message to me from whoever killed Randy Axelrod. I think the killer's after *me* now."

Too frightened to think straight, I couldn't stand the idea of talking to Detective O'Reilly or Detective Martinez. O'Reilly would probably speculate that, at some point, I could have fired bullet holes into my own van to make myself look innocent. Martinez would probably hint that if I'd simply come to the station house sooner, this somehow wouldn't have happened. I called the police station and asked for the only officer I knew for certain would be friendly to me—Linda Delgardio. The dispatcher informed me that Linda wouldn't be on duty again until early tomorrow morning. I left Linda a message and told the dispatcher that I needed some assistance as soon as possible.

A ruddy-cheeked, blond officer arrived fifteen or twenty minutes later. He retrieved two "slugs" from inside my van and determined that the shooter had most likely been standing on the sidewalk directly across the street. He was unable to find any witnesses, and although he combed the area for another fifteen minutes or so— sweeping the steady beam of his flashlight across every inch—he was also unable to find any "spent casings." He was solicitous in his discussions with me, but seemed ready to simply take down the information and leave until Steve told him about my connection to the ongoing murder investigation. Then he told us to stay put for a minute, and he got into his police cruiser to make a call.

I grew more anxious with each passing minute. The

shooter might return to see if my van was still here. I kept looking behind me and to either side of Steve, certain that some stranger was going to pop out of the shadows and end my life here and now.

The officer finally returned and asked if we could come to the station house to make a complete statement. Before I could reply, Steve said, "Yeah," then looked at me and said, "Let's go."

We caravanned to the station house. Inside, Steve was ushered off in one direction, and I found myself back in the same sterile room as before, speaking to the same detective—O'Reilly. He was still in a foul mood and the same cheap gray suit. Maybe his pants were itchy.

Letting me speak my piece about the bullet holes, Detective O'Reilly glanced at his notes, rested an elbow on the table, and said, "Nobody heard gunshots. That seems strange to me. A crowded place like Eleventh and Lincoln Boulevard at eight p.m., and not a single person reports hearing a gun being fired . . . not just once, but twice."

His routine was missing a cheerful partner to play good cop to his bad cop. I fought back a sigh and replied, "Short of seeing someone actually *fire* the weapon, most people probably would have assumed it was just an engine misfiring, wouldn't they?"

"You're absolutely positive that the bullet holes were put there while you were *in* the restaurant?"

"Not absolutely positive, no. I know for sure that the holes weren't there yesterday, but I guess it's remotely possible that I just didn't notice them when I drove downtown this evening."

"Is it?"

"Like I said, it's remotely possible. I barely noticed the holes in the side of my van when I got into the car at the restaurant. But I *would* have heard the gunshots if anyone had fired a gun earlier, while I was in Randy Axelrod's or my own quiet neighborhood."

"So you're not sure when the bullets were fired at your van after all."

That was what he took away from what I just said? "I'm ninety-nine percent sure that it happened *while* I was in the restaurant tonight," I said firmly.

O'Reilly drummed on the table for at least ten repetitions with each finger. My gaze unwittingly drawn to his hands, I noticed that he had an unusual amount of body hair. The observation reminded me of a joke from my childhood about hair on knuckles being one sign of insanity—and looking for hair on one's knuckles being a second sign. That, in turn, led to me thinking about how bad it would look if I were to start laughing about the detective's hairy hands, which brought on such an urge to laugh that my eyes teared up. My thought pattern made me realize that I was not, as of yet, completely sober.

Finally, he said, "Okay."

"So I can leave now?" I started to scoot my chair back from the table.

He scowled. "We're still investigating the poisoning death. I understand Detective Martinez asked you to come in and answer some questions, yet you never showed."

"I'd already told you everything I knew about that."

"We've noticed your van in the neighborhood quite a bit these past couple days."

"I'm working there, designing Myra Axelrod's rooms."

He considered this information worthy of a notation in his pad. "That'd be the victim's wife," he muttered. "You're now picking out curtains and new furniture for the recent widow?"

"It's what I do for a living, detective."

He gave me a disdainful look. "And it doesn't bother you that the husband of the woman who hired you was recently murdered." It wasn't a question.

"It bothers me, sure, but it certainly doesn't stop me from doing the job I was hired to do."

"Did it occur to you, Miss Gilbert, that you might be the key to the whole thing? The final straw that caused someone to break and take Mr. Axelrod's life?"

I gritted my teeth before I replied, "Detective O'Reilly, I don't need to have you try to lay a guilt trip on me."

"Is that what you think I'm doing?" He spread his hands a little in a gesture of innocence.

"I think you're trying to gauge my reactions to upsetting accusations, yes."

He drummed on the table, just two cycles this time, regarding me through both cycles. "It's just that I'm a bit puzzled by your lack of curiosity, Miss Gilbert. Seems to me it'd be human nature to want to know who put your kiddy picture there . . . inside a virtual stranger's wall." He added under his breath, "If everything happened like you claim."

"It *did* happen exactly as I claimed. Myra Axelrod told me the whole story this afternoon. Her husband, Randy, put the picture in the wall, so that I'd discover it there when I was remodeling. Myra's my birth mother, and years ago she put me up for adoption for my own protection. Apparently Randy was prone to violent behavior."

O'Reilly dropped his black Bic pen on the table as if too disgusted with me to be able to keep a grip on the implement. "Let me ask you something, Miss Gilbert. You just got through telling me you had no additional information regarding the ongoing investigation." He retrieved his pen and began to write furiously in his pad. "What do you call your last statement, then? Idle gossip?"

Oops. My cheeks grew warm. "I . . . told you about it now."

He stopped writing and returned to his staring-contest mode. He augmented his side of the contest with non-stop drumming. It was as though his fingers were doing a miniature performance of *Stomp.* At length he said, "Not right away, though. Not voluntarily. Why is that?"

"It seems to further incriminate Myra Axelrod in her husband's death. Apparently I'm related to them. Maybe part of me didn't want to be the one to have to get the police involved in all of that."

"So it appears." Once again he leveled his gaze at me and, for what felt like an eternity, said nothing. I grew to miss the tapping fingers; at least *that* provided a slight distraction. "Anything *else?*" he finally asked.

I felt like a ten-year-old being scolded by the school principal. It had been an oversight on my part not to tell him much sooner what Myra had said, but admitting to an officer of the law that I was slightly intoxicated didn't strike me as all that terrific an excuse for withholding information, even temporarily. "Not that I can think of."

He gave me a sour look and started paging through his notes. I rose and headed for the door.

Just as I grabbed the doorknob, O'Reilly asked, "Ms. Gilbert, what's your blood type?"

It was A-negative, but I turned toward him and asked, "Why?"

"I was just wondering if it was the same as the victim's . . . as Axelrod's. That's all."

"What was *his* blood type?"

Detective O'Reilly rose, leaned past me to open the door for me, and replied, "It's A-negative."

The ruddy-cheeked officer who'd accompanied us to the station now led me to the lobby, which was still dressed up in its paper-products' pseudo-cheer—a cheap veneer if there ever was one. Steve was waiting and mustered a smile as he got to his feet. He rushed over to grab the door for me, and we crossed the parking lot together in silence.

The air was chilly, but the black, moonless sky was still not releasing any snow. This was only my third winter here in Colorado, and I'd originally envisioned the sight of Christmas lights on crystalline snow against a breathtaking mountain backdrop. Friends who'd lived in Crestview much longer than I had warned me that there is almost never any snow either on the ground or falling on Christmas day; with less than a week till Christmas, the weather seemed to be holding true to form.

Relieved to see that my van—bullet holes and all— was still where I'd parked it, I muttered, "At least they didn't confiscate my vehicle as evidence." I turned to face Steve, his features cloaked in shadows, his hands buried in the pockets of his pea coat. "Do you know anything about blood types . . . how common they are, how they're inherited?"

"I just know a couple of random facts. O is the universal donor and, I think, the most common. AB is the universal receiver and the least common."

"Lots of people have type A blood, too, though, right? I remember that it's the second most common blood type. And A-negative?"

"I had a boring teacher in biology. I didn't pay much attention. Why?"

O'Reilly had made me feel like carpet lint. I couldn't bring myself to explain how miserable this was for me.

After eighteen months in her care, my genetic mother had chosen to give me up for adoption to "protect" me from her husband. Then she'd remained with "that monster" for more than twenty-five years. Wasn't nature supposed to infuse mothers with an unconditional love for their babies?

I unlocked my van. "It's not important. Good night, and thanks for . . . everything."

He chuckled a little. " 'Everything' would include . . . what, exactly?"

"For keeping me company while waiting for the police. And escorting me here."

"Yeah. That was downright princely of me." He headed toward his own van, three spaces down. "I'll follow you home, just in case the goon with the gun decides to take another potshot at your van."

Not even a professional bodyguard could truly prevent some maniac with a gun—and surely not one with the skills to dot the *i* in *Gilbert*—from taking me out. "No, thanks. I'll see you soon, though."

He pivoted and said over his shoulder, "Yeah. Great. Maybe next time we can *really* go for a classy evening and visit an *emergency* room together."

Once home, and after a perfunctory exchange of greet-ings with Audrey, who declared that she'd "decided to pack it in early tonight," I dug through every item of personal effects in the box in my closet. Going through my mother's things had been so painful for me immediately after her death that I'd never done a thorough job. I had some of her sheet music for the piano, although I couldn't play myself, and now I was careful to go through each one, page by page. Yet there was nothing—no birth certificate, no records from the adoption agency, no enlightening photographs stashed between the folds of music. There were also no hidden compartments in her jewelry box, no magic potions stored in her perfume bottle, no answers tucked inside the pockets of the coral cardigan she'd worn so often.

I shoved the box into the back of the closet, thoroughly annoyed with myself. I was now deliberately breaking the promise I'd made to Mom. I hadn't actually sought out Myra and Randy Axelrod, but my poking around for clues among her things was undeniably by conscious choice.

It would be so simple, now that I knew that I'd been born in this town, to call the county clerk and get a copy of my birth certificate. Detective O'Reilly was probably going to have that information in his hot, hairy hands five minutes after the clerk's office opened tomorrow morning. Or had he already done so? Perhaps he'd been sitting with me in that miserable room, drumming his fingers, knowing a piece of fundamental personal information about me that I myself wasn't privy to.

With Hildi watching me from her perch on my bed, I began to pace, outraged at the unfairness of it all. What was next in store for me? Only this morning, the *Crestview Sentinel* had run an update to the murder investigation. The brief article was almost an exact duplicate of one they'd published two days ago. Was some nosy reporter going to break the story? So far, my name had been mercifully absent from all news stories on Randy's death. Was that good luck about to end? Would I, along with this entire town, learn who my biological parents were from the newspaper, when it was revealed that the victim's long-estranged daughter had called 911?

Time was running out on me. It was either find out for myself once and for all who my parents were, or get the information crammed down my throat from a grouchy detective or the media. Despite my promise to my mother, it was now imperative that I find out once and for all who my biological parents were.

Myra's story just wasn't adding up for me. If Randy had been this dangerous "monster," why *would* she stay with him all those years, yet give up her child? The implication was that Randy *wasn't* my father. But *Randy* had been the one to find me. Why would he look for his *wife's* banished child?

Maybe *he* was my father but Myra was *not* my mother. Steve Sullivan was right: I *did* look remarkably like Emily Blaire; or at least we certainly shared more physical similarities than Myra and I did. Not that that proved anything. I'd been told at least a dozen times over the years that I was a dead ringer for this person or the next.

Myra had to have other old photographs of herself— pregnant with me, pictures of herself and me at the hospital maternity ward. I could ask to see them. And if that didn't work, I would call the county clerk to get my birth certificate.

The phone rang. The double-short ring indicated the call had been placed to my office number. Not wanting the shrill noise to wake Audrey, I answered quickly, and there was a pause. "Erin, hello. This is Jill McBride. I was expecting a machine to pick up. I didn't realize you'd be at your office this late."

Forcing myself to sound perky, I asked, "What can I do for you, Jill?"

"I have some decorating plans that I'd like to discuss with you."

If she wanted to bring me in after the fact to get rid of the mounted fish or redo Steve's elegant design, she was wasting her breath. "Are you thinking of redoing another room?"

"Not exactly. You mentioned the other day that you

decorate for holiday parties. We're throwing a New Year's Eve bash for some potential backers for Kevin's business. I was going to decorate the place myself, but then I thought, why should I take that on, when you do this sort of thing for a living?"

I was already booked to decorate for one New Year's party, but I could squeeze in a second one. "I'd be happy to do that for you. Let me grab my Palm Pilot." I made a few fist pumps as I headed to the foyer closet; I so loved getting new clients that, even as down as I'd been just moments earlier, it always made me feel as though the cutest boy in school had just asked me for a date. I snatched up my purse from its usual spot on the shelf and retrieved my Pilot. As I paged forward to December 31st, I asked, "Do you have a particular theme in mind, other than the obvious one?"

"The obvious?"

"The new year."

"Oh. That." She giggled. "By 'obvious,' I thought you meant, 'Give us your money.'"

I chuckled. "No, but I'm willing to bow to your wishes. I can string garlands with dollar bills if you'd like."

"Something more subtle, perhaps. Maybe just IOUs as door prizes."

"Have you hired a caterer?"

"Yes, they're from Denver. Super exclusive." She paused. "So much so that I've forgotten the name of their business. I'll give you their business card the next time we meet. You'll need to coordinate everything with them, I assume?"

"Yes. Some caterers bring their own bar carts and serving tables. How soon do you need an estimate from me?"

"Oh, I don't care about the precise amount. I want this to be extravagant and expensive. As they say, the way to get money is to spend money. Just so long as you spend two or three grand, which would, of course, not include the food and beverages, you're my new best friend."

"Easy enough," I said with a grin. My mind was already awhirl with images of crystal garlands and silver baubles that could transform the McBrides' home into an enchanting gala at the Ritz.

"I'm sure whatever you do will be simply *divine*." She added, "Myra tells me you and Steve have given her wonderful proposals for upgrading her interiors."

"Thanks. We're doing our best. We've got my next appointment with Myra tomorrow afternoon, as a matter of fact."

"That's wonderful. It's fascinating to watch how Myra Axelrod is breaking out of her cocoon, now that she's finally free of that monster."

That monster. My father. My grip tightened on the phone. With that one statement, Jill had brought my mood crashing back to the hardwood floor. Carefully I remarked, "Randy seemed a bit abrasive to me . . . though I only spent a brief time in his company."

"The man should have been in jail. He *would* have been, if I'd had any say in the matter. The number of times he put Myra in the hospital . . . it made you want to kill the bastard. And, it would appear, someone finally did just that."

Shortly after eight the next morning, Linda Delgardio returned my call. When I asked if we could "get together and talk off the record" for a few minutes, she warned me that there was no such thing as *off the record* in her line of work. She asked if I still wanted us to get together, which I assured her I did, then suggested that we meet in half an hour at the Major Grind, a coffee shop near the CU campus.

Linda had arrived ahead of me and had managed to claim one of the Major Grind's small, square tables. She gave me a warm smile and wave, which I returned and went directly to wait in line. She was in full uniform, and her long black hair was pulled back and pinned tightly against her scalp. The body English of the mostly college-aged patrons at surrounding tables indicated that they were leery in her presence; the self-consciousness that I felt around uniformed officers was clearly universal.

I got a cup of the house blend and joined her, exchanging hellos as I slipped into the bentwood chair opposite hers. "Erin," she exclaimed, her dark eyes sparkling, "my husband loves the crystal you helped me pick out for my in-laws. Thank you."

She'd bought four gorgeous red-wine glasses: oval-shaped bowls that felt sublime in one's palm, delicate stems, perfectly balanced. *What did it say about me that I remembered her purchase better than I did the woman herself? And I didn't even work at that store!* "You're welcome, Linda."

"Lucky for me that I caught your presentation. His mom's impossible to shop for, but like you said, 'Who can resist beautiful stemware'?"

Had I really said that? Yuk! I forced a smile. "Who, indeed?" *If the answer turned out to be Linda's mother-in-law, there went my one and only potential friendship within the Crestview police force.*

Stalling while I tried to figure out how to tactfully bring up my concerns about the murder case, I blew on the surface of my steaming beverage and took a tentative sip. This particular blend was too acrid for my tastes, yet

I hated the cloying sweetness of sugar in coffee. I should have opted for cocoa.

Linda, meanwhile, was guzzling her coffee. "I've been talking to some of my buddies at work. You turned a few heads there, let me tell you." I widened my eyes in alarm, but she chuckled and said, "In a good way, I mean. That's the thing about being a cop . . . all my work friends are real macho. You've already made something of a name for yourself . . . you're the only witness who's ever brought us a container of poison."

"Is *that* a good thing?"

She merely smiled and gave me hint of a shrug. She leaned back in her seat and regarded me. "So. Some creep fired bullet holes into the side of your van last night. Jeez. Someone's sure been running you through the ringer lately."

"No kidding." I tried to relax a little in my uncomfortable chair and breathed deeply of the delicious coffee aroma that enveloped us. "What makes it all the harder is that Detective O'Reilly seems to think I'm the devil incarnate. He makes me so nervous that I sound guilty even to *me*."

She chuckled again and nodded. "His nickname's 'Oh, *really?*'" Her voice did an uncannily accurate impression of the detective's skeptical intonations, and I laughed, too. "He conducts all his interviews that way."

"He does?" I felt a measure of relief. I took another sip of coffee, hoping to make my next question sound as casual as possible. "So . . . did he tell me the truth? Was Randy Axelrod poisoned by arsenic and not cyanide?"

She furrowed her brow and focused her attention on her beverage.

I went on. "Judging from the articles I've read in the *Sentinel*, Detective O'Reilly's being cagey to the reporters, too, about whether it was an arsenic or cyanide poisoning."

Linda still held her tongue. After a long pause, she set down her nearly empty cup and said, "This is what I meant when we spoke on the phone about our chat being on the record. All I can tell you is, you're right . . . officers *are* allowed to lie to suspects and even to witnesses if that helps us get answers."

I nodded, thinking: *Aside from the police, only the killer knows for sure if it was arsenic or cyanide.*

Linda continued. "Bottom line, this is O'Reilly's case. I can't divulge any facts that could hinder the investigation."

"Nor would I want you to. I have a pretty strong suspicion that . . ." I hesitated, feeling a little manipulative in trying to establish a sense of camaraderie with a woman I barely knew; my actions smacked of the times when new acquaintances first discovered I was a designer and—suddenly all a-bubble with enthusiasm—would invite me to their homes. "I think Randy Axelrod could have been my biological father. I certainly want whoever killed him put behind bars. Even though from all appearances Randy wasn't exactly . . ." Again, I hesitated. "Did Randy Axelrod have a criminal record of any kind?"

"Criminal record?"

"Spousal abuse."

She shook her head. Her expression was grim. "Not that I'm aware of, Erin."

Although I couldn't be certain that she was being honest with me, I had the strong feeling that she was. Myra, however, could have suffered her beatings in silence and never reported them. My questions weren't getting me anywhere. Still, I persisted.

"Linda, would it *really* mess up O'Reilly's case if I at

least knew my standing?" I took another quick sip; the coffee tasted a little less bitter now.

"Your standing?"

"I just want to know if I'm a chief suspect."

Gently she said, "I wouldn't worry too much about that if I were you, since you're innocent."

"It's easy to say 'don't worry . . . you're innocent,' " I snapped, "but when you're in that awful little room and you're getting barraged with questions about your role in a murder. . . . Last night, Detective O'Reilly volunteered information about Randy Axelrod's blood type, to test my reaction. Doesn't that mean he already *knew* Randy Axelrod was my father? Which also means my birth records are now part of Detective O'Reilly's file, right?"

She said nothing and her expression didn't change.

I waved a hand, which may as well have been holding a white flag. "I'm sorry, Linda. I know you can't answer that. It's extremely frustrating to have this police officer treat me like dirt and yet know more about my heritage than *I* do. It's like discovering someone has put a peephole in your dressing room wall."

"Erin." She leaned closer. "You seem like a really nice person. I wish you'd just happened to call me and none of this had happened to you, and we were able to chat freely, as friends." She squared her shoulders. "Right now—" She tapped her badge. "There's nothing I can say to you."

I nodded, more frustrated now than ever. I was close to tears. When I looked up from my cup, Linda was studying me.

"Erin, is there anything you want to tell *me*? Anything that might help us get the killer?"

I mulled her questions, but I'd told O'Reilly everything I knew. "Not really. Anyone in Randy's small circle of *friends*, for lack of a better word, could have murdered him."

She glanced at her watch, then stood up, draining the dregs from her cup. "I've got to get back." She handed me a business card. "I wrote my home address and phone on the back. If *Oh, really?* gets to you and you've thought of something helpful, I can be your go-between."

"Thanks, Linda."

She returned my smile. "Don't mention it. I hope that the next time we meet, it'll be during happier times for you."

"Me, too. Thanks."

She winked. "See ya."

I watched her leave, watched the other patrons sneak looks at her as she passed the plate-glass window to her squad car. Those same curious glances then shifted in my direction. I straightened and started to push back my chair. Only then did I realize what I had in my hands. I had snapped my balsa-wood coffee stirrer into tiny fragments.

chapter 18

> Although logic might tell us that a beautiful presentation doesn't improve the actual flavor of the feast, our tastebuds aren't governed by logic.
>
> —Audrey Munroe

I was surprised to hear Audrey rattling around in the house. By this time on a Tuesday morning, she was usually at the television station in Denver. I stashed my coat and purse in the closet and headed toward the kitchen to greet her, curious about what kind of domestic project she'd have under way today.

It was immediately obvious why she was home rather than at work. Her nose was red and her eyes puffy. Sans her usual elegant leisure wear, she wore a yellow terry-cloth robe, its pockets brimming with crumpled tissues. She wore no makeup and her usually flawless ash-blond hair had a severe case of bed head.

"Morning, Audrey. Feeling under the weather?"

She sneezed.

"Bless you."

"Head cold," she explained unnecessarily, her voice congested and gravelly. "This type of *disaster* is why we tape in advance."

She'd taken out every piece of stemware from the cabinets and was lining them up by height along the granite counter of her kitchen isle. At her feet, she had several more boxes of crystal.

"So you're . . . throwing an enormous cocktail party?"

She shook her head. "Research." She blew her nose. "We're discussing glassware tomorrow. I'll be good as new by then. I'm taking zinc lozenges. They'll knock this thing out of my system in no time." She slid a green-cellophane-wrapped lozenge toward me. "You'd better take one of these now, too, to keep from catching my cold."

"Too bad you got too late a start on the zinc yourself," I muttered, wondering about its effectiveness. I took a seat on a bar stool and stuck the lozenge in my mouth. An artificial lemon flavor waged a losing battle to cover up the metallic flavor. I said, "Bless you," to another sneeze, but she waved me off and grumbled, "Save your blessings for sometime when I really need them."

"I did a presentation on glassware at a store just two weeks ago, Audrey."

"I know." (Her words sounded more like "I dough.") "That's where I got the idea. I'm not feeling terribly creative this morning." She rounded the isle and sank into the bar stool beside me. "In fact, I can't even figure out where to begin." She looked at me with sad—and watery—puppy-dog eyes. It wouldn't be kind of me to ignore her hint that she needed some help.

"Well, whenever I do one of my glassware presentations, I start out by asking the audience to consider how they'd feel about going into a fancy restaurant and ordering a hundred-dollar bottle of French wine, only to have the sommelier serve their wine in a paper cup. And I tell them that the general guideline to identify a glass's function is that chilled, straight-up beverages are served in glasses designed to be held by the stem, room-temperature beverages use glasses that are held by the bowl, and iced beverages are served in large glasses with wide rims and are held near the top of the glass. As long as people keep in mind that the key is whether you want your palm warming the contents or not, it's all pretty much common sense."

Audrey blew her nose and said through the tissue, "That's how you can tell red-wine glasses from white."

"Right. The stem of a white-wine glass is taller and the bowl is smaller because white wine is chilled, so the glass is held by the stem. Plus red wine needs to breathe, which is why its bowl is less tapered than one for white wine."

"Whereas champagne glasses are tall, thin, and tapered, to retain the bubbles longer." Audrey sniffled. "That much I know."

"Right. I always recommend that people buy two

champagne glasses. It's such a minor expense, and I figure that'll encourage couples to partake in the occasional romantic any-occasion celebration."

She snorted. "That never worked on Fred . . . my third husband."

"The one who died?"

She nodded. "Heart attack. If he'd have drunk more wine and champagne, we'd be happily divorced today. Wine lowers cholesterol, you know."

"Mm-hmm. Mentioning that fact is a highlight of my glassware lecture." Unable to resist doing so, I flicked my index finger against the bowl of the nearest, tulip-shaped glass. My fingernail pinged on the glass, which emitted a lovely, pure bell-like sound. "Listen to that, Audrey." Holding the glass up to the light, I said, "I love your crystal. I have such a thing for glass . . . the way it catches the light . . . how it can be so smooth that it's soft to the touch, despite having such a hard surface."

Audrey started to have a minor coughing fit—perhaps to shut me up. When she quieted, I asked, "In any of your travels with the New York City Ballet, have you ever seen an opera singer actually shatter a glass?"

She coughed, then patted her chest. In a gravelly voice, she grumbled, "No, but I'm pretty sure my cough can dent a soda can." She popped another throat lozenge into her mouth. "Did you once sell glassware, along with curtain rods?"

"No, actually my mom ran a bar and restaurant in

line the rim of the margarita glass with salt . . . or daiquiri glasses with sugar."

She managed a sincere-looking smile, despite her illness. "How *do* you do that?"

"To salt the glass, you spread a tablespoon or two of salt on a plate and slice a fresh lime into small sections." Because she didn't have margarita glasses, I grabbed her cocktail glass to demonstrate with an imaginary lime and salt plate. "Dampen the glass rim by lightly running the fruit of a lime piece around the entire rim of the glass. Place the glass facedown in the salt." I gave my glass a twist on its virtual plate, then returned it to its upright position. "Lastly, pour your margarita into the salted glass."

"Do you use a lime for rimming sugar on a daiquiri glass?"

I shook my head. "I use the fruit of the drink itself, such as a strawberry for a strawberry daiquiri. Yummy."

She sneezed, then beamed at me. "Wonderful, Erin. This will be enormously helpful for both of us." She hopped to her feet, showing a sudden burst of energy.

"*Both* of us?" I repeated, suspicion bringing an edge to my voice as I watched her round the island. She opened an over-the-sink cabinet that had been ajar and removed a video camera.

"Yes, dear." She pressed a button on the camera. "I videotaped our conversation . . . as the first step toward helping you conquer your camera phobia."

Instantly livid, I grabbed the edge of my bar stool to

prevent myself from storming toward her. "So you've been faking sickness just to—"

"Not at all. I really *am* sick as a Labrador with a bad cold. I often tape my rehearsals. So when I heard you come in, I merely adjusted the position of the camera and pressed the record button." She wagged a finger at me. "Use whatever's going on in your life to best advantage in your performance—that's an old acting tip." She peered at my slack-jawed face. "You're very photogenic, Erin, and you'll make a terrific expert guest for occasional appearances on my show. And as I've told you before, it will be splendid publicity for your business, as well."

"But . . . but . . ."

"Just wait and see." She popped the tape out of the camera and presented it to me as though it were a trophy. "In a month or two, I'll have molded you into the Katie Couric of interior design!"

chapter 19

Later that afternoon, Myra was, for some reason, a bundle of frayed nerves as we sat on her sofa and looked at her photo albums. With each page that I turned, she ducked her head and peered anxiously on the flip side, then relaxed momentarily. These particular pictures were from five years ago. I'd asked to see this house as it looked when she'd first moved in, which can be insightful for my designs and, in this case, might allow me to ease into asking to see pictures of myself as a newborn.

"This was at a barbeque more than four years ago," Myra said of the current spread. "It rained, so we moved everything inside."

"You'd never know it was that long ago. Everything looks exactly the same. You had that nice All-Clad stainless-steel teakettle back then, I see."

"That was a housewarming present from the McBrides, just for moving across the street," she replied. "It probably cost more than all of my cookware and utensils combined. But all you have to do to tell it was four years ago is look at how much darker my hair was. Randy forbade me to color it. Maybe now I'll indulge myself."

"I don't know if you should," I said honestly. "It looks nice."

She primped a little. "Thank you, Erin, but white hair on a woman is just not appreciated in our society. Maybe I'll dye it blond. I've always wanted to be a blonde, like Jill."

With Myra so uneasy, I flipped through two more pages of shots from this same party, which showed the six of them—the Axelrods, McBrides, and Hendersons. Every room was identical to how it looked today—just with four or five fewer years of wear and tear on the house and all the occupants. For three couples who claimed to despise one another, there were a lot of sincere-looking smiles.

As I turned the next page, Myra snatched the album from my grasp and slammed it shut. But not before I caught a glimpse of a photograph which stunned me. It was of Myra with a black eye. She'd been holding the camera herself, at arm's length. "We're getting into more recent history now, which won't do you any good as far as the house goes," she explained.

What a bizarre picture to preserve in an album, along with vacation shots and mementos from happier times! Had Myra kept the shot in this album as some sort of passive-aggressive warning to Randy never to hit her again? I shuddered.

My thoughts raced as Myra put away her album. Myra and Kevin might have been lovers. A bottle of arsenic had been found in Kevin's workshop. Could he have grown tired of waiting for his lover's husband to pass away and decided to hasten things? Had he been willing to commit murder and leave his wealthy wife for Myra?

"Could I see some of your . . . earlier albums?" I asked.

She gave me a warm smile. "Of course you can." She grabbed another album. "This is clear back from when Randy and I first got married." She handed me the album and sank into the seat beside me.

Her nervousness was now gone as I scanned the first few pages of these pictures—wedding photos. I thought I glimpsed a little of myself now in Randy's young face. He'd been trim then, and athletic-looking. In one shot in particular—his head was tilted and he was laughing— the resemblance was striking.

"Do you have any baby pictures of me in here? I've never seen pictures of myself as an infant."

She frowned and said quietly, "Randy destroyed them. All of them that he knew about, that is. I'd hidden a couple . . . that one that you discovered in my chemistry textbook, and the one that Jeannie took with you standing by the umbrella stand. Randy must have found that one." Her voice was thick with emotion, and her eyes suddenly brimmed with tears. "I'm so sorry, Erin! He claimed the pictures of you were too upsetting for me to have around the house." She took the album from me. "All the while, *he* was the one who couldn't stand to have photographs of a child who wasn't—" She broke off and rose, stuffing the album back in the bookcase along with the others.

I *had* to have been his child; the matching blood types and facial characteristics between Randy and me were impossible to refute. What other ending could there *be* to that sentence—*who wasn't cute? Blond? Bilingual? Worthy?* Too confused and tense to remain seated, I stood up as well. "Who wasn't *what*?"

She shook her head and said quietly, "I shouldn't have gotten into this subject, Erin. It's too painful."

"Who wasn't *his*? Is that what you were about to say?"

Myra frowned and nodded. She balled her fists. "I never should have married that man in the first place. But you just can't believe how easy it is to settle for things, Erin. How you can keep telling yourself that things will improve . . . that they're not really so bad." She released a halting breath. "It was just a fling, but that's what opened my eyes. I should have run away before I had you. After all, Jeannie made it as a single mom. She even managed to buck the odds and get approval to adopt you."

Myra got that sad yearning in her eyes again as she looked at me. "You were just a baby when you were taken away from me. I thought you'd be gone forever . . . but here you are. I tried to believe that you'd remember me. You weren't even two by the time Jeannie graduated from CU and left for New York. That's when I lost track of you. But Jeannie and I agreed it was best kept that way—no contact whatsoever."

"Why?"

She spread her arms. "Fear of reprisal from Randy. He forbade me to contact you, ever. At the time . . . I didn't dare defy him. You'd recently had that accident, which gave you the scar under your chin."

I ran my thumb along the underside of my chin. My scar there was tiny and not noticeable.

"You'd slipped on some ice and landed so hard you needed stitches, poor thing. I was hysterical—demanded they do a blood test. I guess I actually thought you might need a transfusion. Anyway, that's when we both found out that . . . that Randy—my husband—wasn't your real father."

"I see," I murmured, though none of this was making any sense. Randy's and my blood types were the same. Myra was lying. It was impossible for blood tests to have revealed that Randy was *not* my biological father. She sank into the turquoise chair; shaking, I reclaimed my perch on the sofa. The slate-colored walls of this ugly room were closing in on me.

"I never told Kevin about you," Myra said wistfully.

"*Kevin?*" My stomach turned. All those leering looks he'd given me! "Are you saying that Kevin McBride is my . . ."

She nodded. "Kevin was a student of mine at CU. In my Intro to Chemistry class. Randy and I were having troubles. Already. If only I'd listened to my heart then . . ." She sighed. "But Kevin was just a kid. *I* was the married lady. It was my fault, not his. I never even told him that he was your father."

I rubbed at my aching temples, struggling to make sense of this, and failing. "So Randy knew all along that . . . that you'd had a child with Kevin McBride? And you lived just a couple of houses down the street from one another?"

"No. Randy never knew who your father was, just that he was a former student of mine. After I quit at CU, Kevin and I stayed away from each other for many years. He claimed it was just a coincidence that he and Jill happened to buy a house in the neighborhood some fifteen years ago." She fidgeted with the hem of her skirt. "Kevin and I had our chance a long time ago. Despite the way it looked when you . . . saw us together, we're simply good friends. Now *he's* married and I'm alone. But I'm happy this way. It's what's best for everyone."

"I suppose so," I muttered. My stomach—and my thoughts—were topsy-turvy.

"Erin, you wouldn't believe the excuses I had to make up to explain giving up my own child. We started telling people that it was *me* who was too unsound mentally to . . . to handle taking care of a child. Even though it was Randy's fault—*Randy's* violent behavior—all along. You can't imagine how horrible it was."

"It must have been," I mumbled automatically. But all I could think of was how preposterous her whole story was. Surely the truth had to be the polar opposite of what she was now telling me; I had to be *Randy's* daughter, and not Myra's: the blood types proved it. Was she crazy? Had my reappearance somehow provoked her to kill my biological father?

"I hated Randy so much for forcing me to give you away. You were just a baby! You didn't choose your parents or who you were going to live with! It was one thing to take it out on me, but I couldn't risk his taking out his anger on you, too."

I wanted desperately to get out of the conversation, out of this house. A matching desperation—for forgiveness—was apparent in Myra's pleading eyes. I obliged and said, "You did the right thing, Myra. The only thing you could do."

Myra started sobbing. She cried, "I'm so glad you understand!" She moved over to the sofa beside me, pulled me into a tight hug, and murmured, "Not a single day has gone by when I haven't thought of you, hoped and prayed that you were all right."

"Thanks," I muttered hollowly.

"I'm so glad you've come back into my life. Whatever else Randy did to me, at least he found you and brought you back to me."

"Yes, but . . . right now I kind of need to get going." I needed to run from this crazy woman. "This is a work day for me, after all. . . . Christmas is coming and . . ."

"Of course." Grabbing a tissue from her skirt pocket, she dried her eyes. In a pitiful voice, she went on. "We're both grown women now. I'm not expecting you to fill in the gap that my husband made for me more than twenty-five years ago. You're no longer my little girl, and you never will be."

In a daze, I made my way to the door. Only once before had I felt this numb: when my mother had died and my body and my heart had gone on autopilot.

"Take care, Myra. I'll be back tomorrow morning, with Steve, just as we scheduled. We'll show you our presentation boards then."

She was studying me with a peculiar look on her face. "Erin, I didn't kill him, if that's what you're thinking. I would never kill him or anyone else. It had gotten simple, our lives together, finally . . . pleasant, even. His heart condition seemed to mellow him out. Life-threatening illnesses have a way of doing that. We'd ridden out the bad times. We were as happy together as we'd ever been."

"I'm glad," I said impassively.

"So, I'll see you tomorrow, then?"

"Bright and early. Or at least early. It's looking a little cloudy these days. The weather, I mean." God, but I couldn't think straight; my words were coming out all chop suey.

"Maybe we'll have a white Christmas for once," Myra said absently. "That would be so nice. Wouldn't it? Do you like Christmas?"

"Yes. It's my favorite holiday." I forced a smile. "See you tomorrow."

My heart was pounding. At least I'd finally made it out the door. I took a couple of deep breaths and steadied myself. I glanced across the street. A white four-door Impala was parked in Carl's driveway again. Emily's car. Emily Blaire, whom I resembled physically.

With my head spinning, I made my way across the street. It was possible that Myra was watching me, but I wasn't about to look back to see. There was nothing to lose at this point that hadn't already been lost; I had to talk to Emily Blaire.

Randy and Emily could have had the fling that resulted in my birth. If so, maybe the sight of me, of her husband's out-of-wedlock child now grown up, had pushed Myra over the edge to murder her husband.

A second possibility hit me as I reached Carl's porch. Carl had once said that his wife was having an affair with his neighbor *again*. What if those love letters were indeed from Randy—not to his current wife, but rather to his ex-wife? Taylor, Emily's son, could have found those letters in her house at some point and put them in Carl's wall for some reason. And Carl might, upon their discovery, have learned that his beloved Emily and his one-time friend Randy had been lovers.

Carl could have been incapable of hiding how greatly this news had upset him. So he'd covered his reaction by *pretending* that he thought the letters were from Debbie.

I rang Carl's doorbell.

Had Carl murdered Randy? Had the letters revealed that I was the child of his ex-wife, Emily, and his now-despised neighbor? Had he become so enraged when he learned this that he'd murdered my father?

Emily opened the door. She was wearing her coat—a chocolate-brown microfiber parka. The strap of her tan Naugahyde purse was slung over one shoulder, and her keys were in her right hand. She paled a little at the sight of me, but opened the storm door as well. "Erin. Hello. Are you okay?"

"I'm fine. I just . . . feel a little sick to my stomach. Must have been something I ate. I'll be fine, though. Really."

She searched my eyes. Hers were a deep brown, just like mine. "You should take some ginger. There's a type of ginger tea that works wonders for settling upset stomachs. I know Randy used to have some. Myra probably still has some of it in her kitchen."

I forced a smile. "I'm feeling a bit better already. It's nothing. Really."

She gave a nervous glance over her shoulder but remained in the doorway, donning a smile. "I was just about to head home. Carl's working at home today. In Debbie's basement office. His mood's finally improving. You can go on downstairs if you—"

I shook my head. "I was actually coming over to talk to you."

She met my eyes, and the forced cheer seeped from her face. "I see. I guess . . . we're overdue for a conversation, actually. I have some things to discuss with you as well."

I heard footsteps on the walkway behind me, and quickly turned. Myra wasn't wearing her cardigan sweater or a coat, and her breath was forming little clouds of condensation.

"Hello, Myra," Emily said pleasantly.

"Emily." Myra's voice sounded ice cold, yet she asked, "How are you?"

"I'm fine, thanks. It's Carl who's not doing so well. He's paying the price for being such a hothead. I'm sure you've already heard this, but he managed to fracture bones in his hand and his foot. He's right downstairs in the office, if you need to speak to him."

"Uh, yes. Thanks. I wanted to ask him something, and . . . I didn't realize you were here."

Emily shifted her vision to me. "Erin, maybe you and I could go for a stroll around the pond?"

"That sounds good," I replied. Just to the north of the neighborhood was a pond with a surrounding jogging trail.

"On second thought," Myra said, her voice becoming shrill, "my question for Carl can wait. Let me grab my coat and I'll come with you. Erin, I had some more ideas about the house that we should discuss right away before I forget."

"Emily and I were just about to have a private conversation, actually, Myra." Despite my intention to be gentle, my need to be away from her made me curt.

"Oh." Myra's face fell.

"I'll stop by before I leave, though, and we can discuss your ideas then."

"That's okay," she said, her voice deflated. "You're obviously too busy for me. We'll talk when you and Steve come tomorrow."

"Good seeing you again, Myra," Emily said, gracious despite Myra's bizarre behavior. Myra hadn't even maintained her pretense of wanting to ask Carl a question.

Myra gave Emily a long look. "Should I be welcoming you to the neighborhood? You're not moving in with Carl again, are you?"

"No, of course not. I was simply helping him out a little. He asked me to run some errands for him and grocery shop. He's not terribly handy around the kitchen even when all his limbs are fully functional."

"That's true, I suppose. That was one thing he and Randy had in common. Though I don't need to tell *you* that."

Another hint that it was possible that I was Randy and

Emily's child. Quite an incestuous little community of "friends." "See you tomorrow morning, Myra," I said.

She gave me a pinched smile. "Yes. I'll be looking forward to it."

Feeling Myra's eyes on me as we walked away, Emily and I headed off together toward the pond. "How did you get to know Randy and Myra?" I asked her. "I thought Carl and Debbie only moved near them five years ago."

"They did. But I met Randy through work many years before that." She gave me a sad smile.

"You knew one another from work? Do you write for *Denver Lifestyles* or something?"

"No. I worked as an aerobics instructor for Randy at his fitness studio."

"Randy owned a fitness studio?"

"Four, actually, before he sold them. Ironic, since he let himself get so out of shape."

"How long ago was this, when you worked for him?"

She hesitated. "I suppose it must have been at least twenty-five years ago, come to think of it. Hard as that is for me to believe." Although she, too, kept her voice light, her fists were clenched tightly as we walked side by side. "Why?"

Mentally I screamed at myself: *Ask if she's your mother.*

"Myra claims that she's my biological mother."

Emily made no reply. Her jaw was now clenched as tightly as were her fists.

"Do you know if that's true?"

"If Myra says it is, why would you doubt her?" Her tones were clipped, and she didn't look at me.

We'd reached the pond. Some less-ravaged part of my mind could still recognize and appreciated the beauty of the place. The water had iced over in a shade of pearly white that matched the puffs of condensation of our breaths. The wispy shapes of the now-dormant grasses and weeds—thistles, cat-o'-nine-tails, milkweed—stood in resonating contrast to the backdrop of snowcapped mountains and the darkening sky.

"Myra's story doesn't make sense," I replied abruptly. "My blood type and Randy's match, yet she claims he wasn't my father."

She stopped walking. I paused as well, and our gazes met. "My son, Taylor, spoke to me about this already, and I talked it over with Carl. We're all in agreement. You've got to leave us alone, Erin. For your own good, as well as everyone else's."

I gaped at her. "What do you mean, 'leave us alone'? All I've done is accept a couple of clients and try to do my job to the best of my ability."

She swallowed hard. The chilly breeze ruffled her brown shoulder-length hair. "I realize that, Erin. I'm not saying that you've done anything wrong. But someone is playing a very dangerous game with you, and we're all getting sucked into it. You're the only one who can put a stop to it."

"How?"

"By walking away from the job at Myra's."

I grimaced.

"Please, Erin. I'm begging you."

I was simply in this too deep to stop now.

Emily pleaded, "I don't have a whole lot of money, but I will take out a loan if I have to. I'll pay you double whatever your personal profit will be from Myra's job."

"Why is this so important to you?"

"My son's getting in over his head, thanks to this god-forsaken neighborhood! I know Taylor's a grown man, and I should let him make his own decisions, but last time I did that, he wound up in jail!"

"For dealing drugs. Which I never touch. So how

could my working in the neighborhood possibly hurt him?"

She pursed her lips. "It's too chilly for a stroll. Let's head back." Without waiting for my input, she whirled and started back down the path.

"It was *you*, wasn't it, Emily? You're my mother." There was a hitch in her step, but she kept going. I had to trot to catch up with her.

"No." She shook her head. "Myra and Randy raised you till you were eighteen months old. Then they worked out a private adoption."

"Was Randy my father? Did the two of you have an affair? And then he and Myra agreed to raise me as their own, but it didn't work out?"

Each word of mine seemed to hurt Emily physically, and she wrapped her arms across her chest. She picked up her pace. "Randy's dead now. Let the past alone, Erin. Leave Myra's job. You're very talented. There will be other opportunities for you."

"I can call around, check out the story myself. Even though the adoption was twenty-six years ago, there are records."

She stopped walking and turned to face me. "Please don't."

She stood there for a moment in silence, then strode toward a sandstone bench overlooking the pond. I followed at a short distance. She sat and faced the water. Though she said nothing for what had to be two or three minutes, I stayed a step or two away and waited. Finally, her voice deflated, she said, "Myra is telling you the truth, to the extent that she's capable."

"So she *is* my birth mother?"

"No. But she's managed to convince herself that she is, for half of her life now."

With a heavy sigh, Emily reached into her purse and

extracted the necklace and the letters. Carl hadn't burned them after all. She held them out and said, "These belong to you, Erin. The letters were written to you by your mother—by me—while I was still pregnant with you. Randy promised me all those years ago that he'd give them to you on your eighteenth birthday."

chapter **20**

My heart leapt to my throat. Unanticipated emotions struck me with tsunami-like force, and I started to cry. I dropped down onto the bench beside Emily Blaire. Staring at the letters and necklace still in her hands, I whispered, "Carl gave those to you?"

"Not exactly. Carl told me he'd burned them in a drunken rage, but I know him too well to believe that, and I finally found his new hiding spot this morning. That's why I've been so eager to help him out these past few days, so I could search his house for them."

It felt wrong to take the letters, somehow. As if, once they were in my possession, all of my relationships would deteriorate the way the three households had. "How did you even know he had them?" I asked.

"Taylor told me that the last time he'd seen them, they were on the floor next to Randy, while Taylor was trying to resuscitate him." She shoved the letters and necklace in my lap, and I grabbed them before the breeze could scatter them. "Taylor didn't recognize my handwriting at first. I was just eighteen at the time, and my writing's changed. The cameo is a family heirloom and was the most valuable thing I owned. It was all I had to give you."

She paused as if expecting me to respond, but I couldn't. Besides, what could I say? *Thank you . . . it's just what I always wanted?*

"Randy insisted he and his wife would give you a much better life than I ever could. That his wife had recently lost a baby and couldn't have another one, but they were having trouble with the adoption agency. I was just too young and naïve to ask myself *why* they were having trouble. So we agreed I'd give up my parental rights and never see you again. In exchange, Randy promised me he would give you every possible advantage in life, and that he'd tell you about me and give you my letters when you turned eighteen. I was so stupid to believe him!"

So. My birth parents had shuffled me around like an odd-looking table lamp that didn't quite blend with their home decor. I dried my eyes. "If it's any consolation, Emily, my mother was a terrific parent, so everything's worked out just fine." *Although, truth be told, I have some problems with intimacy, thanks to my father deserting us when I was twelve.* But there was no need to make her feel as cruddy as I did right now.

"That's good to hear, Erin. I'm really glad. You know, if it hadn't been for a few strange twists of fate, I might never have known that you weren't still with the

Axelrods. If my ex-husband Carl hadn't bought my ex-lover's house . . ."

I clicked my tongue. "You really think it was a twist of fate that Carl bought Randy's house . . . not something that Randy contrived?"

She winced. "At your age, it's probably hard for you to believe this, but he was once handsome and charming. I knew he was married, but he told me they had an open marriage, and I wanted to believe him. When I got pregnant, though, Myra suddenly became this tragic figure — a woman who wanted to be a mother more than anything in the world and was willing to forgive her husband and raise his out-of-wedlock child as her own." She rubbed at her eyes. "I tried hard to forget about you. I moved to Denver and had a fiasco of a first marriage that resulted in Taylor. I met Carl shortly after my divorce."

"Carl knew about all of this, right? He had to have known those letters were written by you and that—"

"There were gaps in what Carl knew," Emily interrupted. "I only told him that I'd been involved with a married man and that I'd had a baby I put up for adoption. Carl didn't find out Randy was my baby's father until recently . . . a month or two ago. Supposedly, he and Debbie got into a row, and she told him in anger."

"How did *Debbie* know?"

"I'm not sure. Debbie and I are not exactly close friends. I'm hardly in a position to ask."

I risked only a darting glance at the letters in my lap, still feeling that they were cursed. "Why did you sign them with the letter *M*?"

She pursed her lips and said nothing. Finally, in a half-whisper, she replied, "I was all of nineteen . . . trying to write to my unborn baby, who I knew, by the time she read my words, would've grown into a young woman my age who I'd—" She stopped, swallowed hard, and said through tears, "Erin, I knew we'd never see each other, never know each other. I couldn't bring myself to sign 'Mom' and was sure you'd hate me as 'Emily.' Signing as *M* was all I could manage."

I turned away and concentrated on breathing in and out to keep myself from sobbing. I believed every word she was telling me, but there were still some ragged edges to her story. After a minute or two, I said quietly, "Carl told me just the other day that he suspected these letters were Debbie's . . . perhaps written to her by Randy."

She frowned. "He read them and knew that they were from me to you . . . to my daughter, that is. He hasn't figured out yet that *you're* that daughter. Once he found out that Randy was the 'other man' from my past, he managed to convince himself that Randy had destroyed our marriage and was the culprit behind his current marital woes, and that now *Debbie* was having an affair with him."

"Which she wasn't? Having an affair with Randy, I mean?"

"I doubt it."

I swept the hair out of my eyes impatiently. "Everyone's lied to me from day one. Myra said I was her and *Kevin's* daughter!"

"Well, that's probably exactly what she wants to believe."

I stared at the letters and necklace in my lap. "Is this why Randy was killed? Is it because of me?"

Emily got up and gave my shoulder a quick squeeze. "I don't know, Erin. But . . . please don't take that chance. Cut off ties with Myra now and walk away from this job. For your own good, as well as mine and Taylor's."

It felt as though I were trapped inside a tornado, battered and flung about helplessly by forces that far exceeded my strength. Despite my inner turmoil, I managed a bland: "I'll think about it."

Taylor Duncan was my half brother. What a jarring discovery *that* was. I would have to content myself with the notion that he'd inherited many of his bad traits from his father's side. "Does Taylor know that we're half siblings?"

Emily nodded, her expression grim. "Taylor saw you slip the baby picture into your pocket. He put two and two together and confronted me."

Putting two and two together must have been a major challenge for someone who equated counting five boards with higher math. "He figured everything out just from seeing the letters and the picture?"

"I'd worn the cameo for my high school graduation picture, which has been sitting on my mantelpiece at home for years now."

I thought back to Taylor's statement the other night as he left my office. "Does Taylor think Randy hid the necklace and photograph there so that *he* would discover it?"

"Don't go there, Erin," she snapped. She glared down at me. "Let's get one thing clear right away. My son had nothing whatsoever to do with Randy's death."

Surprised and offended, I said, "I'm not suggesting that he did."

We walked back in stormy silence. I slipped the letters and cameo in my satchel and watched as Emily drove away. Neither of us waved.

Good God, but I had no idea what to do now! One thing was certain—I was putting the letters in a safe place and not so much as glancing at a single word unless and until I felt good and ready to read them. I hadn't been allowed to make one choice regarding my own fate ever since I'd started working here, but at least I could determine when and where—*and if*—I read a handful of letters from the woman who'd given birth to me. That meant that I was not giving them to the police anytime soon—not even to Linda Delgardio.

This was one of those times when I most needed to be involved in a solid relationship, but I wasn't. My two closest friends in Colorado were currently vacationing in New Zealand. I was alone in my little rowboat, adrift at sea, enduring a horrid storm.

Even so, Myra Axelrod had to be hurting worse than I was. She'd realized that Emily would tell me the truth during our private conversation. Myra must be panicking—terrified that I'd hate her forever for lying to me. She must have a tenuous grasp on reality to begin with, or she never would have spun those lies in the first place. It might break her heart if I did what I so dearly longed to do right now—get into my van and drive away.

I swapped my satchel for my purse from the van but then stood on the sidewalk, frozen with indecision. I was torn: I felt desperately sorry for Myra, but even so, I was angry at the woman and more than a little repulsed.

Ahead of me, Jill McBride was crossing the street. She was wearing a beautiful thick white wool coat that probably weighed a good third of what she did. She was all smiles as she approached.

"Erin, I spotted you out here. I thought I'd bring you the caterers' card I promised."

"Thank you." She gave me the card and waited as I clipped it onto my Day-Timer's calendar.

"My daughters are home from college, and I want to show them off to you. Why don't you come over now just for a minute? Just to say a quick hello?"

Much as I didn't feel up for meeting anyone right now, I could mindlessly bluff my way through a few minutes of idle chatter at the McBrides' house and give my-self time to calm down so that I could do the right thing by poor Myra. I forced a smile. "I'd love to. Thank you."

As we started up the walkway, the garage door opened, and someone backed out in a silver Lexus. Two very at-tractive young women—both blondes—were inside. The driver rolled down the window as we approached and said, "Mom, we're going over to Kelsey's house."

"Honey, I wanted you to meet Erin Gilbert. She's an interior designer and is helping me decorate for the party."

"Hi," the two girls said simultaneously. Their faces were identical. "It's nice meeting you," the passenger called out. "See you later, Mom," added the driver as she slid the window shut. They drove off.

"Well, that was certainly a waste of time," Jill said with a cheery laugh. "However, since I dragged you over here, you might as well let me show you the portion of the house that you'll be decorating."

"Sure. Though I'll need to take a second look when I've had more time to mull over my ideas." *And give my-self time to formulate some,* I added to myself.

"Of course." Numbly, I followed her inside. She changed into her indoor shoes, and I removed mine. Jill was wasting her time showing me her home in my cur-rent frame of mind; there was no way I would be able to remember a single thing I'd see.

She gestured with both arms to indicate the foyer and said, "Now here, of course, I want something really eye-catching, right from the first moment our guests step in-side."

"As well as something to draw them into the living room."

"Precisely. I'll, of course, have a butler and maid for

the evening." She laughed. "I can always instruct them to give the guests a good shove, right into the living room."

Kevin, talking on a cordless phone, entered the room. He looked at his wife, saying into the phone, "Yeah, she just got home." He put his hand over the mouthpiece. "It's Rachel. She says it's urgent."

Jill sighed. In conspiratorial tones she told me, "This is one of our biggest benefactors, so I have to take this. I'm so sorry."

"That's all right. We can set an appointment and—"

"Kevin, be a doll and take Erin on a tour of the public areas."

"Public areas?"

She clicked her tongue. "Show her where we're going to host the New Year's party," she snarled, and yanked the phone out of his hand. All brightness and cheer, she trilled, "Rachel! Darling! How is Bixby?"

As she wandered out of earshot, Kevin said with a roll of his eyes, "A snippy cocker spaniel," as if in explanation. Presumably Bixby, not Rachel, was the ill-tempered dog. "Let's see. We're inviting a hundred fifty, so we'll probably have about a hundred guests."

"They're not going to have to take their shoes off, are they?"

"No. For large parties, Jill just grins and bears it, and we have the carpet cleaners come do their thing the following day."

"Good. I had visions of needing to incorporate two hundred shoes into my decorations."

He chuckled. "The place would look like a bowling alley. Come on."

The floor plan was ideal for hosting a large party and Sullivan's room would be a great hang-out spot for the men, with its lack of breakable or soft items. There were plenty of open spaces where a crowd could gather for group toasts or functions. There was a circular flow throughout the home, with the ability to enter a room from one direction and leave in the other. The house had plenty of sitting areas, an enormous kitchen and dining room, and that all-important covered back porch for smokers.

Getting more into the spirit of the task than I would have imagined possible, I envisioned a unifying color palette for decorations. I wanted to stay away from the too-common red and green for a holiday party, but reds are an excellent color choice for parties—the warm hues stimulate appetites and conversations, plus they enhance skin tones. Maybe red and silver in the main rooms . . . Also, scarlet was a color that invited people to spend money and take risks. Why else would you see so much of it in Vegas?

We circled through the public rooms and returned to the front room. Kevin gave a nod to Jill, who was now clucking sympathetically at whatever the caller was saying, and he led me up the stairs. "Our cloakroom will be upstairs, and I'm sure we'll have the occasional guest who will want to nose around and pretend to need the bathroom."

"With a hundred people eating and drinking, they probably *will* need to find an open bathroom."

"Were you thinking of decorating up here, too?" he asked.

"Yes. But on a much smaller scale. If there were no decorations except in the public areas, for your guests it would be a bit like peeking backstage and seeing that the scenery is two-dimensional. But if there are any rooms you truly don't want guests to enter, it's fine to simply lock them. Or you can decorate over the doorknob so that it's clear that the door's not intended to be opened."

Kevin nodded. "Now that the twins are home, they'd probably like to make their rooms off-limits."

He opened a door to one bedroom and brushed against my breast as he supposedly tripped on the carpet. I hadn't had anyone else over the age of eighteen pull such a ridiculous grope move on me.

"Whoops. Automatic reaction," he said with a sly grin. "Lost my balance. Good thing *those* were there." He wiggled his eyebrows and eyed my breasts.

In no mood to take any guff, I snarled, "You know, I should warn you that *I* have an automatic knee-to-the-groin reaction. I wouldn't suggest trying that on me a second time."

Jill entered the room. Those indoor shoes of hers certainly made her light on her feet. By the expression on her face, it was obvious that she'd overheard my threat to Kevin.

"Rachel's all handled," she said evenly to her husband. She turned to me, her eyes chilly. "Has Kevin shown you everything you'd like to see, Erin?"

And then some, I thought. "Yes."

While escorting me downstairs, she referred to her Palm Pilot and said, "Let's you and I meet again at ten a.m. on the morning after next, shall we?"

"Let me check my schedule." I stepped into my shoes, grabbed my own electronic calendar from my purse, and said, "That works. We can kick around some ideas then."

"I'll be looking forward to it."

That makes one of us. This neighborhood was a nicely decorated hellhole, and my brief encounter with Kevin had been my kick in the rear to get out of here. I needed to get home to my marble fireplace, afghan, and cat. I headed out the door, vowing to decide about Myra and her design job tomorrow.

Myra, however, was pacing alongside my van. She

looked at me with hollow eyes and asked, "Did you have a nice talk with Emily Blaire?"

"Yes, thanks," I murmured.

"Good. That's good. It's lucky, because she's not always all that lucid. She's on medication, you know. Zoloft or something, I believe Carl told me. She has a tendency to . . . to fabricate when she's under stress."

"Huh. That's too bad." *Please, God, let me just get home.*

I tried to unlock the door to my van. Myra grabbed my hand and pressed it between her palms. Her own hands felt clammy despite the chill in the air. Her pleading gaze made it apparent how desperate she was to connect with me. "Erin. Jeannie did the only thing she could to keep him away from you—moving clear across the country with you. Randy had found you again. I couldn't let him hurt you again. He nearly drowned you as a baby. If I hadn't come into the bathroom right when I did and pulled you out of the tub . . . I did it for you." She squeezed my hand painfully. "I know it doesn't look like it to see how he lived, but Randy had amassed a small fortune from selling his business."

"The fitness studios he used to own?"

"Yes. So you mustn't worry about your inheritance. I'm contacting my lawyer and getting Randy's and my will changed to leave everything to you."

"My *inheritance*? Why would I . . ." I paused when I saw the tears in her eyes. "*Please* don't contact your lawyer about the will, Myra. That's just not something we should be worrying about. I don't want any money that I haven't earned."

"Oh, but you *did* earn every dime, Erin. You wouldn't even be alive today if . . ." Her taut features crumbled, and she burst into sobs. "He didn't mean to try to drown you, Erin. He was *drinking*. Sometimes he had problems with the alcohol. To tell you the truth, I did, too. Sometimes the booze was all that seemed to help me get through the day, living with one man, loving another man I knew I could never have. I had *you* to take care of, and that meant things were never going to change. He never meant to actually hurt you, Erin. And he never would have if it weren't for the problem he sometimes had with drinking. It was just an accident. Believe me, Erin. It was an accident."

I knew she was reversing *her* role for Randy's—who was no longer here to defend himself—but I couldn't help but feel horribly sorry for her. With all the sincerity I could muster, I said, "I'm sure it *was* just an accident. If he were here today, I would forgive him to his face, Myra. I swear to you, I would forgive him." Her eyes were searching mine with such desperation that I continued. "At times, we all fall way short of who we want to be. Every one of us does. So you've got to find a way to forgive as well."

She gathered herself, pursed her lips, and nodded, but then backed away, pivoted, and walked straight into her house without a backward glance. Dear God, what an odd woman! Had my words gotten through to her at all?

I drove toward Audrey's house, willing myself to keep going and act as though my heart hadn't just been ripped out. My brain was filled with images of newscasts with distraught family members telling the TV journalists, "I just need to know what happened." Suddenly, knowing the truth seemed vastly overrated. I wish with all my heart that I'd never taken Carl's assignment in the first place.

O'Reilly's disdainful words and attitude while discussing my job came back to me. Was I kidding myself by thinking my line of work was anything more than trivial indulgences? What possible good could ever come from making someone's wrecked household slightly prettier? In Myra's case, wasn't I just slapping a bright yellow coat of paint onto cracked walls and a crumbling foundation?

I parked in front of Audrey's house and stopped to really look at its stately exterior. For once, I desperately needed Audrey to be home. Sure, she hadn't shown much interest in my life, but *I* was the one who'd been stingy with personal information. Didn't I need to at least give her a shot at listening to my woes before I wrote her off as self-absorbed? Clutching my briefcase and its precarious contents, I trotted up the slate walkway and unlocked the door. The house felt uninhabited, but I called out, "Audrey?" just in case.

No answer. My heart sank.

I grabbed a Ziploc bag from the kitchen and slipped the letters and necklace inside the bag. I went upstairs to my room, opened the closet, and looked at the box of my mother's things. Putting Emily's letters and cameo in it didn't feel right to me, but I needed to put the bag and contents out of sight. I dropped them into the pocket of a jacket that I never wore and shut the closet door.

Hildi, who was obviously punishing me for my negligence of late, waltzed into the room and gave me a low meow that meant: *Oh. You still live here, do you?*

My cat's demeanor changed when I slumped down onto the floor, too drained to bother making my way to the chair or my bed. Though her pace didn't alter, she switched her direction and, instead of passing by me, she nuzzled against my arm. As I stroked her sleek black fur, she climbed into my lap, and I could no longer hold the tears inside.

Hildi, who'd never seen me like this because I'm not a big crier, looked at my face as if surprised, then pressed against my chest in her own version of a hug. Returning the hug, I murmured into her soft fur, now wet with my tears, "I *do* forgive Myra."

Later, I paced the living room and called Steve Sullivan to warn him that things were indeed getting too hot for me to handle, as he had predicted. He asked what I meant, and I told him about my conversations with Emily and Myra, and the all-too-obvious conclusion that it was *Randy* who'd realized he needed to protect me from *Myra*, and that this had led to my adoption all those years ago.

"The thing is," I told him in a calm voice, though I kept needing to clear my throat, "now that some of Myra's defense mechanisms have broken down enough for her to tell me about *Randy's* nearly drowning me as a child, I'm worried about *her* being alone tonight."

"She's not alone," Steve replied. "I just called over there to ask about whether or not she wanted to keep that wing chair of hers in the family room, and Debbie answered. Myra sounded just fine when she got on the phone. She told me that she and Debbie had rented some chick flick and were just about to watch it together. You don't need to worry about her, Erin."

Don't worry. There was that phrase again. It always caused my internal worry barometer to rise. "As long as she's got a friend there, she'll probably be fine," I reassured myself.

"How about you?" he asked.

"Pardon?"

"Is Audrey Munroe home?"

"Not yet."

"Are you okay alone?"

"Sure. I've got Hildi."

"Hildi?"

"My cat."

"You have a *cat*?" He spoke the last word as if my favorite animal was a four-letter word. "Doesn't it scratch up all your furniture?"

I rolled my eyes but replied, "See you tomorrow morning at Myra's. We'll play it by ear, okay? If I do decide I need to bow out, I'll do so as gracefully as possible."

"I hope you don't. Because if you go, I go."

"Why? We're not really partners."

"Maybe we should think about changing that."

"Are you serious?"

There was a pause. "Well . . . you're better with accessorizing than I am. I've got a broader scope of creative vision than you do."

I lowered the receiver momentarily to look at it in dismay and annoyance. Was his assessment of our respective abilities accurate? Maybe, but I felt infinitely better when saying it to myself rather than hearing it from Sullivan. "I *am* better at accessories. I'll grant you that much."

Another pause. "Let's just drop the whole thing for now . . . maybe think about it this summer, though. If my business is still afloat by then."

"You're in such a tight squeeze that it might *not* be?"

"Think I'd be talking about us teaming up otherwise?"

"Yes!" I snapped, stung and all too willing to lash out. "And you'd know that if you were smarter! I'm great to work with. My clients *love* me. So do cats. And they're a lot better judge of people than most humans are, by the way."

"Woof, woof."

I hung up on him, not really sure what he meant by barking at me, but quite certain he'd intended it as an insult. As Hildi rubbed against my legs, I assured her, "Ha! That cat-hater is never going to work with *me*, sweetiekins. Don't worry."

The last two words reverberated, making me wince.

I slammed the phone into its stand on the mahogany console so hard that I could still feel the reverberations in my hand. And yet my brain insisted on rehashing the conversation from Sullivan's viewpoint. I was always yelling at him. I was terrible to all the men in my life, no matter how hard I tried to be otherwise. Not that I *knew* many men. My main clients were usually women, their husbands taking a backseat. My father had deserted me. My biological father had been murdered. Kevin McBride was a lecher. Carl Henderson considered me his personal curse. Maybe I was *everyone's* curse.

A kitchen cabinet hinge creaked. Glass clinked against glass. My feet were still glued to the antique pine floorboards when Audrey entered the living room, saying, "There you are, dear. I've had the most exasperating day, from the . . ."

Her voice, still a bit husky from her head cold, trailed off as our eyes met.

She blinked twice, then said, "Here," and held out the glass of red wine. "You obviously need this more than I do."

I hesitated, then accepted the glass. Although the liquid went down easily enough, it seemed like a pity that she was wasting perfectly good wine on me in my current state. She was waiting for me to say something, though, so I forced a breezy tone and said, "Nice. Is this a Beaujolais?"

She continued to study me skeptically. Quietly, she asked, "Did you get some terrible news over the phone just now? Did someone close to you die?"

I managed a feeble scoff. "My biological father. Last week. Randy Axelrod was . . ." I stopped, unable to continue, unable to move my feet.

After a lengthy and painful pause, Audrey asked, "Have you eaten dinner yet?"

I shook my head.

"Here's what you'll do." She put her hand on the small of my back and nudged me gently toward the kitchen. "While I'm concocting some fabulous repast for us, you'll help me polish off that marvelous bottle of Bordeaux, and you'll talk to me."

"I'm fine, Audrey. I'm just a little—"

"You'll start at the beginning and tell me how you came to be reacquainted with Mr. Axelrod."

"It's a long story," I protested.

"And I've got lots of time. Plus a wonderfully stocked wine cellar."

Steve was waiting for me on Myra's porch the next morning, with a big smile on his face, a portfolio that no doubt contained the preliminary presentation boards under one arm. Did the man *have* to have such a freaking gorgeous smile? Not to mention the bedroom eyes and Adonis body. "Morning," he said as I made my way up the steps. "I got you a little I'm-sorry present." He held out a steaming to-go cup from Starbucks. "I didn't know if you drink coffee or tea, so I got hot chocolate."

"Thank you. That's my favorite."

"I knew it. Sweets for the sweet."

I grimaced a little, and he said, "Too much?"

"A little bit. Yeah." I took a cautious sip of the steamy beverage, which tasted downright sinful.

He gestured at the door. "You ready?"

"Absolutely."

He rang the doorbell. There was no answer. We waited, then he pushed the button a second time. "Odd," he murmured.

Terrible suspicions engulfed me. Myra could indeed have killed Randy and now, overcome with guilt, she'd taken her own life. If so—if she was dead—it would be my fault for not contacting the police the moment I suspected she was suicidal. I set the cup down on the stoop. "Steve, I've got a bad feeling. See if it's locked."

He turned the knob; the door swung open. "Myra?" he called.

"Christ," I muttered, rushing past him into the house. "Myra? Are you here? Myra!"

I went straight through to the kitchen and scanned the room, but she wasn't there.

"You'd better be the one to check upstairs, just in case she's not fully dressed," Steve said.

I ran up the stairs, my heart pounding, calling, "Myra?" once again. I entered the master bedroom. The bed, with its white chenille spread, was neatly made.

I found her, sprawled on the floor in the master bathroom, still wearing her nightgown and robe. She was lying on her stomach, her face toward me.

One glance told me that she was dead.

chapter **21**

My knees wobbled and everything went gray. I slumped against the doorjamb, trembling violently. There was a stench in the air that was horridly reminiscent of my mother's bedroom at the end of her life.

Suddenly I could see myself alongside my mother's bed, could hear her loud, rasping last breaths. The one person on this planet who'd always prevented me from being truly alone would no longer be there for me. As her body gave up the struggle for oxygen, I held her hand and silently railed at her, "How can you leave me!"

My head cleared enough to realize that a different tragedy was unfolding around me. All I could manage was a weak "Steve." He raced up the stairs and through the doorway.

Myra's eyes were dull and unseeing, yet somehow I felt they reproved me as Steve knelt and felt for a pulse. "No pulse. Her skin's cold."

"She's dead." My voice sounded foreign to my own ear. "I should have done something last night . . . called the police . . . had them check in on her."

"She wasn't alone last night; Debbie was here, too." The color had drained from his face. "We don't know what happened. We don't know that she committed suicide. And we don't know that she poisoned Randy. Erin, we need to call the police."

"You call. I can't . . . think straight." A shudder ran up my spine. "God, Steve. She'd said something yesterday about changing Randy's and her will to make me their sole heir. If she's done that, the police are going to think I killed them both."

"You're innocent. You don't have to worry." He put his arm around my shoulders and guided me out of the bathroom. He, too, was shaking as we made our way to the phone on the nightstand. He grabbed the phone and started to sit down on the edge of Myra's queen-sized bed, then thought better of it and leaned a shoulder against the wall. He dialed 911.

There was a noise from below us as someone opened and then closed a heavy door. Debbie called up the stairs, "Myra? I'm back from Safeway. I got everything on your list."

My head felt ready to explode. I pushed against my temples with the heels of my hands. I knew I had to tell Debbie the terrible news.

Steve was speaking to the dispatcher on the phone and looked at me. I held up a hand to signal that I'd handle this, and left the room.

Debbie turned and smiled at me as I entered the kitchen. "Erin, hi. I thought you were here. I saw your van. Did you leave a cup of . . ." Her voice faded. "What's wrong? Where's Myra?"

"Something awful has happened. Steve Sullivan is upstairs, talking to the police."

"The police? Oh my God! Is she . . . hurt?"

I grabbed both her arms before she could pass. "She's dead, Debbie."

She yanked free from my grasp, staring at me in disbelief, then wobbled and dropped into a chair at the silver-speckled Formica table. "But . . . that's not possible! She was perfectly fine when I left to run some errands. She was *healthy*. She can't be dead! How could she be dead?"

"I don't know, Debbie. We had an appointment scheduled. I got scared when no one answered the bell, so we let ourselves in. I found Myra on the bathroom floor."

"But . . . but nothing looks any different. Shouldn't something have changed if . . . I can't believe this is happening." She stared into my eyes. "I . . . should go up there, shouldn't I? She shouldn't be alone till . . . someone comes for her."

"Steve's upstairs. The police will be here very soon." I took a seat at the small table across from her. I couldn't stop shivering.

"I don't understand," Debbie moaned. "How could she die just a week after . . ." Her eyes widened. She shook her head. "Nobody had any reason to hurt her, Erin. She lived such a quiet life here with Randy. She didn't have any enemies."

Could this have been an accidental poisoning? I wondered. "Did she have breakfast this morning?"

With a vacant look on her face, she answered,

"Scrambled eggs and toast. But she made them herself, and I was right there in the kitchen with her." Her speech was slow and her voice quiet. "And we shared the eggs. The police tested everything in her kitchen for poison and didn't find anything."

"Did she have coffee?"

She shook her head. "Tea. Myra drank tea. Always. But it was a new box. She told me the police took her tea, even though Randy never touched the stuff. He was a coffee drinker, like me." She sank her head into her hands. "God. I've been going out for coffee every morning till today. The first couple days, it made me too nervous to drink Myra's, in spite of the police tests. Today *I* drank her coffee, though, and used her sugar. Myra said that they'd all been replaced."

There were sirens now in the distance. Debbie blinked back the tears. "Carl's at work. I've been packing up my things. I found a rental place with immediate occupancy. Only . . . I didn't want to just leave Myra like this, so I went and bought us the makings for dinner tonight . . . for my last night here. I was going to . . . to make the two of us dinner."

Steve came into the kitchen. His face was still ashen. "The police are pulling up outside." He looked at Debbie. "I'm sorry that this has happened."

Debbie began to cry softly. "She was a good friend. I can't believe this is happening." She looked up at me, still in shock. "Erin, come over to my old house later today, if you can. We need to talk."

My eyes misted a little with relief when Linda Delgardio entered the house in full uniform, along with three uniformed male officers. Linda promptly took me into Randy's office to interview me in private. Myra had cleared everything—including the umbrella stand—out of the room, but we dragged in two of the rosewood chairs from the dining room.

"For once I wished I smoked cigarettes," I muttered as I took a seat in the stripped room.

"I know what you mean." Linda sat down in the chair in front of mine, gave me a reassuring smile, then flipped open her notepad. "Tell me what happened, Erin."

"Steve Sullivan and I had an appointment here at nine to discuss our design ideas for Myra's house, so . . ." I paused, then asked tentatively, "Is it all right if I start further back . . . rehash the stuff I already told Detective O'Reilly?"

"Of course, Erin."

So I went into everything from the beginning, including the entire story of Myra's telling me that I was her daughter and how Emily Blaire had refuted that. Just as I was about to describe Emily's giving me the old letters and cameo, though, I fell silent. I didn't want to surrender them to the police. A friend had once had her stolen silverware recovered, only to have it be declared police evidence and locked away for two years. Emily had intended for the letters and necklace to be given to me almost ten years ago. There had to be some point at which I was allowed to keep those small mementos from a mother I'd never known and a childhood in Colorado that I'd never experienced.

"You believed Emily Blaire's story?" Linda prompted, breaking into my thoughts.

"Completely."

"Why? Did she show you any proof?"

"She was just much more convincing than Myra. And Myra's story about discovering I wasn't Randy's through my blood type was nonsense." I felt my face growing warm at my failure to mention the letters. Worse, Linda was looking at me so intently that she seemed to detect something was wrong. "I feel really guilty, because part of me knew I should have called the police last night. Myra was so upset—despondent—that I thought she might even be suicidal. But I found out that Debbie Henderson was going to be with her, so I convinced myself she would be fine."

"You suspect that Myra committed suicide?"

"I'm *worried* that she might have . . . and that maybe, if I'd taken action last night, it could have been prevented."

"Did you notice anything when you found her body that made you sus—that made you worry this might have been self-inflicted? Empty glasses on her nightstand, pill bottles, powder spills?"

I shook my head.

She glanced back through her notes, then gave me a long look. "Is there anything else?"

"Not that I can think of. But I still have your card." I rose, and she did as well.

"Don't hesitate to call me, Erin. If something else occurs to you."

I forced myself to hold her gaze. My heart was pounding. I was hiding evidence from the police *and* lying to a new friend. "I won't. Hesitate, I mean."

Linda excused herself to speak with one of her fellow officers. I retrieved my coat, anxious to get away.

"Miss Gilbert?" a male officer called, causing me to all but jump out of my skin. I clenched my teeth. He handed me a slip of paper. Steve had written: *Get in touch ASAP* and had included his home address and phone number. "You're the other decorator's partner, right?"

"Right."

"He said to call or come over later if you wanted." The

officer smiled a little. "Are those your real last names—Gilbert and Sullivan?"

"Yes."

"Lucky. That makes your business name real easy to remember."

I made no comment and put the piece of paper in my pocket. "Is Mrs. Henderson still here?" I asked.

"No. Said she was going back to her own house."

"I'm going to go check on how she's doing. Thank you, officer."

I headed across the street, glad to leave Myra's house, but with a growing sense of foreboding over what might be in store for me next. The way things were going, Debbie was probably going to drop some bombshell on me—perhaps insist that *she* was my birth mother and that Henry Kissinger had been my father.

I rang the Hendersons' doorbell. Debbie's eyes were red and puffy when she came to the door. "Erin! Come on in."

She closed the door behind us, then rounded the railing by the door and, without a word, plopped into the La-Z-Boy recliner in the living room. She blew her nose while I took a seat on the off-white wool bouclé love seat against the front window. It was chilly, so I kept my coat on; Carl must have set the thermostat at sixty degrees while he was gone.

"I'm trying to shrug everything off and keep packing," she muttered, and dabbed at her nose with a tissue. "Suddenly I'm having a rough time with dust. Pretty ironic, wouldn't you say? That was such a catalyst for me, clueing me in that my marriage really was over, once I found out that Carl couldn't even remember which wife had allergies." She sighed. "You know, Erin, I was the only girl of the two hundred or so at my twenty-fifth high school reunion who'd never been married. I felt so sorry for myself. For my thirtieth, I was married and tried like mad to convince Carl to go with me, but he refused. Said he'd be bored stiff. It's just as well. This way, five years from now, when I'm unmarried once again and, once again, attend my thirty-fifth reunion alone, I won't have to put up with everyone asking me what happened to that tall, grumpy fellow I was with last time."

I had no response. She was having such a rough time in her life—her marriage ending, first Randy and now Myra dying. Maybe griping about something as trivial as a high school reunion was what she needed to do to get herself through this impossibly difficult day. "Did you tell Carl yet about Myra?"

She grimaced. "No. I guess I should call him at work. I so wanted to be able to just slip away without having to see him . . . to be all moved out by the time he got home. The moving men are coming at four." She sighed again. "It's a really small, one-bedroom place, so I'm just taking the bedroom stuff, the kitchen table, and the living room furniture. Carl can keep everything else. At least for now."

"I thought you were keeping the house and Carl was going to be the one to move out."

"Carl's such a stick-in-the-mud, I figured it'd be faster and less painful if I let him stay here till the judge decides who gets what." She stared at her hands in her lap. At length, she said, "I had a bit of business to wrap up with you before I moved out, though. I wanted to tell you that the wall that the police destroyed looks good as new now. Carl hired Taylor. He already managed to repair the bedroom wall and rehang the wallpaper."

"Really? I still have that extra roll in my van. Taylor never asked me for it."

She gave a one-shoulder shrug. "Carl must have

bought more. It's his money to throw away as he chooses. The point is, I'm going to have the moving men take the bed, night table, and dresser this afternoon. I thought you'd like the chance to take your photos for your portfolio now, while the room's still intact."

"Yes, I sure would. That's really thoughtful of you. I'll do that right now, if you don't mind."

"Go ahead."

I fetched my digital camera from my satchel in the van, then went upstairs and shot my photographs from every angle. At first, I thought the room looked precisely the way it had before the police ruined the wall, and then I noticed the outlet cover plates. Taylor had merely reused the ones that I'd created to match the original wallpapering job; now that the paper behind it had been rehung, the pattern on the plates no longer matched.

Cursing under my breath, I trudged down the stairs. It would take me thirty minutes, tops, to remove the old paper from the covers and recover them, as opposed to letting the thought fester in my brain indefinitely that the outlet plate covers were loused up in a room that I'd so carefully designed.

I found Debbie in the kitchen, packing up the blue willow dishes. "The room looks great, doesn't it, Erin?"

"Taylor did a pretty good job. But the wallpaper on the outlet plates needs to be redone. I'll have to get my tools."

"Please don't bother. I noticed that, too, I'll admit, but Carl sure won't."

"It won't take me long, and I just can't knowingly leave a mistake like that."

"Suit yourself, but there's no need to do it right this minute." She shut the packing box, grabbed her coffee mug, and headed, once again, for the living room, as if she could only handle the task of packing in short spurts. "I'm sure the outlets won't show up in the photographs that the *Denver Lifestyles* photographer's taking."

"Pardon?" I followed her.

"He's coming at two o'clock this afternoon." She reclaimed her seat. "I'm now officially editor in chief at *Denver Lifestyles*, so I can dictate the photo shoots. Now that Myra, the in-name-only owner, has passed away, I no longer feel obligated to keep my role secret."

"*Myra* was the owner of the magazine?" I asked, dropping back into my seat on the sofa, stunned.

Debbie nodded. "Though it was Randy's money. He and Myra had temporarily split up, and I guess Randy's buying a business for her was part of his means for winning her back. Although he gave me quite the shaft in the process."

"Randy bought the magazine from *you*?"

"He didn't buy it, no. When we bought the Axelrods' house and first got to know them, Myra told me that he was independently wealthy. I'd already come up with the idea for starting the magazine—back before I'd even met Carl, let alone Randy. I couldn't get the financing I needed, though, so . . . one day I mustered up all my courage and presented everything to Randy to see if he'd be willing to invest in it. He said he'd look into it and let me know. He kept putting me off for months, then he finally let on that he'd already gotten everything off the ground and had made himself editor in chief and would hire me as his ghostwriter only."

"Jeez! You couldn't sue him?"

"He said that people couldn't copyright their ideas alone, so there was no way I *could*. At first I told him where to shove it, of course, but my technical writing business wasn't going well, and he assured me that he'd help me find work plus pay me very generously as long as I kept quiet, et cetera. And he told me that if I *did* try to sue, I'd only be hurting Myra, since he'd made her the owner."

"That must have made you furious." I wondered if I'd misjudged Debbie; maybe she was hiding a murderous rage.

She set her coffee mug down. "Yes, but that's all ancient history. An amazing thing happened. Apparently Randy wrote a codicil to his will at some point. In it, he confessed that he'd gypped me out of my idea for the magazine and that I'd been his ghostwriter for years now, so he wanted ownership of the magazine and some back pay the company owed him to go to me instead."

"That's wonderful."

"Well, it's *good*, at least. We aren't talking about a huge amount of money, but it will be enough for me to cover my rent and deposit on my one-bedroom apartment in Longmont." That was a small town nearby.

She managed a small smile. "What this means as far as you're concerned is a bit of good news during a dreadful day. We're going to run a feature story about you and Steve Sullivan and the rooms you two completed. Originally my story was going to include your design in Myra's house as well, but for obvious reasons I'm just going to nix that part and run the story of the contest, which I've officially declared a tie."

"Thank you, Debbie. It will be a terrific boon to both Steve's and my businesses. I'm sure he'll be happy to hear about this."

"That reminds me. Jill wasn't certain that she would allow photographs to be taken of Steve's work, since she says the room is her least favorite in the whole house."

Poor Steve! He needed all the publicity he could get,

or his business might fold. "That's going to be a major stumbling block to your magazine piece on our contest, won't it?"

"I think Jill can be persuaded to change her mind easily enough. I can always agree to run a separate story next year that shows her entire house, and—"

The doorbell rang, and Kevin McBride burst inside. He was panting and flushed. He was wearing a jogging suit and was sweating profusely. For once, he didn't give me a leering eye. Rather, he ignored me, gripped the short length of railing that ran adjacent to the door, and gasped, "Debbie! What's happened at Myra's house?"

Debbie clasped her hands and held them to her lips, studying Kevin's face, her eyes tearing up once more. "Oh, Kevin," she said. "You'd better come in and take a seat. I'm afraid it's Myra."

He stayed put but tightened his grip on the rail. "What does that mean, 'it's Myra'? *What's* Myra? Is she missing? Did she have an accident?"

Debbie looked at me with pleading eyes.

"She died this morning," I told him. "I found her when Steve Sullivan and I went to her house for an appointment."

He shook his head. "No. No. She can't be dead." He doubled over and plopped down on the hard tile in front of the Hendersons' door. Debbie rushed to his side and knelt in attempt to put her arms around him. Pushing her away, he cried, "What the hell is happening? I don't understand any of this!"

"I know," Debbie soothed. "It's impossible to fathom." She got to her feet and returned to her chair, hanging her head.

Kevin rose, supporting himself with the banister as he made the short trip into the living room to join us. He took a seat beside the La-Z-Boy on the carpeted step to the living room. He looked at me, his expression tight. "Was it natural causes? Or was she . . . killed?"

"I don't know," I replied quietly. "There wasn't any blood, but she may have ingested poison."

He rocked himself slightly, saying nothing. Debbie reached down to put her hand on his shoulder, and he held it there, his hand on top of hers. At length, he said to her, "I need to speak to Erin alone for a minute."

Debbie gave me a quick glance, then said, "I've got some more boxes to pack up in my office. I'll be back in a few minutes."

Kevin promptly got up and began to pace in front of the smoked-glass coffee table between us. "This has something to do with those letters you found in the wall upstairs."

"I don't know if that's the case or not. What makes you think so?"

"Myra said as much. A couple of days ago. That time that you and Debbie came into the kitchen right when I was trying to slip out the back door. Myra said she could never tell me what happened right after she and I broke up, but that it had something to do with you." He stopped directly in front of me, his hands fisted, his expression one of fury. "What the hell was she talking about? Was it all spelled out in those letters?"

"I don't know. I never read them. All I know is that when I spoke to Myra last night she told me something strange."

"What?"

"That you and she had a baby together. Twenty-seven years ago. And that *I* was that baby."

His anger promptly deserted him. He shrank into the recliner that Debbie had just deserted and muttered,

"Oh, my God. Myra. She'd had some . . . troubles with . . . delusions and depression. I had no idea it was that bad."

"I feel so sorry for her," I said in a near whisper.

He met my eyes. "Myra taught my chemistry class my freshman year at CU. Thirty years ago. We fell in love. When she got pregnant, she didn't know if it was Randy's or mine, but she told me we had to end things . . . that either way, this was going to be her and Randy's baby. Only the baby died within a few days of her birth." His eyes flew open wide. "Hey. Come to think of it, they named the baby Erin. Maybe that's why Myra got it into her head that you were really *her* child, when she deluded herself into believing that her baby had lived."

"You were just a college student then, right, and not a neighbor? So . . . are you positive that Myra's baby died?"

"Absolutely. I went to her funeral."

"Huh," I muttered, though my mind was racing.

"I've always loved Myra. All these years." His bark of laughter was hollow. "She'd made it perfectly clear it was over as far as she was concerned, and I never forced it, but I'd drive through her neighborhood sometimes. . . . When a house went up for sale just a couple of doors away from hers fifteen years ago, I insisted to Jill that we move. Jill was furious—our other house was much more to her liking, which is to say, godawfully ostentatious." He shook his head. "I guess I always believed that one day, Myra would leave Randy for good and we'd run off together. But it just wasn't meant to be."

Debbie cautiously entered the room. "Actually . . . I'm pretty much finished packing up the basement."

Kevin squeezed his eyes shut. "I can't believe she's gone," he said softly. "Myra was a wonderful lady. She was just too fragile, and life never gave her a decent break." He grimaced. "My car's still two miles away, over at the gym. I've got to jog back, get cleaned up, and get home. Jill will be sending out a search party before I know it."

"I'm sorry for your loss," I said to him, though the whole matter of stringing his wife along while he professed to be in love with Myra was reprehensible. Maybe he didn't love either of them, but merely their money—money that Myra hadn't actually possessed until she inherited it from Randy.

As Kevin let himself out, he said to someone outside, "Carl's not here, but Debbie's in the living room."

There was one quick rap on the door, and Taylor strode into the house. He gave a little nod and said, "Hey, Debbie." Apparently nobody used proper etiquette when entering this home. "Kevin practically bowled right into me just now. He's sure in a mood."

Debbie's eyes had widened in surprise. "Taylor. What are you doing here?"

"Carl didn't tell you? He hired me to move you and your stuff out in my pickup."

"No, he didn't tell me. I already hired movers."

"Looks like I wasted a trip," he grumbled.

"It's okay," Debbie said. "You can keep Carl's money and take a load of books over for me, since you're already here."

"Fine by me." Taylor eyed me, then waggled his thumb over his shoulder. "What's going on across the street? There's a shitload of police cars over there."

"It's Myra," Debbie said solemnly. "She died this morning."

He frowned. "Jeez, that's too bad. She was pretty friendly to me. Lately she was, I mean. It was weird. Before her old man got offed, she acted like she hated my guts. Now all of a sudden she's all 'Taylor, how nice to see you again!' "

"She seemed to be a bit unpredictable," I muttered.

"Yeah. If by that you mean she's, like, totally wacked."

"Taylor!" Debbie chastised. "Myra Axelrod was a good person and a personal friend of mine. Don't talk about her that way!"

"Sorry. But, shit, you know as well as anyone that she was one of the crazier people on the planet."

"Is that true?" I asked Debbie.

She sighed. "In a way, the poor thing."

Taylor pulled out a chair from the dining room table and dropped into it, straddling its banister-style back. "One time, back when I was house-sitting, she wandered into Carl's house. She was—"

Debbie snorted. "When you say 'Carl's house,' you mean mine as well, don't you? Meaning the house we're all sitting in right now?"

"Yeah, but, like, you're moving out." He returned his attention to me and continued. "It was the middle of the night. She's wearing, like, this shiny red bathrobe and pink fuzzy slippers. She looks at me, and she says, 'What time is it?' And I go, 'Nine thirty,' or whatever, and she says, 'Is it that late? I was looking for my daughter. Is my daughter here?' I just want her out of there, so I tell her, 'No, but I'll send her right home if I see her.' Then she just thanks me and leaves."

"Oh, that poor woman!" Debbie cried. She looked at me and explained, "She lost a baby girl in childbirth many, many years ago and then could never have another child. Randy said the whole thing made her mind just snap, and when she got stressed, she'd get delusional and . . ." She shook her head. "This all seems so disrespectful." She scowled at Taylor and asked, "Why didn't you tell Carl and me about Myra when we got back from Europe?"

Taylor growled, "God, Debbie. I don't know. Maybe I

was a bit distracted by being *hauled off to jail* at the time! Must have slipped my mind!"

Debbie winced. "Of course, Taylor. I'd forgotten."

"Yeah. Just like you forgot to warn me about your Looney Tunes neighbors. If you'd told me how weird the Axelrods were and that they had a key, *I* would never have been arrested. I wouldn't have been so casual about leaving my stuff out."

She clicked her tongue and bolted upright in her seat. "Taylor Duncan! One of these days you're going to have to learn that to be an adult means taking responsibility for one's own actions. It is nobody's fault but your own that you got arrested for selling drugs! Not mine and certainly not your stepdad's for not warning you about Randy. Not Randy's for turning you in. *Yours* for committing a very serious crime in the first place!"

"Hey! You're not my mother! You're not even my step-mom once removed anymore!"

"Thank God I'm *not* your mother, because if I were, your drug use and dealing would have broken my heart! Just like you broke Emily's heart! And Carl's, too, for that matter! They've given you everything, and if you ask me, which nobody ever does, that's been their only failure in parenting. And what have you *ever* given them in return, Taylor? Aside from grief, I mean. You've given them lots of grief." She shot to her feet and took a step closer to him. "Since I'll soon no longer be distantly related to you through marriage, it's high time I told you something that's been festering in me for the last couple of years. Get your head out of your ass and *act like a man*! Take responsibility for yourself. Start doing the right thing by your family members!"

Taylor sat in stunned silence. It was clear from the red-cheeked expression on his face that her words had hit him hard.

"I'm going to finish packing up the kitchen now," Debbie said to me in a calmer voice. "Are you sure I can't get you anything?"

"No, thanks." I rose. "I should get going. Any minute I'm sure the police are going to want to talk to me again about Myra's poisoning."

Taylor's jaw dropped. "She was *poisoned*?"

"Actually, I don't know whether she was or not. I simply assumed she was."

He leapt to his feet, dragging his palm over his shaved scalp, and went to the front window. There he parted the sheers to look at Myra's house.

Confused at his reaction, I followed his gaze. There were now a half-dozen official-looking cars and vans parked by the house, including an unmarked white van. Myra's body was being put into the van; I could see the black body bag from here. "Taylor, maybe she wasn't poisoned. All I really know is that she looked similar to how Randy was when we found him."

He gestured at the activity across the street. "Which officer is in charge?"

"I don't know. Probably the guy in the brown suit. But what's going on, Taylor? It's far too early to know if Myra was poisoned. Her death could have been from natural causes."

He ignored me, threw open the door and marched outside. Though dumbfounded by his behavior, my instincts warned me that he was about to do something dreadful. I charged after him.

"Taylor!" I shouted. "Stop!"

He continued to storm toward Myra's house and the man in the suit, whom I began to suspect was merely the coroner; he was obviously anxious at a man of Taylor's titanlike stature striding toward him and was giving nervous glances to either side as if hoping for police support.

"Taylor? What are you doing?" Debbie called, trailing behind us.

"I have a confession," Taylor said as he neared the man in the suit. "I did it. I killed them."

"Them?" the man in the brown suit repeated, glancing back at Myra's house in obvious confusion.

Taylor was visibly trembling. "Randy and Myra Axelrod," he said. "I poisoned them both."

chapter 22

Taylor, don't say another word!" I cried.
What was going on in his thick head? His
confession was rubbish; just minutes ago he'd had no
idea that Myra was even dead. He suddenly decided he'd
murdered her only *after* I'd blurted out that she'd been
poisoned. He must have assumed she'd ingested something he'd targeted for Randy, but the food and cooking
implements had been thoroughly tested last week. How
could that be possible?

The man in the brown suit was gaping at us. Three
uniformed officers drew closer, frowning. The eldest officer—a burly, bald man—asked Taylor, "You murdered
that lady?"

"No! He's talking crazy." I grabbed my cell phone out of my coat pocket, gesturing for Debbie, who raced across the street toward us. "Do you have Emily's number?"

She grabbed the phone from me. "She'll be at work at her Pilates studio by now. I know that number by heart."

Swatting at Debbie's hand in an attempt to knock the phone from her grasp, Taylor shouted, "Don't call my mother! Leave her out of this!" Debbie took a step back and continued to dial. Taylor grabbed his head, looking panic-stricken.

"How old are you, son?" the officer asked him.

"Twenty-one."

"He's only twenty," Debbie interjected.

The officer muttered, "Legally an adult, either way."

Where was Linda Delgardio? *She* would listen to me.

Debbie thrust the phone back to me. "It's ringing. I'm going to go grab *my* phone and get Carl out here. He's just talking nonsense," she told the men. "He didn't kill anybody." Then she turned and asked, "Did you, Taylor?"

"Don't answer that!" My heart was pounding. I couldn't bear the thought that my talking through my hat had inspired Taylor to make a false confession.

The phone was ringing at Emily's Pilates studio. I gestured emphatically at Debbie to hurry back across the street. "Tell Carl that Taylor needs a lawyer."

The officer said to Taylor, "Let's just head down to the police station. I'm going to put some handcuffs on you. No big deal—it's standard procedure." He looked over his shoulder. "Lennie? You want to pat him down and read him his rights?"

I covered my ear as a woman answered the phone.

"Emily?"

"Yes."

"This is Erin Gilbert. Taylor just confessed to the police that he killed both the Axelrods."

"What!?" she shrieked. "That's not . . . Myra's dead, too?"

"I found Myra's body this morning in her house. And a minute ago I mentioned to Taylor that she may have been poisoned, and he suddenly charged up to the police and confessed."

"Where is he now? *Where's my son?*"

The burly officer was guiding him through the patrol car doorway with one hand supporting the top of Taylor's head, and he was so large that getting him into the backseat was a tight fit. "They're putting him in a police car now."

"Stop them! Erin, he's your kid brother! Don't let them do this to him. He's innocent!"

I swore aloud. What exactly did she expect me to do? Throw myself down in front of the patrol car? Launch myself spread-eagle on the windshield? "Emily, I don't see how I can stop this."

"Oh, for Christ's sake! Do *something*! Let me talk to whoever's in charge!"

I sprinted up to the nearest officer—a younger-looking man with a full head of hair. I thrust my phone out, and said, "This is the mother of the person you're arresting. She wants to talk to you."

He took the phone from me. Mr. Brown Suit, meanwhile, got into the unmarked white minivan and drove away, no doubt anxious to get as far away as possible from this insanity.

I wrapped my arms around my chest, wishing I could get Taylor away someplace private to speak to him. Debbie jogged back across the street, announcing, "Carl's on his way." She stopped beside me. In a half whisper that none of the officers could overhear, she continued. "He thinks Taylor must be tripping . . . blaming himself because of a drug-induced hallucination."

"Taylor seemed completely lucid to me." By his standard, at any rate. He must be trying to protect his mother or his stepfather. That was the only reasonable explanation I could come up with.

The young officer returned and handed me my cell phone. Debbie started to say that Taylor's stepfather would arrive soon, but the officer cut her off. "He'll be at the station on Thirty-third and Chestnut."

We watched the patrol car drive away, Taylor turning his face away from the window. Debbie stamped her foot. "He must be protecting his mother," she said, as if reading my mind. "I mean, yes, it was terrible of him to get into drugs and everything. But Taylor? *Kill* somebody? No way."

"You think Emily Blaire *is* capable of murder?"

"I think that woman is capable of any number of things," Debbie growled.

I shivered, not entirely due to the cold. I didn't want to believe that my birth mother had actually poisoned the Axelrods. That possibility was far more upsetting to me than my belligerent half brother Taylor as the prime suspect. I buttoned my coat, my mind racing.

Emily had been here that first day, when Taylor was unloading the wood and found my container of cyanide. Maybe *Emily* had actually been the one to take the cyanide out of my van. She could also have made some remark about the Axelrods to Taylor. He could have been provoked into making a false confession to protect his mother.

"You didn't see Emily in the neighborhood this morning, did you?" I asked Debbie.

"Well . . . no, but then, I wasn't watching. I was packing up my basement office—which, as you've seen for yourself, gives me no view of the street whatsoever—then I went to Safeway."

"That probably *is* what Taylor's got in his head, though . . . the thought that he'll take the rap for his mother." I didn't want to add that he was probably trying to do the right thing by his family, as Debbie had recently harangued him to do. Or that it was every bit as likely that he was protecting his father, Carl, not Emily.

Had Taylor rashly confessed to a crime he didn't commit, in the mistaken fear that his mother was guilty? Or did I just not want to believe that my biological half brother, not to mention my biological mother, could be guilty of such a heinous crime?

Debbie gave my arm a gentle squeeze. "Erin, I really don't want to be here when Carl comes home. I'm going to take a couple of boxes of stuff out to my new place. Couldn't you please stay and talk to him?"

"But can't we call him on his cell phone and tell him that now to save him from—"

"He never turns it on when he's driving. Just tell him that they've already taken Taylor to the police station. Please?"

That seemed the least I could do, considering that if I'd never blurted out my theory that Myra was poisoned, Taylor wouldn't be in this mess. "Okay."

"Thank you, Erin. I promise I won't forget to come back by two to show the photographers your and Steve's rooms."

She fled into her house, and less than a minute later, she was backing out of the garage. My attention was soon drawn to the McBrides' house. Jill was dumping armloads of clothing into the front yard. She noticed me and gestured for me to come over. I tentatively ventured toward her. The mounted fish was on the lawn, along with what had to be Kevin's entire wardrobe.

I didn't know what, if anything, she knew about Myra and hoped with all my heart that she wasn't calling me over to ask. If so, I cut Jill off at the pass and asked, "What's going on?" despite its being quite obvious that she was tossing Kevin out.

"I'm hastening my husband's departure." Her voice was even and calm, although her eyes were red. She took a couple of steps toward her house, where the beautiful coffee table that Steve had designed was now wedged in the doorway. "Myra's death was the last straw."

"Why?"

"Please be a dear and help me with one end of that table. The twins will be home from their ski trip tomorrow afternoon, and they can help me move that silly new chair of Kevin's outside then."

Damn it! The photographer would be here soon. Just because she was emptying her husband's closets didn't mean she had to immediately tear up Steve's impeccable den design. "Jill, I just . . . wouldn't feel good about helping you to move your husband's things."

"I've already carried the table out to the front porch," she said, as if my concern were merely one of logistics.

"It's really not my place to get involved in any sense in a marital dispute. And didn't Debbie contact you about the story she wanted to run featuring Steve's and my room designs? The photographer's going to be here in just a couple of hours."

She scoffed. "Do you honestly think that *I* would allow a room in *my* house, one that has a *dead fish* over the fireplace, to be displayed in a magazine for all the world to see?"

"Steve could replace the fish temporarily with something more . . . reflective of your refined tastes."

"I can't be bothered." I bit back my response as she continued. "If you're reluctant to choose between Kevin and me, I must remind you to consider which side of your toast bears the butter. You haven't forgotten about our meeting tomorrow morning to cement the plans for the New Year's party, have you?"

"But the purpose of the party was to raise capital for your husband. You're . . . still going to hold that party?"

"Of course. I'll simply change the theme. We'll go back to the traditional idea of—" She stopped abruptly as a silver BMW pulled into the driveway. Leaving the motor running, Kevin got out of it.

"Hey! That's all my stuff!" he cried as though his wife had to simply be confused about its ownership.

"I heard about you and Myra!" Jill shouted back. "I've known all along!"

He started to come toward her, protesting, but she held up a hand. "Stay where you are. You come any closer, I'll get a restraining order against you!"

"But . . . it's my house! What on earth are you talking about?"

"You killed Randy, Kevin! You wanted Myra so badly, the two of you cooked up this plot to get rid of him. Then something backfired on you and she wound up dead as well."

"That's nuts! I did nothing of the kind!"

Her features twisted with rage. "I've put up with your games long enough, Kevin! I had our phone tapped. I've got recordings of you and Myra, making your plans. I've already turned them in to the police!"

"You what?! That's just . . . Jill! I never once discussed murdering Randy with Myra! Or with anyone!"

"Save it for the police when they play back those tapes for you. I've lived with this knowledge of you and your affairs for years now. I won't live with the knowledge that you're a murderer."

Kevin gaped at her.

Jill leveled her finger at him and continued. "And if you think I'm going to let you stay here, share my home with a murderer, you're even a bigger bastard and fool than I believed!"

Just then, car tires squealed as someone made too fast a turn onto the street. Carl's red Subaru whizzed past us, came to a stop in front of Myra's house, then backed up the half block to pull even to us.

Carl rolled down the window on the passenger side of the car. "Erin, is Taylor inside?"

Before I could answer, Kevin thrust himself between us, gripping both sides of the open car window. "Carl! Jill's thrown my stuff outside on the lawn! Can I stash everything at your place till she calms down?"

"Yeah, sure. Just let me talk to Erin."

"Do you have a spare key?" Kevin asked him.

Carl tried to wave him aside. "Use the combination and go in through the garage—six-three-eight. I have to find out where Taylor is!"

"He's at the Crestview police station," I called to him over Kevin's shoulder. "I think Emily is on her way there, too, if she hasn't already—"

Carl tore off, swinging the car around. Jill whirled and stomped back into her house. Kevin got back into his car and sat behind the wheel in shock.

I knew how he felt. My birth father had been murdered, and now so had his wife. My birth mother or my half brother was very possibly the killer. Steve needed and deserved the publicity from *Denver Lifestyles*. He was in a better position to appease Jill than I was, and there was little time to salvage the room before the photographer arrived for the shoot. I looked again at the slip of paper where he'd written his address and phone number. My afternoon's assignment was in the general area of his house, and this message was best delivered in person.

I got into my van and dialed the now-empty house across the street. I left a message on Carl's machine explaining that I needed brief access to his bedroom this evening to make the repairs to the outlet covers.

Afterward, I shook my head, shocked at myself. This whole neighborhood was going to hell in a handbasket, but *first* I was fixing the outlet plates. Now *I'm* losing a grip on reality!

Steve's house turned out to be a bungalow near Foothills Park that, just in terms of the location and prior to seeing the interior layout, instantly had me fighting the green-eyed monster yet again. Although the above-ground portion of the house couldn't be more than twelve hundred square feet, he could walk to the hiking trails inside fifteen minutes. He also had a wonderful wraparound deck with a gorgeous view of the mountains over his privacy fence.

He had an old-fashioned antique brass door knocker; even in my battered state of mind, I appreciated the solemn sound that it made under my fingertips. I felt a flutter of nervous anticipation as I heard someone unlock the door.

Steve was still wearing all-black clothes, the top two buttons on his shirt open. Unless I was fooling myself, his eyes lit up a little at the sight of me. "Hey, Gilbert. I waited for a while, but the police seemed to want to keep you talking forever."

"You missed yet more excitement after you left."

"What happened?" he asked, stepping aside to let me in. He shut the door behind me, crossed the stunning oak floor, and eased into a forest-green chaise longue. A vintage iron floor lamp stood beside the chaise. The only other furnishing in the loftlike room was a stunning, down-filled sofa covered with ultrasuede. No doubt this had been one piece that he'd appreciated too much to give up when Evan had wiped him out and skipped town.

"They hauled Taylor down to the police station."

"They arrested *Taylor*?"

"Yes. He confessed to the police that he killed both Myra and Randy."

"Whoa. Well, it's great that the killer's caught."

"Except that I don't think he's the killer. I think he's lying to protect either his mom or Carl."

"You think one of *them* did it?"

"Not necessarily, just that *Taylor* believes one of them did."

Steve let out a confused sigh. "Man. And sometimes I think *my* life's screwed up." He met my eyes. "Don't just stand there, Gilbert. Grab a seat on the sofa. It's not like I've got too many seating options."

The instant I sat down, I could tell from the dreamy comfort that the sofa used top-of-the-line eight-way hand-tied coil construction. I noticed, too, that although the walls were bare, telltale nail holes indicated that pictures had been removed.

"You sold off your paintings?" I asked.

He winced. "A couple of them. And some photographs. The portraits I did of my ex-girlfriend were just too painful to keep around."

Though I tried to cover my reaction, Steve had been watching me so intently that he must have noticed my eyes widening.

"Your ex-*girl*friend?" I echoed.

"She ran off with Evan. Turns out *she* was his actual business partner . . . or partner in crime, really."

"Oh, my God. That must have been hideous for you!" So why was my heart singing?

"Yeah. I . . . kind of left that part out before. I didn't want you to think I was playing you for sympathy." He sighed. "So, Gilbert." He made a sweeping gesture to take in his spartan living quarters. "You like the way I've decorated for the holidays?"

There wasn't a speck of decoration in the place. "Festive," I pronounced with a nod. "Hosting a big holiday bash, are you?"

"No point in jazzing the place up for the holidays when I'm going to be heading home to Wisconsin. To my parents' place, that is. I'm leaving tomorrow afternoon."

I felt a too-familiar pang. My mother used to put together the most wonderful Christmas celebrations. "That sounds nice," I said and heard the wistfulness in my voice.

"Are you . . . sticking around Crestview for Christmas?"

"Yeah. I've got some close friends with little kids who've kind of made me their unofficial aunt, so I'll go there on Christmas day. I've got two final decorating jobs for Christmas Eve parties, plus a pair of New Year's Eve parties. Decorating, lifestyle tips—that sort of thing is something of a sideline for me." Ashamed of my self-pity, I was rambling to cover for myself, even though I suspected that I'd told him all of this before. "More than enough to keep me busy."

"Good for you."

I shrugged. "It's a living."

"Yeah. I'm sure it lets you while away the hours, stringing popcorn and cranberries."

He was patronizing me. I replied evenly, "Actually, remind me to show you sometime how to make a chain out of strips of construction paper."

"I don't mean to make light of your jobs."

"Make fun of them as much as you want, but those referrals sometimes lead to major design contracts. Which brings me to why I'm here. Debbie's taking over at

Denver Lifestyles and planned to do a feature on her bed-room and the McBrides' den."

"That's great!"

"Not really. You missed the past tense when I said that's what she *planned* to do. The photographers are ar-riving in less than two hours, and Kevin's blue marlin is now out on the lawn. Along with his clothes."

"Marital strife?"

"And then some. Jill threw him out, accusing *him* of having murdered Randy so that he could run off with Myra. So she's chucking all his possessions, too. It's not looking good for your coffee table. Nor the Barcalounger. Maybe there's something you can say to her, though, to convince her to let her husband's room be featured in a magazine nevertheless."

He furrowed his brow. "Oh, cripes," he muttered, de-flated. "No way."

I gave him another moment, then asked, "Ever notice that Chippendale wing chair in Jill's formal living room?"

"Mahogany with claw-and-ball feet and acanthus-carved knees?" Brightening a little, he picked up on my thought pattern and said, "I'll take out the recliner, and she'll love the coffee table once she sees the Chippendale next to it. But that won't be enough, Erin. The woman's pure ego. The only way she'll agree to a photo op of Kevin's den is if *she* were the focal point. If only there were a large portrait of her someplace to hang over the mantelpiece."

"There is," I said with a grin. A sight that had scarcely registered during my quick tour of her house had re-turned to my mind's eye. "An oil painting that looks like she's in her late twenties. Top landing, east wall, directly across from the master bedroom. Haven't you ever been upstairs in their house?"

Ignoring my question, Steve hopped to his feet. "Will it work in the room?"

I closed my eyes for a moment to picture it. I couldn't judge the dimensions, but the colors of the mat, wood frame, and portrait background would be striking against the fireplace and the surrounding green walls. "Well enough for our purposes," I answered.

Steve was already collecting his things for a hasty departure.

I rose, too, "I'd better run. I've got to get to my party-decorating job."

"Yeah. Hey, if I don't see you before then, have a merry Christmas." He was too busy searching for his keys to look at me. Were he a customer, I'd have had a useful lifestyle tip for him—place a side table near the door to house the keys and any other paraphernalia he regularly needed for work.

"You too, Sullivan." I let myself out, wishing I could cancel my afternoon job and instead reflect on Myra's death—examine my feelings in privacy. But my next clients were hosting a dinner party tonight, and their lives weren't going to be put on hold because of my problems.

My work was completed on time, and, showered by well-deserved praise that felt undeserved even so, I left my clients to their lovely home and their lovely evening. Rarely had I felt so alone. But, I knew if I went home now and Audrey was there, my floodgates would likely open. Last night's heart-to-heart had been hard enough; I couldn't handle two of them in a row with someone I was only just getting to know. I went to my office instead and left a message on Emily's phone at her studio to please keep me posted regarding Taylor.

A few minutes after six p.m., someone opened the door to my office and started up the steps, and I watched the stairwell, expecting this to be a holiday shopper in search of a public bathroom, which, at this time of year, tended to comprise a sizable portion of my visitors. It was Emily.

I greeted her warmly and offered her a seat. She sank into the antique Sheraton armchair with my mother's cross-stitched upholstery. She looked a little flustered but no longer distraught. I asked if she'd been able to help Taylor, and she nodded.

"He's out on bail. He recanted the whole thing once I assured him that *I* wasn't guilty. He'd misconstrued some remarks I'd made in anger . . . after he'd told me about you and what you'd found in the wall. I knew at once that it was all Randy's doing, and I lost my head. I made a crack to Taylor about how I wished I could poison Randy's Budweiser. That, of course, turned out to be a . . . miserably thoughtless remark." She searched my eyes. "Last week, when I found him in the back of your van with a container of white powder, I'd thought it was drugs. To tell you the truth, I was actually relieved when he showed me the label."

"How did my cyanide bottle wind up in the Axelrods' backyard?"

"That was a measure of Taylor's immaturity, but that's all, Erin. He deliberately placed it where he thought Randy might discover it if he tried to examine Taylor's handiwork. He said it was supposed to be a joke . . . a harsh message to Randy not to"—she made air quotation marks—" 'nose around' in Taylor's space."

A bottle of cyanide is a real knee-slapper, all right. I held my tongue, and she continued. "I'm afraid Taylor also pilfered some of the poison . . . claimed there were rats in the trailer park that kept getting into his kitchen . . . or some such nonsense. Again, Erin, he's not evil, just impetuous and immature. He turned the cyanide over to the police, though, thank God. Unfortunately, he's being charged with obstruction of justice now, for making a false confession. But our lawyer's working on it."

"Oh. Good." I paused and added, "That he's turned over the cyanide, I mean, not that he's being charged with a lesser crime."

There was an awkward pause. Finally she leaned forward in her seat and said earnestly, "Erin, I came to see you because . . . I wanted to apologize. That wasn't fair of me to call Taylor your kid brother and expect you to take care of him."

"I understand. You were just trying to help your *son*."

Some bitterness had crept unbidden into my voice, and it had obviously not gone unnoticed. A look of intense pain crossed her features. She averted her gaze, and a teardrop landed on her thigh, darkening the fabric of her pants. "Sorry. I didn't intend to come over here and start crying. It's just been such a shitty day."

"I know. I understand." I fought off the image of Myra's body on the bathroom floor. "It's been a horrible day for me as well."

I held out a box of tissues to her, which she promptly grabbed. Though seeing her in tears was painful, a part of me was unwilling to open my arms to the woman, even though she was my birth mother. There was very likely a double murderer on the loose, so surely my caution was justified.

After she'd collected herself, she said, "You don't know how much I wanted to marry Randy and raise you . . . our child . . . together. That's just not the way things turned out. When I gave custody of you to Randy and Myra, I had no idea that they were going to wind up having their nanny adopt you less than two years later. I didn't even find out about that till a few years ago, when

I ran into Randy and asked about you. I was ready to kill him, I was so angry, but by then, well, it was far too late, of course. He tried to claim that he didn't know how to find me once I'd left Crestview and moved to Denver."

There was a lump in my throat that prevented me from replying. I didn't want to go over this same arid ground one more time.

She sighed and pinched the bridge of her nose. "I didn't mean that literally . . . that I would kill him. That's just the sort of stupid statement that got Taylor into so much trouble, when he took it seriously."

Still frowning, she walked to the window. "I told Randy I would sue him for everything he was worth unless he promised me that he would do everything in his power to locate you and to give you my letters and cameo. It was, after all, the very least I could ask at that point." She let out a sharp, bitter laugh and turned to face me. "He claimed later that he'd tried his best but couldn't find you, but that he would hang on to the letters and necklace and keep looking."

She studied my features. "I'm so sorry, Erin. I know this must be really difficult to listen to."

Swallowing hard, I replied, "Emily, all I know is that two people—including my biological father—are dead. A support beam in Myra's basement nearly crushed me. Bullets were shot into my van. Just yesterday, you yourself told me to stay away. This hasn't exactly been the kind of let's-get-acquainted greeting anyone would want."

Emily's look of inner pain intensified. She nodded and averted her eyes. Then she cleared her throat and said in a low voice, "Taylor's staying with me through Christmas. I live out in Lafayette . . . and I'm listed in the phone book. You should stop by for some . . . eggnog or cookies. Or perhaps dinner. Nothing would please me more than to . . ." She faltered.

"Thank you for the invitation," I said. "I'll try to at least stop by."

"You really should, Erin. But we'll understand if it's too hard for you." She crossed the room and started down the stairs, saying over her shoulder in a choked voice, "Merry Christmas."

I battled the lump in my throat well enough to say, "Merry Christmas to you, too, Emily. And tell Taylor merry Christmas for me as well."

I heard the door open and then shut behind her, but she made no reply.

chapter **23**

J ust as I turned off my computer and prepared to leave for the day, Carl called. To my surprise, he asked if I could come to his home immediately to fix the outlet covers. He added, "I already got the covers off the outlets and started soaking them in hot water, like you told me to in your message." Despite deeply regretting my having left that stupid message with him, I decided to get this job over with once and for all.

As best I could tell in the dark when I drove past, Kevin's belongings had been removed from the McBrides' front lawn. I wondered whether or not Steve's efforts had proved fruitful and the photographer had been allowed to shoot the pictures for Debbie's article.

Amid the twinkling Christmas lights on the surrounding homes, every lamp in Myra's house, including the ones on the front porch, was illuminated. Yellow police tape blocked access to Myra's front door, and two police cars were parked in front of her garage. The sight gave me a chill.

I pulled into Carl's driveway and collected my supplies. I poured a minute amount of powder for wallpaper paste into a recycled margarine bowl, stashed a mixing spoon, Phillips-head screwdriver, scissors, sewing chalk, architect's scale, and X-Acto knife into my purse, and carried the roll of wallpaper along with a small plastic cutting board. Thus burdened, I made my way up the walkway and rang the doorbell. Carl opened the door and said, "Evening." He didn't smile, but at least his voice didn't sound hostile. He backed up to let me in. Though his arm and leg were still in casts, he was now able to walk without crutches or a cane.

"Hi, Carl. This is just going to take me a few minutes."

He nodded but said nothing.

I glanced at the living room, which Debbie had emptied out, and only then remembered that the bedroom I'd worked so hard on would have been ransacked now as well.

"Is Kevin here?" I asked, a little nervous. After all, I might be alone in the house with Carl. He'd stopped just short of clobbering me the last time we were alone together.

"I don't know where he is. Probably bending a bartender's ear."

I went up the stairs and felt a terrible pang when I entered the bedroom. Debbie had left the television and its stand. The round, skirted table was still in the corner, along with the bentwood side chair. Carl's clothes from the missing dresser were heaped on the floor. The bed was gone. Debbie had even taken the curtains, rods and all. The wonderful tiger maple nightstand was gone, as was the oil painting of the French village.

This must be how an ice sculptor feels after an Indian summer unexpectedly turns her creation into a puddle. That I was here to put the finishing touches on a wall made me as though I were desperately trying to carve my name into the last remaining lump of ice.

I found the outlet plates in the sink and easily scraped off the wallpaper, then mixed up my tiny batch of wall-paper glue. While I was kneeling in front of the wall—cutting out with scissors the new general sections of wallpaper that I would need—Carl joined me upstairs. He dropped into the bentwood chair.

"The police released Taylor," he reported. "He told me he was innocent, and I believe him."

"I think he's innocent, too. His confession seemed bogus to me right from the start."

Using the sewing chalk, I held the outlet plate in place against the wall and traced around it. With that drawn rectangle as a guide, I found the precise location on my new section of paper and traced around the outlet cover a second time. As a double-check, I used my architect's scale as a straightedge and my chalk to draw an X within this rectangle, making sure to cross the points of the diagonal corners. Leaving a suitable margin, I sliced around the rectangle with the X-Acto blade. All that I needed to do next was paste the rectangle onto the plate cover, making sure that the margins were even and that the center of the X was in the center of the hole in the cover, cut out the holes, and fold the margins under the edges. I repeated the procedure for the cable outlet, and—minus the X—for the circular phone jack cover.

Carl let me work in silence—so much so that I wondered if he'd fallen asleep. But as I was wiping away my chalk lines, I glanced back at him and saw that he was watching me with a gloomy expression on his face.

I decided that I needed some answers from him, and because this was the last time I hoped to see the man, this was my only chance. The moment I'd erased my last chalk line and tightened the last plate into place, I turned resolutely to face him. "Carl, I had an interesting chat with your ex-wife yesterday. Emily gave me those letters and the necklace. She said that they were intended for me all along."

"*You're* their daughter?" He sighed. "I should have guessed. You look a little like Emily, now that you mention it. And I guess that's the only way somebody could have gotten hold of your picture. Plus, Randy had been so insistent that I hire Erin Gilbert and nobody else. He'd been acting so weird. But I figured he was just yanking my chain, like always." He grumbled, "God, but I hated that guy's guts. I didn't kill him. But I sure don't miss the jerk, either." He let out another heavy sigh. "Myra's another matter, though. Whoever killed *her* deserves the electric chair, as far as I'm concerned."

Because I now knew for certain that Randy Axelrod was my biological father, I felt compelled to defend him a little. I asked, "Did you always find him intolerable? Or did your opinion of him lower when you found out he had fathered your first wife's child?"

"I was never all that crazy about the guy. But learning about him and Emily was the last straw." He cursed under his breath and shook his head. "I never should have let her get away. That woman is the love of my life. I dragged

Debbie down the aisle with me, hoping I could get over Emily. But I never did." He gave me an appraising look. "You're lucky to be related to her, Erin. Emily's a hell of a woman."

How was it possible for me to feel "lucky" regarding my birth mother in the light of the events during the past week and a half? I said instead, "You read Emily's letters. You had to know all along that they were written by her to her daughter. Why did you mislead me into thinking they were love letters from Randy to Debbie?"

He shrugged. "Debbie's and Emily's handwriting is so similar that at first I was convinced the letters *were* written by Debbie. Then when I found out that stationery belonged to Randy, I realized they were probably sharing the same stationery at some point. I was jealous; I must have gotten my two wives confused in my head."

I glared at him. "That doesn't make any sense at all, Carl. I don't believe that for a minute."

He grimaced. "Truth is, I just . . ." He began again. "I figured it was Emily or Taylor who killed Randy. I wanted to make myself look guilty rather than let one of them get arrested."

"Just like Taylor confessed to a crime he didn't commit to protect his mother? What *is* this? You both immediately assumed that Emily had murdered someone, and you both made false confessions to protect her?"

There was another long pause. Finally he answered quietly, "I'd like to believe she's innocent, too. But . . ."

Unsettled, I rose, rinsed out my bowl, and gathered my materials and tools. "I'll let myself out."

Carl remained silent, staring at the wallpaper in his decimated bedroom.

"Have a pleasant evening, Carl," I muttered as I headed down the stairs.

I felt bone weary when I got home. There was a hand-written note from Audrey taped with a big fat Christmas bow on my bedroom door. It read:

> E—I've gone to Colorado Springs for some final filming of my Christmas special. I won't be back until late tomorrow night, but you can reach me on my cell phone. Eat the tortellini salad in the fridge . . . leftovers from today's show. Yummy!

There was also a message on my voice mail from Jill, who sounded like a petty dictator: "It is absolutely imperative that you show up as scheduled for our meeting to discuss the final details of the New Year's party. We'll run out of time otherwise."

I didn't return the call; instead, I decided to sleep on the matter. The morning brought no particular insights, however, and I debated whether or not I could withstand continuing to work in that neighborhood. My resolve to help the police ferret out the killer was fading like fabric overexposed to direct sunlight, especially now that I was so deeply worried that Emily could be the person they sought. Two people had died and, judging by the bullet holes in my van, the killer had a gun.

On the other hand, Jill was paying me handsomely, the work itself was fun and relatively simple, and in no way could my going over to someone's house to help them plan a New Year's party be construed as walking into a lion's den. I could be in and out of there in an hour, at most.

Resolved, I drove to Jill's house and rang the doorbell. I was anxious to see if her portrait was now hanging in the den and made a mental note to check out the room as soon as possible.

She greeted me with a gracious smile, asked me to come in, and took my coat. We both happened to wear navy-blue linen skirt suits that were almost identical. Except for the fact that hers was, no doubt, a size zero—unless American fashion designers are now into assigning negative numbers. "We're dressed like twins," I commented with a smile as I stepped out of my shoes.

"Yes. My daughters would be so pleased," she said, without interest. "The invitations for the party have already been mailed."

"Okay." I retrieved my Palm Pilot, pen, and notepad from my purse and left it next to my shoes.

"Since it's too late to cancel, we're changing the theme," Jill said. "Instead of looking to filch their money for Kevin, I'll be inviting my friends to celebrate my new-found freedom."

"Good for you," I said heartily. "But . . . if the invitations already went out, aren't you inviting mostly venture capital folks? Not necessarily the friends you'd want to celebrate changes in your personal life with . . . ?"

"True, but we'd already invited our old friends as well. This way I can make it clear to Kevin that when the marriage is dissolved, I'm the one who gets to keep our mutual friends."

"Oh, good." Was hoarding one's friends "good"? I wondered to myself. "Why don't we start by—"

The door slammed open behind me. Startled, I whirled around. Kevin McBride entered, looking disheveled and desperate. He stared past me at his wife. "Jill? Can we talk?"

"No!" Instantly her features mutated with fury. "You can't just barge in here anymore! This is *my* home, not yours!"

"Sorry. I'll . . . go back out and ring the darned doorbell."

She put her hands on her narrow hips. "Just say whatever you have to say to me, then leave."

He gave me a little glance, but ventured, "You were right, Jill. I'm going to mend my ways. I'll give up all the running around. And the attempts at starting up new businesses. My inventions never work, anyway. If you want me to, I'll get a real job. I'll grind it out, just like all the other worker ants. It'll be hard, but I'll manage. Somehow."

"Too bad you didn't face that hurdle ten years or so ago," Jill grumbled. "Maybe by now you'd have cleared it."

I started to step back into my shoes, saying, "I'll give you two some privacy—"

"No!" Jill cried. "Don't leave me alone with him! He might hurt me!"

Kevin bellowed, "Oh, come on, Jill! You know I didn't really kill anyone! You were just saying that to get attention!"

"I did no such thing! I *saw* you, Kevin! Carrying the arsenic over there!"

"*What* arsenic? I told you before, that was a plant. Somebody stashed it in my office to set me up. Probably Taylor."

She marched toward him, and I flattened myself against the wall. "Kevin," she snarled, "you've said your piece, and my answer is no. Now, either you leave of your own free will, or I'll force you to go. Do I have to call the police?"

"Fine. I'm going. But don't think I'm just going to give up on everything we've had together." He stepped onto the porch.

"You already *did* give up on us. Before we ever even met. You *always* loved Myra. I was just your consolation prize. Your *wealthy* one."

"That's not true!"

"Goodbye, Kevin." She slammed the door in his face, then threw the deadbolt, using a key that she then pocketed. She turned on her heel to face me. Placidly, she gave me a practiced smile and patted the pocket containing the key. "Unfortunately for my soon-to-be-ex husband, I changed all the locks first thing this morning. Sorry about the interruption, Erin. Now where were we?"

"We were about to talk about New Year's themes," I replied, hiding my reaction to her odd coldness.

"Indeed. I want bright and wild. I'm thinking Mexican."

"Mexican?" I echoed.

"Yes. It will be completely different from anyone else's New Year's party that way." She gestured at the wall. "One of those champagne fountains will be here, but instead of champagne, we'll do margaritas. We'll suspend piñatas from the ceiling. Gorgeous reds and deep greens everywhere. Salsa music. Big sombreros for everyone instead of those silly cardboard cone hats."

I had a feeling that her party guests, who were no doubt expecting a black-tie affair, would feel as ridiculous donning a sombrero as they would a cardboard party hat. Jill would need to be talked down from this. "Okay. Let's do another walk-through of your house and think about this. If everyone's going to be wearing large sombreros, that's going to affect the width of the aisles. We'll need to look at moving out any fragile items that might be at the same height as a big brim."

"Good thinking," she replied cheerfully.

Lucky that *one* of us was thinking. Normally, I would never dissuade a client from throwing a Cinco de Mayo party on December 31, but the idea of sombreros and piñatas and salsa music seemed totally out of character for the blue-blooded Jill McBride. What she *really* wanted was just to get as far away from her original vision of the party hosted for her husband as possible.

"Let me get you a nice cup of coffee, and we'll get started," she announced.

Again with the beverages, I thought, as she led the way to the kitchen. The pocket doors to the den Steve had decorated were shut, delaying me from seeing if her portrait was now hanging over the fireplace. "Just a glass of tap water would be fine," I said as we reached her glorious kitchen. I watched her pour herself a cup of coffee and me a glass of water from the tap on the refrigerator. "Jill, what do you think about decorating each main public room with items from a specific country? The party theme could be New Year's celebrations around the world."

"Oooh. I love that idea, Erin!" She grinned at me. "No wonder Debbie is so fond of you. You're a creative *genius!*"

"That's more than a little overstated, but I'm glad you like the idea. It will be fun."

"I know just the place to start." She gestured for me to lead the way through the doorway ahead of her. "My formal dining room is French provincial."

Rococo, actually, but I was more than willing to go with the philosophy that the customer is always right now that she'd anointed me with the creative-genius title. We entered the room. She had a stunning Savonnerie rug under the elegant walnut table, which, even without its leaves, seated eight.

"I'll talk to the caterers. Heaven knows I'm paying them enough to buy me their flexibility." With dramatic gestures, she said, "In here we'll serve bonbons, French champagne, petit fours . . ."

"And," I interjected, "we can put a cake on the table, with the phrase 'Let them eat cake' written in frosting."

She raised an eyebrow and curled her lip, and I added humbly, "Or not." This woman had a rather hefty dose of attitude for someone who, left to her own devices, would have her guests in sombreros and wielding sticks.

Jill indicated the buffet behind me. "I told the caterer that he could use my French Louis the Fifteenth buffet from which to serve hors d'oeuvres. Of course, that was with the understanding that I'll have *his* head if he damages it."

I considered pointing out her pun about "having his head" and Marie Antoinette but decided her reaction to "Let them eat cake" didn't bode well for her sense of humor. Turning my attention to the buffet, I replied, "That's a beautiful piece. Mind if I take a closer look?"

"Not at all."

I opened the center breakfronts and glanced at her impressive array of fine china. "You're just going to allow him to use the marble surface on top, right? You're not going to want to remove your china, surely."

"Heavens, no. That would be far too impractical."

"I agree." As I started to close the doors, I noticed how elevated the cabinet bottom was compared to the outside bottom edge. "Oh, wow! I've never seen this done on a buffet before! This has one of those hidden drawers underneath, like some Chinese wedding cabinets."

She chuckled. "Oh, that's right. So it does. Very astute of you, Erin. I'd all but forgotten that was there. We've never used it."

Without thinking, I grabbed on to the eight-by-thirty-inch piece of wood just below the breakfront doors and pulled it toward me. The drawer slid open easily.

Inside was an unlabeled baby-food jar half full of white powder. Beside the jar was a stainless-steel All-Clad kettle, identical to Jill's kettle, currently occupying the left back burner on her stove, and identical as well to the one that she'd given Myra five years ago as a house-warming present.

I had to stifle a gasp. My mind raced. In a heartbeat, the whole murder scene flashed before my eyes. No *wonder* the police hadn't found poison traces in Myra's kitchen. The tea water had been spiked. The tainted kettle had been swapped in and out of the Axelrods' home. Myra had told me that the McBrides had copies of her keys.

Myra had been the big tea drinker, not Randy. Had she been the killer's target all along? Randy's poisoning could have been an accident; Emily had said something to me the other day about his drinking ginger tea when his stomach was upset, and he'd felt ill that afternoon.

Kevin had had access to this drawer, too, but there wasn't a doubt in my mind now that Jill, and not Kevin, was the killer. She was standing right behind me, well aware that I'd just stumbled across the contents in that little jar of baby food, as well as evidence that revealed how she'd gotten away with murder.

Now all I had to do was pretend that I was clueless, get the hell out of here, and call the police. I shut the drawer, rose, pasted a broad smile on my face, and turned back to face Jill. "Looks like you've got some pots and things you stuck in the drawer at some point and forgot you had."

To my horror, she had donned latex gloves. Reaching into the inner pocket of her jacket, she removed a small, silver gun.

She aimed it at me.

chapter 24

Pity, my dear," Jill said. "I truly liked you. I should have known better than to let you examine that particular antique. My mistake. I can tell by the look on your face that you just now put it all together."

"I have no idea what you're talking about!"

"That's the difficulty of your being in a career in which you make a living by noticing all the trivial nuances that the rest of us tend to dismiss. To my credit, I *did* try hard to scare you off, you realize."

She must have meant by shooting bullets into my van. Yet *she* was the one who'd hired me for this party planning job. Had she expected to just scare me away from Myra, all the while keeping an eye on me? "I don't even know what you're talking about," I tried again. The longer I could keep her talking to me, the longer I could stay alive.

She chuckled. "Oh, come now. I'd been planning this for quite some time. Kevin's undying love for her had gotten ridiculous . . . intolerable. Even Debbie noticed. So I had to get rid of Myra. That damned support beam didn't seem to want to fall, even after I nearly sawed clean through it in two places during Thanksgiving. When Kevin and Carl presented Debbie and me with tickets to the spa, it was perfect. I wouldn't even *be* here when Myra drank her standard two cups of tea on Sunday morning. I was going to tell Debbie that I'd had a premonition so that we'd come rushing home and I could sneak over there to get rid of the evidence."

At least she's still talking to me. She had the key to the front door in her pocket. Maybe I could get out through the back door in the kitchen. She was blocking my exit to the kitchen, though.

"The trouble was," Jill continued, "for whatever reason, Myra didn't *have* tea that Sunday, probably because she was so flustered at *your* impending arrival. And, as luck would have it, Randy apparently started feeling sick to his stomach. So, apparently, the die-hard coffee drinker in the family made himself a cup of ginger tea."

She let out a puff of indignation and shook her head as if expecting me to share in her disgust at her misfortune. "I had no choice but to lie low for a few days, swap the kettles, and stash the contaminated one back into its secret place. *Then* that damned husband of mine had to go and force my hand by plotting his escape with his beloved widow, despite having you and the police snooping about. As if I would simply step aside . . . let them humiliate me like this . . . and leave *me* for another woman."

"So you *killed* Myra rather than lose Kevin to her?"

Through clenched teeth she growled, "Didn't I just explain that to you, Erin? Weren't you *listening*? I am younger, prettier, thinner, and wealthier than Myra! How would it look to have my husband leave me for someone like that . . . that *cow*? My *life* would have been ruined. You, of all people, should understand that much!"

"Why would *I* understand?"

She raised an eyebrow and scoffed. "Your entire living is based upon self-image. You give your clients the illusion that they can rub shoulders with gentility . . . with old money, like my people. You should understand how crucial a person's image is. Without it, we all might as well never have left the Cro-Magnon cave."

I wondered if she was right, if my career was a sham. I mustered up the nerve to state firmly, "You're not going to be able to get away with any of the murders if you kill me, too."

"Oh, but there's where you're wrong, Erin. I was prepared for this. I *always* prepare for all possible contingencies. I've planned everything down to the last detail."

She took a step toward me. I backed into the hallway. I desperately needed a weapon. My purse was in the foyer. I'd removed the bulky items from last night's repair job, including the scissors.

Jill continued. "There's that ridiculous expression 'God is in the details.' Quite the opposite is actually true. It's the devil who's in the details. Such as your happening to notice the minor detail of the false bottom in my buffet. That, too, was a contingency for which I prepared myself."

Think, Erin! There had to be a way for me to get out of this! Jill must have been planning to make shooting me look like self-defense. She was a deadeye shot with her gun. What if I turned and ran? Shooting me in the back wouldn't be self-defense.

Try as I might to convince myself to turn and run, my eyes remained riveted on the gun in her hands. "Randy's death was an accident, and you had extenuating circumstances for killing Myra," I said, taking a step backward. "Every woman juror will be on your side. A good lawyer will paint you as . . . as another Princess Di. But if you shoot me in cold blood like this, it's all over for you."

She shook her head. "It will look like self-defense. The gun will go off as I try to wrestle it away from you. Myra told me about how you were her long-lost daughter and that Randy had put your baby picture in the paneling. That will be the headlines—embittered young woman takes revenge on her biological parents for deserting her and abusing her late, adoptive mother."

"Abusing my *mother*?"

She sneered at me. "Myra told me that Randy was his typical belligerent self when your mother was working for them as a live-in au pair. I tearfully told the cops that Myra once confided in me that Randy raped your mother, and that I'd unfortunately had a little too much to drink in your company and let that slip. You took the news so hard. You hated Randy, and Myra, too, for not stopping him."

"Those are bald-faced lies!"

She cocked her eyebrow. "Anyone who can refute them is dead. Or will be soon."

"Except Myra *isn't* my biological mother. My mother's alive and well. She'll tell the police that I knew who my true parents were. If you kill me, the autopsies will prove every word of her story. Your manufactured motive for me as a murderer goes right out the window."

She paled a little and her lips parted in surprise. "Oh,

my God. You're *Emily Blaire's* daughter. Of course! I should have recognized it myself. You look just like her."

"Face it, Jill. Your best chance is to let me go and turn yourself in . . . plead temporary insanity."

"I have my daughters to think about. I cannot allow myself to be arrested for murder, let alone have everyone think my beautiful daughters are the product of a crazy mother." She smirked. "With *your* background, you must know precisely what *that* would be like."

I clenched my teeth, enraged.

"Emily can be bought off," she said decisively. "I'm quite certain that's how Myra got custody of you in the first place. I'll simply pay Emily to keep quiet about your having been aware that Myra wasn't your mother."

I was still a full twenty yards from the foyer. Damn these oversized houses! "That's never going to work, Jill. I already told the police—"

"I'll make it work! I get whatever I want!" Her eyes flashed. "Your birthright doesn't change my story of what Randy did to your adoptive mom and why you killed them. If anything, it makes your motive for killing them stronger. So you came to my house; we argued when you realized I knew you'd killed the Axelrods. Then you pulled a gun out of your purse. You threatened to shoot me, and, when I tried to get the gun away from you, it went off."

My last hope for talking her out of this was lost. Heading to the tile foyer was a risk. She probably wanted me to get off her precious white rug before shooting me.

She chuckled as she came toward me. "I don't know what good you think backing away from me is going to do you. Did you forget? I've got the key to the deadbolt in my pocket."

I spun on my heel and raced to the foyer, grabbing my purse as I ran to the front door.

"Really, Erin! Are you going to smack me with your purse now? You never carry so much as a nail file in your purse!"

Keeping my back turned so that she couldn't see, I grabbed my X-Acto knife and flipped the blade into position. The one-inch blade wouldn't be lethal, but it would sure hurt.

"Reaching for your cell phone? You'll be dead before you can get the first word out." She stood directly behind me, just a step away. "Now be a dear and turn around, and we'll get this over with."

"You won't be able to explain bullets in my back."

"Turn around, or I'll make you turn around myself. I work out for a solid hour each and every day, Erin. Everyone's always underestimating my strength. Yet another reason the police would never suspect that I'd be able to saw through a support beam directly over my head."

I gripped the knife tightly in my fist, praying that this would end peacefully—that I wouldn't have to fight for my life. "Don't do this, Jill. There's still time to turn yourself in and get leniency from the courts."

To my astonishment, there was a pause. In a choked, small voice Jill said, "You're right. My God. What am I doing?" There was a metallic click. "I'm putting the safety on the gun and putting it down."

This was a trap. She'd cocked the gun, I was sure. She wanted to trick me into turning around of my own volition.

In one motion, I brought my arm back and whirled to face her.

The gun was still pointing right at my face. I slashed at her neck and then stabbed her in the chest. My unexpectedly swift pivot distracted her for the fraction of a second that I needed.

Crying out in shock and pain, she pulled the trigger as she staggered backward. The bullet whizzed past my ear.

She dropped the gun and sank to her knees. Screaming in pain, she looked up at me, in an obvious state of shock. "You *stabbed* me. I'm *bleeding*."

I snatched up the gun and pointed it at her. Then I retrieved my cell phone and dialed 911. "Stay right there. The paramedics will be here soon."

Hours later, I returned home from the police station. I'd told my story countless times. All I wanted to do now was pour myself a glass of Châteauneuf-du-Pape, draw myself a steamy, lavender-scented bath, and do my best to drown out all memories of the worst day of my life.

Unfortunately, two weeks ago, Audrey had temporarily converted the house's only bathtub into a terrarium, and I'd brought my last bottle of my favorite red wine to a dinner party two weeks ago and didn't want to resort to dipping into Audrey's wine-cellar stock. I would have to settle for a shower. Afterward, I decided I'd curl up on the velvet sofa with a good book, my great cat, and a bottle of Michelob.

There was a padded envelope beside Audrey's door with UPS handling tags. Probably a Christmas present for Audrey—a book or a couple of CDs—and then I read the labels. The envelope was addressed to me, from a lawyer's office in Denver. Judging by the contents' size and weight, there was something bulky inside.

In haste, I let myself into the house, tore open the mailer, and removed a videotape and its accompanying typed note. In legalese wording, the note explained that this had been sent to me in fulfillment of the wishes of Randal James Axelrod upon the event of his death.

I went straight over to the VCR in the den and, still

wearing my coat, was soon seated in front of the television set.

After a few seconds, the screen showed an empty Chippendale side chair with celery-and-white striped upholstery. I had not seen such a chair in his house, and the background was a blank white wall. Randy, wearing a short-sleeved shirt and jeans, rounded the camera and sat down in the chair. He looked to be the same age as he was at the time of his death. His hair was neatly combed. He appeared to be a bit nervous as he stared into the camera.

"Erin Gilbert. Hello. You may or may not recognize me by the time you see this tape. If you don't, that probably means the end came for me sooner than I'd hoped. You see, I have a serious heart condition, and my life expectancy doesn't look so good right now. Anyway."

He chuckled a little and shook his head. "Whew. This is even harder than I thought it'd be. Let me introduce myself. My name is Randal Axelrod. My friends call me Randy." He scoffed and said under his breath, "Actually, *everybody* calls me Randy, at least to my face. I've done some things I'm not very proud of in my life, but I'm thinking, maybe there's time to make amends, starting now. . . . Or maybe not. I can't figure out how to approach you."

I tried to merely listen and to quiet the sarcastic voice in my head that was retorting: *Whatever you do, don't put my baby picture inside the paneling of a room I'm remodeling.*

"See, it's tough," Randy's taped image explained, "because my wife, Myra, isn't at all well, and sometimes she does stuff to herself . . . hurts herself and makes up these wild stories. But"—he gestured nervously with both hands—"I guess that's my problem, and you must be thinking, 'Who is this moron, sending me a tape of himself?' " He smoothed his mustache. "Anyway, Erin, what I'm trying to tell you is . . ."

He leaned toward the camera and stared straight into the lens. "The point I'm trying to make is, Erin, I'm your father. I know that's a title I don't deserve. I realized a long time ago you were best off *way* the hell away from . . . me." Again, he shook his head and laughed. His smile faded quickly. "But you should know I *did* at least arrange to provide a scholarship for you at that school in New York you went to."

I was so shocked by this revelation, I paused the tape, rewound, and listened a second time. I hadn't misheard. My full scholarship at Parsons had come courtesy of Randy Axelrod. My eyes misted.

He dragged his hand over his mouth and along his jaw. "Anyway. If we never meet, I just wanted you to know that it's not like I never did anything for you, all these years. I know, paying for your college anonymously sure wasn't much. But, well, that Jeannie Gilbert . . . she just seemed like the kindest, most loving young lady I'd ever met, and I knew she'd be a much better parent than . . ."

He stopped, seemingly unable to continue. Finally he cleared his throat and muttered, "You take care, now." He got up and came toward the camera. The picture faded to black.

I sat there staring at the black screen, stunned, numb, unsure of how to react. Maybe I was just too drained from the events of the day to feel much of anything just now. I decided, though, to simply take his word for it that Myra had injured herself and not continue to believe that he had abused her. Randy Axelrod might not have been nearly as bad a person and a husband as she, and everyone else, had led me to believe.

Hildi, meanwhile, decided to come join me on the

sofa, and I welcomed her warm, sleek little body onto my lap. I pressed the rewind button and watched the entire tape a second time, looking for myself in Randy's features, mannerisms, speech patterns.

Questions whirled in my mind; I knew they would likely remain unanswered. If Randy knew Myra was as unstable as she was, why didn't he come to my office in private, like any reasonable person would have done? Why play the game of hiding everything in the wall? Maybe he was just so hopelessly stuck in the rut of his own manipulative, controlling behavior that, try as he might, he couldn't change.

I shut off the tape. Picking up on my vibes that I was about to get up, Hildi hopped off my lap and pranced toward the bedroom. I garnered the strength to remove my coat and hang it up. I picked up the phone and listened. The dial tone indicated that I had a message on my voice mail. Though I silently chastised myself, as I dialed my voice mail I foolishly hoped that the message would be from Steve Sullivan.

"Hi, Erin," the message began. "I was just thinking about you and decided to call." My father. "My wife and I were talking . . ."

I rolled my eyes at the "my wife." He always called Angie that, "my wife," as though I didn't know my own stepmother's name. Which was not to say that I knew much else about her, even after their having been married for thirteen years now.

". . . if you'd like to come out to Los Angeles for Christmas. I know it's short notice, with Christmas just three days away, but you might be able to catch a flight from Denver tomorrow or the next day. We'd be happy to pick up the tab. My wife pointed out that it's been . . . well, that I should have been more accommodating, as far as your getting to spend time with her and my daughter. Anyway, I don't suppose you can manage to take me up on my offer at this point, but maybe next year. I've got to run, but think about it. See if you can get a flight. If not, Merry Christmas. Maybe you could call me . . . us . . . tomorrow, and let us know if you can come out." There was a pause, then he said, "Bye," and the message ended.

I returned the phone to its stand. This was a first—an invitation to come visit during the holidays. He was, of course, ambivalent about the idea or he would have made the offer sooner so that I could actually accept. Still, he'd opened the door a crack. . . .

My mother's words returned to me. Whenever I lamented about having such an absentee father, she used to tell me: "Just because someone doesn't love you the way you wish to be loved doesn't mean that they don't love you with all that they've got." Although it had taken me years, and sometimes the wound still festered, I had finally come to accept that basic truth. My father loved me as best he could.

I curled up on the sofa, hoping Hildi would return to the room and join me. It struck me that finding a family, a home, a safe haven, was really what my life was about—what had motivated my choice of careers. I'd been trying to find a way home, to help my clients find their way home. That might not be as noble an occupation as some, but neither was it as trivial—as driven by image and mere status seeking—as Jill McBride had made my career choice sound.

The doorbell chimed. I swung open the door without looking through the sidelight, figuring it was probably a police officer with yet some more questions for me. On the doorstep stood a young woman. She held an enormous arrangement of exotic flowers in a large porcelain vase. "Erin Gilbert?" she asked.

"Yes."

"These are for you."

She handed them to me. Surprised and delighted, I carried them over to the side table in the parlor, near the French doors, saying over my shoulder, "Wow! They're absolutely stunning!" I stared at the amazing flowers and the outstanding, elegant arrangement—bird of paradise, protea, red anthurium, dendrobium orchids, heliconia. The elegant design looked like something that I might have assembled for my wealthiest of clients. Audrey's oak table was suddenly boasting some three hundred dollars' worth of exotic tropical flowers.

The delivery girl stepped into the foyer. "Here's the card." She handed me an unmarked envelope in the standard two-by-three-inch size. She smirked. "The guy who sent them insisted that the plastic spear we stick into our arrangements would ruin the lines or something, so he wouldn't let us use one."

My God! There was only one person I knew would possibly care about a removable card holder ruining the lines of a floral arrangement. I opened the envelope and read:

Hey, Gilbert—Keep in mind that my
offer to form sullivan & GILBERT
Designs stands.
               Have a merry Christmas.
                         Sullivan

I beamed at the card. Compared to the bottle of cyanide on my birthday from my ex-boyfriend, this was the proverbial gift of the Magi.

The delivery girl fidgeted with a lock of her spiky maroon-dyed hair and said, "My shift ended a while ago, but, you know, everyone loves flowers. I just figured I could make one last trip before I called it a night."

A hint for a tip, if ever there was one. "Thank you so much for bringing this out tonight. Let me just grab my purse."

As I fetched my bag, I glanced over the girl's shoulder at the darkening sky. "Oh, look! It's starting to snow! And the forecasts all week call for the temperatures to stay below freezing. This is going to be just what I pictured . . . a white Colorado Christmas!"

She gave a quick glance back and shrugged. "Nah. We never get a white Christmas in Crestview. It'll prob'ly quit in another ten minutes."

She gestured with her chin at the flowers. "Your boyfriend insisted on doing the arrangement himself, so he came in the shop first thing this morning and did it. You're lucky. He's really *hot*."

I found my wallet and extracted a five-dollar bill, saying, "He's not my boyfriend."

"He *isn't*?"

I met her gaze. She had a glint in her eye. Aside from her unnatural hair color and excessive body piercings, she *was* attractive. I knew at once that she was thinking about getting Steve's number and address off the receipt and contacting him. Almost simultaneously came the realization that I wanted to discourage her from doing so.

I raised my eyebrow and said with artificial significance, "Steve is an interior designer."

"Oh," she said casually, then said, "Oh," again in a lower, disheartened voice.

I felt guilty enough to grab a second five from my billfold and double her tip, but not so guilty as to correct for having deliberately misled her. The man had just sent me flowers; I was under no ethical obligation to fix him up with the delivery girl.

I lost track of the time as I stood and stared out Audrey's front window at the falling snowflakes. The sky had turned from royal blue to black. A halo of light from a streetlamp in the distance carved its own miniature world of falling snow out of the darkness.

Before I could make any excuses and change my mind, I retrieved the handful of letters Emily Blaire had sent me, the child she had never known. I brought them downstairs, and curled up on my favorite sofa. Hildi promptly hopped onto the far cushion, then tucked herself into my lap. I unfolded the first letter.

My hands were trembling. I took a calming breath, murmured to myself, "Confidence and optimism," and began to read.

about the author

Leslie Caine was once taken hostage at gunpoint and finds that writing about crimes is infinitely more enjoyable than taking part in them. Leslie is a certified interior decorator and lives in Colorado with her husband, two teenaged children, and a cocker spaniel, where she is at work on her next *Domestic Bliss* mystery, *False Premises*.

If you enjoyed the debut of the *Domestic Bliss* mystery series, DEATH BY INFERIOR DESIGN, you won't want to miss the next mystery featuring the design team of Gilbert & Sullivan—and their wonderful decorating tips!

Read on for a tantalizing look at Leslie Caine's second Domestic Bliss mystery

FALSE PREMISES

a domestic bliss mystery

by

Leslie Caine

Available now
in paperback from Dell

FALSE PREMISES

For the second time in the past thirty minutes of our girls' night out, the waitress arrived bearing drinks that Laura Smith and I hadn't ordered and didn't want. Within those same thirty minutes, we'd also been approached by two less-than-sober men asking if we were sisters. With Laura's drop-dead-gorgeous looks, that question was, at least, flattering to me, and, thankfully, Laura hadn't paled in horror. However, this latest drink offer was an unwanted interruption of a serious conversation.

Laura frowned slightly and asked the waitress, "Are these from the same guy as the last time?"

The baby-faced waitress, who had to be at least twenty-one in order to work in a bar in Colorado but looked all of fifteen, indicated with a jerk of her chin that the drink buyer was seated behind her. There, at a long brushed-aluminum bar illuminated with futuristic halogen lights, the wall completed the large room's interesting color transition from the lemon yellow of the opposite wall, through peach, apricot, orange, and pumpkin, into tomato red. "Nope. A new one. And he has a buddy." She cocked her eyebrow and grinned. "They're both kind of cute, I gotta say."

Without so much as a curious glance in the men's direction, Laura replied, "Please tell them thanks, but no thanks . . . and that we're lesbians."

I hid my smile. The girl gave a slight nervous laugh, as if unsure of whether or not Laura was serious, said, "All rightly, then," and turned away.

We were no more lesbians than we were sisters—just friends grabbing a quick bite and a glass of wine before we dashed off to hear a talk on home decor. After a dry spell, I had a new man in my life, and Laura was living with Dave Holland, a bespectacled thirty-something with a receding chin and hairline. Judging from the fortune that Dave had amassed, he must resemble Bill Gates in more ways than just phsycially. I'd met Dave and Laura nearly six months ago, when Laura had hired me to decorate their gorgeous home in the foothills of the Rockies.

Laura leaned closer. "Getting back to our conversation, Erin, this was your *adoptive* mother who died, right?"

"Right. Just over two years ago from a congenital lung disease. How long ago did *your* mother pass away?" I asked.

"Fifteen years ago."

Because we were the same age, my mental math was

automatic, and I cried, "So you were just twelve at the time. How awful!"

Laura merely nodded, so I persisted. "She must have been fairly young. Was it an accident?"

Laura shook her head, her gaze averted. She adjusted her signature silk scarf a little, drained the last of her Chablis, then answered quietly, "Murder."

I fought back a shudder. "She was *murdered*?"

The pain the recollection had brought to her was plain to see in Laura's expression. "By my father. He killed my little brother, too, then took his own life."

"Good Lord. That's horrible! I'm so sorry." Reaching for the only possible positive spin, I said, "Thank God *you* were all right, though."

She gave me a sad smile and didn't respond. In a near whisper, she said something that sounded like "I'm a slow bleeder."

"Pardon?"

She hooked a manicured finger in the knot of her gold-and-indigo scarf, slowly untied it, and reaveled the puckered skin that ran across the base of her neck.

Her throat had once been slit.

Another chill ran up my spine. In that instant, I vowed never again to feel sorry for myself and my lonely and at times difficult childhood. My heart ached at the unfathomable pain and horror that she had endured.

"Oh, my God," I murmured. "Laura. I'm so sorry."

In the light of her personal history, I was all the more impressed at how warm and welcoming she'd been to me from day one, when she'd hired me as her interior designer. Since that time, Laura had become more of a personal friend than a client. She'd been remarkably knowledgeable as we'd selected the million dollars' worth of antiques for her home. And yet, when she'd suggested that we go bargain hunting at a Denver flea market, she'd been every bit as comfortable and in her element while dickering over the price of a stained porcelain teacup as she was selecting a hand-crafted seventeenth-century armoire.

Now I understood the origin of the depth that I'd sensed in her and had found so compelling—the occasional sadness that passed over her features during quiet moments. She seemed to be unaware and unaffected by all the heads that turned her way whenever she walked by, and she noticed and found joy in the same details I did—in the beauty of sunlight catching an aubergine glass vase, the hue of purpleheart wood, the softness of the finest chenille, the amazing artistry and craftsmanship of Scalamandré wallpaper.

With the color rising in her cheeks, she retied her scarf.

"Did you want to tell me about it?" I asked, all the while thinking that if she said yes, I might have to signal the waitress and say that I'd changed my mind about accepting those drinks.

Laura sighed and fidgeted with a lock of her shoulder-length brown hair, a slight tremor in her fingers. "No, but thank you. Talking about it only brings back all those memories I try so hard to forget." She put her hand on top of mine on the table and, with forced gaiety, said, "Let's never mention it again, all right?"

"Of course."

She glanced at her watch. "Oh, shoot! We're late for your landlady's presentation!" She hopped to her feet and briefly insisted on leaving an overly generous tip, until she accepted my reminder that this evening was completely my treat. The waitess benefited from Laura's and my exchange; I now felt compelled to give her the same oversized tip.

"Actually, there's no rush," I told her as we left. "I've been to a couple of these events before, and Audrey's always too busy signing autographs and chatting with her legions of fans to begin on time."

Audrey, my landlady, hosted a local television show three mornings a week, *Domestic Bliss with Audrey Munroe*. The name of her Martha-Stewart-like show was more than a little ironic. Having shared Audrey's mansion on Maplewood Avenue for nearly six months now, I knew her to be indefatigable, irrepressible, and endlessly entertaining—but her domestic life was far from blissful. Audrey allowed me to live there rent free in exchange for the never-ending task of helping her to redecorate her home, which she did on frequent and often- bewildering whims. (It took three months until she finally realized that it had been a mistake to turn the one bathtub in the house into a terrarium.) A former ballerina with the New York City Ballet, she was now in her mid-sixties, although she'd recently informed me that she'd decided to welcome her birthdays by "awarding myself negative numbers each year from here on out." I'd replied that, some thirty years from now, she was going to be a very old-looking thirty-five-year-old, indeed. She merely shot back: "But a wise one!"

It was a beautiful April evening, and the crisp air lifted my spirits, so I did not mind that the gentle breeze occasionally blew my auburn hair into my eyes. The sky was a lovely indigo; the slightly deeper violet shapes of the mountains were just discernible in the distance. Laura and I meandered along the brown-brick pedestrian mall, window-shopping as we made the journey to Paprika's. I soon realized that were were being followed: a bearded and dreadlocked man in Birkenstocks, grungy blue jeans, and a wrinkled, once-white long-sleeved shirt and sheepskin vest had left Rusty's Bar and Grill seconds after we had and was now lingering behind us, matching our pace stride for stride.

In mock secret-agent tones, I said to Laura, "Psst. Don't look now, but someone's on our tail."

She immediately looked back, as did I. The man turned away casually, as if waiting for someone to catch up to him.

"I wonder if that's our would-be drink purchaser, who now thinks we're lovers."

She laughed, "Oh, heavens, I hope not. I might have to ask you to kiss me." She again glanced back as we continued on our way. "Although by the looks of him, he'd probably be turned on."

"Oh, he looks harmless enough to me . . . though he's sure not your typical Rusty's patron." Rusty's had become the latest hot spot in Crestview; our midsized college town seemed especially prone to sparking trendy hot spots.

"True. And he *really* doesn't look like the crystal-stemware, copper-pot type, so I'm sure we'll lose him when we get to Paprika's." She added as if in afterthought, "Not that I could blame him. The personnel there isn't up to snuff."

"What make you say that? I *love* the staff at Paprika's."

Laura gave me a warm smile as she opened the door for me. "That's only because *you* love everyone, Erin."

A moment later, the man followed us inside the upscale kitchen store. Annoyed and slightly disconcerted, I whispered to Laura, "I'm going to confront the guy and ask why he's following us."

She touched my arm. "Let's just ignore him."

In the center of the first floor of the store, merchandise displays had been removed or shoved aside, and in their place sixty folding chairs had been set up to face the table where the illustrious Audrey Munroe was soon to hold court. Only three chairs were empty. As an interior designer, I, too, had been featured at a couple of these special evening presentations but hadn't drawn one quarter of this crowd.

We rounded the seats toward two available chairs in the front row. From the back of the makeshift auditorium, Audrey was currently entertaining a large percentage of the customers, who were craning their necks to listen in as she joked with an elderly couple. My landlady was wearing an elegant two-piece black dress, perfectly tailored to flatter her trim, petite frame. She gave me a little wave. Beside her stood Hannah Garrison, the manager of Paprika's. I could tell by Hannah's plastered-on smile that she'd been trying in vain to urge Audrey forward to begin her talk.

Hannah spotted me, grinned, and started to head over to say hello. Her smile faded mid-step and mutated into a glare when she saw my companion. Puzzled, I glanced over my shoulder at Laura. She was eyeing Hannah with a haughty smirk. Her expression seemed odd; I'd never seen Laura act the least bit haughty. Apparently Laura's dislike for the "personnel" included the store manager— and was mutual.

Hannah hesitated for a moment but was soon beside me as we reached the two empty chairs. Tonight she had strapped herself into an ill-fitting skirt suit that wasn't flattering to her short, buxom frame. "Thank you so much for coming, Erin. It's always so great to see you." Her body English hinted that she was trying hard to ignore Laura's presence on the other side of me.

The implication that it was *never* great for Hannah to see Laura seemed to hang in the air. I replied, "Likewise, Hannah. I love to come here."

"How are you, Hannah?" Laura asked pleasantly.

Although Hannah's smile was rigid, she replied, "Fine, Laura. And you?"

"Things couldn't be better. Thanks for asking."

As if it were a facial tic, Hannah's lip curled for just a split second, then she shifted her gaze to me. Her arms were folded tightly across her chest, and Laura still wore the Cheshire-cat grin. The tension was so palpable that I babbled, "You've got quite the crowd here tonight."

"Yes, we do," Hannah replied in hushed tones. "Which is really good timing, because we've had a bit of trouble lately."

"Oh?"

"Paprika's has managed to become the target of a . . . " Her voice faded as she caught sight of the new patron in the second row, directly behind us. The bearded, scruffy man who'd followed us from the bar was apparently having some trouble getting comfortable. The front leg of his folding chair was missing its inch-tall base.

Hannah grimaced and said under her breath, "Speak of the devil." While Laura and I took our front-row seats, Hannah rounded our row and said quietly but firmly, "Please, sir. Not tonight. It isn't fair to Ms. Munroe, and there's no way she's going to mention you or your cause on her television show, no matter *how* big a scene you throw."

"Huh?" he muttered.

"Tell you what," Hannah said, her tone now patronizing. "Why don't you come to my office first thing tomorrow morning? You can air all of your grievances regarding Paprika's merchandise to me personally at that time."

He harrumphed and, again, seemed to deliberately turn his face when he felt Laura's gaze on him. "You don't *sell* these crappy chairs here, do you? 'Cuz some-one's likely to fall out of one and break their neck."

"I'd be happy to get you a better chair, sir, in exchange for your promise that you'll listen quietly to the presentation. Please, just for tonight, keep your personal opinions about how we Americans should spend our money to yourself. Okay? Would that be too much to ask?"

I cleared my throat, hoping that I could catch Hannah's eye and give her a wink. She might want to let this all slide. The attention of the sixty or so people had shifted from Audrey to Hannah and Dreadlocks' conversation, which, to my mind, was defeating her purpose.

"*Look* at this!" As if to demonstrate his concern about the chair, he wobbled from side to side, the chair legs clanging against the tile floor with each motion. "This chair's totally *useless*." He then hopped to his feet and bent to examine the offending leg.

As he leaned over, the back of his shirt lifted a little, and I caught sight of an object tucked into his waistline. I stared in alarm as the man continued. "See? Here's the problem. This chair leg's busted."

Cupping my hand over my mouth so that only Laura could hear, I whispered, "Look! The guy's got a gun!"

Laura gasped. The sudden sound caught Dreadlocks' attention; he turned, and the two stared at each other. Laura yelled, "Get a grip on yourself! Stop hassling the poor woman! She made a perfectly reasonable request that you speak to her tomorrow!"

Why on earth was Laura so aggressive to an armed man? I shot a pleading look at Audrey, who cried, "Goodness! Look at the time," and rushed forward. "Let's all take our seats"—she nodded to the still-standing dreadlocked man—"such as they are, and we'll begin talking about table settings."

As much as I wanted to set the tone by facing forward in my seat, Laura maintained her attempt to stare down the armed man. She and I had to get out of there right then, I decided; Dreadlocks wouldn't dare follow us with this many witnesses.

"Here," I said, offering him my chair. "Why don't you take this one, and—"

"You need to leave," Laura snarled at him. "Now!"

"Take it easy, miss. I'm just minding my own business, trying to learn about table settings. If *someone* could just *get* me a *freakin'* chair with four legs and same height, you *won't* hear another—"

He made a broad gesture and accidentally smacked Hannah in the chest. She gasped and stepped back.

Laura cried, "That does it!" Kicking her seat aside, she grabbed the man's arm and in one swift motion flipped him onto the floor, upsetting a display of cutlery in the process.

The store patrons gasped and shrieked. As for me, I couldn't help but stare at the man's hair. It had shifted. As if merely checking his skull for injuries, he grabbed his head with both hands to center his wig. He struggled to his feet, and the weapon fell from his belt. A middle-aged woman in the seat next to his cried, "Oh, my God! He's got a pistol!"

Everyone began to clamber to their feet. Already racing for the exit, Laura whipped out her cell phone and cried over her shoulder, "I'm calling the police! I'll be right back with them!"

Audrey's crowd, shrieking, followed her. The man stuffed the gun into the back of his pants and shouted over the pandemonium, "Wait! It's okay, everyone! I'm an undercover *cop*!"

The panic eased a bit.

"Ladies. Please. As an officer of the law, I have no intention of firing my gun, I assure you." His voice was authoritative even as he made placating gestures. "If everyone could please just take their seats . . ." The patrons began to honor his request, shuffling a trifle nervously back toward the chairs. The man glanced at Audrey. "Real sorry, ma'am. I'll get out of everyone's hair now." He left in the same direction that Laura had gone.

In the front of the room, Audrey rang a small brass bell. "I hope everyone enjoyed my pre-show entertainment, provided to you courtesy of the Free-for-All-Players of Piedmont, Colorado. Be sure to check your local papers for their next performance. I hear their 'Instant Shakespeare' is especially enjoyable. But right now it's time to talk table settings."

Everyone chuckled with relief and began to reclaim their seats in earnest. There was no way I could simply sit down and listen to Audrey's presentation. Much as I wanted to believe that the wig-wearing man was truly a police officer, he hadn't shown his badge, he'd called attention to himself despite claiming to be undercover, and he was following Laura again.

As I started to make my way toward the exit, past Hannah, she grabbed my elbow. "Are you all right, Erin?"

"Fine. But I'd better go check on my friend. Even though she's probably already on her way back here with a uniformed officer."

Hannah clicked her tongue and grumbled, "You obviously don't know Laura very well. There's no way she's coming back, let alone with a cop." She turned on her heel and stepped beside Audrey to introduce her to the audience.

I furrowed my brow, mouthed "Sorry," to Audrey, and left.

I trotted in the same direction Laura had headed and circled the entire pedestrian mall twice. She had vanished. So had the "undercover cop."